Foxhaven Chronicles
Volume One

Raven's Eye

Carolyn Houghton

Carolyn Houghton

Elyse Wheeler

Elyse Wheeler

DANCING CROWS
PRESS

ISBN 13: 978-1-951543-00-6

Library of Congress Control Number:2019914951

Cover art and drawings of Pyewacket by Colin Wheeler, MFA, ABD Strickenbrow.com or strickenbrow@gmail.com

Authors' photos by Keith May mayphotoanddesign.com

Dedications

Carolyn

I am dedicating this book Celia Walsh. My daughter has presented eight-dimensional training on how to realize there are no boxes. I love your gallantry, humor and compassion.

Elyse

Colin, you have kept my imagination alive and flourishing from play in a refrigerator carton, D&D, unusual themed birthday cakes, and many costumes to long talks over lunch as you finish your PhD. I am proud of the compassionate and creative man you have become.

Acknowledgements

We are so pleased to thank Meg Carroll, PhD who valiantly plowed through the first draft of 220,000 words. Her insightful comments and gentle critique helped to remove over 100,000 words to arrive at the final version. Be of good cheer! We'll find a place for those scenes in the next story.

Carolyn

My friend, Fred Richards, has given me stalwart support through the final writing time here in Georgia. He is a wise counselor. I'm so happy I can call him my friend.

My gratitude to all my wonderful friends who were willing to make music and art through the years. Doug Chambers, John Goddard, Erik and Mark Endresen, Wally Greeley and Wes Riley added deep harmony to my everyday life. Carol Talanian, Sue Jannetty and Lindsay Auer were friends throughout the best and worst of times.

Three heart friends left the world much too soon. I miss you, Susan Martin Houghton, Linda Goodard Brown and Heidi MacLaren. You are cherished on this side until I can see you again. Hopefully, I won't be waving up at you.

Elyse

My heart found a home in the Carrollton Writers Guild. My thanks to all who have supported us as we crossed the finish line with our first novel. Especial thanks to Stephanie Baldi, a supporter and friend beyond compare. And to two gentlemen who gave of their time and encouragement: Bob O'Kelley (a big heart and lots of enthusiasm) and Ken Boekhaus (great insights and precision). And to my bass playing friend, Lisa Wilson, who said we got the band right.

Circle of Twelve

(in order of appearance)

Saminthea Fairmont-Ramhill: Sami is the youngest child in the Fairmont family (from New York society) with sister Colby and brother Michael. She was an anxious child diagnosed with agoraphobia at a young age. She was mentored by Kay Kasavina and went on to study art history in Paris under Kay's guidance. She is married to Charles Ramhill.

Niki Kaye: Niki is Kay's younger brother who ran away from home when he was 13. Spending ten years on the streets, he pursued his passion for music absorbing every style he could find. Drawn to the band's rehearsal space by their music, he became their manager, using his survival skills to promote the band.

Charles Cognac Ramhill: Charlie is the drummer (though he is proficient on many instruments) and founder of the band. He left England on poor terms with his older brother. He is passionate about his music and his wife. He is also temperamental and tends to jealousy.

Jeffry Conray, PhD: Jeff is the second son of the Conray of Texas. His father's family are Native American while his mother is from New Orleans society. Jeff earned a PhD in chemical engineering and worked for the family oil company before joining the band.

John Beauregard MacIntyre: At the age of fourteen, Mac was brought to the Conray ranch when he was found wandering along the Texas highway. Raised as part of the Conray family, he is Jeff's best friend. Dedicated to the bass, he strengthens the band members. He gave up a career in architecture to pursue their mutual dream of music.

Colby Fairmont: Colby is Sami's older sister. She is a talented cellist but is too shy to perform professionally. She is impulsive and passionate. She is very protective of Sami though a little jealous she married first. Raised in New York Society, she is well versed in manners and finds her occasional oracle pronouncements unsettling.

Jessica Hamilton-Ramhill: Jessica was born and raised on a ranch outside Chicago. She was on horseback before she could walk. Jessica, Colby and Sami are family friends as their fathers are business competitors and colleagues. She is married to Damian Ramhill, Charlie's older brother.

Kay Kasavina: Kay grew up on the Ramhill estate where her father served as a tutor to the Ramhill daughters. She completed her degree in art history and pursued her PhD in Paris. She is a practitioner of psychometry—the ability to sense or "read" the history of an object by touch. She has come to America to work with Tori Madison.

Victoria Madison: Tori was born and raised on the coast around Charleston, SC. Inheriting the family business of interior design, she left the traditional path and specializes in finding the rare, the odd and the unusual for her wealthy clients. She is headstrong and competent preferring the low country wilds to the drawing room.

Scotty Miles: Born in Scotland, he is the second son of Laird McMillan. He befriended Charlie Ramhill while they were at Eton. A savvy businessman, he left the family business to give a try at music.

Chris Thomas: Young Scotty found Chris as a babe on the moors. Abandoned in the middle of nowhere, the McMillan clan adopted him. He is talented with wind instruments and calming the wild things. He adds soaring descants and counter melodies to Charlie's songs.

Chad Alton: Chad lost his parents in a random bombing with antisemitic overtones. Raised by his Uncle Bernie, a luthier and rabbi, Chad studied to be a luthier in his uncle's shop. Music and the road called him away. He plays lead guitar and is a student of the Kabbalah.

Other Characters

Pyewacket: Pye is Niki's scruffy cat named after the beautiful Siamese cat in *Bell, Book and Candle*.

Maeve: Maeve is a Lurcher, a large dog usually the cross between a sighthound and a working dog. She is large dog with great intelligence and speed.

Carleton and Celeste Fairmont: The Fairmonts are Sami's foster parents. Carleton is a self-made millionaire industrialist, inventor and alchemist.

Harry: Harry is the family retainer and guardian of the mistress of the house of Foxhaven.

Nigel Ramhill: Nigel is the younger brother of Lord Edward Ramhill. An inventor in his own right, he is skilled at playing the bumbler.

Lord and Lady Ramhill: Edward and Genevieve are Charlie's great, great grandparents. Lord Ramhill is a sorcerer and Lady Ramhill is a witch.

Adrian Ramhill: Adrian is Lord and Lady Ramhill's only son.

Gordon and Serena Matheson: Serena and Gordon are Sami's biological parents. Serena is a member of the local coven and Gordon is an inventor and alchemist.

Thomas Westfield: Westfield is Lord Ramhill's steward.

Anna Simpson: Anna is a new maid in the Ramhill Household.

And

Foxhaven: Foxie is the ancestral home of Sami's maternal progenitors.

Prologue

December 21, 1905

Gordon Matheson urged his roan gelding into a fast trot. He settled his black sloucher hat against the sleet. "Damn you, Ramhill! And this foul weather." The horse swiveled his ears and plowed through the gloom. "What possessed Edward to drag me to his club tonight?" The gelding snorted. Gordon shrugged deeper in his overcoat. His wife and their newly arrived babes safe at home spurred him on, kicking the gelding into a canter, disregarding the treacherous footing.

A high-pitched keen split the air. The hair rose on his neck, icy fear slipping down his back. The gelding shied sideways, slid in the mud and struggled to keep his feet. Gordon rose in the stirrups giving the horse his head to regain a footing. He leaned low over the withers and urged the gelding to greater speed.

The house lights appeared beyond the open wrought iron gate. The Christmas tree in the parlor window did not calm him. The gelding stumbled in a deep rut. Gordon flew over the horse's head, rolling in the giant paw prints leading away from the house and into the woods.

"Where are you, you bloody beasts?" He yelled at the empty pedestals, the stone foxes missing. He leapt the steps and charged through the open oak door.

Harry sprawled, face down, in the foyer, his long red hair loose from its leather binding. Gordon leapt over him and careened into the parlor.

His wingback chair lay on its side, pushed against the wall, its legs splitting the wainscoting. Blood spread across the scorched floor, burn marks leading from the fireplace. Demon-magicks and sulfur fumes filled his mouth, burning and acrid.

"No!" he bellowed. Kneeling beside Harry, he rolled him onto his back, pulling at his collar to reach the carotid artery. Harry's eyes flew open, unfocused, the deep mahogany orbs rolling back.

"Harry!" Gordon pulled his fingers away sticky with blood. He stripped off his coat and draped it over the older man. "Harry, where is Serena?"

Harry stared at the ceiling. "Master Gordon, she's gone. They've taken her." He closed his eyes.

"Harry, stay with me, man. Where are the babes?"

Harry pointed at the oak stairs, mumbling "den". Gordon sprinted for the rooms behind the stairs.

"Den? This is the library. Harry, what do you mean?" He stood just inside the darkened library, his senses prickling.

He put both hands on the wall. "For God's sake, Foxie, help me. I know you don't care for me but where the blazes is the den?"

Frustration rang in his voice. Pivoting, his muddy boots slipped on the oak floor, sending him skidding on his knees toward the opposite wall. He slid through the wall into a narrow passage, a small round opening into the underground bowels. The air carried earthy odors and a sweet, familiar scent. On hands and knees, he forced his shoulders down the narrow passage.

He scrabbled into the inky darkness, his fingers digging into the cool earth. His outstretched hand felt soft fur. He clawed his way, his shoulders no longer rubbing against the tunnel walls. Swiping a wide arc in the darkness, his hand strafed a wool wrapping. He grabbed a fistful, pulling away the swaddling blanket. He stroked her cheek, her warm skin soft against his palm.

His held breath escaped in a rush. He laid his head down between his outstretched arms giving thanks to all the gods he could name. He reached to each side, seeking the second bundle, knowing in his heart, it was in vain.

He drew her to him, backing out inch by inch. She wiggled, waking from the deep sleep. He smelled Harry's wild magick on her breath. *To keep her quiet*, he thought for once grateful for the retainer's strange ways.

He edged backwards, able to move a few inches at a time. Hands grabbed his ankles pulling him from the close quarters. He twisted to kick stopping just in time, Harry's pale face staring at him from beyond his boot.

"Is she all right, sir?" Harry croaked, the blood on his neck attesting to the heavy blow.

"She seems to be, Harry." Gordon rolled to a sitting position and cradled his daughter in his arms. Her bright amber eyes stared up at him. She fought the confining blanket. "Tell me what happened."

Harry sank back against the wall. "Four demons came down the chimney. Madam felt them coming and bade me hide the babe." Harry rubbed his face, running shaking fingers through his hair.

Gordon noticed the single lock at Harry's temple, gone white all at once.

"When I returned, they were dragging her out the door. I tried to stop them, Master Gordon. One hit me from behind. I am so sorry." Harry collapsed in on himself.

"Harry, you did your best. And my son?" Gordon rocked back and forth, not certain if the movement was for Saminthea's comfort or his own.

"With his mother." Harry hung his head, "She fought them, sir. The foxes awoke, trying to stop them. I heard their cries before I lost my senses." Harry struggled to his feet. "We have to go after them!" He staggered against the wall.

"Harry, we have to secure the baby and the house."

Harry shook his head. "But…"

Gordon rolled to his knees and rose, clutching Saminthea to his shoulder. "I know. I don't like it either but it is what Serena would want." He patted her back to calm himself as much as the babe.

"Carleton. Carleton will help me."

Pulling a small bronze top from his pocket, he tossed it to the floor. The top half spun clockwise. The bottom rotated the opposite. Soft whirring filled the room, growing in intensity.

"Work, damn you. He promised me it would work." Copper-colored mist flowed from the edges until a cloud stood five feet in the still air.

A figure stooped, stepping through the opening. He ran his fingers through his salt and pepper hair and brushed the copper dust from his jean jacket. "I've got to work on this. It should be large enough to step through comfortably. And you didn't believe it would work." His laughter died in his throat. "Gordon...?" His face paled.

"Carleton, I fear I need to call in that favor sooner than I wished." Saminthea mewled, fretting in her blanket. Gordon patted her. "Serena has been abducted. I need you to protect my daughter." He looked around the room. "And the house."

Before Carleton Fairmont could reply, Gordon dropped to his knees beside the drying blood and pressing Saminthea's small palm into the middle. "Dearest, I do not know the ritual your Mother would have used to pass the keys to you but this will have to do." He closed his eyes. "With your mother's blood, I seal you to her and her to you." He turned the baby and stared into her eyes. "These chambers are the chambers of her heart. Never forsake her. Her love will protect you." He kissed Saminthea on the forehead. Rising, he placed her in Carleton's arms. "I have to go. Harry knows what to do. Take her away. Keep her safe."

Carleton cradled the baby to his chest. "Gordon, do you think eighty years will be far enough?"

Gordon chuckled. "It will have to do."

Carleton reached into his pocket, pulling out another brass device. "Then you'll need this to come to us."

"I never believed the first one would work."

Carleton laughed, "Why am I always saddled with a doubting Thomas for a student? You have to believe ... or it doesn't work. That's alchemy for you." He clapped him on the shoulder. "Go. Find them. I'll protect Sami and Foxie."

Gordon grabbed Harry in a tight hug then lunged for the front door.

"Mr. Gordon, let me go with you." Harry called.

Gordon leapt into the saddle. The gelding sidestepped, throwing mud. "No, Harry, you need to keep her safe. They'll be hunting her. You're the only one I trust." He wheeled the horse and kicked him into a gallop. Darkness swallowed him.

Carleton's firm hand pulled Harry back into the house. "Harry, I've learned a little about babies from my own two. I wager she'll be hungry soon. Shall we proceed?"

An open field bordered by tall pines and hardwood, windswept, breezes cold and damp filled Harry's senses.

"That's it, Harry. The right place for Foxie to wait." Carleton bounced Sami on his shoulder, her face puckered into a cry.

Harry nodded, his words lost in his aching heart. He beckoned Carleton to follow. Standing in the fire-scorched parlor, he raised his eyes to the heavens. He grasped Sami's bloody hand, his ululation splitting the air.

The house shook, the earth bucking around the foundation. Gordon braced himself, holding tightly to the baby, his ocean sailing experience lending him stability. All colors in the house swept toward them leaving a grey shell behind. The whirlwind circled them. Carleton stepped through the portal onto the open field, Harry followed close behind.

For a heartbeat, the spectral cloud hesitated, then slipped through the opening. It rose high into the air as if inspecting the clearing in the forest. Swooping down with tail flashing, all four paws pierced the ley lines. The house reformed, the foundation groaning, shifting stone and mortar to bind to the earth. She settled into her new home.

Carleton nodded. "Well done, Harry. Now let's go home."

CHAPTER 1

Foxhaven languished alone for twenty-five years, suffering rats in the cellar and bats in the attic. Cold winters and rainy summers warped the doors and dimmed the red oak floors. Her heart decayed in the lonely nights. Now, after the long nightmare, she wrapped her solid arms around her young mistress returned at last. She would not allow the evil from without to gain entry again.

DECEMBER 20, 2010

Sami Fairmont-Ramhill wiped her hand across the mist on the pane, searching the dark skies. The screech ripped through the air, pushing her back from the sill. She edged toward the window, arms wrapped tightly across her chest.

In the dappled light, Pyewacket crouched, his black fur speckled with sleet, nose raised to scent the air. His tail twitched.

"Pyewacket, come back. It's not safe out there," Sami pleaded.

The small cat rose, ears perked and, with one last glance in her direction, disappeared into the overgrown lilac bushes lining the driveway.

She shivered, reliving the stalking terror ... in the darkness beyond the garden, hidden overhead on the city buildings, shadowing her steps down the streets. The swaying branches outside hid their secrets well.

The sleet shifted to snow, swirling against the pane. Sami frowned, worrying about Charlie's drive ... about his resistance to living in the decrepit house so far from the city. After their elopement, her father—*foster father*, she corrected herself, a now familiar lump forming in her throat—gave her the keys to the Victorian house. The porch leaned, the doors wouldn't close, and small bones littered the floor.

But it's better…getting better every time he comes home. She surveyed the library shelves, Charlie's guitars suspended on brass hangers, sheet music tucked into mahogany magazine holders found in the basement, and the walnut desk's satin sheen restored.

He preferred the cold-water walkup near where his band rehearsed. She saw the shadows in his eyes, scaring her he worried about their precipitous marriage. She almost gave in. But she struggled to hide the fear she felt when she left their apartment and walked to the Museum each day. Once inside, she loved the granite halls and the objet d'arte she studied and prepared for display. But in the evenings, shadows nipped at her heels, the walk back longer, her heart pounding with each step. She counted each heartbeat.

Moving to the country house released her from that struggle. She danced through the rooms, feeling at home for the first time in her life. She still feared the dark shadows in the woods.

But he's willing to come here for me.

The aged Victorian creaked, the heating system groaning to life. Each warm exhalation lifted her blonde wisps, caressing her neck. She stretched her arms to the high ceiling. She twirled, her circle ritual with the swirling air dispelling her worry, the white cotton shirt billowing out from her slim frame. Stopping in the foyer, she pulled Charlie's shirt tight around her shoulders, anticipating his warm embrace. The lights flickered on in the oversized parlor. She paused in the doorway caressing the vine-carved door frame. The wood thrummed under her palm, beating in time with her heart.

The wind from the chimney blew the fire into a welcoming blaze, beckoning her. She traced the walnut carving under the mantel. Rampant foxes pranced, paws on the engraved word Foxhaven, tails swishing amidst the braided holly.

You'll keep it out, won't you? You'll keep me safe. She leaned her head against the mantel.

The fire flared again, warmth blossoming up her legs.

She lifted the Bohemia crystal brandy snifter, firelight reflecting through the facets. A treasure from the attic, the high Baroque style thrilled her … her touch confirming its history. *Circa 1735.* Charlie would appreciate its elegance. She poured the amber liquid in the snifter and placed it on the mantle. Behind it stood their wedding picture, the couple side by side, their fingers entwined.

Blowing a kiss at her grey-eyed groom, she dashed for the kitchen. Cold wind from the open back door met her at the threshold but Niki's wide grin warmed her. The door swung closed behind him.

She grabbed him by the shoulders and spun in a circle with him. "Niki, is it all ready?"

Niki laughed, allowing her to turn him. "As best I can do. He'd better be pleased by this. Your father spent a fortune on the equipment." He swept his blond bangs from his forehead, his blue eyes glittering.

"Don't worry. Dad's got it." Sami brushed her lips across his cheek. "I'd best get the stew on to heat."

"He's almost here?" Niki reached for a low ball and poured vodka neat.

"So she says." She stirred the steaming stew. "Though the icy roads may slow him down." She paused, pursing her lips. "Niki, I'm worried about Pyewacket being out there."

Niki raised his glass. "Don't worry, he knows what he's doing."

"But, Niki, there's—"

"Sami, we won't let anything happen to you." Niki set his glass on the counter and wrapped her in his arms.

"But you go away with the band, just like Charlie does." She laid her head on his shoulder.

"The band has to travel. They're building a good reputation and a following. I can almost smell a record deal." He kissed the golden locks and hugged her tighter.

She unwrapped from his arms and reached for the ladle. "Why do you do this? Manage them? I've heard you play. You could be performing."

"Not my thing, Sami. I don't want to be out front. I get what I need from helping them. They're my way off the street."

She surveyed his clean black jeans, slate-grey sweater and black leather jacket. "I can't believe you ever lived like that."

He finished his drink. "I'll do anything not to go back there." He shivered, a haunted shadow crossing his face.

Sami glanced away, not wishing to intrude where he wasn't ready to go. He'd talk to her when he was ready. They all did. She raised her head, the question nagging her but swallowed. "You won't. You have a home here. Charlie loves you... and you put up with his idiosyncrasies"

"He's a blinkin' genius." He poured another ounce in his glass. "I doubt he cares a whit about me. I'm convenient. And I produce."

"He cares. He just has a hard time showing it." She searched for words to lighten the mood. Niki saved her from her quandary.

"Now, if you were Foxie, where would you hide the caviar?" Niki opened a cabinet. The next door swung open, hitting him on the shoulder. "Thanks." He chuckled and picked up the small glass jar. "Want some?"

CHAPTER 2

Charlie Ramhill's asthmatic MG ran exactly twelve miles over the speed limit. He drummed his fingers on the steering wheel anxious for the drive to be over. *Home.* He'd been making this drive for over a year. *That's the first time I've called it that.*

Humming a melody, he considered a song for the next gig. He yawned, his jaw cracking. *I should have helped them load the equipment. I wish she'd travel with us.* He rolled his shoulders. *Gods, I miss her.*

The remaining miles rolled by in rhythm to the remembered drumbeats—his perfectionist percussive imperative. *Will I ever get this love song finished?* He tried out a melody to fit the words, his rich tenor filling the car.

> I can't help but be amazed
> Finding my joy mirrored in you
> I'm the one who sees the darkling moons
> But now I'm asked to join your luminescent dance.

He turned into the drive. Snowflakes careened across the windshield. He stopped, peering into the gloom, pale lights in the distance. "Welcome to my demented Oz." He wondered what she was wearing then chuckled, knowing the answer…his shirt her preference over the designer clothes her mother provided, a belated trousseau.

The car coughed, wheezed and died. *Damn it, I'd best keep my daydreams in the boot until I've navigated this gauntlet.* He turned the key, ground the starter motor until the engine caught. Putting it in gear, he edged it between the lilac's bony fingers. He gritted his teeth, staring down the narrow lane dimly illuminated by feeble headlamps,

There, there on the right side. He eased the car down the drive. Glancing up at the security pole, he cursed under his breath. *Light is out again. Niki is here which means his damn cat is, too.*

He glanced at the shifting branches inky black in the falling snow. The wind drove the flakes dancing in swirls along the muddy drive. The underbrush writhed in the gusts.

So where are you, your feline devil? Charlie squinted his eyes. The car rolled, quickening the pace. He hunched his shoulders against the thickening in the air, a pressure from above.

A heavy body slammed onto the hood, darkening the windshield from edge to edge. Leathery wings beat on the slick glass. Claws scrabbled for a purchase.

"What the hell?" Charlie stomped on the brakes, killing the engine. The writhing form slid, claws screeching along the hood, and landed beyond the projected light.

Acrid stench flooded the vents, gagging him. The bitter taste on his tongue recalled memories he thought long forgotten. He coughed, retching, his breath fogging the windshield.

He wiped his gloved hand across the glass, banging his knuckles against the rearview mirror. Through the porthole, he searched for the apparition, scanning in all directions. Seeing nothing, he leaned his forehead on the steering wheel, his knuckles stinging.

I left this horror behind in England. Why...? The question hung unfinished.

Childhood memories, the dark manor house, his relief at being sent to away to school and the dreaded summers at home flooded his mind. He spent many days visiting school chums rather than to be with his father and brother.

He knocked his head on the wheel, then raised his eyes to the road. Stretching his fingers, he wiped his face. "Okay, Ramhill. Be reasonable. This is the Colonies. There is water, a lot, between here and there. You're tired at the best ... and hallucinating at the worst."

He started the car. "Either way, you have to get down this damned drive."

A few feet farther along, a black ball unrolled in the headlights. Pyewacket's deep green eyes shone red in the light, melting snow glistening on his fur. He flicked his paw, flinging mud, and ran his tongue over the pad before limping to the brick wall beside the cast iron gate. He leapt into the darkness beyond.

"Damn it, Pye!" Charlie pounded his fist on the steering wheel, fuming when the windshield fogged over again. "What is the phrase Sami repeats," he said aloud welcoming his own voice in the chaos "Breathe deep, seek peace. What I need most right now, peace." Peace, a foreign concept in the loud music, the crowds, on the road… all the chaotic elements rendering his life how he wanted it.

He cringed at the grinding gears. The car crept through the gate, stopping even with the front steps. Turning the ignition, he realized the car sat on the left side of the drive. Five years in America and he parked on the wrong side. He considered pulling over but his fatigued muscles argued against it…even stronger, his drive to be within the house and into the light.

The driver's door closing punctuated his deep sigh. He searched for the cat while he pulled out his case. *Claws in my knee are not on my agenda.* Inhaling the cold night air, cinnamon and clove sang on his tongue raising his desire for a warm fire and a strong drink. *She always knows when to pour the brandy to be properly warmed. Is Pyewacket her early warning system?*

The first wooden step to the porch groaned. *F sharp*, he mused. He stepped up. *A flat.* He stepped back down, his adrenaline surge waning with the notes. *Hmmm, from the first to the third ... C, and the first, the second ... discordant but possibilities.* Perhaps he was welcome after all, this amusement just for him. He jumped from step to step, playing his offkey hopscotch. Etude des l'Escaliers Avant, he anointed the piece. His unfinished symphony resonated in his head, forcing the darkness behind him.

He turned the brass knob, unlocked as usual. He frowned. Concern for her safety didn't impress her. Touring with the band for weeks at a time, he worried about her alone. Growing up in a household filled with dogs—hunting dogs, herding dogs—the presence meant security. Sami refused a dog along with locking the door. *For a woman so resistant to ever leaving the house, she shows no fear someone might come in.* He chewed his lip, deciding the discussion should wait until after the holidays.

The heavy oak door swung open, warm air wrapping around him. The entry floor and stairway—lustrous red oak and bright mahogany—gleamed in the candlelight. Golden candles flickered in the swirling air. *The color of Sami's hair.* His throat tightened. The wind gusted from behind, battering him aside and setting the flames dancing. He drank in the silence. *Home ... our home ...* the feeling lifting his heart.

Niki's lilting tenor from the kitchen broke the moment. Sami's crystalline laughter responded to Niki's story. The sound swept over him, igniting his jealousy and sending the candlelight spiraling, increasing the RPMs before setting him down hard. Niki always made her laugh—free, full-hearted laughter—so different from her response to him or to his band mates who joined them in this retreat.

He drove away his irritation at Niki's easy manner with her. Niki's gift wasn't limited to Sami. The light in Niki's boyish face always sparked a celebration. Niki focused on each equally.

Charlie shrugged off his coat, trying to hang his worry on the coat hook. He found the snifter on the mantle. *The temperature of a woman's skin.* The touch drove the cold from his fingertips. He savored the rich aroma. Anxious to hold Sami in his arms, he paid the entrance requirement with the short moment alone.

She insisted he take a deep breath and appreciate the beauty unveiling before him. At first, the ritual irked him, fueling his concern regarding her obsessive-compulsive behavior. Now, he looked forward to the moment, the fire warming his legs, the brandy burning his throat, quiet all around him. He marveled at his good fortune.

Studying the room, he searched for changes ... what she accomplished over the weeks he was away. A wind rose inlay gleamed in the firelight where the floor had been scorched from a long-distant fire. He imagined her slim fingers smoothing the wood, her love caressing him.

Charlie downed the amber liquid and sprinted for the kitchen. He swung around the jam and swept her into his arms, the ladle in her hand clattering to the floor.

"I don't know which feels more welcoming to me, the warmth of this kitchen… or holding you. It's good to be home." Charlie lowered her until her feet touched the floor. Sami pulled his head down and kissed him, long and deep.

"Hmmm, the way I like my brandy." She licked her lips. Blushing, she gazed up at him from under silky bangs. Her amber eyes gleamed with reflected light from the copper pots hanging over the kitchen island.

He buried his face in her hair. This first moment overwhelmed him no matter how many times he arrived.

He looked up and met Niki's eye. "I see you are still blowing out the security light like your namesake in that old movie."

Niki's smile grew puckish.

"You just arrive?"

Niki looked away from Charlie's gaze for a moment. "Yeah." He sipped from his glass. "I talked with a guy who owns a club in Baltimore. He has a cancellation on his holiday schedule."

Charlie sighed, torn between excitement at the growing reputation and bone-deep fatigue. "Don't book us until after New Year's." He caught a fleeting frown on Sami's face when she glanced at Niki. Concern clawed at his throat.

"You know New Year's is a big deal in the industry and I'm tracking the record producer who heard you in Boston last week. He's interested but wants to hear the band again before the year's end." Niki dropped a lemon slice into his vodka.

Charlie tracked Niki's hand. *How often is Niki here when the band isn't?* He shook his head. He desperately craved time alone with Sami.

"How was the gig in New York?" Niki's voice pulled Charlie to the present, his weariness crashing down on him.

"Fine. Not a crowd but some music reporter types. Scotty pays attention to those things." Charlie reached for a glass, splashing scotch into the crystal.

Sami snuggled under his arm, running her hand across his chest. "Why don't you go shower? I'll have dinner ready by the time you're done. Mulligan stew. Perfect for you vagabonds."

He spun her in a dance turn and sang out. "I've wined and dined on mulligan stew"

Sami put her hand on Charlie's cheek and sang the refrain, "And that's why the lady is a tramp."

Charlie grabbed her shoulders, staring at her.

"What?" She laughed.

"I've never heard you sing. You have a lovely voice."

Sami's ears reddened. "You inspired me."

Charlie pulled her into a tight embrace, pouring all his love into his kiss. She responded, sending his heart pounding.

Sami pulled free. "About that shower …." She picked up the ladle.

"What?" Charlie chuckled, echoing her earlier question. "Oh, right."

The aroma set his hunger rising but his shoulders craved hot water. He brushed his lips across her forehead. "Be down in a minute. Stew smells wonderful."

The golden candle flames in the hall reminded him of the gift still in his topcoat pocket. He pulled out the ring box and opened it. The faceted amber ring caught the flames, glowing for the only woman who could fill his heart. *I won't wait until Christmas.*

At the threshold to the kitchen, he heard Sami's lowered voice, "Niki, you have to be careful. I told you he would notice if you were here early."

"Sorry, Sami. I had to get here before he arrived. We needed the time."

"I haven't figured out how to explain all this to him." Her tone switched to light teasing, lifting the mood. "And you're a lousy liar."

Charlie froze.

Niki laughed. "Of course, he won't understand." Niki affected a formal British accent. "A certain rigidity in the thinking, you know. Comes from all the stiff upper lip and boarding school training."

"Stop it, Niki. Charlie's very open-minded. But this may be more than even he may accept. I don't know how to tell him."

"The Ramhills have their secrets, too."

"Niki!"

"Sorry. I'll be more careful. What can I do to help with dinner? It smells fantastic."

Leaving the ring box on the hall table, Charlie dragged his bag up the stairs.

CHAPTER 3

Jeff Conray tightened his grip on the steering wheel. Wind gusts pushed against the Rent-a-Wreck truck, threatening to send it onto the shoulder.

"Jeff, you're a real lady's man but, boy howdy, were you put in your place this afternoon." John "Mac" MacIntyre grinned.

Jeff chuckled, remembering the flashing brown eyes. "She was so pretty when she stamped her feet and shouted at me." He rolled his shoulders and reflected his foster brother's smile.

Heavy, wet snowflakes careened past the windshield, the old wipers struggling with the sleet and snow. Mac slouched against the passenger door. Jeff felt Mac's stare, the pressure adding to the oncoming migraine. The road conditions required his full concentration but he always felt Mac's presence.

"Well, the Yankee do-gooder put herself in an interesting place— offering you sandwiches—thinking you were homeless, starving and probably diseased to boot." Mac shifted in the seat, easing his broad shoulders into the corner.

"I was starving. Why'd you think I took the sandwiches?" Jeff put a little whine in his voice.

"I can't wait 'til we hit it big and can act like the rock stars we're supposed to be rather than day laborers. I thought she was having a heart attack when you invited her to Four Seasons for dinner. What were you thinking?" Mac chuckled.

"Man, where else would you take a babe wearing an Armani leather jacket and Gucci boots? Chang's Chinese Emporium all-you-can-eat for $6.95?"

"Okay, okay." Mac held up his hands. "I should know better than get between you and a good-looking woman."

"You've your groupies dogging your footsteps." Jeff smirked remembering their high school football days when they gathered athletic letters and cheerleaders as easily as plucking spring blue bonnets along a Texas highway. Another wind gust rocked the truck. Jeff pulled it back into the lane. "Good thing we tied everything down."

"Hey, how come you and I do the roadie work while Chris and Scotty escape?" Mac frowned. "I can understand Charlie hightailing out to get to Sami."

"Think those pipsqueaks could pick up this stuff? Charlie'd have a breakdown if they handled his drum kit. And we own the speakers. I don't want to explain damage to Niki." His tone softened "Wish she'd said yes."

"You'd like that just fine. Leave me cooling my heels. I sing praises for the pretty wet hen who shat all over your parade 'cuz I don't like arriving at Sami's at 4 am. Getting down that driveway gives me the creeps … like I'm rolling over my own grave." Mac shuddered. "Those front steps! Creeeek… Groan… Squeeeeek."

Jeff chuckled at Mac's characterization. "As Da would say, all it needs is the application of a hammer and some nails."

"Charlie may be a great drummer but driving nails isn't in his wheelhouse." Mac shrugged. "And don't distract me from a good scare. That driveway has booglies all the way." He stared out the windshield. "Hmm. Wonder if we could write a Halloween song." Mac's long fingers plucked invisible bass strings.

"Sami's more interested in the inside and keeping Charlie happy. We all do better when Charlie's happy. Better arrangements and new songs—translation—closer to solid work. You're the one who wants rock star perks."

"Drummers are supposed to be extroverts." Mac grumbled. "And he takes out all his frustration on Niki. Man, he can be cutting."

Jeff knew Mac wouldn't let a good pout go without a fight.

"He is happy … when he's drumming or when he's with Sami. Charlie's moody. I, for one, will put up with a creepy entrance if the lady inside keeps our resident genius happy. Besides, she feeds us better than anyone I know besides Ma."

"Even better than Sandwich Lady?"

"Colby," he said drawing an 'ooooh' from Mac. He ignored the sound. "I'll take her to Four Seasons someday."

"Yeah, sure. As if you'll ever see her again."

Jeff raised an eyebrow and shifted the conversation to the day's performance, a point by point analysis. Mac hunkered down, rolled up his sweatshirt and tucked it under his head. Jeff suggested changes to each song, recalling each note and beat.

Mac's responses shifted from a grunt to a soft snore. Jeff's voice trailed off. *Never fails.* Nothing kept Mac awake once the truck rolled. Mac slept anywhere, at any time if given the chance. But he awakened at the slightest change in the environment, leftover from his runaway past. Mac found an immovable force in Jeff's mother and, under her watchful eye, he'd stayed put on the Texas ranch. Jeff nursed more than one black eye that first summer when he stumbled across Mac's hiding places.

John Grey Wolf, Jeff's Native American grandfather, taught him to reach out to Mac's spirit first, nudging him awake from afar. Their talent evolved into outright telepathy, an ability they exploited on the football field. Jeff doubted his grandfather approved or maybe the old man laughed at his grandson's ingenuity.

I hate to tell Charlie I'm going home. When Grey Wolf demanded to see a tribal member, he tolerated no argument. Jeff's frown deepened. *Worse is telling Mac he isn't welcome.* The old man begrudgingly allowed Mac to attend ceremony when Jeff's mother made it clear Mac was family. *But he isn't clan.*

The traffic thinned, headlights sparse in the deepening gloom. *Another hour.* He pushed his palms against the steering wheel and rolled his shoulders, his flannel shirt whispering against the seat. In his peripheral vision, Mac's aura flared near waking. Jeff reached out to him, soothing the aura until Mac slipped into a deeper sleep.

Jeff sipped at the tepid coffee fighting off the tedium induced by the dark road and winter weather. The mile markers slipped by in time to the roaring tires. A light flashed in the side mirror. A silver Mercedes roadster, invisible in the gloom, emerged from behind the truck. Throwing sleet as it accelerated, it pulled past and cut in, narrowly missing the front bumper. Jeff swerved toward the shoulder.

"Damn!" He swore under his breath. Mac opened one eye. "Idiot driver tried to play tag."

Mac stretched, placing his knuckles against the cab roof, arching his back. He reached for the thermos and poured a cup, refilling Jeff's.

What's on your mind, buddy, other than courting the Sandwich Lady? Mac's question vibrated in Jeff's head.

Jeff didn't respond.

Mac tried again, out loud. "Hmmm, whatcha thinking 'bout? The Sandwich … er … Colby?"

"No." Jeff hesitated but knew how persistent Mac could be. "About family."

"Ol' home week, huh?" Mac paused. Jeff waited for Mac's outburst.

"No … hell, Jeff, every time you go down memory lane, it's 'cuz you're going back to Texas." He stared at Jeff, a frown on his face. "You are, aren't you? Just when were you going to tell me?"

"Quit reading my mind," Jeff snapped at him. Mac's projected distress softened Jeff's tone. "Now," he added.

"Not trying … don't have to. Just noticing the pattern … what I'm good at." Mac resurrected his earlier pout. "Bet I'm not invited to this party." He looked younger than his thirty-two years, his face tight with pain.

Jeff took a deep breath. "No, you aren't." He went on before Mac could protest. "Charlie will have my hide over this. I know Niki has worked overtime to get us a good long run."

"What's wrong with Grey Wolf? Doesn't he know we're a team? I've done all the damn sweat lodges and spent my time in the wilderness. Why aren't I good enough for him?" Mac's exposed feelings vibrated.

"Man, I don't have any choice."

"Of course, you do. Don't go!" Mac accentuated his statement openhanded on the dashboard.

Jeff took another deep breath, concentrating on the road. The exit sign flashed by. *Great Spirit, Mac, how can I make you understand?* Just doing "all those things" wasn't like fulfilling a graduation requirement. Incorporating the experiences themselves into the spirit path required surrender…not Mac's way. He squinted against pain and hunkered down to weather Mac's distress.

"Remember the last time I didn't go?" In Jeff's peripheral vision, Mac's face paled. "Remember the nightmares? And the things going bump in the night…things that don't belong in New York City? Grey Wolf isn't a subtle man when he's crossed and he's good at showing his displeasure."

"Okay, okay," Mac relented. "Your grandfather is a mean son-of-a-bitch. When do you have to leave?"

"Soon." Before Mac could respond to the non-answer, he pleaded, "Please, Mac, don't say anything. I'll tell Niki. The band will need another guitar, either rhythm because Scotty can pick up lead or a damn fast learner for the lead." He swallowed, dreading the scene. *Why do I feel like a kid caught truant?* He'd followed the family plan—going to graduate school, working for the company and on the ranch—that is, until he left to pursue music, his dream. Even after a moderately successful year with Charlie, he still felt his life wasn't his own. He looked down at his white knuckles, his internal argument manifest.

The truck slid to a stop at the bottom of the exit ramp. He turned onto the two-lane road through the small village, dark storefronts lining the street. The Quick Mart lights stood out in the falling snow. A silver Mercedes roadster parked in front, steam rising from the hood.

"There's that damn car. I'd stop and give the driver a word or two if I wasn't so hungry." Jeff shrugged. "Those ham sandwiches looked good. Too bad she knocked them out of my hand."

The truck continued down the slick road, the wind velocity increasing. Jeff kept both hands on the wheel. *Reminding Mac about the ghoulies and ghosties wasn't a good idea. Sami's house is scary enough itself.* They'd driven to the Victorian house on every break and he couldn't remember a time when the weather cooperated ... through the spring and summer, driving rain ... now sleet turning to snow. The gloomy property wasn't welcoming at night in any weather.

They left the last house lights behind, traveling farther into the woods. The truck slowed to a crawl as Jeff turned the truck into the narrow drive... skeletal limbs clawing at the sides. He stopped, staring at the faint lights in the distance.

What's up, buddy? Mac's thought nudged at him, fear in the communication suggesting Mac didn't want to say it aloud.

I feel something, Jeff responded in kind, *and it's angry.*

The truck dipped and jerked in the ruts. The lights grew closer.

"Jeff! Watch out!"

A monstrous shape appeared from the overgrown branches. The blackness hung in the air for two heartbeats before diving towards them. Metal on metal screeched through the truck.

Jeff swerved and stomped on the brakes. The truck rocked to a stop, nose buried in the bushes. Jerking the gear shift into park, he glanced in the side mirror before throwing open the door. He stepped out on the running board, searching the trees behind them. The wind wiped the dark branches, driving snow obscuring the drive.

Back in the cab, he glanced at Mac. His face ashen, Mac peered through the windshield. An unspoken *what the hell was that* hung between them. Jeff heard Mac's explosive breath.

"Okay, so was that some gentle reminder from Grey Wolf?" Mac's eyes continued to scan the darkness beyond the windshield. "We were just talking about him."

"I doubt it. He knows I'm coming."

"But I was trying to convince you not to go."

Jeff faced him. "Look, we've been working hard the last three weeks without a break. I'm bone-tired. Everything is exaggerated."

"Jeff, that was no hawk—they don't hunt at night—and it was way too big even for a great horned owl. I know they're in these woods ... I've heard them. But ..." his voice trailed off.

"Okay, something's out here." Jeff gestured at the dark driveway. "What, I don't know." He ground the gears forcing it into reverse.

"Whatever it is gives me the heebie jeebies. It's not natural." Mac rubbed his face. "I'm back in the swamps where the *best* thing that's bad is the alligator. Hurry, Jeff, let's get to the house."

Jeff urged the truck back onto the drive. They rode in wary silence. As the truck passed through the gate, a black streak ran across the headlights and leapt over the brick wall. Jeff jerked the wheel again, slamming on the brakes stopping inches from Charlie's car.

Mac jumped, banging his head on the roof. "Yikes! What the hell?"

"Pyewacket, that's the way to lose another life!" Jeff yelled at the cat.

Mac grabbed his chest. "Go around on the grass! Get me in the stable before my heart stops!"

Jeff gunned the engine and the truck lurched. "Bet I left ruts in the grass this time."

"I'll fix them with a teaspoon if I have to...just hurry, Jeff." Mac braced against the doorframe. The truck hurtled toward the open stable door.

CHAPTER 4

Charlie stood with the scalding water running down his neck and shoulders. Sami's hand appeared through the shower curtain with a lowball. His wet fingers secured the glass. Turning off the water, Charlie pulled back the curtain.

Clutching the warmed bath sheet to her chest, she ran her eyes over his wet body. She blushed along her jawbone, the highlighting increasing his desire. He sipped the scotch, set the glass on the sink and stepped out. She wrapped the towel around him, entering his arms.

"You'll get wet," he murmured into her hair.

"I don't care." She held on tighter. "I missed you."

Charlie's heart stopped. Tightening his embrace, he willed away his dark thoughts. He waited for her to speak. *I will give her anything she desires.*

"How long has Niki been here?" He bit his lip, wanting to take those words back. *Why didn't I tell her how beautiful she is?* He missed her answer, too busy with his own thoughts. "Sorry, I didn't hear you."

"He arrived this morning." Escaping from his grasp, she pushed him to turn so she could dry his back. "He checks in to make sure I'm okay. Charlie, he's excited about the deal he's got for you."

How often? He bit his lip to prevent the question from escaping. Relieved she couldn't see the grimace on his face, he shook his head.

"You're throwing water on me." She laughed and reached up to dry his hair.

He twisted back around, pulling her tight against his chest.

"Why the second scotch? Trying to get me drunk?" He leaned down and ran his tongue along her neck. She arched against his arms, letting her head fall back. He nibbled across her collar bone nosing aside her shirt. Her scent rose from between her breasts. He inhaled, his knees weakening.

She raised her head, pushing him away.

"I have clean clothes laid out for you." She opened the door to the bedroom.

Charlie tucked the towel around his waist. The chilly bedroom air raised goose bumps on his skin. He grabbed the clothes from the bed— his favorite black jeans and a soft cream cashmere sweater—a gift from her on their first Christmas together.

"I've some news." The fabric muffled her words.

Charlie struggled to free his head from the clinging sweater. He broke a sweat at the possibilities. *Is this what she meant ... something I can't accept?* He sat down on the bed and reached for a sock. Taking a deep breath, he looked at her. "Okay, shoot."

"We're going to have company for the next few days."

"Company? We planned on the chaps so that's not news. The bad news is I won't have much time alone with you." *Again, the blush. Two years married and she still blushes.* He tried to catch her hand but she picked up a hairbrush and ran it through his dark hair.

"I had a call from your sister-in-law ... the Lady Jessica," she announced. Straightening her spine and holding her head at a dignified angle, she continued in a thick British accent. "She deigns to grace us with her presence while on her sojourn to visit sister Anita."

"Lady Jessica?" He succeeded in trapping her fingers and pulled her into his lap. He felt his tension, building over the past weeks, subside. "Sami, it is just Jess. She is as pretentious as ... as ..." Charlie grasped for a good analogy. "As Pyewacket. She has kept my stodgy brother in line for ten years now." He leaned his cheek against her soft hair. "I'll be glad to see her."

A warm breeze floated through the room, stirring the crystals on the chandelier. Charlie teased her when she moved the chandelier into the bedroom. Now he treasured the crystal droplets. He grew dizzy watching the colors change and the light dance across the ceiling.

Sami stirred in his arms. "Colby will arrive tonight. Dad and Mother are cruising the Mediterranean. She didn't want to go."

He held his breath. Celeste Fairfield expressed her negative opinion of a man who would prevent her daughter from having a proper wedding. It would have been the season's crowning event. Growing up among the English Peers, he had no taste for pomp and circumstance. Still, he worried he had stolen an experience that couldn't be replaced. *Colby ... fine. Not Mater and Pater. Carleton is a good bloke ... but Celeste ...* He hugged Sami tighter.

"Why does Pyewacket hate me?" He shrugged at her sharp look.

"Charlie, he doesn't. Why do you say that?"

"He leapt at the MG when I came down the drive. Scared me almost into the ditch." He drummed his fingers on her back, uncomfortable with his admission.

Sami wiggled free. "I hear the truck." She pivoted and disappeared into the hall.

He grabbed his boots and ran down the backstairs. He tripped on the last step, and caught himself on the kitchen counter.

"Graceful," Sami said. She filled three mugs with mulled wine.

He stood on one foot to pull on the boot, trying to hide his embarrassment.

"Charlie, we need to try that move out on the dance floor." Sami grabbed his shoulder to steady him.

No, not embarrassment. He swung her around under his arm, planting a kiss on her nose as she turned. *Joy when she teases me. I like it.*

He accepted the mugs, kissed her forehead, hearing her hum as his lips met her skin. *Maybe she did miss me.*

CHAPTER 5

Kay Kasavina waved at the Volvo SUV when it slowed in the airport traffic. The redhead behind the wheel grinned, pulled to the curb and waited for her to stow her bag in the backseat. Kay shut the passenger door and sighed. "Tori, it is so good to be on the ground."

"Kay, I can't tell you how glad I am to see you in person. Video conferencing is a great invention but it can't beat the real thing." Tori Madison glanced at her watch. "The way I figure it, we have just enough time to find a hostess gift and make it to your friend's in time for a fashionably late supper."

Kay's stomach flipped at the thought of food. She sank back into the leather seat.

Tori pulled the SUV into the airport traffic. "Now as to a gift. I need a better picture in my mind. It's a traditional Victorian? Not a painted lady?"

"No, it's traditional." Kay held up her phone. "I have a photo."

Tori glanced at the image. "There are pedestals flanking the steps but no statuary." Tori changed lanes. "Just the clue I need. We should find something to live there."

"Tori, I know you are interested in antiquities. But you want things for your business, not a museum. I'm trying to figure out where I fit in. How did you become an interior decorator?"

Tori winced. "Designer, sweetie. You'll have half the industry mad at you calling them decorators." She checked the mirror, merging into traffic. "My Mama. She was a social climber. My Daddy came from old money … didn't give a damn about society in Charleston. Mama couldn't find a way into their drawing rooms except by selling them fabulously overpriced gewgaws."

"The words you choose suggest you don't like the business."

"Mama's in the grave and I've changed things. I don't worry about the curtains or the couch. I find my clients the oddities … the structural antiques to make the house unique or the special items worth the dollars they throw at me."

She exited the highway and pulled the SUV into the parking lot of a large warehouse. The sign over the loading dock read "Arsenault Brothers, Purveyors in Antiquities and Oddities." Red lipstick appeared in her hand. "I enjoy the hunt. Your authentication will help me justify the cost to my clients. Will make them feel special."

Through the open bay door, dust motes danced in the breeze, glittering under dangling, naked bulbs. Tarpaulins covered spiky protuberances. The sound of their heels on concrete echoed to the high tin ceiling. Tori turned off the main aisle. Kay followed her, flanked by lawn ornaments, angels, naked children, crouching lions and more.

"No …no … no … maybe." Tori trailed her fingers across each object they passed.

A tall ebony-skinned gentleman, dressed in impeccable white tie and evening tails, emerged from the shadows. "Welcome, Miss Victoria. We have missed you." His voice rolled with a Jamaican lilt.

"Lucius, dear friend." She stretched up to kiss him on the cheek. Then she wiped the lipstick from his skin with her fingers. "Always a joy to see you. Let me introduce my new partner just arrived from Europe."

Lucius bowed to Kay, shaking her hand at the same time. "It is a pleasure. Miss Victoria has sung your praises."

"My pleasure as well. You have an interesting inventory."

"My brothers have a yen to travel. They find the items and depend on me to keep them in money."

"How many brothers, Mr. Arsenault?"

"Lucius, please. I have four who work for me here and three on the road."

"Kay." Tori's voice sounded from the distance. "Come look."

Lucius guided her through the aisles to Tori's location.

"What do you think about these pillars? Not for Sami. I have a client restructuring a portico."

Kay laid a hand on the carved pillar. Descending bombs whistled in her ears. A child's scream as she is ripped from her mother's arms. Dirt cascading back to the ground. Kay shuddered. She rubbed her hands to clear the energy. Backing away, she bumped into another pillar leaning against the wall. The stone vibrated but no visions came.

Kay cleared her throat, trying to find her voice. "Would these do?"

Tori examined the new pillars, walking from side to side and eyeing their height. "Yes, they will. The patina is lusher. Lucius, dear, will you have these shipped?"

She brushed against a large grey tarp. It rippled and sent water down her leg. She jumped away. "What's under here?"

"My apologies, Miss Victoria. This pair has been here a long time … since my grandfather's time. They were shipped home from England by a soldier during the War. He found them in Scotland when he was on leave. He died from mustard gas before he could return to the States. The family couldn't stand to keep them." He pulled the tarp back and revealed two statues with reddish amber carnelian eyes.

Tori knelt next to the statues. "Hello, darlings. Have you been waiting for me?"

Two foxes peered from under the edge. The Reynard stood rampant. The vixen crouched, powerful back legs bunched to jump, her tail held high. "How unusual. If Sami doesn't like these critters, I'll be surprised." She looked at Kay.

Kay nodded, amused by Tori's enthusiasm and pleased knowing Sami would treasure them. "Tori, the house is named Foxhaven."

Tori grinned. "Damn, I'm good." She stroked the two foxes. "I will take these beauties with me today, Lucius."

"We will miss this pair." He ran a hand down the Reynard.

"I suppose the price will be premium because they keep you amused?" Tori arched an eyebrow at Lucius.

His grin widened, "For you, missy, never—but if you were our only customer, we'd not be in business long."

"Oh, Lucius, you say the sweetest things!" Tori patted his cheek.

"Do you have time to see our new arrivals? We have a beautiful carved bench from Tuscany … eleventh century."

"I'd love to stay, Lucius, but Kay's friend expects us."

"Then we shall load them immediately." Lucius' whistle split the air. Two young men, broad and muscled, appeared dragging a flatbed cart.

In a few moments, the foxes nested in the back. Tori guided the Volvo onto the entrance ramp to the northbound highway.

"I call those beauties a good start!" Tori glanced at Kay. "Now you've time to nap."

Kay closed her eyes, the motor's drone soothing her to sleep.

CHAPTER 6

Colby Fairmont paused, her knuckles inches from the heavy oak door. *I hope I'm not imposing.*

The door flew open and Sami pulled her into the bright hall.

"I've missed you!" Sami unbuttoned Colby's coat. "How was the drive?"

"I'm so glad to see you!" Colby kissed Sami on the cheek. "Where's Charlie?"

Their voices entwined, punctuated with hugs. Sami peeled Colby's coat from her shoulders, spinning her out into the hall.

Colby looked around. "This is so elegant." Without drawing a breath, she continued, "I'd love some tea. You must have some now you've landed an English aristocrat. So what if he doesn't have the title." They entered the kitchen, the careening monologue continuing.

Sami poured hot water over the tea ball waiting in the cup. She slid it across the island.

"It was so strange coming up. There was some snow but it wasn't slick until your exit. Then snow, rain, sleet, fog. I swear, Sami, I expected a tornado to appear … anything to slow me down. I had to stop at the Quik Market to ask directions. Couldn't find anyone who knew the way. How can you've been here this long and no one knows where you live? I had to just go on instinct."

Sami shrugged.

"God, I can't stop yattering. I'm just so glad to be with someone who loves me." She swallowed the last words in a throat-tightening sob. "I feel so unlovable and stupid about people and will never ever find anyone." Colby shuddered, gasping for air. "I was horribly rude to the most handsome man. All I wanted to say to him was 'Where the hell have you been? I've been waiting all my lifetimes for you.' Oh,

Sami, I'm such a yutz!" Colby punctuated the last statement with a careful sip. "This is delicious, by the way."

Sami's laughter set the crystal goblets singing in counterpoint.

"So, should I leave now that I've exposed all my latest neuroses? You are the only one I've ever trusted and probably ever will since I'll be an old maid." She gazed off into the snowy evening. "Maybe I'll join the NASCAR circuit. I'm a good driver. I can concentrate on motors, not on his shoulders…"

"My turn?" Sami asked.

Colby gazed at the floor, dark bangs curtaining her eyes. "Yes."

"You're here for the holidays. You will enjoy yourself."

Colby looked up at her emphasis.

"The way you handle the Mercedes, NASCAR has nothing to teach you!"

"Oh, my God. You listen to me." Colby exclaimed.

Sami stirred the stew. "I always will … even when you are talking nonsense. Tell me about this man."

"He's taller than Dad with long dark hair tied back with a leather strap and the brownest eyes." She sighed and sipped her tea. "A great smile with a dimple right here on his cheek." She pointed a manicured nail at her right cheek.

Sami poured her own tea, her face averted.

"I didn't even get to see Charlie's band! You talk so much about them! But the hungry mob wanted more sandwiches." She tapped her fingers on the table. "They ate like locusts. Every time I tried to get away, an empty tray came back and someone barked at me for more. It was awful … hot and messy and miserable." Colby threw up her hands. "What made me think helping the homeless would be fun?"

Sami nodded, remaining silent.

"I snuck out with a tray and Charlie's band was gone. Men were carrying equipment in all directions." She rolled on. "It was chaos, one band onstage, another in the wings and then these two ... roadies, do you call them?" She looked at Sami.

Sami nodded.

"They were moving things into a beat-up truck. I offered them sandwiches." Her face reddened. "He snatched two and said, 'Will you go with me to The Four Seasons tonight?' I was shocked." She picked up speed. "I suffered through two hours working like a galley slave and he has the gall to accept free food ... free ... and make such a ridiculous offer. Looked me up and down with a grin on his face!"

Sami choked on a sip.

"Are you okay?"

Sami grabbed a napkin.

"Who did he think he was talking to? Some naïf off the street with no idea the requirements for such an offer? Reservations at least, not to mention the cost. He was dressed in blue jeans with holes above the knees and a stupid flannel shirt covered in dust and more than a little sweat. What a joke. At my expense." She burst into tears.

Sami handed her another napkin. "Colby, I doubt he meant any offense. It sounds like a nice offer even if all he could afford was coffee."

Colby cried louder. "I was so mean to him. I called him a cad. When his friend laughed, I was mortified, I knocked the sandwiches from his hand." She hiccupped. "Imagine Mother's distress if I showed up with a gorgeous, penniless man! He may be my last chance!"

"You know Jon loves you. He has since kindergarten."

Colby looked away.

Sami grabbed Colby's hands pulling her up. "Enough wallowing. Upstairs with you. I put together a bedroom just for you. Even a queen-sized bed because *I* don't expect you to be alone forever."

Colby drew a sharp breath. "Sami!"

"Don't look askance. I'm a married woman. Try it. You'll like it." She smiled at her sister's wide eyes. "Up the back stairs. I'll get your bags."

"Have Charlie's roadies do it. Isn't that what they're for?" Colby said, Granddame Fairmont's influence in her voice. She climbed up the dim stairwell. "Which room is mine?" she called back. "It's rather spooky up here."

"The first on the left." Sami yelled up the stairs.

***

She muttered under her breath. "Charlie's roadies."

Sami opened the back door and stared at the stable. Niki appeared from the dimly lit interior. He nodded, striding toward the front drive. The Mercedes fired to life. The headlights illuminated the auto bay beside the stable then went dark. He crossed the yard carrying a valise and a cello case. Sami rolled her eyes. *How do I explain he moved the car without the keys*?

Niki climbed the porch steps. "Hotwire. No challenge at all." He hefted the cello and edged by her, kissing her on the nose. "Let me guess. Cello in the parlor and run the valise upstairs. Right?"

"Thank you." she said turning her eyes back to the stable. After a moment, Niki came up behind her. "What's Jeff wearing?"

"Jeans. Red flannel shirt. Why?"

"No reason." She wrapped Charlie's shirt tighter around her shoulders. "So many secrets. My teacher—my friend—is coming tonight."

Niki inhaled sharply. "Sami, that's great." He snatched the door open.

"It is, Niki." Her hand on his arm arrested his exit. "It's time for our secret to be revealed."

Niki nodded.

CHAPTER 7

Charlie stopped just inside the barn door. He marveled at the effortless way Jeff and Mac moved the heavy sound gear and stowed it in the empty stall.

"Come on, Niki, help us," Mac called from the back of the truck.

Niki stepped by Charlie causing him to jump. Niki grabbed the snare drum Mac held out. "If you guys make a little more noise, you could revive *Stomp*."

"Don't think his Lordship would play on a garbage can." Mac untied the bass drum, handing it off. He jumped off the tailgate.

Charlie glared at Mac. Jeff stepped up beside him.

"Charlie, we have to talk…there's something in the woods."

Charlie continued to stare at Mac. "It's your imagination, Jeff. Nothing more."

"Charlie …."

Charlie pivoted to face Jeff. Looking up into his face, he whispered, "Don't ruin the holidays for Sami."

Jeff shook his head but returned to the unloading. He shrugged at Mac's raised eyebrow.

Niki pushed a wheeled crate to the back wall. "Mac." He looked over his shoulder. "There isn't room for all the equipment. You guys pick up more?"

"No." Mac eyed the barn. "Hey, something's different."

"Can't be, Mac," Charlie called. "No one would have changed anything out here." The long hours on the road pressed down on him and, for the first time, he wished they would all go away.

Mac paced off the distance from door to back wall. "It's shorter by thirty feet." He surveyed the aisle. "Yep, you're missing two stalls on each side. I don't remember a door at this end."

Charlie turned on his heel. "What the hell are you talking …" He studied the double sliding door. "Bloody hell." He stalked to the door. He paused. "Sami may not be ready … best leave it alone."

"Come on, Charlie," Mac stepped up beside him. "Curiosity will kill me." He reached for the handle.

Charlie slapped his hand away.

"Ow!" Mac rubbed his fingers. "Damn, you're strong for being so scrawny."

Charlie drummed his fingers against his leg and stared at the door.

"It is her house." Niki said under his breath.

The blood drained from Charlie's face. "May be, kid, but I am the man in her house." Charlie grabbed the handle and yanked the sliding door into motion. The door rolled back revealing a dark space. Charlie stepped in. Forty track lights warmed to daylight. Mac pushed in behind Charlie, his mouth dropping open.

"The Saints, man! What a space. I couldn't have designed this better myself." Mac studied the architectural detail.

Egg crate soundproofing in crème Brule lined the walls and a dozen microphones hung from the high ceiling. An electric piano and unopened boxes with labels from major companies filled the room. Charlie stared at the gleaming drum kit on the raised platform.

A glass partition defined the sound booth. Niki ducked around Mac. Charlie blocked his path. "Unless Sami is ready for us to see this, it isn't right." Charlie treasured the changes he discovered in the house, the furniture restored for him. *Has she even been out to the stable?* Confusion rattled his thoughts.

Niki looked Charlie in the eye, steel in his voice, "Charlie, did you ever consider she wants to surprise you? Just enjoy it." He walked away.

CHAPTER 8

The house telephone rang. Sami listened to the raucous sound. She took one step at a time toward the study, counting the rings—*eleven—twelve—*

Trailing her fingers across the reconditioned walnut desk, she tried to ignore the sound. It was a small surprise compared to the studio but any change brought a twinkle to his eye, his delight evident in his gentle caresses and passionate kisses.

I've lost count and it's still ringing. She lifted the receiver, steeling herself for her Mother's voice. She hadn't given the number to anyone else. Her father let it ring three times, hung up and called back in a few minutes so she knew to expect his baritone greeting. *And when to prepare for you.*

"Hello?"

"Sami, why were you so long?"

"Sorry, Mother. I was in the kitchen."

"Put a phone in there. Why do you have to live where there is no cell service?"

Sami remained silent.

"Sami, are you there?" Her voice grated shrill in Sami's ear.

"Yes, Mother."

"Sami, did you hear a word I said?"

"Sorry, Mother."

Celeste harrumphed. "Lady Ramhill will arrive within the hour. We met her plane and escorted her to luncheon. That was hours ago so you must have dinner ready when she arrives. Harold is driving her down."

Harry, not Harold. "Thank you. Have a wonderful trip."

"Not so fast, young lady. Listen to me. Use the silver and china … in the dining room. You want to make a good impression, don't you?"

"Yes, ma'am" Jessica Hamilton was a childhood friend in the Fairmont home long before she became Lady Ramhill and, upon Sami's marriage to Charlie, her sister-in-law.

"Pay attention. Send Harold back tonight."

Sami responded before she could stop, "But the weather is getting worse. Harry will have to stay the night…"

"What a lovely situation. We have never been invited to visit but Harold can stay the night." Venom dripped through the line.

"But he's getting old. I worry about the roads in this weather. You're invited … next summer when the gardens are done. I still have so much to do." Sami stopped protesting.

"Your father has important business with Lady Ramhill's father. Be thoughtful for him if you won't do it for me. I must go. He hates to be late for his scotch."

"I will, Mother." The line went dead before she finished speaking. *Damn it, Daddy*—she adored him but they fought about the telephone—*I don't want it*. She slammed down the receiver.

A hum in the air tickled her face. She closed her eyes, calming as the touch thrilled her skin. She lifted both arms and allowed it to guide her into the parlor. Opening her eyes, she looked down at the inlaid wind rose. She sank to the floor, a handkerchief discarded—her long blonde hair hiding her face. *One heartbeat, two heartbeats, three heartbeats*, a responding pulse from the wind rose.

"Sami," Colby's voice startled her. "Are you all right?"

"Yes," she said.

"Why are you on the floor?"

"Mother called."

"You have a phone? I bet she badgered Dad. She just can't stand being unable to spread her *bon mots.*" Her voice lost the cutting edge. "You will give me the number, won't you?"

Sami rose from the floor and embraced Colby. "Of course, I will." She twirled Colby around.

"Stop," Colby squealed. "You're learning to dispel Mother's pall."

"I've help … you and Charlie. Now, there's work to do. That outfit is wonderful, but you have to change."

Colby waved her hand at her cashmere sweater and the cream wool pants. "What's wrong with this?"

Sami laughed. "Nothing at all, but we're dressing for dinner … with a capital D." Her tone grew imperious. "The Lady Ramhill is gracing us with her presence and the Queen Mother has decreed I will impress her properly." She laughed. "We have to fulfill her desire and take pictures … lots."

"But I didn't bring anything formal!" Colby protested.

"Open the armoire's other door. Pick the color you like best. I have shoes to match everything." She herded Colby toward the stairs. "And there will be earrings in the top drawer."

***

Charlie burst through the kitchen door. "Sami, how did you do it?"

She stopped him with her finger on his lips. "Do you like it?"

"It is magnificent! It is bloody well the most fabulous studio I have ever seen." He pulled her to him. "How did you know what to buy? You can't spend your money on me. It cost a fortune."

Sami's hand on Charlie's chest slowed his wild search for more words. "It's not from me."

"Then whom?"

"My father. It's a wedding present, to show his appreciation that you make me so happy."

"But he doesn't know anything about the music industry … does he?" Charlie hesitated, his fingers drumming on her back. "How could he pick out the top equipment?"

"Niki."

"What about Niki?" he demanded.

Sami tried to pull away but he held onto her arms. She froze.

"Charlie, they went to Nashville, Austin, New York … anywhere Niki thought the best equipment could be found. Niki spent the last month working day and night to have it ready. Pyewacket even carried a screwdriver in his mouth."

"You have been out there?" His fingers tightened on her arms.

"You know I haven't." Her tone chilled him. She peeled his hands from her arms. "Your friends are hungry." She stretched up on tiptoe to kiss him on the nose. "Just answer me again, is it what you would want?"

He dropped his forehead to press against hers. "Yes"

"Good. Then …" her tone indicating she would not entertain any argument, "tell them to dress for dinner. There are clothes in the armoires."

He raised an eyebrow.

"Dinner is formal. In the dining room. One hour."

She pushed him out the back door.

CHAPTER 9

Niki stood at the corner of the house, his collar turned up against the cutting wind. He drew back when Charlie exited the back door and headed for the barn.

There goes his lordship. You won't drive me away. He swallowed the bile in his throat. *I'd never hurt Sami, you suspicious bastard!*

He pulled his coat tighter. The wind swirled up the snow. He ran a finger down the scar on his cheek, a souvenir from the Ramhill family ring. Unbidden, the touch swept him back to the last argument with his father. As a refugee, his father, though an educated man, was lucky to hold a position as a tutor for the Ramhill daughters. Niki was just another servant's child in the household where Charles Ramhill embarked on his musical education, graduating with honors.

Niki loved the land … spending nights in the forest, playing his own tunes on a handmade wooden flute. When his father announced Niki, at age thirteen, would attend boarding school, he begged to stay then ran to hide in the stable. Lord Ramhill and his son's fiancée entered the stall to view his hunting horse. In his cups, the Lord cornered Jessica, attempting to kiss her. Niki rose from the straw and grabbed Lord Ramhill's arm. The Lord backhanded him, sending him under the hunter's legs. Niki reached out to the horse he loved. Years under the crop made the small push to frenzy easy. The stallion trampled Lord Ramhill. Niki fled into the winter storm, stumbling through the mud.

A plaintive cry gave voice to his scrambled emotions. Tiny claws scrabbled up his leg. Scooping up the starving kitten, he tucked it into his coat and never went back.

What conspiracy brought me to that garage in New York? The music laid a geas on his heart, compelling him. Only when he saw Charlie did he start awake. Recognition did not flicker in Charlie's eyes. Niki hated the compulsion shackling him to the band. But he used the skills that kept him alive … sweet talking bar owners, trading favors for studio time, wheedling the DJ's. *They're on the way to something big. Lucky bastard.* He slammed his hand against the post, jarring the bones.

Headlights alerted him. He stood still against the weathered siding. A silver limousine whispered through the storm to the front steps. The elderly chauffeur opened the passenger door. Jessica Hamilton-Ramhill rose from the interior, hair as black as night, the white-streaked lock over her left eye blowing in the wind.

"Thank you, Harry." Her voice washed warm over Niki. "Will you give me your arm to the door, please?" The pair mounted each step with intense concentration.

Niki chuckled at her deception. He'd seen Jessica leap on her horse and turn it on two legs. The soft pressure against his calf broke his concentration.

It's out there again, Niki. Pyewacket rubbed figure eight against Niki's legs.

A chill ran down his spine. He scanned the clouds straining to feel the presence eluding him. "Looks like a cold night for us, old friend."

Pyewacket arched his back, hissing at the falling snow.

Niki put his hand on the weathered clapboard. "Help me, Foxie. Give me a clue," he implored then headed for the forest, his black shadow at his side.

***

Charlie opened the front door and Jessica swept into the hall, a swirling wool cape and flashing teal silk suit. She enfolded Sami in a tight embrace. "Sami, so good to see you." She turned to Charlie, grabbing his hand as he closed the door behind Harry.

All movement stilled as she ran a hand along his cheek. He turned into her palm, kissing it. "Charlie, you sly dog. How did you ever convince Sami to marry you?" Before he could respond, she placed a finger over his lips, "Don't answer. It'll be a lovely story over dinner. I'm famished." She kissed him lightly on the lips.

She pulled Sami into a second embrace. "I'm so happy for you."

Sami hugged her. "Colby's here, too."

"Colby?" Jessica looked about for the other Fairmont sister.

"You'll see her at dinner." She slipped away, running to hug the elderly gentleman carrying the suitcases toward the stairs.

He swept her into his gnarled arms admonishing her as he hugged. "Now, Miss, you've made me drop the lady's bags. I'm sure there's some fine thing broken." Moisture shone in the old man's eyes.

"Charlie, will you show me the way?" Jessica smiled at him. "I need a bath and drink. Not necessarily in that order." Charlie disappeared into the kitchen reappearing with a crystal tumbler with ice and bourbon. She took it from him. "It's so good to see you."

Hefting the bags, Charlie preceded her up the stairs. He nudged the door open with his foot and edged sideways into the guest room. Over his shoulder, he said, "This is a strange house. Each room has an adjoining bath. Must have cost a fortune in plumbing."

"Magnificent design, if you ask me."

Charlie set the suitcases down and stepped to the door.

"Wait." Jessica wrapped her arms around him, careful not to pour the drink down his back. "You are such a scoundrel. Are you happy?"

Charlie hesitated for a heartbeat. "Yes," he said. Jessica searched his face. Her grey eyes swirled with energy and he knew she read everything in one word.

"Dinner will be ready in thirty minutes. I have my mates from the band for you to meet." Jessica drained the glass and, handing it to him, closed the door.

CHAPTER 10

Colby stood at the cherry dining table running her finger around the Waterford plate. Sami paused in the door.

"Those were a gift from Lord and Lady Ramhill." Sami set the coffee cups on the sideboy. "Remember when we'd sneak into the butler's pantry and talk about the finery we'd have one day."

"Now you have sterling silver cutlery and Waterford plates. A linen tablecloth shot through with gold thread, white orchids in a crystal bowl, amber candles in silver candlesticks. And the crystal goblets." Colby twirled the stem spreading rainbows in the soft light. "I admit it. I'm jealous."

"Colby, I never expected to have a life—or a house—like this." Sami toyed with the cord tying her sleeves.

Colby looked her up and down. Sami wore a vanilla silk dress with cut sleeves, tied with gold cord at shoulder, elbow and wrist exposing the alabaster skin down her arms. The neckline scooped across her collar bone and framed the amber drops hanging from a gold choker. *An elegant home with a handsome husband.* Colby felt her throat tighten with conflicting emotions. She loved her little sister, protected her … was thrilled when she married in a fairy tale romance. *But why did you get all this first?*

"Sami, is all this necessary? I know she's a Lady now but she'll always be Jess to me." Colby picked at her French manicured fingernails.

"Turn around. I want to see every detail."

Colby obeyed. She fingered the rich brown velvet flowing from her shoulders and folding into layers across her breast. The delicate cameo on a silk ribbon stroked her throat and ivory earrings swung in her chestnut brown locks. She felt elegant.

"Charlie's friends are expecting British nobility and appropriate pomp and circumstance they will get. They don't know she's a family friend. I've never seen them in anything but blue jeans or khakis. It'll be fun to see them squirm in tuxedos. Mother wants pictures she can flaunt to all her friends. Especially the ones who never believed I would amount to anything." Rancor harshened Sami's voice but her quick smile dispelled the negative flash.

Colby recalled Sami's discomfort going to the country club for dinners or dances. Mother's cronies' remarks when Sami refused a debutante ball were scathing.

Charlie came through the hallway door. "Sami, you are stunning." He tucked her under his arm. "And you, my dear sister-in-law are exquisite." He pulled her to his other side. "Could a man be any happier than between two beautiful women?" He squeezed Colby tight until she squeaked.

Jeff's baritone voice echoed in the hallway.

> "Don't go down in the woods today,
> You're in for a big surprise…"

Colby stiffened in Charlie's embrace. *That voice, I know that voice.*

Mac interrupted Jeff's solo. "Help me with this tie, buddy. I'd rather eat the scraps in the kitchen if I wouldn't disappoint Sami."

Sami stepped to the door to meet a tall, dark-haired man. He held himself store dummy stiff. "How handsome. Thank you for humoring me." Sami pulled Mac into the room. "My sister's here. I know you'll enjoy her company."

Jeff wove around the pair with a dancer's grace, the silk suit draped smoothly across his broad shoulders. He stopped dead still, eyes locked with Colby, then stepped back toward the door. Before he could duck out, Sami grabbed his arm.

"Colby, I would like you to meet Mr. John MacIntyre," Sami nodded to Mac then pulled Jeff a step closer, "and Dr. Jeffry Conray."

"Hey, it's the Sandwi—ow—ow—" Mac sputtered. Jeff lifted his heel off Mac's foot. Mac glanced at Jeff then coughed behind his hand.

Colby's face grew hot. She swayed, not taking her eyes from Jeff's face. Charlie tightened his grip around her waist and gave her a worried look.

Jeff bowed, pulling her hand to his lips. "It's a pleasure. May I escort you to your seat?"

She nodded. Jeff tucked Colby's hand around his arm and led her to the seat on Charlie's left. His eyes flicked toward Sami, intense concentration in the gaze. Sami turned away, a smile flitting across her face. Colby frowned at the interaction, her anxiety heightened.

Mac stuck out his arm. "Sami, you know I'm not good at this fancy stuff. Just tell me what to do and I'll do it but, please, don't make me figure it out."

Harry appeared at the door to announce Lady Ramhill. Before he could speak, Jessica put her hand on his shoulder and stepped past him.

"Harry, don't make this so formal. This is my family. Not a state function … oh." Jessica observed the table laden with china and crystal, the gentlemen in tuxedos and the women in evening gowns. She wore a dark raspberry, brushed flannel shirt and tight-fitting black jeans tucked into polished boots. A wide leather belt with a brass buckle wrapped around her slim waist.

"Aren't I the country mouse."

"Now, there's my kinda woman," Mac mumbled under his breath.

Jessica stared at him, her laughter filling the room. Her dark eyes sparkled in the candlelight. He stood up a little straighter under her gaze.

"I'll be right back." She stepped backwards.

"Jess." Sami went after her. "Don't change! Please, come eat."

"Oh, no," Jessica called back, her boot heels beating a tattoo on the stairs. "I know my obligations."

Mac grumbled. Jeff stared at Mac who returned the look. The hair on Colby's arms stood up. She sensed mental messages but couldn't interpret it. It felt like *Shut up*.

Jeff laughed and returned his attention to Colby still on his arm. She mumbled something about the kitchen and fled … only to be herded back into the room by Harry, his hands filled with a large soup tureen.

"Sorry, Miss Colby. Please, take your seat so I may serve." Harry proceeded to move toward the sideboard. He leaned close to her and whispered, "Buck up, young lady. You're made of sterner stuff."

She backed her way around the table and directly into Jeff. He caught her elbows and steadied her. She froze on contact.

Jessica made her second entrance.

Mac's appreciative "Ahh" filled the room. Everyone's gaze on him, he colored around the collar.

Once again, Jessica's rich laughter rippled the air. "My concession to protocol," she said, modeling the drop diamond earrings. She unbuttoned her shirt one more button, exposing the diamond and ruby necklace across her cleavage.

Sami hugged her, calling for Harry to bring the camera. "Can you imagine Mother's face. Lady Jessica in jeans surrounded by all this finery." Sami herded them to the fireplace and composed them in best portraiture style. Harry continued taking pictures during the hasty striptease shedding ties and tuxedo jackets.

Jessica cleared her throat. "This is great fun," she said, her tone changing to a meek whine, "but I'm starving."

Charlie pulled out her chair on his right. She snatched up her fork and looked down the table at Sami. They grinned at each other.

Jeff turned to Colby to find her already seated with her eyes on her plate. The place card beside her announced Mac's name in gold script. Shrugging, Jeff and Mac switched places.

Harry circled the table filling wine glasses then served tomato bisque with sherry-sour cream and dill.

Charlie held up his glass. "My friends, my precious wife." He nodded to each friend, landing last on Sami. "On this beautiful winter night, welcome to the first formal dinner in our home." He paused. "With thoughts to our errant knights, Scotty and Chris, everyone I hold dear is here tonight. Thank you for this blessing. To your health and to our growing popularity!" He sipped the fine vintage. The formalities aside, he turned his attentions to dinner. "Sami, what happened to the mulligan stew?"

"It'll do for lunch tomorrow. This seemed more appropriate tonight." Sami looked over at Harry. "And I had great help in the kitchen."

"Excuse me, my lady." Harry placed a Caesar salad at Jessica's place.

"Hmmm. Sami, this is delicious." Jessica speared a crouton. After a few bites, she turned to Charlie. "How did you and Sami meet? It couldn't have been in the dives you frequent."

Charlie glanced over his wine glass. "It was All Hallows Eve in New York City. About four in the afternoon and the dark clouds loomed. A cold wind howled between the buildings."

One cue, the winter storm exhaled down the chimney, sending the flames roaring in the fireplace. The heavy drapes flapped against the windows, dark wings in the night.

"This is better than 'it was a dark and stormy night.'" Jessica glanced at Sami. Sami's eyes were fixed on the covered windows. "Charlie, do go on."

"In mid-block, just beyond the Metropolitan Museum, the heavens opened up. I dove into a doorway. A blonde juggernaut plowed into me, knocking me back into the corner." Charlie watched Sami in his peripheral vision. "She hit me so hard I couldn't breathe. Then she tossed her head throwing water everywhere. When she shivered, I opened my coat and enfolded her."

Sami pulled her eyes back to Charlie's face. She looked aghast at his rendition.

"I looked into her eyes and fell madly in love ... prayed she was single or that I could find a good hit man if she wasn't."

Jessica smiled at Sami. "What did you think, Sami?"

"I was wet so I figured any port in a storm." She shrugged her shoulders. Everyone laughed at Charlie's startled look. "One minute, the wind held me back so hard I couldn't take a step, then whipped around and pushed me down the street. The next moment, I'm wrapped in his arms, a complete stranger but I wasn't afraid … of him." She paused, playing with her salad.

Colby stared at Sami remembering the fear dominating Sami's life.

"When the rain stopped, he offered me his arm and we went to a cafe for tea. He talked from the minute we sat down, telling me about his music, the concert he'd been to the past weekend … like we were old friends. I didn't say five words in the first hour."

"Dear Lord, five words in the first two hours!" Charlie interjected. "I kept talking, trying to find a way to keep her from leaving. Her face was so pale, I thought something warm might help. I was a blithering idiot, telling her things about my life I hadn't thought about in years. When I mentioned a recent visit to the museum, she looked at me and told me she was an intern there. I managed to get her to talk about the show she was working on—"

"Poor man hasn't gotten a word in since." Sami picked up the story. "I said I'd rather a hot toddy. He had the good grace to look shocked but relieved at the same time. I finally found the courage to actually meet his eyes." Sami's voice grew husky, "I prayed he wouldn't leave me."

"Then wine, dinner, coffee." Charlie laughed. "I hired a cab and we rode to West Virginia. Got married in twenty-four-hour wedding chapel just over the border … just before midnight."

"A cab?" Jessica glanced from Charlie to Sami. Sami shrugged.

"I was afraid if I dropped her hand, she would disappear like in some O Henry story."

"I, for one, am delighted with the outcome. My brother-in-law marrying my childhood friend. Now I can call her my sister for real." Jessica tipped her wine glass in Sami's direction.

The conversation swirled around Colby. She knew the story. She twisted her napkin in her lap. She had always accepted Sami's shyness but did not realize how deep her fear. In her home, she was at ease with these men. Colby mentally stamped her foot. *Mother groomed me— the perfect hostess, comfortable at the club, at dinner parties. But here, in this room, I don't belong.* She glanced at Jeff, studying his sharp profile. *It's his fault.* She looked back at her plate. *I can't keep my eyes off him.*

Harry replaced the empty salad plates with lamb and roasted potatoes.

"Sami, this meal is wonderful. Where'd you learn to cook like this?" Mac bit into the potatoes.

"When I was in school in Europe, we ate cheeses and fruit during the week but on the weekends, my mentor and I put together elegant meals. There was nothing she wouldn't try. She said there was more in the world to learn than art."

Colby's fork bounced against her plate and fell to the floor. She and Mac leaned to retrieve the errant silverware, bumping heads. Shaking his head, Mac reached out to help right her in the chair. Tears prickled behind her eyes.

"Sorry, ma'am. I've got a hard head. Are you hurt?" Colby, face turned down, hid behind her auburn hair, waving him away in silence.

"Did you bring your cello?" Charlie covered her hand with his. "Are you working on a new piece?"

She gulped, looking around the table. Sami had Jeff's full attention and Jessica leaned to engage Mac in conversation. Drawing a shallow breath, she replied. "Yes, *Sonata for Unaccompanied Cello*. Samuel Adler's early work. It's challenging." Sipping the Beaujolais, she glanced across the table. Jeff's eyes looked in her direction.

She choked, coughing into her napkin. Charlie patted her on the back. Harry placed a glass of water wrapped in a fresh napkin in her hand. When she lifted her head, Jessica and Jeff were engaged in a debate over thoroughbreds versus the Western working breeds. Charlie warned Jeff he was in dangerous waters discussing horse flesh with Jessica.

She turned her attention to Sami's conversation with Mac.

"Mac, I need a favor."

"Whatever you want, baby girl," he said.

"A Christmas tree lit with candles and hung with popcorn and cranberry strings," Sami said. "Mother always had the perfect tree. She'd call the florist, announce the theme of the year and, poof, it appeared the next week. When Twelfth Night was over, it was gone. I want something more homemade."

Harry placed a dark chocolate mousse with raspberry sauce in front of her. "I bet we can find one on the property. Would you go with me to find it in the morning? Charlie won't get up before noon."

Mac nodded, tasting the mousse, then looked around. "Hey, where's Niki? With his sweet tooth, no way he'd miss this mousse."

Charlie waved his hand without looking away from Jessica. "I'm sure he's fine. Off plotting with his cat to attack my car's bonnet. He'll show up when he wants … like a bad penny."

Mac glared at Charlie. "You think that comment's funny? He works his ass off yet you treat him with contempt."

Charlie turned cold eyes on Mac. "Mac, you don't know anything about it."

"Damn it, Charlie, you don't know where he's been. He's a street kid. Never feels welcome. With your silver spoon upbringing, there's no way you can understand."

Sami placed her hand on Mac's arm but he shrugged it off.

"Ladies," Mac nodded to each. "Forgive my outburst. But I need to find my friend." Jeff edged his chair back.

Sit down, Jeff. I can handle this.

Mac disappeared through the swinging door into the kitchen.

***

Sami's dress rustled behind Mac. His stony face softened. She pulled a down parka from the closet. Slipping it on, he wondered why Charlie's coat would fit him… that thought and Sami's quiet movement around the kitchen eroded his anger. He tried to recapture his fury as he buttoned the coat.

Sami held out an insulated cooler. "He's in the studio. It's really his space," she said, her voice low. "Charlie's the guest."

Mac looked into her eyes trying to catch the will-o-wisp in that simple statement. "You're the world's best, Sami. I'd say I was sorry for speaking my mind but I'm not. He needs to remember how much Niki does for us."

Sami turned away. "If you find Niki smoking, don't give him a hard time."

With a curt nod, he stepped out into the driving snow.

CHAPTER 11

In the control booth, the oscilloscope peaked and waned to the music's rhythm and intensity.

Headphones on, his feet propped up on the soundboard, Niki closed his eyes, the magic sweeping him away. Smoke wreathed his head. For a minute, he surfaced to reality, leaving a mental sticky note, to air the studio before the guys woke. He rarely slept but cat napped throughout the day.

He hummed along, his fingers absently casting silver and gold strands dancing in the smoke. He peered through slitted eyelids, inhaling again.

Sami will forgive me tonight. She needed him for all her errands and covert messages, her eyes and hands in the outside world. He turned up the volume and set the lights spider-webbing across the walls, rising with the orchestra's swell. *In the Hall of the Mountain King*, the music swept him away.

"Poor, poor Peer," Niki mumbled. "Peer lost every opportunity in his life due to ego and, ultimately, threw away his heart's desire."

Niki, you listening to that sad music again? Pyewacket leapt into his lap.

"What is the difference between troll and man? Man, be thyself. Troll, to thyself be … enough." He rubbed Pyewacket behind the ears.

He laughed remembering the cold night he hid in the public library in London until the lights went out. He'd unrolled himself from the small, dark hiding space. *Reading by moonlight in the mausoleum of lost thoughts.* He'd found the recording in the archives and listened to the aging tape all night.

"The Boyg is asked 'Who are you?' He responds 'Myself.'" Niki stared into Pyewacket's eyes.

I wish you'd leave that alone. It depresses you. I'm going hunting.

Pyewacket squirmed away.

"Be careful." Niki flicked Pyewacket's tail earning a withering look.

"Who am I?" Niki asked the dark studio. He shivered, trying to drive away the memories, cold nights on the streets and the icy hands on his body, feelings leaden in his gut.

"Tomorrow, I'll face Charlie's ill will … tell them about the gig in Baltimore on New Year's Eve." He rubbed his eyes. "Tomorrow, I'll deal with Jeff going to Texas. *" Though Jeff hasn't confessed yet.* "Yes, Miss Scarlet, we will think about that tomorrow. But tonight, damn, I wish I had a drink."

Niki drifted in and out, his twilight world spinning around him, the thing out in the dark not far from his mind.

CHAPTER 12

Jessica touched Colby's hand. "Would you mind if I spirit my brother-in-law away for a few moments? We've business to conclude before everything shuts down for the holidays."

Jeff pulled her chair out. "Thank you, Jeff." She smiled at him, then the two left the dining room.

Turning back to the table, Jeff pushed in Charlie's chair.

Colby scooted through the swinging doors to the butler's pantry. She stopped. "Come on, Colby girl. Like Harry said, you're tougher than this."

Pushing the door open just enough to peer into the dining room, she studied his face. He extinguished the candles, pinching each wick between his fingers.

"Why do you pinch the flame rather than blow it out?" She stepped through the door, her knees shaking but congratulating herself for speaking at all.

Jeff smiled at her. "Two reasons. First, in my clan's beliefs, one never attacks one element with another. Fire." He pointed at the candle then at his lips. "Air. Two important elements."

She couldn't take her eyes from his lips.

"Second, blowing the flame spreads wax on the tablecloth and that would make Ma mad." He chuckled. "You don't want to see my Ma mad."

Colby thought a moment, realizing the humor in his statement. "Oh," she said.

They stood silent, the fire crackling in her ears.

"I … well … I …" She shrank under his gaze. Searching for another topic to avoid the inevitable, she said, "Do you and Mr. MacIntyre communicate telepathically?" She winced at her audacity, expecting a scornful reply.

Jeff chuckled. "Charged and found guilty."

She waited another heart beat for him to explain.

"We have since we were young. My Grandfather taught me to reach out to him and we discovered Mac could respond." He stepped forward.

Colby backed up, keeping the table between them. Jeff stopped.

"It came in handy on the football field." He reached over the table and snuffed out two more candles. "How do you know?"

"My father and my brother do it, too." She rubbed her arms. "It makes the hair on my arms ruffle." She had never admitted that to anyone before. *Why him?*

She drew a deep breath, stood up straight and marched around the table. "I wish to apologize for my horrid behavior. I'm not normally such a shrew though I admit I'm not as nice as Sami." The formal tone drained away, "I don't feel too terrible about it though since I haven't met anyone else who is either." She looked down at the rich Bijar carpet. "You were kind to stop your friend from blurting out about my bad manners. Will you forgive me?" She held her breath, her knees tensed to flee.

"If you will forgive me," he replied. "I didn't consider the impression I made on you … that it would seem impertinent. I would still like to take you there, someday. I will make reservations."

Colby inhaled. She stretched up on her toes and kissed him. The room spun, a sandy-haired toddler flashed through Colby's mind. *A little girl.* She slipped away before he could embrace her and rushed from the room, the kitchen door swinging against the wall.

***

Charlie escorted Jessica to the wingback chair in the study. His mood darkened with Mac's comments. *Sure, Niki is a vulnerable kid who has been kicked around. Just the type to appeal to Sami's tender heart.*

Jessica drew her hand away from his arm, taking his anchor against the swirling emotions.

Everything's so perfect—what the hell is going wrong? Am I losing her?

"Charlie. Charlie," Jessica's voice became sterner with each repeat. He looked at her. She pointed to a brown folder on the desk. He unwrapped the security string and pulled out the thick document.

"What is this?"

"I've found a buyer willing to pay what I thought your parcel is worth. All I need is your signature and your last holdings in England will be dispersed."

Charlie felt a pull in his chest. *My strings to England. The last shouting match with Damian.* He flipped through the pages.

"Hesitating?" Jessica studied him. "Would you prefer to review the papers in detail?"

"No." Charlie sank into the swivel chair. "Jess, I trust you. I need a pen." He pulled open one drawer after another, searching. *Pen ... I have to find the pen. If I can find the pen, I can find the right way to tell Sami how much I love her.* He pawed through the drawer without seeing the contents. *Maybe she will understand if I write her a truly good love song. But nothing ever seems to measure up.* His father was probably right. Nothing he did would ever be enough to make anyone happy. *Pen ... I have to find a pen. It will solve the problem.*

"Charlie, stop!" Jessica commanded in her best arena voice.

He paused, his hand on the next drawer, startled that she was standing beside him. She held out a Waterman pen and turned to the signature page. He scrawled his name. Air escaped his lungs and he rocked back in the chair.

Jessica tucked the document in the folder and laid it aside. She settled on the edge. "I'm glad you trust me ... but I don't sense much trust in this house at the moment. What's going on?"

"What do you mean?" He stared at the desktop, his fingers tapping against his leg. *One. Two. Three. Four.*

"Your words at dinner. If I hadn't been looking at your face, I could have been back in England. That snide, paranoid comment sounded like your brother … not you."

He scowled, his anger returning. He stood and stalked across the room. *The words won't come—or will too fast and harsh and ruin everything.*

Her strong hands grasped his shoulders and turned him to face her. Darkening storm clouds grew in her eyes.

I love your eyes, the violet gray twilight or, as now, lightning in the dark clouds. Just don't look at me that way. Charlie surrendered and embraced her. She hugged him. After a long moment, he stepped back.

"I am afraid I am losing Sami. When I got home, Niki was here … apparently has been here several times. They share an easy way with each other … physically …"

"You mean, they hug each other?" Jessica prodded.

Charlie's neck burned. "Jess, I have seen him hug or kiss her every time I've turned around tonight. Sami and I haven't had ten minutes alone."

"Charlie, we just hugged for the second time tonight."

"That's different."

"How?"

The scowl returned to his face, hurt in his eyes. His hands clenched, unclenched and his fist beat against his leg. *One. Two. Three. Four.*

"Remember the week I met you in Buenos Aires? We toured the city and bought things for your apartment. We visited the horse dealers. We ate fantastic meals and drank more than a little wine."

Her words pulled him back to a time which drained the poison from his heart. He smiled at dancing the tango with her, staring so intently in her eyes with the required serious demeanor then exploding in laughter… the music dying away. She had slipped from his arms and left him bereft when she accepted the invitation of the horse breeder who hosted them for the next dance.

"Yes, I thank you for that time, Jess. You saved my life."

"Maybe but we were comfortable with kisses and hugs and …" she looked at him through her dark lashes, "the tango." He smiled, pleased she valued the same memory. "But we didn't cross any line." Her last words were pointed directly at him.

Startled, he retorted, "Of course, we didn't." *Where is she going with this?*

She leaned against the desk.

"When I returned, Damian flew into a jealous rage. It didn't matter the meeting with the horse dealer had been planned for months before you left. He was livid I'd spent time with you. He raged for days insisting we'd planned it. Nothing calmed him. He told me the conversation—" she laughed, bitterness imbedded in her voice, "—I always thought a conversation had two parties involved—the conversation was over and we would not speak about it again."

He reached out for her, understanding his brother's capricious wrath. She waved him away. He dropped his hands to his sides.

"Charlie, don't be so self-absorbed. I'm telling the story." Her smile belied her correcting tone.

He nodded, his eyes averted.

"He's been impossible ever since. Ignoring my career, one he encouraged. I grew up in the horse industry and it's my passion. He owns the finest horse stables in the British Isles." She slammed her hand flat on the desk top. "Due to me. I work with—compete with—and associate with more men than I do women."

Charlie stared at her strong hands. *I don't like the way this story is unfolding.*

"He always trusted me … seemed to value my independence. But now, it's the same qualities he wanted that are driving him to be a possessive bastard. He questions my driver, pesters my secretary regarding my appointments and whereabouts. Even has me followed. All the while expecting me to present a perfect appearance in public and … to find passion in his bed." She shook.

This time, when he reached for her, she molded herself into his arms. They stood for a long moment without words.

"Charlie, at this moment, I'm running away from his paranoia and distrust and I find myself running into the same seeds here." He held her tighter and buried his face in her hair, smelling rain and ozone.

"Jess—"

"Wait. I told your brother when I return from this trip, we'll discuss the issues. If we can't find a way back to the relationship we had before—understanding that I have friendships with both men and women—he'll be heading to the same divorce court as his stuck-up friend in the palace."

He admired the steel glinting in her eyes and laughed

She joined him, laughing long and deep.

"Sounds so damn melodramatic, it makes me want to retch." She gasped trying to catch her breath. "Charlie, that is the laugh I remember. Please, don't let this fester. We haven't talked about Sami but I've known her since she was a child."

He stared at her.

"You can name all the titles in England but you don't know a thing about the social structure on this side of the pond. All the right families know each other. Our fathers are business associates and sometime rivals. We vacationed together in the Hamptons... Mother dragging us up the social ladder while Dad made the money." She sat on the corner of the desk.

"Coming from the Midwest, our blood isn't quite as blue as the old New York families. I was eleven when Sami was born. Her giggle set us laughing helplessly. Colby and I spent hours entertaining her. She tagged along with us and she brought the sunshine with her." Her face darkened, "Before everything changed for her." She looked back at him. "Harry adores her ... will lay down his life for her."

He nodded.

"So, you bring her these handsome men. I've noticed no women." She raised an eyebrow at him. "Her heart is reaching out to each in a different way. I see the child in her again. Don't take that away by not trusting her. I saw something new in her tonight, the devil in her eyes."

He laughed again, easier this time.

"Help her conquer the fear. She needs people who care. Men ..."

Charlie scowled.

Jessica punched his arm. "Men and women. She needs to be able to love them, too."

"Okay." He studied the desk under his hands, noticing the magnificent wood for the first time. He sensed the hours she'd spent sanding it to glassy perfection and staining it rich amber. *I've got to hold on tight but let her breathe. I've got to know her better ... then sit at this desk and put all the revelations into music to celebrate her soul.*

He embraced Jessica again, his love spilling over them.

A breath shifted the shadows. Charlie glanced toward the doorway and wondered how much Sami had overheard.

CHAPTER 13

The ice pellets scratched at Mac's face, blinding him. *Hmm. It should be about sixty feet. Where's the stable?* Glancing over his shoulder, the white billows obscured the house. Mac felt the hair on his neck rise, unseen eyes upon him. Scuffing the ground with his toe, he searched for the shallow ley lines running from the house to the stable. He stepped, slipping on the ice. He bent his knees, trying to plant both feet.

MRRWOW! My paw, you big lummox!

Mac danced in a circle, looking for the cat.

Sharp claws sank into his pants leg above his boots.

MWWOW WOW WOW! This way.

Pyewacket clung to Mac's leg.

Straight ahead...get going...it's out there again.

Mac stumbled, dragging the weighted leg.

I should see it by now ... unless you're leading me astray, Furball.

His foot contacted the ley lines, a sharp jolt racing up his spine. Pyewacket shifted, climbing higher on Mac's leg. Growling rent the air.

Hurry, Mac. Hurry. We don't want to be out here alone with that thing. It's hunting.

Hunting what?

Mac's thought stopped abruptly, his outstretched hand connecting with the stable door. Grabbing the handle, he jerked the door open far enough to slide into the dark space. He rubbed his face with his free hand. Dim light filtered through the partially closed door to the studio.

Pyewacket leapt from his perch, racing for the door. He slid a paw in the crack, pulling at the heavy panel.

Wait, Pye.

Mac squatted down, rubbing Pyewacket's back.

What thing?

Pyewacket stiffened, projecting the vision. Mac jerked backward, hungry, red eyes staring at him. The abomination roared, foul breath gagging him. It wheeled away on dark leathery wings.

Mac shook his head, expelling the sight.

Pye, what does it want?

Pyewacket shivered, digging at the door.

Mac pulled and the studio door whispered open. He shrugged off the heavy coat and slipped into the sound booth.

Niki leaned back in the chair, eyes closed, headphones on and smoke surrounding his head. Mac sniffed the air, too sweet for tobacco.

Damn good thing Jeff didn't come. Mac chuckled.

"Finding your inner Rastafarian, Nik?"

Niki snatched off the headphones and rolled from the chair without looking up. His lips pursed in a tight line, eyes glinting in the light.

Mac realized too late Niki didn't recognize him.

Niki pivoted, landing his heel square in Mac's solar plexus. Mac slammed back against the wall. He doubled over, willing his lungs to fill. Between gasps, Mac raised his head. Niki stared at him.

Mac inhaled, letting out a shuddering guffaw. "What a fool I am! Best side kick I didn't see coming!" He gasped between labored breathes. He reached down to right the cooler. "Well, it's your dinner. Glad I didn't bring out any pineapple upside-down cake. It'd be pineapple-right-side-up cake now."

Niki scrubbed his face with both hands.

Mac plowed on. "Listen, buddy, don't take Charlie seriously. He's a jerk when he's worn out. Let's be honest …a jerk most of the time but a bigger one when he's tired. You're doing a great job promoting us and we suck at that."

Mac attempted to straighten up.

Niki's foot hooked Mac's knee. Mac slid down the wall, covering his head with his arms. Nothing happened. He lowered his arms, found Niki sitting cross legged beside him, the open cooler between them and vodka bottle in his hand.

"At least, you didn't break the bottle." Niki didn't smile.

"Me? Me break the bottle?" Mac sputtered.

"Why did you laugh at me?" Niki rifled through the cooler retrieving glasses. He poured two fingers, setting the glass near Mac's hand.

"Laughing at myself, Niki … and wanted you to know I wasn't coming back at you. I was a street kid until Jeff's mom gathered me in. Life like that … it's simple in its own way, isn't it?" Mac paused, studying Niki's face. "Stupid to walk up on you. Guess my instincts are a bit rusty. I missed you and Pyewacket at dinner."

Niki glanced at Mac's broad smile. "I don't care about Charlie. I wanted to be left alone."

Mac stared at him and the silence stretched out. Niki finally shook his head, throwing his long bangs into his eyes. Mac waited. Niki remained silent.

Mac gave in first. "Well, okay. How about a sandwich and …"? He pulled the cooler closer and dug out a plate covered in clear wrap. "Ooh, red velvet cake. A little squashed." Mac gingerly pushed up from the floor, snagging the glass. He stepped back into the studio and, balancing the glass on the music stand, picked up his bass. Niki recognized the note pattern before Mac started to sing.

Niki grabbed a sandwich and joined in on the keyboard.

CHAPTER 14

Charlie drummed his fingers on the desk. He ran his hand from one end to the other, finding the rich tone consistent throughout. *Nice work. Okay, I am an ass. I need to apologize with grace.* He closed his eyes and rocked back in the chair. His shoulders slumped. *Get up and go find her—or Niki. Damn, I am not sure how to go about this. He is unpredictable. And if Mac is there, he'll hover over Niki like some giant troll defender.* He grimaced. *Why don't I let the band go ... just stay here with Sami?*

"Because I am a damn adrenaline junkie. Cannot get enough without the band." Even when his body screamed from exhaustion, the bottomless pit loomed. Time alone with Sami refreshed his soul but without the stage time, interaction with other musicians in rehearsal, smoky clubs and performance spaces, his personal demon scrambled up his spine.

He looked around at the dark oak bookcases, the high ceilings. *Her fortress—she won't even go into town. At least in New York, I could get her out to a restaurant now and then.* He slammed his hand down.

"No wonder she'd want Niki's company." He rubbed his stinging palm.

He closed his burning eyes and replayed their first entrance. She insisted he carry her across the threshold. She spun around in every room, a whirling dervish transported by the space, the light, the air in the house. To his eyes, each room looked more decrepit than the last. He bit his cheek to bleeding rather than declare the house should be condemned. She plowed through with broom, dust pan and mop until midnight and arose after a few hours rest, energized and excited. The oak floors gleamed under her gentle hand. The windows, old glass, shone with rainbows.

Encouraged by her elated mood, he tried to take her out to explore the Upstate New York countryside, the villages and boat yards along the Hudson. She refused to walk even to the stables. Sami sat with him on the porch in the evenings, listening to him play his guitar. Her foot never touched the ground.

"Charlie, I know you aren't asleep." Sami's soft voice sounded close to his ear. Without opening his eyes, he reached out and pulled her into his lap, holding her head against his chest. His arms tightened around. Fear clutched at him.

She pushed away, looking at his face. "Your heart just skipped a beat."

He swallowed hard, his throat tight. "Sami." He ran his fingers through her hair, tucking a stray lock behind her ear. "Are we okay? There's a shadow over us tonight."

She smiled, "Okay? I think we're fuckin' fantastic!" She flushed bright pink, guilty for borrowing Mac's oft-uttered phrase. She hid her face against his chest. He squeezed her until she wiggled for breath.

"Charlie, I love you." Her muffled words thrilled him. "Are you upset about Niki being here when you're away?"

He searched for words.

Sami raised her head. "You are. Niki is … he's my first friend … after Kay. I love Mac and Jeff and … them all. But Niki found time for me."

"Sami, I overheard you in the kitchen. Then I saw you two …" He stopped, teetering on the edge. He wouldn't enumerate each episode, remembering Jessica's warning.

"Niki's the little brother I always wished for. Yes, he wasn't telling you the whole truth but it was for my sake. And to keep the surprise. He's worked hard on it. A little selfishly, I know." She looked up at him through her long lashes. "He loves all the wires and switches and things. Dad was amazed watching Niki fit it all together."

He raised an eyebrow.

"Yes, my father was here, too. He came down after every shipment and spent several hours out there. He adores Niki, even tried to convince him to apply to college … his alma mater, naturally. Niki refused. But I know my father. He won't be discouraged easily."

Charlie smiled at her torrent. *I do trust her. I still need to face Niki but I am safely in her heart.* He kissed her, pouring all his love in the tender contact.

"Air, air!" She fought away from him. "Charlie, about what you said at dinner—"

Her intense stare sobered him, "I know, I know. I was a rude bastard. Dire thoughts, love, but I was wrong."

Before she could speak, he went on. "I will find Niki. I will apologize. You know the Ramhill despair. Jess reamed me out for it. And bless you, my love, for refraining from doing so. Sami, I would rather die than lose you." He tightened his embrace and kissed her again. She relaxed against him. Moments passed before she once again pushed away.

"I'm not being a good hostess, so let me go. Niki's in the studio. He looks up to you, you know."

He stared at her, eyes open wide.

"Don't believe me. He wants the band to go places and he's working hard to make that happen." She rose from his lap, straightened her dress and, blowing him a kiss, disappeared through the study door.

"Sami," he called dropping his voice, sensing her beyond hearing, "I love the desk. Thank you." A warm breeze brushed his cheek.

CHAPTER 15

Jessica paused to remove her earrings and necklace. Dropping them on the hallway table, she pulled out her hairpins, black locks falling down her back. She entered the kitchen and tiny track lights warmed to a soft glow. Harry stood at the sink, illuminated by a single spotlight.

"Harry, you're a jewel. Celeste will miss you."

"Thank you, my Lady. It is a kind thing you say."

The fresh coffee aroma pulled her to the coffeemaker. "Bless Sami. She's learned to be a musician's wife." She looked out at the light from the stables, glowing through the snow.

Perching on the stool at the counter, she thought about the luncheon with Sami's parents. "Harry, I don't understand Celeste's fixation with all things proper. As if I'm not drowning in it myself." She smiled at the contradiction.

Harry dried his hands. He opened the cupboard over the bar sink.

She stared into her coffee cup. "Lady Jessica, my foot. I'd give it all to her if I could…or to Colby. That would be her wish, wouldn't it? Social standing for her eldest daughter."

"May I offer a little addition, my Lady?" Harry's soft voice by her ear startled her. "My apologies, ma'am. I didna mean to fright ye. I've a fine Irish whiskey here, to complement the coffee."

She held out the cup.

"What perverse fate delivered Sami into his arms? At least, Charlie has the good sense to stay away from the dear old chaps and their conniving wives." She lifted her cup, inhaling the rich dark aroma. *Oh, how I envy her*, Jessica thought. "You would make a great bartender, Harry. You listen in silence then offer a balm for the heart."

"I do my best, my Lady." Harry patted her hand.

Wind blew the back door open, slamming it against the wall. Harry stepped toward the door.

Jessica rose, cup in hand. "I'd like to see the studio."

"My lady, please," Harry stopped her. "Let me get you a wrap and walk with you. The storm is ferocious."

She smiled at him. "Thank you, Harry. I'm warmed by your fine Irish whiskey." *And my dear one*s, she addressed the windling who swirled around her, caressing her with a warm breeze. "You will stay, won't you, Harry? With Sami, I mean."

Harry nodded. "I'll na'e leave home again."

Jessica patted his arm then stepped off the porch. Her windlings shouldered the sleet and snowflakes aside, the corridor closing behind her. An old blues tune, one she remembered from her father's collection, met her at the door

Muddy Waters. She felt the music spill over her. Dry leaves, swept from the corner, circled her. The wind returned to stroke her face.

It's okay, Dervish. She addressed her eldest wind.

The leaves dropped back to the ground, falling snow covering them over. A gust pushed between her shoulder blades moving her toward the studio door.

Okay, I won't wallow in my misery here in the dark. I get it.

She stood in the shadows, engrossed by Mac's precise fingering on his bass guitar. A blond man sat at the keyboard. His straight bangs hung over his eyes obscuring his features. She waited, willing him to lift his head.

As if at her command, he reached for his glass and, finding it empty, held it out to Mac for more.

Jessica stared at the face, the young man grown from the boy who had dogged her heels years ago. *This is unexpected but not surprising. Too many coincidences for any of this to be random.*

Everywhere she turned that summer, she found feathers, stones, or flowers, tucked into the stall railing, on her dresser after the maids had straightened the bed clothes, or in her tack box. Her stallion, Damian's engagement gift, shone like silk from brushing. A fondness grew in her for the shy boy who wouldn't speak to her beyond a quiet *yes, miss* or *no, miss.*

That winter's eve, she walked out alone while Damian enjoyed cognac with his schoolmates. She startled when his father appeared in the stable door. He cornered her in the stall, pressing too close. Niki exploded from the shadows, grabbing the large man by the shoulders and pulling him away from her. He backhanded him, his ring slicing across Niki's face. Lord Ramhill grabbed a riding crop.

She ran toward the manor. Her steps faltered at the stallion's angry bellow but the winds pushed her toward safety. Damian welcomed her into his arms, reveling in her disheveled hair and flushed cheeks. His friends teased him about his wild American beauty.

A groom discovered Lord Ramhill's body. The coroner ruled it an accidental death—a known drunkard and a spirited horse with blood on its hooves. Niki disappeared. His parents appealed to Damian for help but his absence rated little notice by the new Lord. The winds brought her whispers here and there but they were capricious and she failed to track him down.

Now, in this strange place, with people I hold dear, you appear. She studied Niki's face, disturbed by the gauntness highlighting the pale scar from eye to jaw.

Mac ran a riff, giving Niki a rhythm pattern to follow. She stepped into the room. Mac's fingers stopped. "Lady Jessica, good evening." His words slurred. He attempted to bow, shifting his feet to maintain his balance.

"Forgive my intrusion. I couldn't resist the chance to hear you play." She glanced in Niki's direction. "I'm glad you found your friend."

Mac cleared his throat. "Forgot my manners, ma'am. Lady Jessica Ramhill, let me introduce you to Niki Kaye, the best manager a mangy band could ever want." He motioned to Niki to stand up. Niki rose, avoiding her eye.

She extended her hand. "A pleasure to meet you, Mr. Kaye."

"No, my Lady, the pleasure is mine." Niki swayed on his feet but held on to her hand. She squeezed tighter, sealing her promise to be silent.

"Please, continue. I grew up near Chicago. I've a fondness for the blues."

Niki's face lit up, a twinkle replacing the conflict in his eyes. He offered her his glass. She polished off the remaining vodka then refilled it, leaving it on the piano. Mac smiled, his fingers picking up on the song.

"Will you show me how to play?" She slipped between his chest and the bass, the strap still over his shoulder. Niki looked down, concentrating on the keyboard.

"Okay." He settled the bass before her. Jessica leaned back against him and placed her hands in the correct position.

"Guitar?" He asked.

"Uh huh," she said, her concentration on the neck.

"It's different because there are four strings." He placed his hands over hers, matching finger to finger. "You pluck the strings with your thumb and index finger."

Niki played the melody. She fingered a run without rhythm. Her laughter rang through the studio. She turned within the strap and pulled Mac's head down, brushing her lips across his cheek. Mac staggered back a half step.

Jessica slipped under Mac's arm. "Mac, thank you. Most instructive. But now, you gentlemen have more serious endeavors to undertake. Good night." She walked into the dark stable.

The first chords from *Midnight Rider* rippled through the air.

CHAPTER 16

The Volvo's lights illuminated the narrow drive, overgrown lilacs swirling in the wind. "Spooky," Tori noted. She maneuvered between the bushes and around the pot holes. "Does this place really reflect your young friend?"

Kay ran her fingers through her hair, feeling worn. "No, not at all. Sami is brightness embodied. I am certain in the spring, this is lovely."

Tori scanned the drive. "Kay, there's something out there. Something big." Tori slowed the car to a creep.

Kay peered into the darkness, dread for Sami clawing at her throat.

"It's hunting. Frustrated because it can't get to its prey." Tori leaned to stare up at the tree tops. A deep growling emanated from the back.

Kay glanced back over the seat. *My imagination,* but she reached for the ley lines feeling the muddied energies. The car emerged into the open yard. She felt the flow increase, released from the strangled hold in the forest. The lights from the house glittered off the falling flakes, the golden glow welcoming.

"That's more like Sami," Kay commented, loosening her fingers from the door handle.

"Right." Tori pulled up by the front steps. "But I'm glad we found the foxes. They will be elegant on those pedestals."

The door opened, shedding light on the car. Sami ran down the steps, flying into Kay's arms when she stood from the car.

"Kay, I can't believe you're finally here. Come in." She grabbed Kay's hand pulling her around the car. "Ms. Madison, come in." She grabbed Tori's hand and bumped the driver's door shut with her hip. She led them up the steps and into the warm foyer.

Harry arrived from the kitchen. "I will get the bags, Madam." Jeff came down the stairs and joined Harry heading for the door.

The front door swung open, banging against the wall. The wind extinguishing several candles. Lightning highlighted the SUV. It rocked from side to side lifting off the wheels.

Tori raised her voice to be heard over the wind. "Be careful with my housewarming gifts. They're in the back."

Kay followed them to the door, the wind whipping her auburn hair around her face. She felt it important to watch over the two men. Inner guidance she would have ignored before her months with her mother's people.

Harry launched into the storm. The old man slammed into the bumper. Jeff skidded to a stop as another wild gyration peaked, the roof contacting his chin, knocking his head back.

Harry worked toward him. "Be careful, sir. Stand aside when the door opens. They have the scent in their nostrils. Nothing will stop them."

Jeff swung the tailgate open with polished expertise from the rodeo. Two dark shapes exploded from the car. Massive stone heads twisted in all directions, nostrils flaring. A guttural yowl raised the hair on Jeff's neck. The vixen leapt toward the frozen gardens, her mate close behind.

Pyewacket careened into Jeff. Righting himself, he pushed against Jeff's leg to launch down the drive. Jeff staggered, grabbing for the cat.

Pye, come back. Jeff shot his command at the flying cat.

They're after it. Pyewacket snapped, his black tail tip lost in the falling snow.

Dead black eyes and leathery wings lingered in Jeff's mind. He slipped sideways, fighting for momentum to follow. He felt a strong hand grab his arm and pull him back.

"No, Dr. Conray. Let the favored ones do their duty. They'll drive it off." In response to Jeff's raised eyebrow, Harry held out the Gucci bag. "Let us escape from the cold and wet."

Jeff retrieved the worn brown valise from the backseat and followed Harry up the steps.

The door closed behind the them. Colby hurried down the stairs, her arms filled with towels. She tossed one to Jeff, ducking her head not to meet his eye. She wrapped another around Harry's shoulders, smoothing back the grey lock plastered on his forehead.

Charlie stood with his arm around Sami. "What was out there?"

"Fox statues … animate." Jeff scrubbed at his hair, the leather tie dropping free, his hair spilling over his face.

Charlie stared at Jeff. "You're kidding. Animate? Loose on the grounds?"

"They're guardians, Mr. Ramhill." Tori said. "I would never gift anything that could bring harm."

"You." Charlie turned on her, pulling Sami closer. "You brought them?" His face reddened.

"Yes, I did. You shouldn't worry about them. It's what they're chasing that's the danger." She glanced at the parlor's dark windows.

"What are they chasing?" Charlie glared at Tori. She shrugged her shoulders.

Sami placed both hands on Charlie's chest. "Charlie, it's probably the fox. I saw the vixen just before you arrived. Besides, I have Pyewacket."

Charlie stared at her, his jaw working. "That furball!"

"And now the guardians. Don't forget them." She slipped from his grasp. "Miss Madison, thank you for bringing my new protectors. I want to hear all about where they found you." She held out her hand to Kay. "First, come upstairs and freshen up. Then there are sandwiches in the kitchen."

She nodded for Tori to follow and kept up a chatter as they ascended the staircase. Kay glanced back finding Charlie and Jeff carrying the bags.

Charlie dropped Kay's bags on the luggage rack, then motioned to Sami.

"Kay, I'll be right back to help you unpack."

Kay kissed her on the forehead. "Don't worry, Sami. I am more tired than hungry so you go on. I'll nap awhile." She followed them to the door and peered through the crack.

In the hall, Charlie pulled Sami into his arms. Kay heard their voices. She pushed the door tighter but kept her ear to the crack.

"Sami, how can you stay so calm? Animated garden statuary? It is terrifying."

Sami did not reply.

"And what do you know about this woman who brought them?"

"Tori is Kay's business partner. I trust Kay's judgment." She pushed him toward Jeff leaving Tori's room. "Charlie, you and Jeff go enjoy the studio. I know you're dying to try out the equipment." Sami's tone indicated she would not discuss the issue any longer.

Charlie's voice held resignation. "Come on, Jeff. We've been banished to the stable." They descended the back stairs.

Kay leaned her forehead against the door. *So, Sami's nightmares are coming true.* A tear ran down her face and splattered on her hand on the door knob.

A vibration ran through the wood. It pulled the knob from her hand and closed the door tightly. Warm air pushed her toward the bed, the counterpane sliding back as she approached.

We'll deal with this, won't we? She sighed. Her heavy lids closed. Warm fingers stroked her forehead.

CHAPTER 17

Sami tapped on the oak door to Tori's room. "Tori, is everything all right?"

"Sami, please come in. This is a lovely room. I love the Morrison wardrobe." Tori took a finishing swipe with her lipstick.

"Thank you. It came with the house. Kay is done in for the night. But come down to the kitchen if you're hungry."

"Always!" Tori draped a sapphire scarf around her neck. "You're generous to allow me to visit."

"Not at all. You're Kay's friend," Sami paused for a heartbeat. "And I hope you'll be mine."

"Mama would say sharing a meal is a good start." Tori followed Sami down the back stairs to the kitchen. She pulled out a chair and held out her hand to Jessica. "We haven't met. I'm Tori Madison."

Sami started an introduction but Jessica cut her off, "Jessica." She glanced at Sami. "Just Jess ... we've been friends since childhood.

Tori's eyes narrowed for a moment. She looked from Jessica to Sami.

Colby rose with her empty cup in hand. "May I pour you some tea?"

Tori glanced toward the bar sink. "Perhaps something a little more bracing?"

Harry appeared in the door with a bottle. He offered red wine to each lady.

"Ah, excellent vintage." Tori reached for the sandwich tray, taking two.

"Tell me, Tori," Jessica caught her in mid bite. "What is your profession ... that Kay is working with you?"

Tori swallowed. "I started out in interior design … apprenticed to my mother in Charleston. We know all the wealthier families since Charlestonian society is so inbred."

Colby snickered, drawing a look from Sami. Sami knew what Colby was thinking…about the New York Society in which they were raised.

Tori arched an eyebrow at her. "I accosted my friends when they started their own homes." She chuckled and looked around the table. "I like buying luxurious and decadent items…using someone else's money."

Sami wrinkled her forehead. "But the items are theirs, not yours…"

"I know, sugar, but once I've seen it or touched it," Tori tapped her head. "It's in here forever. I can visit it anytime I want and I don't have to worry about breaking it or, God forbid, dusting it."

Laughter rippled around the table.

Harry snorted. Sami caught his eye and he coughed, his hand over his mouth, a gesture she knew meant he was amused. She excused herself from the table and motioned for Harry to follow her. Leading him to the hallway door, she stood close.

"Harry," she whispered. "Colby and I will clean up. Find your way to bed. I told Mother I wouldn't let you drive in this weather." She looked down at her hands. "I don't want to be alone any longer…when Charlie goes on the road…and you're my dearest friend. Would you consider staying?" Her voice shook.

"*A chroí* … dear one" Harry raised her hands to his lips. "I've been here for you from the beginning and will go on until the end." She hugged him tightly.

***

She returned to the table to find Tori toying with the empty plate

Sami studied Tori. *What in the world has Kay gotten into?*

Colby returned with another plate piled with sandwiches.

Tori's eyes lit up. "You're gonna make some big starving man very happy."

Colby flushed and held out her wine glass to Jessica.

Jessica refilled the glass. "Are you still seeing Jon McGann?"

Colby winced but her voice stayed light. "Jon's finishing medical school at Johns Hopkins. He'll pursue a specialty in infectious disease."

"And?" Jessica raised an eyebrow.

"And what?" Colby looked back at her. "Oh, you're just like Mother."

Tori chuckled. "Family dynamic?"

"Jon and I've dated casually for years … since early in high school. Our mothers pushed us together. I enjoy his company but I'm just not ready for anything, yet." Colby glared at Tori.

Not convincing, thought Sami.

Jessica looked out at the stables. "Will they be out there all night?"

Sami laughed. "Probably. Once they start, the curse has to run its course. I don't expect Charlie in before three." Her wistful tone prompted laughter and she blushed to the hairline.

"Newlyweds," Jessica jibed. "On that note, I'm off to bed." She kissed Colby on the cheek, "Good night. I hope you'll find time to play for me tomorrow." Colby nodded.

"Very well then, ladies, me, too. I've been shown the best hospitality, a good snack, fine wine and wonderful company. My sincerest thank you." Tori rose. "Good night."

"Harry will be up early." Sami said, "Breakfast can be early or late." She glanced at Colby. "All I have planned is tree trimming and dinner."

Tori nodded. The sisters listened to their footsteps up the back stairs.

"Sami, I couldn't see in the dark. What were those things outside?" Colby asked.

Sami cleared the dishes from the table. Colby waited while she loaded the dishwasher. Finally, she returned to the table.

"Do you remember when I told you—and Mother and Dad—about the thing I saw in the garden? With dull red eyes and dark wings?"

"Sami, you were five." Colby patted her hand. "You had a vivid imagination."

"It wasn't my imagination." Sami stuck out her lip, feeling like a petulant child. Colby covered her mouth with her hand. Sami glared at her, knowing she was hiding a laugh. "Laugh if you like. It's better than Mother increasing the medication." She played with her napkin. "Dad believed me. He hunted in the woods."

"So did Mick." Colby's tone softened.

"Yes, and came back with a claw the game warden couldn't identify." Mick was excited over the find, carrying it to school for his friends to see.

"Dad said he made it go away. I wanted to believe him … but I knew there were more out there somewhere. I think another one has found me here. Even staying in the house hasn't helped." Sami's hand shook.

"Is that why you're afraid to go out?"

Sami nodded.

"But those things from the car?"

"If Jeff says they're guardians, then that's what they are. I'll be safe—safer—with them here." Sami shredded the napkin, working to quell her fear.

Colby leaned over and hugged her. She rose.

"May I make you some chamomile tea?" She stretched, gazing at the lights in the stable. "You certainly have different friends than what Mother planned. I congratulate you." She filled the kettle with water.

Sami remained silent.

"You've grown, my dear sister. Seeing you so comfortable with Charlie's friends is the best Christmas present. He's helped you find the key to who you are." Colby continued to fill the silence with her chatter.

She looked around the kitchen trying to puzzle out the secret. "Now let's see. If I were chocolate truffles, where would I be?" She pulled open a cabinet door and grinned. "Ah-hah."

"You've an unerring nose for chocolate." Sami shook off her despair. "Charlie's more than I ever dreamed. But it isn't just Charlie. It's them all."

Colby rummaged in the cupboard for the tea.

"What happened in the dining room?" Sami's eyes twinkled.

"We talked."

"About what?"

"Nothing much." Colby kept her back to Sami. "I apologized." The words eked out.

"Oh, come on. Did you kiss him?" Sami spun her around. Colby's cheeks flamed.

"No … er … yes. Don't be so smug. I'm still mad at you for setting me up." Colby poured, her hands shaking, spilling water on the countertop. She wiped up the water and carried the teacups to the table.

Sami dimmed the central light and lit the candles. "It was just too good to pass up. Your description painted his face in my mind and when Niki told me what Jeff was wearing, I knew it had to be him. Besides, what harm did it do?"

"Harm?" Colby set the cup down with a crash. Her eyes flared and Sami sat back. "Harm? You made me feel like a fool. Awkward, bumbling idiot! I've never been shy a day in my life and it … it was awful." Her face softened. "Sami, I'm so sorry. I thought I understood what you go through but I didn't. Not really. Tonight, I wanted the ground to swallow me. I don't want to feel that way ever again!"

"Colby, you won't have to. You're the most courageous person I know—you and Kay—and Jessica—the strong women in my life. I'm so jealous the way you're at ease with everyone and everywhere."

"Not everyone." Colby looked down at her cup. "Not with him. I don't understand why except I just fall into a petrified trance when he's in the room." She shook herself, looking back at Sami. "Tell me what you know about him."

"He grew up on a ranch about a hundred miles outside Dallas. His father is full blood Native American and his mother is from New Orleans … society, you know. He's got an older brother, Matt and a younger sister, Suzie. He adores her. From his description, she's wild and tough. She's a competitive barrel rider at the State level this year. Far cry from your English training, isn't it?"

Colby nodded.

"From what he's told me about his mother, I'd love to pit her against ours some time." She giggled. "Okay, he's quiet. Doesn't say much but with me at least, he knows what to say when I need it. He has a rich voice and often sings lead. They all sing wonderfully. I haven't heard Chris sing much because he plays wind instruments." She grabbed Colby's hand.

"I've had so much fun when they're around. The house is filled with music—instruments, singing—even Charlie walks through the house humming. Wait until tomorrow. Tonight was strained. Tomorrow will be better. Please tell me you aren't mad enough to leave."

Colby sat up straighter in her chair. "No," she said, squeezing Sami's hand. "No, I wouldn't leave for the world. I came to enjoy Christmas with you. I'd be silly to go home to an empty house. I wouldn't even have Harry. Mick's in Paris with his fraternity buddies, so, you're stuck with me. I have to be back in the city for New Year's."

"I hoped you would stay."

"I made a promise last summer. I completely forgot about it until Jon called me over Thanksgiving. He has reservations for dinner at Four Seasons." She paused, agony written on her face. "Why does that restaurant keep popping up to haunt me?"

Sami laughed. She rose, yawning, "Your prescription worked, doctor." She looked at the candle. Air swirled and extinguished the flame. She touched Colby's shoulder finding it rigid. Colby stared into her teacup.

"His family's curse reaches for you."

Sami started at Colby's dead voice.

"The shadows may destroy him."

The teacup handle broke off in Colby's hand. She jumped.

"Oh my God, this is the third cup I've broken this month. Damn it!" Colby slapped the cup off the table, the delicate china shattering on the floor. She stared at the remnants. "I said something, didn't I?" She looked up at Sami. "I know I did."

"Colby, it's okay."

"No, it's not. I hate this. I'd rather be shy than crazy!"

Sami pulled out a broom. Colby snatched it from her hand. "I'll clean this up." She swiped at the shards. "Then I'm going straight to bed and I may not get up 'til the day after never."

CHAPTER 18

December 21ˢᵗ

Mac staggered in from the studio, the grandmother clock chiming two. He stretched, neck bones popping, and scrubbed at his eyes. He groaned, knowing in his bones Sami would rise with the dawn.

Moving silently into the parlor, he knelt on the wind rose. He reached out to Jeff. Charlie's complex melody captured Jeff's entire attention, Charlie's aura overlaying Jeff's, the two heads close together. Mac nodded, awed by the ease Jeff allowed others in his personal space. He drew a deep breath, pulling into himself and exhaling residual anxiety.

The ley lines need to be stronger. That thing can't be allowed to get in. He reached out feeling for the lines and gathering the energy to him. *This home understands timing, heartbeats—love.*

Keeping his voice low, he spoke in rhythm with the thrumming from the wind rose. "Spirit in this place, help me protect your daughter. Give her the freedom to discover your graceful landscape."

He sat in silence enticing the energies in the earth to come, envisioning them flowing with light. "Happy Winter Solstice, loving spirit."

He ran his fingers over the smooth inlaid wood. "This is a damn good design, isn't it?" Mac patted himself on the back, pleased Sami worked his art into the floor repair. He stood, hopping on one foot then the other, removing his boots. He dropped on the couch and fell into a deep sleep, not feeling the blanket settling over him.

***

"Mac!" Sami kept her voice soft, sensing he would wake with a headache from the night before.

Mac's eyes stayed tightly closed but his mouth twitched.

"Mac, the Christmas tree?"

"G'morning, little irresistible force," Mac mumbled, opening his eyes. He swung upright. She wrapped his fingers around a mug. He took a sip, the steam rolling across his face. She stood still, holding out a plate filled with steaming cinnamon buns.

"You must have been up for hours." He picked up a sticky bun, licking his fingers. "What time is it?"

"Nine o'clock. I let you sleep in. Here are your boots." She glided across the room. "Harry brought down the tree stand." She spun around pointing to the green cast iron stand.

Mac held his head, his eyes rolling. "Anyone but you and I'd lie right back onto this couch. Do you swear your first born will be a bass player?"

Sami nodded. She pulled open the heavy curtains, bright sunlight reflecting off the snow. His boots in place, Mac stood and reached for his jacket. Sami handed him gloves and a purple knit stocking cap.

"Those are always too small for my big head." He laughed, handing the cap back to her.

"Try it. It's the first one I made. I bet I got it right." Sami put on her coat and donned a yellow cap.

Mac pulled on the cap. It fit all the way down to cover his ears. He nodded to her as he opened the front door. A tree saw and a length of burlap lay on the porch. He reached for them but straightened, staring at the snow-covered gardens directly in front of the house.

"It worked! Do you see them?"

Sami stared at the fresh snow, shaking her head.

"The strings of gold running across the ground. They surround the property almost—almost—" Mac turned around looking in all directions, "almost a complete rose. There are a couple of breaks but those can be mended."

"I don't see them—" she whispered. His face fell. She took his hand. "It's enough you do. You'll keep me safe."

Mac stepped off the stairs without looking. His foot broke through the icy layer and landed on the nearest line. A warm tingling radiated through his gloved hand and into her fingers. "I may not see them but I feel them. All the way up my arm."

Mac took a deep breath, smiling at her. "Okay, baby girl, let's go."

She looked back at the house. *One heartbeat, two heartbeats, three heartbeats,* she counted against the rising panic. The foxes raised their snouts and scented the air. Their action reassured her. She turned her back on the house and walked toward the trees, her breath wreathing her face.

Mac scanned the tree line toward the west. He pointed at a young Balsam fir. "There."

From the corner of his eye, he noticed a rippling movement in the snow. He stood still but the disturbance was not repeated. He transited from one leylines to another. He paused at the tree line.

"I know you can't see it but the line is broken here." He pointed to the right. "And there. I'll work on closing the gap." Stepping toward the trees, he stumbled, dropping the saw and the burlap.

Sami held tight to his hand, trying balance him. The darkness pulled the warmth from her, dark claws grasping for Mac's chest flashing through her mind. She pulled his arm over her shoulders, backing up with all her weight. His foot refused to release from the ground. A sharp bark startled her, the vixen appearing in front of them. She leapt, landing all four feet on Mac's chest, pushing him backwards to the ground. Sami tumbled beside him, the snow puffing up around them. Mac twisted and wrapped his arms around her.

Large red-gold eyes stared at him, a pinkish tongue lolling out one side of her muzzle.

"Holy shit!" Mac swore. "Jeff wasn't kidding. They are alive."

Wiggling in his arms, Sami reached beyond him to pat the vixen. "Of course, they are!" Mac stared at her, his mouth hanging open.

She pushed herself away, both hands on his chest and rose brushing the snow from her coat. "What was that? That thing reaching for you?"

Mac rolled to hands and knees keeping his eye on the grinning vixen. His face grimaced. "I don't know but I'm going to fix that ley line as soon as possible. It felt like what we saw…" He shuffled his feet.

"Saw when, Mac?" Sami fixed him with her eyes.

Mac shrugged.

"Mac, tell me."

"When we came in last night. Something … something large flew down on the hood." He shrugged again. "But, Sami, it was dark. There was a wind. It could have been a falling branch. Besides, Charlie didn't want us to talk about it."

Sami stamped her foot. "Charlie doesn't know everything." She took a step toward the trees, feeling through the snow with her toe. "You should have told me."

"But, Sami, he's protecting you."

"He doesn't know what from." She looked over her shoulder at him. "Are you coming?" She glanced at the house. The morning sun played red off Harry's long white hair. Harry raised a hand in return, his stance suggesting he would be right there until they returned.

"Sami, let's go back to the house. I'll get the tree later when Jeff can help me." He pulled her hand. The reynard stepped in front of him preventing any movement toward the house. "Move, Fido."

"Mac, his name is Reynard. We're so close. I'll need time to decorate it."

"But didn't you feel that—"

"I think that tree will be perfect." She smiled at him, shielding her eyes from the light.

Holding Sami's hand, Mac slipped between the trees. The reynard paced at his side, the saw and burlap in his mouth.

"Will it fit in the parlor … with enough room for a star?"

"Yes, if I trim it correctly." He ran his hands through the needles and held his palms to his nose. "Is that the Christmas scent you wanted?" She copied his gesture and nodded her approval.

"Okay." He knelt in the snow then crawled under the tree. "Ugghh! Snow on my belly. Remind me to wear a longer coat next year. Hand me the saw. You'll have greens to use." Snow fell from the shaking branches, burying Mac deeper. "Almost done." The low hanging branches muffled his voice. One more cut and the trunk gave. The tree settled on its side.

He stood, shaking the snow from his legs. Sami brushed the snow from his back and the nape of his neck. "Where's that sack?" he said, looking around. Sami held it up.

"Good, we've got our very own Christmas sleigh for your beautiful tree. I guess I always wanted to be a reindeer though I probably have more in common with Brother Moose." Mac hefted the tree onto the cloth. "Argghh. Now the snow is down my neck. Sami, it's not nice to laugh at me. I haven't even complained about all the needles. Sticky! Wouldn't be caught dead doing this for anyone else."

Grabbing the burlap sack in their mouths, the foxes kept pace.

Sami threw a snowball at Mac's back. "I've got more coffee waiting for you. And ham and eggs. You'll feel better."

Black smoke issued from the bare oak's canopy, spreading into voluminous wings. Foot long talons glinted in the bright morning light. The creature rose silently, angling to put the sun at its back. It dove.

***

"Scotty, wake up." Scotty Miles stretched, palms against the car's roof. Chris Thomas's voice roused him from uneasy dreams.

"Mac and Sami are in the field. There's something there. Up high." He pointed ahead.

Scotty scanned the lawn, blinking against the morning sun. Chris sped the late model sedan along the drive. Reaching the house, he slammed on the brakes, the car skidding on the ice.

Scotty threw open the passenger door before the car stopped. He pulled his sword from the sleeve across his guitar case, narrowly missing Chris's ear and ran toward Mac and Sami, his eyes searching the sky.

"Mac! Get her in the house." Scotty pointed toward the diving shape. The strident screech raised the hair on Scotty's neck.

Mac dropped the burlap sled, putting himself between Sami and the menace. "Run, Sami!"

Sami stared at the descending monster, her feet unmoving. Kay and Tori exploded from the front door, running behind Harry. Kay sprinted ahead, grabbing Sami and forcing her to the ground in a crouch. She laid her arms over Sami, covering her. Pyewacket launched over Kay's back. He clawed at the air. His growl echoed down the drive.

Scotty skidded to a stop in front of Mac. "A tree saw will only give this beastie a manicure, Mac. Get them out of here."

Harry ran up behind Scotty, brandishing a metal poker from the fireplace, his white hair flowing around his shoulders loose from its ties. "I'll stand with ye, son." Snouts raised, the foxes stood on either side, Pyewacket balancing on the Reynard's back.

Scotty spared a glance in their direction. *Great gods, what are those?* He shifted his stance, knees bent, his sword held loosely in his hand.

An unearthly cry split the air, drawn out for moment after moment. Scotty resisted the urge to cover his ears. He focused on the creature. Wind from its wings swirled ice crystals and snow across Scotty's vision. He blinked rapidly, maintaining eye contact with the monster.

A flash in Scotty's peripheral vision distracted him from the diving monster. A gun's retort cracked the air, then a second.

The creature wheeled, fighting to stay aloft. Blood, India ink black, sprayed across the snow. Steam rose from each drop. Gaining the tree tops, the creature disappeared into the dark branches.

A tall, red-haired woman ran through the snow. She held the gun at her side. "Are you kidding me? A sword?" The woman stood a respectful distance from him.

Scotty eyed the gun in her hand as she twitched it up toward his chest, then checked her movement. "Nice shooting. You've scared it off but you can't kill it with a gun. You have to separate head from body."

Her lips hardened into a red line. "I'd strongly recommend we get into the house before that…" she scanned the sky above the trees.

"Demon." Scotty filled in the gap.

"Demon?" Tori's eyes grew larger, the pupils dilating.

"Actually, a lesser demon. Nine feet long. Too small to be very powerful." Scotty shrugged.

"Lesser?" Tori glanced at Kay. She helped Sami up from the ground. Placing her arm around Sami, they ran for the house. Tori turned toward them.

"Down!" Scotty shouted, pointing to the returning demon. He gripped the sword with both hands. The demon wheeled cutting to Scotty's right, attempting to get beyond him, its obsidian eyes reflecting Sami as she ran between Kay and Harry for the house. Charlie and Jeff came down the steps two at a time. Charlie plowed forward to reach Sami and Kay.

Niki ran around the edge of the house. He knelt, pushing his hands through the snow over the ley line. The ley lines burst into sheets of gold light shooting high into the sky. The demon dove through the closest line, screaming. It swung its head, right to left, searching for its prey.

Scotty took two steps and leapt into the air. He swung, blade contacting the leathery neck. Its wings beat at a frantic pace, knocking Scotty away from the flailing body. Head first, then scaled body plowed into the snow. Oily steam rose from the corpse. Scotty rolled to his feet, and approached the demon. He knelt on one knee, his head down. The foxes flanked him, lowering to their bellies in the snow.

Tori stepped toward him but Chris laid his hand on her arm. "Leave him be."

"There's blood on his face…"

"I said, leave him be, woman."

After a moment, Scotty raised his head, tears glistening on his cheeks. He stood, lifted both hands and spoke in a guttural tongue. The demon burst into flames, showering the group with black ash. Scotty grabbed Chris by the forearm in salute. He looked up to see Niki slip back around the house out of sight.

"What in the hell?" Charlie enfolded Sami in his arms, his voice ringing across the lawn. Kay stepped aside.

Jeff shepherded the pair toward the house, Harry staying close beside. "Charlie, we told you last night there was something out here."

"And you should have told me." Sami stopped, unmoved by Charlie's pull on her arm. "It's been out there for days. Pyewacket was stalking it."

"Pyewacket? Against that thing?" Charlie's lips twitched toward a smile.

"Scoff if you will. Now, you've seen it." Color returned to her face. She stamped to the steps. "I know it isn't even noon but I need a drink." She disappeared into the house. Harry ran behind her.

Tori stepped up beside Kay. "I hope you'll explain this to me." she said, her voice low. "And who is that gorgeous man?"

CHAPTER 19

Mac heard "Ring of Fire" rolling from the kitchen, Jeff's baritone underscored by Harry's agitated brogue. *Great, Johnny Cash. That means chili!* From the door, he joined the chorus.

"Dr. Conray, sir … please leave the kitchen. You are in my way, sir. I prepare the meals for this household."

Jeff pivoted around the small gentleman and continued pulling spices from the cupboard.

"Mac, onions, please." Mac shouldered into the kitchen space, sandwiching Harry between the two. He pawed through the vegetable drawer, tossing three large onions over Harry's head.

They broke into the next verse.

"Dr. Conray … Mr. MacIntyre, please, you're making a mess." Harry pleaded.

"Harry," Jeff patted the old man's back. "Sami is aware we're talented in the kitchen. See." He held up two bags filled with fresh jalapenos. "She stocked for the occasion." He brought the song to a close, his accent countrified and filled with laughter. Mac provided harmony.

Harry covered his ears and wailed. "My ears, good gods, man. Ye make a banshee cry in pain!"

Jeff spread the onions and jalapenos across the cutting board and thumbed the knife's edge. "Harry, beat a hasty retreat."

Mac broke into "Blue Eyes Crying in the Rain".

Harry ran from the kitchen.

"What did you do to Harry?" Sami stepped out of the back stairs. She sniffed, her head turning toward the stove. "Oh, no need for explanation. Chili."

Jeff swept a deep bow to her. She laughed. "Mac, would you help bring down the ornaments from the attic?"

"You're on your own, buddy. Duty calls." Mac followed Sami up the stairs.

Chili complete and simmering, Jeff scooped coffee for another pot. His back to the door, he heard her clear her throat. *Definitely female.* He turned from the coffee machine.

Colby stood in the door. He scrambled for something to say. *Any word would do.* His tongue stuck to the roof of his mouth.

"Might I have a cup? Or is it a personal shrine?"

"Let me." He grabbed the pot. Dripping coffee sprayed across his hand. "Damn." He fumbled the pot back into the holder. *Okay, don't turn around until she's quit laughing.*

He stuck one hand under running water and grabbed the dishrag with the other. He reached to swipe at the wet counter. She pulled the cloth from his grip.

"I'll get it," she said, "Keep your hand in the water."

He couldn't meet her eye, knowing the twinkle would match the amused edge in her voice.

"Okay, Conray, get a grip," he mumbled. Drying his hands, he turned to the refrigerator for fresh cream. Colby ran into him on her way to the sink. She staggered back a step. He grabbed her hands to steady her.

"Keystone Cops. My grandfather's favorites." Jeff inhaled.

"You bring out my clumsy side."

"Enough with the shenanigans, young mistress and master." Harry burst the bubble surrounding them. "Miss Colby, help me roust this bounder from my kitchen!" He brandished a broom.

Jeff stepped past Harry, dragging Colby, her hands still in his. "I surrender. The kitchen is yours. Please, just stir the chili now and then." He executed a dance turn and tucked her hand in his elbow escorting her to the table. Pulling out the chair, he spoke to Harry,

"Please, kind kitchen master, would you provide this young lady with a full coffee cup since I've failed miserably?"

Harry poured coffee, refilled the cream and pushed the tray across the island to Jeff.

"Thank you, Harry. Everything is perfect." Colby took a sip.

Harry lifted the lid from the chili pot and backed up. "By the gods, that concoction fair to removed my eyebrows! How can you eat this?"

"It's a bit spicy, Harry but without the Scotch Bonnets my mother prefers, it doesn't measure up to hers. With bread, it makes a meal to stick to your ribs." Jeff chuckled.

Harry wiped his face. "It gets to the ribs once the stomach is dissolved." he muttered. "Perhaps I should throw it at the beast next time."

Colby's eyebrows drew together. "What happened out there? I heard shots … and an unearthly scream. Sami's in the parlor with brandy and wouldn't tell me."

Jeff glanced at Harry.

"We got the first look at what is hunting Miss Sami." Harry wiped the counter for the third time. "A demon, Miss Colby."

"A lesser demon." Jeff added. "Scotty killed it."

"She always said something was after her." She shivered. "Then it's over?"

"One can hope so, Miss." Harry busied himself at the sink, not looking at her. Colby shivered, a look of doubt on her face.

"Sami wants classical music this evening. Niki wants us in the studio to talk about it." Jeff gathered up her empty coffee cup. He hoped addressing her passion would dispel her anxiety.

"Do you play classical guitar?"

"No, or rather, not well." he said. "I love classical music. Ma plays it all the time. Drives my dad crazy. He prefers country."

Colby pushed back her chair. "Shall we go meet Mr. Kaye? I've heard about him but I haven't seen hide nor hair." She smoothed the front of her skirt. "Harry, coffee for the illusive Wizard, please. My cello is in the front room." She disappeared through the door with Jeff behind her.

***

Harry found a large thermal mug. He reached out to Pyewacket.

Cream and sugar, Mr. Pyewacket?

Black, Mr. Harry. Cream on the side, if you please. The deep throated purr filled Harry's ears.

Already prepared, sir. Please let Mr. Kaye know they are on their way.

***

Jeff juggled the cello and the coffee. Colby carried her music case.

Gleaming snow mounds lined a cleared path to the stable. Colby walked across the driveway, aware Jeff was close behind.

"Niki, we've brought coffee … and cream. Pyewacket, where are you?" Jeff called. Black fur streaked from behind the drum kit and climbed to Jeff's shoulder. The cat rubbed cheek to jaw. Setting down his load, Jeff lifted Pyewacket by the scruff, rolling him over in his arms, belly up. "This is Pyewacket, rapscallion, and Niki's best friend. Pye, straighten up and meet the lady properly." Pyewacket squirmed over in Jeff's arms and aimed jade green eyes at Colby.

She felt thoroughly examined and measured.

Pyewacket launched, landing close to Colby's feet. Purring loudly, he wound around her legs.

"Give him the cream and you'll have a friend for life." The suggestion issued from the speakers. Colby glanced around for the floating head. Finding none, she filled the small bowl. Pyewacket rose on hind feet, paws guiding the bowl to the floor.

Can't be too careful, gracious lady.

Colby stared at the cat. She glanced at Jeff but his back was to her as he set up the music stands.

Niki appeared at her elbow. She shied away from his sudden proximity. He bowed, reaching past her to grasp the mug from the ledge. She anticipated his first words. "Welcome to Oz."

He picked up her music case and snapped it open, leafing through the sheet music. "Too stuffy, too Avant Garde ... too hard without more rehearsal time. Are you proficient at all these pieces?" He studied Colby.

She flushed, resenting the scrutiny by both cat and master. Straightening to full height, she looked him in the eye. "Most. I'm still working on some."

His twinkling eyes fascinated her, a gentling light shining on her. *Okay, down girl, no judgment here. No wonder Sami likes him.* She smiled back.

"You're good. We need something less highbrow. Jeff, did you bring your violin?"

Jeff pulled the case from behind the guitar stand. "Sure, but Niki, I can't keep up with that." He pointed at the sheet music arrayed on the piano."

"Trust me." He handed Colby her cello and waved her to a chair. "How quick a study are you?"

"Quick enough, I'd say." Her hackles rose again. "Why?"

"Try this." Niki played a melody line on the piano. Colby hummed the notes, fingering the neck. She played the sequence, slower but without error.

"Great. Jeff, here's the part for the violin." Niki ran through a quick sequence.

"Okay, let me try." After a few tries, Jeff completed the sequence. "Niki, this isn't classical even if you've transcribed it for violin and cello."

Niki laughed, "Wondered how long it would take you to catch on."

"Niki, it's wonderful choice. 'Celebrate Me Home'. The chorus goes like this." Colby played the chorus line, repeating it twice.

Niki smiled and she warmed under his attention, launching into a second chorus with embellishment.

No wonder Charlie's conflicted, she thought. Right now, she would do anything to get Niki's approval but she understood Charlie's jealousy. *Even Jeff wants Niki's approval,* noting his concentration on every note. As the two finished the song for the fourth time, Niki picked up a flute from its battered case.

"This time with the descant." He counted them in then added a high mirror to the melody, switched to harmony then back to echoed melody. Colby's heart caught in her throat listening to the three instruments and their voices wing through the song. She had never worked with anyone who pulled so hard on her ability and made her feel she could reach for more, even on this simple piece.

"Amazing." Jeff lowered his bow.

"Niki, I've never played so well. Thank you." Colby shook out her arm. Niki nodded and rifled through the sheet music on the piano. Pulling a sheet from the pile, he turned to Colby. "Let's try this one." He turned the music stand toward her.

"Niki, this is a solo. You want me to…" Her voice trailed off. He nodded. "Okay." She pursed her lips.

A few notes into the piece, Niki joined her on the flute in counterpoint. Each note from the flute pulled her to her next note, filling her with desire to match his fluidity with her strings. She lost herself in the music.

"Niki, where did you learn to play?" she asked when the music faded.

Niki put the flute into the case. "I learned … years ago." He picked up Pyewacket and disappeared out the door.

CHAPTER 20

The freezing rain returned to coat the heavy snow fall. Mac took his coffee to the parlor, admiring the tall Balsam fir waiting for its finery. Tori and Kay sat by the fire, deep in conversation.

"Good choice, Mac." Jeff stood at his elbow.

"Yeah, I think so. It makes Sami happy."

The sharp bark of a fox echoed across the field. Mac started, leaping to the window. "That's the same bark from this morning. Jeff, Pyewacket's out there. See, he's running on top of the wall. What the hell?"

Both foxes ran to the gate, Vixen slightly in the lead. Mac pivoted, moving toward the door.

Remembering Harry's admonition, Jeff stopped him. "Wait. Let them investigate first."

Mac turned back to the window. A dark shape stumbled out of the woods. The figure moved awkwardly encumbered by a large backpack and a case. The foxes flew past it momentarily hiding it in a plume of snow. Another bark sounded, farther from the house. Pyewacket skidded to a stop and hunkered down on top of the pillar. The figure resolve into a man dressed in a winter fatigue jacket.

"Good thing he's got a hard-shell case." Jeff noted

Pyewacket leapt, aiming for the man's shoulder. The man dodged. The cat flew by scratching at the air, trying to change direction. The man overcompensated, the icy footing winning where Pye failed. He landed on the ground in full snow angel position. His guitar case flew from his hands, landing across his chest. He sat up, setting the guitar case aside and rising to his feet.

He called out, "You want to play ninja, huh? What's the matter, won't the foxes play with you? Come on then." He crouched, scanning for the cat. Pyewacket came in for a second attack, lighting a snarling grin on the man's face. Catching the cat by the scruff of the neck, he flipped him into the air. The man's quick motions wound Pyewacket into a fuzzy tumbleweed. Pyewacket screeched. He bowled the cat toward the gate. Snatching up the guitar case, he sprinted for the house. Behind him, the foxes nipped at his heels.

Mac opened the front door. Pyewacket shot through the front door, yowling. He ran to climb Jeff's pant leg, missed the grab and slid against the wall. Jeff scooped him up and planted him on his shoulder, grimacing as wet fur rubbed the back of his neck. He scratched the damp head, resettling him so fewer claws engaged.

***

Sami shot from the kitchen, eyes wide as she took in the figure in the door. Mac stepped up beside her at the ready. She studied the young man, the tips of his sandy hair coated with ice and sticking out from the knit cap.

"Ggood afternoon, mmma'am. I hope you don't mind the frolic with your cccat." His stuttering voice—scratchy but melodic— echoed in the hallway.

Velvet sandpaper, Sami thought. *A most engaging smile and a very nice moustache.* "Won't you come in? You look very cold." His whole frame shook.

"Oh no, ma'am, I don't want to dirty your beautiful floor. I'll be jjjust fine. Thanks."

"You're hurt." Sami motioned toward his arm. "Did Pye do that?"

Chad stared at the bloody tear in his coat, swaying slightly. "No, ma'am. It was the thththing in the woods." Kay and Tori joined the group.

"Come in. Take off that wet coat. What's your name?" Sami mentally cringed. *Charlie will declare a first-class victory if he finds I've let a stranger in. Especially after this morning. But the foxes let him pass—and Mac and Jeff are here.*

"I'm Chchad Alton." He rubbed reddened hands together.

Frostbite. I doubt he can remove his boots by himself. Time to call in the professionals. She motioned to Jeff who relieved Chad of the guitar case and backpack while Mac steered him into the house swinging the door shut with his foot. Chad stared up at the two men, struggling to resist through chattering teeth. Harry appeared from behind her shoulder carrying a wooden stool from the kitchen. He placed it just inside the door.

"Harry will help you."

Harry maneuvered Chad onto the stool. "Sir, those leather laces are quite swollen and with my arthritis, it would be a help if I could cut them free. We will find others to replace them. My name's Harry."

Chad looked at the wrinkled face and sighed, dropping his shoulders from about his ears. He sat shivering as the Harry pulled off his boots.

"Ooof! There you go, sir. Here are slippers. I'll put these boots by the fire. Won't you let me have your coat, too, sir?" Harry kept up his mesmerizing conversation.

"Nnno thanks." Chad shivered, his feet prickling as the warmth penetrated. "Jeez, I was feeling okay until I got in here."

"Yes, sir. How long have you been wandering around?"

He looked around, "What time is it now?"

"Just after noon." Harry pulled Chad to his feet. "Hand over the coat, young man." The last took on the tone of an order and Chad allowed Harry to peal the wet canvas from his shoulders. They shambled down the hallway and disappeared into the kitchen. Sami followed behind.

Chad sat at the table, shivering. Stripped down from the multiple sweaters and army fatigue jacket, the new arrival had a thin wiry build. His shaggy hair hung in his eyes, dark circles blooming beneath.

Harry held tea with brandy to his blue lips.

Sami studied him, the circles under his eyes illustrating profound fright and fatigue deep in the human soul.

"Is the llittle ccat okay?"

I'm purrfectly fine. murmured Pyewacket, cozied in Jeff's embrace.

"I've lost mmy fricking mind." Chad stared at Pyewacket.

"Quite so, young sir." Harry said, holding the cup to his lips again.

Scotty draped a blanket across his shoulders. "What are you doing out here?"

He drew a deep breath, fighting to stop his teeth chattering. "I'm lost." He looked around the kitchen. "Hey, where's my guitar?"

Jeff opened the hard-sided guitar case.

"Careful with that." Chad tried to rise, his shivering abating but Harry pushed him back into the chair.

Jeff held out the guitar. "This is a beauty. I've never seen this combination of wood before."

Chad clutched the guitar. "It's my master work. Uncle Bernie's a luthier. I've been working with wood since I went to live with him."

Sami sat down beside him. "How did you end up out here?"

"I had a little trouble with the band. They decided I should hit the road. They stole my Fender. Joke's on them. It was made in Mexico. The guy at the QuikMart said the manager for "Numina"—you know, the new band—lived near here." He looked from face to face. "Niki Kaye. You know him?"

Jeff nudged Mac to close his mouth. He glared at Jeff.

Chad fingered the strings on the guitar. He struck a dark blues beat. "So, I got lost last night…" He chanted with the beat.

> Walking strong toward your light
> I felt a swoop, a sweeping
> Something unseen gliding toward me.
> The light was lost.
> It's so dark in this forest deep.
> I'm so lost and bewildered

He paused, his eyes darkening. Mac tapped on the table—a hesitation on the third beat. Chad nodded.

> Thump, what was that?
> The sky is flick flick flickering
> And snow is getting deeper
> The trees are growing thicker

> I hear my heart beat
> I feel my blood flow
> All I can say is, oh no
> Don't you take my soul

> Why was I pulled to come this way?
> What is that above me?
> Shadows aren't feeling right here
> I am falling into a nightmare

Mac's beat strengthened the song, hitting hard on the pauses, then more insistently working the tension as the song meandered and cascaded Chad's weird path to safety.

Harry picked up the teacup, added more brandy and handed it to Chad. He fumbled with the guitar, accepting the cup. Jeff saved the guitar as it slipped from his grasp.

"Don't mind Harry. He worries over us all." Jeff tucked the guitar back into its case. "Pretty good for impromptu. Charlie will want to hear more."

Chad looked from face to face. "You guys play?"

"A little." Scotty said.

"Come on." Mac brightened. "Wait till you guys see Charlie's wedding present. Out to the stables we go."

Sami picked the blankets up. Kay held out her hand, reaching for one to fold.

"Sami, have other things like this been happening?" Tori put the tea cup in the sink.

Kay and Sami glanced at each other.

"Did I miss something?" Jessica appeared in the kitchen door.

"Just a lost lamb being chased by the demon." Tori responded.

Jessica raised an eyebrow.

"Tori, to answer your question, I've been watched …" Sami hesitated looking to Kay for support.

"This isn't the first time Sami's been protected by stone creatures. You should have seen her at Notre Dame."

Jessica laughed. "Imagine the horde crawling down the walls to mingle with the tourist."

"You're being awful dismissive about this. There was a demon out there." Tori glared at Jessica.

"And you're being presumptive. You have no idea what I've seen. Or been through." Jessica turned sharply and disappeared back to the study.

"Tori, it's okay. Jess is right. We don't know each other. And these events are unsettling. But," her voice brightened, "I want to sort out the ornaments for tonight." Sami glanced at the stable. "Even though, they won't be in for hours now they've a new playground."

CHAPTER 21

Pyewacket wound through the many legs to streak into the studio. Leaping to the sound booth's window sill, he settled into Buddha cat pose, bright eyes gleaming.

Scotty and Chris explored the studio, their instruments arranged on the stands. Chad stared, open mouthed, at the abundant musical equipment.

"Man! What a place!" Chad burst out.

Scotty performed introductions. "Chad, this is Chris Thomas with wind instruments array. He can play anything you blow into, over or on."

Chris played a run on the piccolo. Chad felt the hair rise on his neck.

Scotty continued around the room. "Behind the drums is Charlie Ramhill." Charlie straightened up from adjusting the foot pedal and looked Chad over.

"Sami is his wife. This is their home."

"Oh, yeah … that angel." Chad sighed.

Charlie fixed a baleful eye on him.

"Nothing meant, sir. Just thought maybe I'd dreamed all this. Wait, if it's your home then Niki Kaye doesn't live here? I was told he did …" His voice trailed off seeing Charlie's glare.

"We all do from time to time." Charlie cleared his throat. "Since Sami let you in the house, I suppose you are welcome."

Scotty finished the introductions, Jeff on lead guitar, Mac on bass. Scotty picked up his guitar. "And I play rhythm. Why don't you show Charlie what you can do?"

Red flooded Chad's face. He snapped open the guitar case and settled the strap over his shoulder. Without looking up, he played the first notes of *Estudio Sin Lu*. The haunting Segovia piece swirled through the air.

Charlie twitched the drumsticks but remained still. He made notes in the notebook on his lap. Jeff clapped, bringing more color to Chad's face.

"Yeah, but can you do anything with an electric guitar?" Niki's voice lilted over the sound system. Chad peered at the slight figure in the sound booth, his face hidden in the shadows.

"Sure, I can, kid." Chad responded in a loud voice. "Trade for a minute?" He handed his guitar to Jeff and accepted the electric guitar. "How about some Carlos Santana? G okay with you rhythm and bass guys?" He looked at Mac and Scotty.

They nodded and he charged onward. "Drummer boy, join in whenever you stop napping, okay?"

Charlie looked up. He picked up the drumsticks and set the rhythm. Jeff picked up his spare. He studied Chad's fingering then added harmonics.

In a moment, Niki exited the sound booth. He waved for them to stop.

Taking the guitar from Jeff, he ran through several chords, a complex pattern on the strings.

Chad stared at him. He ran the first few chords then fumbled. "No, wait … do it again."

Niki handed the guitar back to Jeff and walked away.

Jeff replayed the sequence at full speed. At Chad's intense stare, he played it again slower. "Don't worry. You'll get used to it. He doesn't do anything twice."

They launched into the piece finishing it without interruption.

"Charlie," Niki's voice issued from the sound booth. "Try your new piece. I want a mike check with vocals."

Charlie nodded and gave the downbeat. Mac and Scotty joined in.

Jeff leaned over to Chad. "Key of E. He likes to make it interesting." He nodded toward Charlie. "Here's the melody." Jeff played several bars. "Got it?"

Chad ran his fingers silently over the frets. He nodded.

"Can we get on with this sometime today?" Niki demanded over the intercom.

"Pushy little twit, isn't he?" Chad said.

Jeff grinned and nodded to Charlie. Mac and Scotty joined in with rhythm and counter rhythm. Jeff launched into the melody line with Chad following. Jeff stepped up to the microphone. His rich baritone voice rumbled through Charlie's elegant lyrics. Mac added his deeper tones to the chorus.

Charlie varied the rhythm in response to the melody, smiling. Jeff and Mac brought the words to life. The flute rose in descant.

Twice more, Niki stopped the group, each time suggesting a change.

"Jeff," Chad whispered during one break. "He's got balls or are his ideas always this good?"

Jeff just smiled.

They worked through the material and each new piece pushed a little harder. Jeff showed him each melody line, giving him one or two tries. Sweat beaded up on Chad's forehead. Soon they were all drenched.

Charlie set down the drumsticks. "Enough! The sun is setting. Nik, you got enough for the demo tape now?"

"Sure, Charlie. After a little blending." Niki stepped out from the control booth.

"Thanks. The studio gives every note life. The acoustics are beyond my wildest dreams."

"Thank Sami's father." Niki picked Pyewacket up and settled him on his shoulder.

Charlie stopped them. "I know your touch when I see it. I mean it, thank you."

Niki shrugged.

"Niki? Demo tapes?" Chad groaned. "Man, am I dense! You're Niki Kaye? Oh, shit, I didn't mean to be disrespectful. But you're Niki Kaye? I thought you were a manager, not a sound guy. Aren't you supposed to be greasy and wear polyester with gold chains? Thought you'd be older but I mean I don't have a problem with you being so young …"

Pyewacket hissed at Chad.

He grinned. "Actually, it's a I-can't-shut-up problem." He smacked his forehead. "Wait, that means …that means, you guys are Numina. Oh, wow."

Jeff cuffed Chad across the back of his head. "Stop while you're ahead. I need a beer … and a shower before we join the ladies for dinner."

CHAPTER 22

Scotty held out his hand to Kay. "I thought I recognized you. We met on the Ramhill estate many years ago."

"You and Charlie rode out on his father's hunters and ended up mired in the bog … didn't make you any friends at court." She laughed at his chagrinned expression.

He smiled, a twinkle in his eyes. "Ah, but it was a ride well worth the price." He lifted her hand and bent to kiss it without taking his eyes from hers. She felt a blush rising under his frank appraisal.

"Hey, you can't monopolize all the beautiful women." Chad ambled in from the back hall. He shook water from his hair.

"You looked much recovered, Mr. Alton." Kay extended her hand.

Chad wrapped her hands in his. Her fingers felt his silver ring before the light from his heart chakra surrounded them.

"Shalom Aleichem, " she said in a whisper and the energy from her heart chakra flowed down her arm. The two energies touched, danced for a moment and pulled back leaving a tingle.

"Aleichem shalom." Chad responded. "I hope we have time to talk later." He looked around at the stares. "What? What? Can't I appreciate a beautiful woman?"

Sami laughed. "Dinner is informal. You're welcome in the kitchen or the dining room … or the parlor."

Harry handed Chad a bowl for each hand. He sniffed one then held them out to Kay.

"Mulligan stew or chili. I'd say from the way the spoon is melting, the chili has a Scoville rating equal to taking-your-life-in-your-hands. It's your choice."

Chuckling at his analysis, she chose the chili. Chad whistled under his breath.

"Wow. I'd better get us something to drink. Harry's made eggnog but with the alcohol content in it, the combination might be flammable. How about red wine?" He grinned at her nod.

Kay picked up the bowls. Hearing Charlie's melodious voice from the dining room, she decided to join him.

As she pushed through the swinging door, Charlie rose from his seat and pulled out a chair for her. She placed the second bowl before the empty chair on her left. Chad slipped into the seat beside her and placed a goblet filled with red wine at her hand. Scotty continued the debate about an obscure French company producing an even more obscure electronics product … a company in which he and Charlie both owned shares.

"Smells magnificent," she murmured. She brought the spoonful to her lips. The first bite burned her throat. She felt her eyes filling with tears. Grabbing the wine glass, she drained it, her action producing laughter from a dark shadow in the kitchen doorway. Mac presented her the choice of water, the open wine bottle or a tall, amber beer.

"Sorry, ma'am. Should have warned you about Jeff's chili. It removes paint and scours the cast iron. Here, this might help." She gratefully accepted the water while he refilled her wine glass. Mac edged between Chad and Kay and sat, pushing Chad from the chair.

Chad staggered to his feet. He turned, threatening to pour his stew over Mac. Kay shook her head. Shrugging, he left for the kitchen.

Kay finished the water, eyed her wine glass. She reached for Mac's beer. She drank half, without a breath, seeing Mac's eyes grow large. She set the mug down. "Thank you." Her voice caught in her throat. "I may consider being his friend when the burning stops." She scooped up another spoonful and ate it without hesitation.

Mac laughed and sipped on his beer. "Ma'am, you're either very brave or very foolhardy. I'd prefer to think brave."

"I like spicy food." She laughed. "I spent time in Burma last spring. Spicy is life there." She swallowed another bite then picked up his beer again, her green eyes watching him over the rim. She leaned toward him and whispered, "I prefer beer to wine."

He rose to refill the mug. "Don't let the pipsqueak take my seat, Kay. I want to continue this conversation. A beautiful woman who likes nine alarm chili and beer. What more could a man ask for?" He winked at her.

A furry body rubbed against her legs and nosed her calf. She reached down and the cat placed his head in her hand. She scratched under his jawbone. A deep rumble vibrated her fingers.

> *He'd like to see you in the study.* Pyewacket wrapped his tail around her leg.

> *I'll never get used to this part*, she responded.

> *You will. You just haven't met many, yet.*

> *There are more?*

She remembered hearing her name with no one near... the Irish wolfhound dragging her away from the peat bog's crumbling edge, repeating her name and encouraging her frozen steps. He led her back through the fog to her mother's wagon. Not every animal, her mother said, just those with auras shot with gold.

> *Who wants to see me?* She asked. She leaned over looking for the cat.

> *It's a surprise.* The cat slipped from under her chair.

"Kay," Tori called her name for the second time. "Are you all right?"

"Yes, but after the chili, I drank my wine and Mac's beer. If I am a little tipsy, I have earned it."

Tori flashed a grin.

> *Hehemmm.* The cat placed both paws on her thigh and grabbed her hand in his teeth. *Wnt y come on.*

> *I would understand you better if your mouth weren't full*, she replied. *And since we are getting intimate, won't you tell me your name?*

Pyewacket dropped her hand and performed an apologetic wash. *"Pyewacket, my lady, at your service."*

Well met, Pyewacket. Lead on.

She rose from the table and followed the prancing cat down the hall. The wood paneling glowed in the deepening evening light. A figure stood in the shadow, his back to the windows. Blond bangs hung in his eyes, his hair curling at the collar. She didn't breathe … didn't dare speak fearing to lose this vision.

Niki.

Yes, Kay, came his response, familiar in her mind.

Fir and fresh rain, scents dear to her, surrounded them. Her throat tightened as the man—not the boy in her memory—embraced her. He buried his face in her shoulder, his arms tight around her. She stood still holding her breath until she felt her knees weaken.

She lifted his head. Deep blue eyes filled with loneliness searched her face for forgiveness. Music swelled up in her thoughts. *Thank God, he hasn't lost the music.*

Taking her by the shoulders, he held her out.

"You look wonderful, Kay," he said. "I've missed you." Before she could respond, he hurried on, "We don't have much time before Sami calls us. The people here don't know much about me and it's best that way."

Niki turned away from her, pacing, energy building up in his aura. It flared from red to gold and back again.

"I need to be who they think I am right now. I can't go back and revisit all the things that happened. Do you understand?" His voice pleaded with her.

She nodded. "Just tell me I'm not walking in a nightmare … one where I turn around to find you gone."

He moved so quickly to grab her hand she startled, shivers running down her frame. "Kay, I'm sorry I ran away."

She squeezed his hand hard. "Niki, stop. When we were children, I always wanted to know everything you were thinking and feeling. I envied your freedom, the way you defied Father, your escape into the countryside. You're much more Mother's child than I am. I've been so worried." She brushed the hair from his eyes and he leaned into her palm. She felt the soft stubble along his jaw line. "Niki, I love you."

Pyewacket leapt from the desk, twining between their legs.

"Niki, how did you get involved with Charlie?"

"His music, Kay. Charlie doesn't recognize me." He paced again. "And something else about him … something binds me to him." Niki balanced Pyewacket on his shoulder, his tone lightening. "I'm glad you're here. Especially now with the demons out there."

"How does Scotty know to name it such?"

"I don't know. Scotty carries a deep magic in him." He stroked her arm, an old habit from the years falling asleep as she sang to him. "And a deep hurt."

She pulled him into a tight hug, careful not to upset Pyewacket.

Mac appeared in the door. "Hey, pretty lady. Nik, I didn't know you were in here, too. Sami's ready for everyone." Kay chuckled at Mac's obvious scrutiny.

Niki held Kay's hand. "Mac, I'd like you to meet my sister."

"Ma'am, it's easy to see you got all the beauty and brains in the family." Offering his arm, he winked at Niki, "But you, little bro, may have a future in matchmaking."

Kay's laughter wrapped around Mac's chuckle as Niki trailed behind the pair to the parlor.

CHAPTER 23

Sami ran to them, her arms filled with crystal orbs. She spilled them into Kay's hands. "Kay, here. These need to go on the tree. Chris is getting out the candles. Charlie and Jeff are working on the candleholders. It is a fire hazard but it'll be okay."

Grabbing Niki's hands, she spun him around eliciting a hiss from Pyewacket who sprang from his shoulder. "Come on, help me untangle the garlands. They're white silk and an absolute mess." She dragged him to the corner by the fireplace.

Tori rolled the butler's cart in. Harry steadied the cups. "My goodness, what a bustle! Maestro Harry has been teaching me about wassail and, I do declare, it'll put starch in your shorts."

Harry grimaced at her. Tori delivered each cup with running commentary.

"Charlie, that's just perfect. Jeff, put it a little higher. "Kay, what a beautiful silk blouse. It matches your eyes perfectly. Jessica, are those earrings a family piece? They are exquisite."

"Where's Scotty?" She asked no one in particular. Shrugs all around was the response.

"Niki, this is perfect. Thank you."

Charlie turned at Sami's voice in time to see her throw her arms around Niki and kiss him on the cheek. He bit his lip. A movement in his peripheral vision pulled his gaze to Jessica's face. She stared at him for a moment then she handed Jeff another candleholder. As he looked away, Sami appeared so close, he startled back.

"Charlie, look." She held out her hands. "Niki made this for the tree." He examined the small, white feathered figure. Dark obsidian eyes stared back at him, smoke deep in the interior.

"It's *Athena noctua*, the little owl of wisdom. Will you put him in the tree?" Sami pointed high in the tree.

"Of course, darling." Taking the little figure from her, he reached up. As he secured it, the sharp talon pierced his finger drawing a crimson drop.

"Damn, it's sharp." He glared at the owl.

Sorry, Niki's voice sounded close in his head. *I should have trimmed his claws but you know magic often requires a blood sacrifice.*

Charlie looked around to answer him but couldn't find him in the room.

Scotty arrived with his arms filled with holly. "Tori, will you help me put this on the mantle?"

She carefully removed the boughs from his arms and placed them around the candles on the mantelpiece. "What, no mistletoe? What is this holiday without mistletoe?"

Scotty grinned. "Abracadabra!" Two large bunches of mistletoe appeared in his hand. Tori clapped.

"Yeah, Scotty," Jeff laughed, "I'm glad to see it's mistletoe, too. It looked like you'd grown a leafy tail." He snatched the mistletoe from him and hung a sprig on a hook over the parlor door. "Sami, you have hooks in all the right places." He stood there, the mistletoe hanging over his head.

Colby stepped around Jeff, her hands laden with long cranberry strings. She stopped short. Everyone was looking in her direction.

"What?" she said, staring at each face in turn, resting on Charlie.

His lips twitched up at the corners.

"What?" She repeated, irritation creeping into her voice.

A hand closed on her shoulder and turned her around. Jeff pointed at the mistletoe over his head. She tried to pull away but he held her firm. Sighing, she closed her eyes and lifted her face for a kiss. Jeff placed his lips on hers and executed a perfect ballroom dip, one hand at the small of her back and the other behind her neck. Her eyes opened wide. He lifted her, guiding her into a turn ending with her back against his chest, arms wrapped across her and tangled in cranberry strings. Applause and laughter filled the room.

She stepped away from him, fumbling with the escaping strings. Seeking a seat on the loveseat, she kept her head down with her long hair shielding her face. She focused on untangled the cranberry strands, her hands shaking.

The rhythmic beat of a small drum drew attention away from her. Niki appeared in the doorway, leading Mac and Chris carrying a mountain ash log beribboned in white and red.

"The Yule log," Charlie's smile beamed. "It's perfect." He looked at Mac. "It's rowan. How did you find it here?"

"It's called mountain ash in the States but it's the same tree." Mac and Chris positioned the log on the kindling.

"Sami, did you arrange this?" Charlie clapped Mac on the back as he straightened.

"Your friends did the hard work." She held out the oil cruet. "I prepared the herbs. Rosemary for friendship, parsley for rejoicing, catnip for courage." She looked around finding the black cat on the hearth. "And for Pyewacket."

He looked up from his grooming.

"Basil for protection."

"A Yule log to last the holiday season." Charlie bowed to the assembled group. "My thanks to you all."

Harry pulled a crystal pitcher filled with mulled wine from under the cart and handed it to him.

Mac eyed the Yule log. "Chris says the tradition is the master says a prayer to protect all those who live in the home. So please pray the house doesn't burn down." He glanced at Sami. "The chimney's clean, isn't it?" She nodded.

Charlie chuckled and held up the cruet and the crystal pitcher. Chanting the words flowing through his mind, he drizzled the mixtures over the log. His hands wove a rhythmic dance. He blessed the log …

the words arcane and bowed to Sami, murmuring softly "With your permission, Mistress."

She nodded, her face solemn.

He lifted his hands. The Yule log burst into flames. Sami gasped, slipping her hand through Charlie's arm and pulling him close.

Pungent scents washed through the room. Kay stepped closer to Niki and he clasped her hand. She leaned against his shoulder, kissing him on the cheek. He closed his eyes.

"You are each the true gift. I am glad for everyone here. You bring the blessings of the hearth, heart, and music to us." Charlie said. "No demons will reign here while we are together." At his final words, the burning log transformed into a dancing blaze.

"Everyone, find a seat, please." Sami pushed Charlie to the loveseat and settled in his lap. "Maestro, music if you will." Charlie squeezed her when Colby pulled out her cello.

"What other surprises have you?" he whispered. She shushed him.

Colby sang the opening line to "Celebrate Me Home", her soft alto counterpointing her cello. Jeff joined in then picked up the violin. Niki augmented the melody with a flute descant.

Sami snuggled under Charlie's arm. Charlie's throat tightened with each repetition. *Home*. He pulled Sami closer and listened with his heart to his friends.

The last strains died into silence. As one, each sighed, laughter punctuating the sacred moment. Harry disappeared from the room pulling Chad with him. In moments, they reappeared bearing tall champagne flutes filled with sparkling wine and sugared fruit and dark chocolate truffles on silver plates.

"Sami, shall we light the candles on the Christmas tree?" Charlie asked her.

She shook her head. She whispered, "The Yule log is for the Winter Solstice. Let's save lighting the tree for Christmas." She accepted a glass from Harry and held it to Charlie's lips.

Colby took up the cello once again, filling the room with elegance. Niki joined in with high airy harmony. Jeff set his violin down on the window table and accepted a champagne flute from Chad. He closed his eyes. Charlie knew that look. Jeff allowed his mind to joyously ride Colby's notes, rising and falling.

CHAPTER 24

Lord Damian Ramhill slammed the door to his study and private collections. "This nonsense! I am sick to death. Where are my things?" He paced, stomping across the room. "Infuriating! The staff wouldn't dare." *Maybe the Tarot will yield an answer.*

He picked up the carved, wooden box from his desk. A cold chill ran down his neck.

"Damn it!" The empty box gaped at him. He threw it against the wall, searching the room. The red silk covering lay on the floor behind his desk chair. He snatched it up.

He learned—by his father's punishing hand—to respect the cards. His great great-grandfather painted the deck during the Golden Dawn. Each subsequent generation the cards with familial power. No one but the heir dared touch them.

"Desecration!" He raged, twisting the silk covering. "I will find the guilty party!"

His eyes swept the floor and over the hearth. The cards lay strewn across the bricks. He gathered them up, shuffling them from hand to hand. He stalked to the mahogany desk. Sitting in the leather chair, he exhaled. He shuffled them, focusing his energy on the cards.

"No!" He shot up from the chair, overturning it. He stared at the deck. The shuffling rhythm ceased too soon with each turn. He spread the deck, noting each card. "The minor arcana. The Emperor, the Fool…" He counted down the major arcana. "The Devil. The damned Devil is missing!"

Slamming his hand on the desk, he retraced his steps. He jerked back the Aubusson carpet, glowing red and blues revealing empty floor.

"Damn it all! I will have it back!"

Kneeling on the hearth, he stoked the fire, sending it flaring from its night banking. "First my ring then my wife. Now my card. I will find out who… they will pay for this!"

The flames licked higher.

He pulled the juniper stump onto the hearth, placing it close to the fire, warming the resin. As the air filled with smoky essence, he relived the bloody ritual at his father's hands. He'd been forced to retrieve the log himself, dragging it a mile from the forest, his hands raw and bleeding.

His father's voice grated in his ears. "The juniper embodies the co-mingling, your blood and the family essence. No rowan must ever burn in your hearth. It will unravel your strength."

Damian pushed back his sleeve and pulled the knife across his forearm. Blood welled, dripping onto the stump. *Juniper will protect you.* The heat intensified with every drop. A cold chill crawled up his arm. He heard faint laughter then his brother's voice from the fireplace.

"… the blessings of the hearth, heart, and music, to us. No demons will reign here while we are together."

Damn. I can't believe he has the power. He sat back on his heels, his eyebrows drawn together. "We will see who is better!" He shouted into the fire. He flicked his hand, blood spattering into the flames. Grabbing the poker, he threw another log on the fire. Satisfied with the roaring blaze, he gathered the ingredients for the incantation.

"I will have my card back. They will not defy me."

Unblinking red eyes followed his movements, a subsonic rumble rolling from its scaly throat. Hot claws ran up Damian's back, twisting his spine until he turned toward the darkened corner where the secret panel stood open. A massive form dragged his bulk through the door. "You only have to ask for my help." The demon sat on his haunches his flaming eyes looking down on Damian.

"I know, I know," Damian stammered. "But there is always a price."

The demon laughed. "Naturally. We have the same goal, you and I. We will never be free of his curse until we have her."

Damian pursed his lips, biting back a retort which he knew would do no good.

"Speechless? I see. Then figure this one out on your own." The demon rose, turning to the open panel. "Perhaps I chose the wrong brother. When you have exhausted your pitiful attempts, you may crawl back to me."

The panel slid shut on silence.

CHAPTER 25

Sami applauded her sister as the last note died away. Colby set her bow in the case. She accepting the warm snifter from Niki and took a seat on the loveseat across from Charlie and Sami.

"Beautiful, Colby. You are gaining mastery every time I hear you play." Charlie looked over at the Christmas tree. "Sami," he whispered. "The tree."

"Oh, my!" She rose and stood before the tree. The candles alit, the tree glistened, the crystal ornaments throwing rainbows around the room. Boxes wrapped in white and tied with gold ribbons nestled at the base.

Charlie put an arm around her. "Decided not to wait til Christmas?"

Her eyes filled with tears. Warm air swirled pine scent around them. "No, I guess she didn't want to…"

"She?" Charlie wrinkled his forehead.

Sami didn't answer. She dropped to her knees under the tree. "We have Solstice gifts to open." She sorted through the pile and handed a box to each. The last item was a long, slender object.

"Harry, this is for you." Sami placed the gift in the old gentleman's hands. He pulled the paper from the rune-carved wood twisted in a tight spiral.

"My walking stick!" he cried. "My walking stick." He clutched it. "Thank you, Miss Sami. Thank you. I haven't had this stick … well, since you were a babe. I thought it lost forever." He danced a step bumping into Chad. He looked at the open box, puzzlement on his face.

"Chad, something wrong? What is in the box?" Harry looked over his shoulder.

"String," Chad rolled the red ball in his hand, "and an etching tool." He rifled through the paper, "several metal discs. Silver, I think."

Harry cocked his head. "These things will have their use, I am certain." He patted Chad on the shoulder. The walking stick remained tucked under his arm, Harry turned, grazing Chad's side. Rubbing his ribs, Chad moved farther away. Niki winked at him before turning back to the fire.

"Sami, this is beautiful." Tori dangled a silver chain. The light from the tree glittered off the twirling cone-shaped amethyst.

Harry inspected the object from a distance. "Be careful, miss. You'd best ask for a few lessons." Tori's eyes narrowed and she pursed her lips. After a moment, she placed the amethyst crystal back in the wrappings.

"Sami, where did you get this?" Jessica glared at Charlie. "Of did you do this?"

"Jess, what are you talking about?" Charlie grimaced.

"This ring." She held up a heavy gold signet ring. "This ring …" she repeated, "is the ring Damian has been ranting about. It disappeared after your father died." she hesitated, "Before Damian started behaving like a maniac." She sank down on the loveseat. "He's convinced someone stole it—that maybe I did—and now it turns up here." She put her face in her hands.

Charlie sat beside her, setting his unopened gift on the hearth. He reached for the ring. She dropped it into his palm. He jerked back, fumbling it.

"It's hot. Fiery hot." He examined it. "The seal of Solomon," he muttered under his breath, his eyes flashing. He peered into the flames, jaw muscles writhing.

Jessica grasped his wrist. Charlie jumped. "Jess, your fingers are so cold."

"Give it back. I don't like it either but somehow it came to me. Don't invite him in." Jessica scooped up the ring, depositing it in her pocket. She wrung her hands. "I'm to bed." She rose, leaving the parlor and taking the stairs two at a time.

Chris pulled a wooden ocarina from a green velvet bag. Prancing foxes chased around its belly, the hand-rubbed surface gleaming in the candlelight. He fingered it.

"The one you lost in the bog?" Scotty looked over his shoulder. "If it's not, then it's a twin."

Chris palmed the instrument.

Scotty held out an ornate watch. "It's a Breitling Navitimer. Remember the summer I had flying lessons? My flight instructor showed me his grandfather's … said it saved his life in World War II. It's an early model. They used a Breitling to time the first flight at Kitty Hawk."

Chris smiled. "Always a boy around gizmos." He hefted the watch. Multiple analog dials decorated the face. "It's a beautiful piece. Bet you know what each one is for." He handed the watch back.

Scotty nodded. He motioned toward Chris' pocket. "How does she sound?"

Chris set the ocarina to his lips. He ran up the scale. All conversation in the room ceased.

"Lovely. Chris, play something, please?" Niki saluted him with his glass.

He launched into the first tune that came to mind, a haunting melody. All motion in the room stilled. When he finished, he wiped the ocarina with his bandana and stuck it in his pocket again. "It's another song calling to home. First melody I could recall."

Kay stood close to him. "Magnificent."

Chris cleared his throat. "Thank you for the compliment." Chris studied Kay's face.

"Romani blood," she whispered, her voice husky in his ear.

He flushed but did not drop eye contact. "I thought you were Jewish … from what Chad said."

"My father raised us in the tradition. The Kalderash were his people but he converted. The rabbi in the village saw promise in him … gave him support for the University. From there, he taught for a family in Dublin where he met my mother." She smiled at him. "She belongs to the Pavee. Niki and I are gypsies on both sides."

Chris blinked twice.

She laughed at his evident confusion. "Don't tell me Mac hasn't spread the word already."

Chris' gaze shifted from her auburn hair to Niki's straw blond.

"My father's blood line wasn't pure, either. And my mother's hair is white blonde." She studied the ocarina. "What a beautiful instrument. Have you played one before or are you a quick study?"

"It's mine." He blurted out. "One I lost a long time ago. I don't know how it turned up here."

"I hope you'll play again." She stepped away and caught Harry as he gathered up the empty cups.

"Do you wish anything else, Miss Kay?" He paused in his search.

"Harry, you're versed on Celtic lore. Do you know anything about this necklace?" She held up a dark silk cord from which hung black raven pendant. A red inset eye twinkled in the firelight.

Harry froze, his eyes glued to the pendant. His face paled. "Morrigan ..." Harry croaked in a strangled voice. He looked away. "Goddess of death ..." He blinked and ducked away, leaving the parlor.

"Now what did you do to scare him, Kay?" Niki spoke at her shoulder. She opened her hand.

Niki stared at it for a moment, reached to touch, pulling back. "Ouch. Not a friendly bird. Melanite, I would guess."

"Also called andradite garnet. Not a common crystal." Kay lowered the figurine into the black silk bag.

"But appropriate. Garnet's the warrior stone."

She hugged him. "What interesting present did you receive?"

"Nothing much." He shrugged.

"Let me see." She urged.

"I'd rather not unwrap it here. It might have the same effect yours did." He kissed her on the cheek. "I must say good night. It's been a long day." Niki dropped his voice and pointed at the bag. "Think long and hard before you put that around your neck."

Pyewacket rose from the cushion in the corner, stretching and meowing. Niki scooped him up. His shadow fell on Sami still seated beneath the tree. She closed her hand, hiding her fist beneath her oversized shirt.

"Sami, thank you for a lovely evening. I pray you have sweet dreams tonight." He kissed her cheek, and, nodding to the others, left the parlor.

Into the space left behind, a larger presence lowered to the floor beside her. Jeff searched her face. "Sami, I don't understand what is happening here. These are powerful gifts. I trust they have a purpose." He studied the double terminated crystal in his hand.

"I don't understand, either," she whispered.

"Yet," he finished.

Before he said more, Colby knelt on Sami's other side. She set down a lemon-sized crystal ball nestled in satin.

"Sami, remember when we used to play in the attic …" She grinned, excitement in her voice. She looked at Jeff. "We weren't supposed to."

"Colby's idea." Sami interjected.

Jeff chuckled.

"I know where your loyalties lay, little sister. Remember the purple satin box we found and I would never let you see what was in it." She toyed with the crystal ball, not looking at Sami. "There wasn't anything in it." She held up the crystal. "This is what I wanted to find. I can't imagine what I will do with it except keep it on a window sill." She stared at the ball.

"Colby, don't look at it too long." Sami nudged her sister.

Colby shivered. "You're right." she said, placing it back into the satin cradle. "I'm too tired to think about it tonight. What did you get?"

Sami revealed a delicate gold locket. Colby stroked a finger over the engraved surface.

"I've never seen one with a fox on it. Are there pictures inside?"

"No," Sami snapped, closing her fist and tucking the locket into her pocket. She dropped her head, blonde hair curtaining her eyes. "I'm sorry, Colby. I didn't mean to be sharp."

"We're tired." Colby climbed to her feet. She offered Sami her hand and levered her to a standing position. "We're still a good team. Good night." Colby clutched the crystal ball to her chest. "Don't wait breakfast for me." She paused in the doorway. "I'm so tired, I may not be down until noon."

Holding up his gift, Mac explained the inclinometer to Charlie. "It measures the deviation from vertical or horizontal to show slippage, say in a building's foundation. It may suggest structural weakness or shifts in the ground."

Sami smiled at the glazed look in Charlie's eye. She touched his arm. "Charlie, I'm going up to bed." She stood on tiptoe to brush his lips. He did not respond, coldness in his eyes. She drew back, noticing his gift sitting unopened on the hearth.

"Good night, Mac." She nodded to each.

"Good night, baby girl." Mac responded. "Just promise me, no early morning excursions tomorrow."

She turned back around giving him her best dazzling smile. "I don't make promises I can't keep," she said. Mac groaned.

Sami found Harry policing the kitchen. She pulled the locket from her pocket and opened it to reveal two pictures. "Harry, are these my parents?"

He studied the pictures. "Yes, your real parents. They love you very much even though they've been gone."

"You're here to protect me?"

He nodded.

"Why did they leave me?" She studied his face then cut off his response. "And why didn't you tell me?"

"Your father went off searching for your mother." Harry looked down at his hands. He swallowed. "She was kidnapped … by the demons. I could na stop them." Looking into Sami's face, he frowned. "I could na tell you before. Mr. Carleton thought it best until you were safely here." He swept his arm to encompass the room. "Until you learned what she has to offer."

"But why are they after me?"

"I dinna know. I would tell you if I did." Harry hung his head.

"We have much to discuss." She stroked his cheek. "I want you to stay forever."

She walked up the back stairs, her footsteps heavy.

CHAPTER 26

The bedroom door slammed. Charlie flung the box on the bed. Sami put down her hairbrush and rose to embrace him.

Pushing her away, he paced the room and beat his fist into his palm. He stopped, fixing her with his gaze.

"What the hell is going on?"

"What do you mean?" Sami backed away from him.

"You know damn well what I mean. Those gifts … you saw Jessica's ring. It belongs to my brother. To each Lord since my however many greats grandfather commissioned it. The pendant Kay received … it was a gift from my grandfather to my grandmother days before she was killed in a freak storm. That …" He pointed to the box. "has been in more Ramhill hands than I dare count."

"Charlie, it's unopened. How do you know what it is?"

"I know!" He threw up his hands. "I touched the box and I knew. It isn't a feeling one ever forgets. I fled England to leave all this shit behind." He stopped, panting then burst out, "Then I come home to deception. And now this! Sami, I never thought you'd do this to me."

"Do this to you?" She shouted back at him, surprising him. "Charlie, I have no idea what's happening."

He started towards her, angered by her tone. He stopped, holding himself rigid but for his hands beating on his thighs.

"Don't glare at me. I can't think when you're angry!" She said, "Is this the behavior Jess is running from?"

She backed up to the bed. Her voice low, she said, "Charlie, when my father brought me to this house, he told me I'm not his daughter. Since then, I've uncovered the secrets in this house and my identity. The house is sentient. It changes and grows. I haven't made all the repairs you see. It … she … heals herself."

He shook his head in disbelief. He saw flames in her eyes.

"How the hell did you light the fire tonight? You didn't have any matches." She shouted at him, "How dare you judge me when you haven't been honest with me either. I was going to tell you everything tonight. I need to tell you." She pulled out the locket. "Tonight, this locket appeared. Pictures of my parents—my real parents—who abandoned me." She inhaled sharply, letting it out with a shudder. "I need to share all these things. After this morning, I need you to hold me and tell me it's going to be all right."

Charlie stepped toward her, his hands tensed at his side.

She put her hands up. "But instead, you burst through the door with murder in your eyes." She sat on the bed, her hair hanging over her face.

"Oh, please." Charlie sneered at her. "Don't try that routine on me. I'm not Mac. Not so easily swayed by histrionics."

She looked up at him. "Do you hear yourself?"

Grabbing her upper arms, he hauled her to her feet. "I know damn well what I am saying. I want this shit to stop and stop now!" He felt the darkness overtaking him, reacting to the hardness in her eyes, amber flaming red and gold.

"Let me go." She said, her teeth clenched. "Now!"

He released her left arm and pulled back. His hand swung toward her. She flinched.

The window panes burst inward, glass flying. A cyclone, raw and frigid, circled the room, pulled at his clothing. Ice crystals stung his eyes. He let go of her and wiped at his face. He fought against the wind to reach the curtains.

The wind died. He staggered, catching himself on the sill, glass shards cutting into his hands. A chill ran through him, blood draining from his face.

He turned. His heart stopped in his chest. Sami stood, stiff and still, her hair a nimbus around her. Her face matched her ivory dressing gown. He started towards her. Sweat ran into his eyes, the room warming with each step.

He heard the wind howling outside the windows. *The windows?* He snapped around to find the curtains hanging motionless over the intact windows. *My God, am I hallucinating?* He stared out into the dark night, his anger driven away. He brought his hands to his face … stopped, holding them out. Blood drops littered his palms. He turned to meet Sami's stare, her eyes ablaze.

A heavy knock at the door fanned his anger back to life and he stalked towards the door.

"Come!" Sami said. Her stare defied him to speak or move. His breath hissed through his teeth. The door swung open.

"Madam," Harry's voice issued from the dark doorway. "Do you need assistance?"

Charlie blinked, the form larger than seemed right for the old man.

Sami stepped into the shadows and touched Harry's hand. "Thank you, Harry. All will be well."

"Yes, Madam." He pulled the door closed.

Sami faced Charlie. "I can't make all this go away. I don't know how. But I'm going to learn."

He started towards her.

"Stop!" she commanded, freezing him in place. "The people here, our friends … and family. Those things they received tonight. It all fits together somehow."

He shook his head.

"You can believe me … or you can leave."

"Leave?" He looked at her face, realizing she—or something that responded to her— would assure his departure. "Leave? You want me to leave my house with this nightmare going on?"

"My house," she said. "Your home … if you are willing to fight for it. And for me. I'm going to learn to work with this spirit because it's my legacy. You can love me or you can run from me … and yourself!" Her voice dropped in volume as it grew in intensity.

He looked at her as if for the first time, wondering if he would ever again see the woman who had sheltered in his arms. His palms stung. Not understanding … not being in control … angered him. The heat rose in his belly again. *How dare she tell me to leave. How dare….*

Cold hands cupped his face, cutting off his thoughts. Icy lips on his. The fire in his belly shifted downward and intensified. He slipped his hands under her robe, her skin silky to his touch.

"Don't go." She murmured against his lips. "I need you."

He held her away from him, his hands around her waist, her robe falling open. He stroked her collar bone and along her breast, leaving red streaks trailing across her skin. Gathering her into his arms, he carried her to the bed, brushing the gift box to the floor. He laid her on the bed and she reached for the buttons on his shirt.

"Sami," his voice tight. "Sami, we need to talk …"

"Later." She unbuckled his leather belt. "We'll talk later."

He leaned over her, running his tongue along her jaw and down her neck, hearing her breathing increase. *Later*, he thought, his blood salty on his tongue.

***

They're asleep, Nik. Pyewacket rubbed against his legs then bounded onto the kitchen counter. *Aww, Harry's too thorough.*

Niki smiled at Pyewacket's disappointed tone. Opening the refrigerator, he scrounged around coming up with leftover ham. He dropped several small pieces into a bowl.

Ooo, ham. Pyewacket tucked into the delicacy.

"What happened upstairs?" Niki motioned to the back stairs.

Lubber's spat, Pyewacket mumbled into his bowl.

Turning the light switch to dimly illuminate the kitchen table, Niki opened the silk bag. A slim card fell onto the table.

"Colorful work. Not bad." He reached down to scratch Pyewacket as the cat washed his face. He held the card down to Pyewacket's eye level. "The Devil. It fits the old man. I'm sure Damian sees himself as the Magician or the High Priest. That smile, the old devil's trying to look beneficent while holding the sword so carelessly. What did Baudelaire write? 'The Devil's cleverest wile is to convince us he doesn't exist.'" Niki held the card up at eye level. "Well, I know you exist and, apparently, Foxie does, too."

Niki, don't. Pyewacket placed both paws on his leg, picking at his jeans.

"What do you think, Pye? Is it the answer to the demon?"

Niki, it gives me the willies. Put it away. Pyewacket paced around under the chair.

"Foxie brought it to me. I can't keep waiting for an answer. Jessica's exhausted. He's draining her power." Niki kept his voice low but his anger rose the hair on Pyewacket's tail.

Niki, you're getting way ahead. Jess is here ... says something for her power. Pyewacket stood on hind legs, paws on Niki's thigh.

"Pye, you saw the strange gifts. There's a message here."

And danger. His claws prickled Niki's skin.

Niki reached for the bag.

The room spun. He blinked. The card burst into flames sticking to his palm, burning flesh. Oily smoking strands emanated from the card. Black coils wrapped up his arm, jerking tight. He pulled back, fighting nausea.

Pye! Help me! Kay!

The ground dropped out from under him. Kay's hand grabbed for his, unable to reach him but grasping the tarot card. The card tore in half, her hand disappearing in the swirling smoke.

Niki, no! Pyewacket screeched, jumping for his shoulder, flames running up his arm.

He doubled over, pain ripping a scream through his gritted teeth. The darkness consumed him.

***

Damian pulled his hand from the fire. He stared at his empty fingers. "It's gone awry! A basic summoning?" He slammed his hand on the stump sending sparks flying across the carpet. "A basic spell. This can't be." He roared out his frustration, rising to pace the carpet.

"Blood," he screamed. "I felt Jessica there … and my ring. She is working with him. I will kill them both. Before I am through, they will beg for release." He stared into the hearth.

A fire-laced form leapt from the embers. Red fur stood in a ruff on her neck. Fangs bared, she launched herself at his face.

He threw his arms up. The heat stole his breath and he staggered backwards… the Devil card flashing across his vision. Blinded, he staggered against the sharp edge of the desk. Glass shattered behind him. Cold wind fanned the fire sending sparks across the room.

He swung to face the destroyed window… his eyes following the fiery paw prints across the lawn and into the early dawn.

***

Charlie strained for any light. He rolled his head to the side looking toward the windows, careful not to pull his arm from under Sami's head. Charlie held his hand up before his face. Nothing, not even a vague outline. He listened to Sami's slow breathing. He ran his hand down her warm back. He thanked all powers they'd weathered the storm.

*I never want to see her like that again…*though the resolution was more deeply passionate than he ever imagined.

He paused, listening. He sifted back through the moments before his eyes opened. A scream echoed through his mind, more remembered than heard. He struggled to sit up.

Dizziness grabbed him. His eyes rolled, seeking a reference point—light, the horizon, the window's edge—anything. He failed. The spinning intensified. He wrapped his arms around Sami rousing her. He gulped, holding down bile and buried his forehead in her shoulder. His stomach rebelled, preventing words. Fear coursed through him. A second scream ripped through the ether. *Is it a memory or a new sound?* The absurd internal debate unsettled him.

"Sami, what's happening?" Panic rendered his whispered words harsh.

She twisted in his arms to face him. "I feel it, too. She's traveling. Taking us with her."

He sought her eyes in the darkness but found inky blackness. Swirling wind surrounding him, scattering his thoughts.

Her voice shook. "She's tracking … someone."

The mental tornado swept away each question he formed. He couldn't find reason in the nightmare. "Why? Who?"

"We'll find out … soon."

"What about the others?" His panic deepened.

"They'll be with us. Anyone in the house will be. They've no choice."

He clung to Sami's voice.

The rotation slowed. Different, yet familiar, stars appeared in the night sky beyond the silvered windows. His eyes drank in the light. He felt her warm breath on his neck. The world righted itself in his head.

"We can't do anything until morning." She shivered. "For now, just hold me."

He didn't need convincing, surrendering to her with all his heart.

CHAPTER 27

December 29, 1910

Chad sat up with a gasp, tearing away the confining bedclothes. His eyes worked to focus on the white-haired retainer.

"It's okay, lad. The dizziness will stop in a moment." Harry helped him sit up. "We'd best be about fixing breakfast. Food will help us all find balance."

"Harry," Chad croaked, his throat dry. "I had the worst dream." He swung his legs off the edge and rose, swaying. Harry pushed him back to a seated position.

"You know the scene in the Oz story … the tornado. The Devil pedaled the bicycle. I reached out to grab the back. Red strings kept tangling in the spokes …" Chad rubbed his face. "And a fox nipped at his heels. What do you think that means?"

Harry chuckled. "I'd blame the salami and sardine sandwich you inhaled last night."

Chad gaped at him. "I cleaned up!"

"Little passes through my kitchen I don't know!" He cuffed Chad on the ear. "Now, will ye fire up the stove? I have cheese biscuits rising." He handed Chad a flint and striking stone.

Chad stared at the objects. "Harry, why do I need these?"

"Because the fire won't light itself. Unless you want to get a brand from the parlor."

Chad reached for his blue jeans. He found heavy canvas pants in their place. "Harry," he called, "where are my jeans?"

"Sorry, sir, you'll have to make do with what she's given you." Harry's voice disappeared into the kitchen.

Chad shrugged and pulled on the strange pants.

***

Jeff alerted to the swirling movement, the vertigo sending pain through his right temple. Wincing, he reached out to touch Mac's thoughts finding him tossing and turning in the next room. He soothed his blood brother's aura calming Mac's agitated dream state. Harry's light footstep prevented his out-of-body tour to find the others. The door edged open.

"I'm awake, Harry."

Harry noted Jeff's upper body bare to the cold air, the white scar running from last rib to sternum.

"A bull," Jeff answered the question in Harry's eyes. "Da set my brother Matt and me to rounding him up. The bull cornered Matt against the fence. I tried to bulldog him but he tossed me, catching me on a horn."

He rose and slipped his arms into the robe Harry held out.

"Never seen Matt move so fast. He came close to picking the bull up shoving him into the next pasture." He tied the belt in a loose knot. "First time I realized he loved me … from the panicked look on his face. We'd bloodied each other's noses the day before scraping over something." His scrutiny grew serious. "What caused the vertigo, Harry?"

Harry accepted the friendship in Jeff's offered tale. "All will be explained, sir. Would you help me wake the others?"

Jeff nodded.

"Meet in the parlor. Chad has hot tea and biscuits to tide everyone over 'til a proper breakfast." He stepped to the door.

"Chad?"

"Yes, sir. He's a good young man and won't be a trouble if he's kept busy."

Jeff chuckled. He rolled his shoulders against tight muscles. He tapped back into Mac's aura, pulling him up from sleep.

Humph, Mac mumbled. *Time to get up already? It's still dark.*

Try opening your eyes. Jeff sent a mental chuckle.

Man, it's brighter with your eyes open.

Heads up in the parlor.

Jeff knocked on Scotty's door.

The door swung open. Scotty stood in the doorway already dressed in wool trousers, the suspenders hanging loose.

"Good morning." Scotty stepped back and reached for a stiff white linen shirt. "Have you looked in your clothespress yet? Sami is playing an interesting game with us. We are in for a traditional Victorian Christmas." He raised an eyebrow at Jeff.

"Harry wants us in the parlor. Will you wake Chris?" He paused, watching Scotty's eyes glitter in the dim light. "Or would you rather rouse Tori?"

Scotty chuckled. "Is it that obvious?"

"She's a beautiful woman. Feisty, too."

He grinned. "I'll get them both."

Jeff went on down the hall. He tapped on Colby's door.

***

Yawns and shuffling feet stirred the dusty morning air. Chris pulled the heavy woolen robe around his shoulders, shivering with first waking. Mac met him in the hall, his own light robe hanging open over flannel pants and they descended to the parlor.

Chad handed each a mug filled with steaming tea. Harry stirred the Yule log to a roaring blaze. Mac settled on the loveseat, stretching bare feet out to the fire. He cradled the mug. Others arrived … Tori, her strawberry blonde hair disheveled in a becoming mop, Jessica, her long dark hair unbound, a waterfall over her shoulders.

Jeff walked in with Colby, her hand wrapped through his arm. He leaned down speaking to her before leading her to the loveseat opposite Mac. He accepted two mugs, Colby following him with her eyes. She swung around to meet Mac's scrutiny, a flush running up her neck.

Chris settled beside Mac. "Mac, what's going on? My stomach's doing flip flops but I dinna feel ill."

Mac kept his voice low. "Don't know but I suspect it isn't good. You're queasy and Jeff's got a migraine. I'd say from looking at the lines around the Lady Jess's eyes, she's feeling some pain, too."

Chris glanced at Jessica. She sat in a wingback chair, staring out into the early morning. Her hair drifted back and forth across her breast. Mac nudged him, pointing to Sami and Charlie standing arm in arm before the fireplace.

"I regret dragging you down here this early." Sami looked around the room meeting each eye.

Mac followed the circuit. "Baby girl, if you're counting noses, Niki and Kay aren't here yet."

"Mr. MacIntyre, exactly the point." Harry leaned heavily on his walking stick, dark circles under his eyes. "They are not in the house. Dr. Kasavina and Mr. Kaye are in trouble and it will take everyone here to extricate them."

Sami cleared her throat. "I'll tell you what I know."

Colby shivered. Jeff placed his hand on her shoulder.

Sami looked at Colby. "I wanted to talk with you privately but ..."

Colby stared at Sami, holding her breath. Jeff squeezed her shoulder and she reached up to take his hand.

"After we were married, Dad brought me here and gave me the keys. He told me he's not my father ... my blood father."

Colby tried to pull her hand away from Jeff but he held it preventing her from rising. Sami's voice caught in her throat. "My birth mother disappeared days after I was born and my father gave me to the Fairmonts while he went to find her ... and my brother."

Colby's eyes grew wide, filling with tears.

Harry cleared his throat. "Saminthea is the heiress to this house. The spirit that abides here draws her power from the matriarch and her chosen companions. You each are here to help protect this family … and the house."

"And she protects those who are welcomed." Sami looked at each in turn. "I'm just beginning to understand what she can do. Now she has brought us to this place and time to find Niki and Kay."

"This place?" Tori stared at Sami. "This time? I didn't see my car out my bedroom window. Where are we?"

"Miss Madison, we are in England in the year 1910."

Everybody went still, nary a breath taken. Harry studied each face.

"I see curiosity more than fear." He bowed to Sami. "Well chosen."

"Yeah, I thought so." Chad broke the silence. "Not the England part but another time for sure. Scotty's getup aside, didn't anyone notice the gaslights? They weren't here last night. And I had to light the stove with a flint."

Jeff laughed, winking at Chad. "Good catch. I hadn't noticed. My mind must still be catching up with my body."

Chad grinned at him.

"Something happened last night … and she moved to protect Niki or Kay. From what, I don't know." All eyes turned to Sami.

"A spell … a summoning spell." Jessica interrupted. She stood, her slim figure silhouetted against the morning light. "I felt it last night." She pulled the signet ring from her pocket. "The gifts, some are from the Ramhill collection. Niki or Kay must have received something of my husband's … an item he valued sufficiently that he wanted it back immediately." She tucked the ring away.

"He has that much power?" Charlie pulled Sami tight against him.

"Yes. That's why my windlings wrap around me. The moving air confuses his sight. Otherwise, he'd watch me all the time."

Charlie winced.

"I suspect he wished to retrieve the object. I doubt he could pull anyone to him. Some other power was involved." Jessica dropped her eyes to her hands and let out a deep sigh.

"Harry, why are we here and now?" Scotty glanced at the other heads nodding at his question.

"The destination and time are normally under the Madam's control."

Mac snorted. Harry turned on him with a withering look. Mac choked on his tea, chuckling under his breath.

"In unusual circumstances, the house will make decisions to protect the Madam's court." Harry stressed the honorific staring at Mac. "Your missing friends must be here ... and now."

"Harry, how do we get home?" Colby asked.

"Trust, Miss Colby. Once your friends are safely within these walls, we will return to your time and place."

"How do you know so much about this, Harry?" Mac's eyes narrowed.

"Mr. MacIntyre, Miss Sami's father requested I protect her. Now, everyone should dress. It is unseemly to be in a mixed group in such disarray."

Tori rose, opening her robe to reveal a floor-length flannel nightgown, the high neck buttoned and arrayed with a lace collar. "Harry, I doubt anyone could find anything indecent about this coverage."

He opened his mouth but she held up her hands in surrender. "I know but my last question is who put me in this dang thing during the night?" She wrapped the robe around her shoulders and swept from the room.

CHAPTER 28

Charlie rubbed the rough towel across his chest. Sami grumbled. "What were these people thinking? I can't put this on by myself. Charlie, I need your help."

He wrapped the towel around his waist.

Sami wore white pantaloons and a lace camisole. She twisted in an attempt to fasten her corset.

"Ahh, well. I have always wanted to be a lady's maid. I have very nimble fingers. May I help Madam with her … difficulties?" He affected a horrible French accent. "Please, I shall mince right ovaair and see what I can do weeth this beeuutiful Americaan lady. Pleeze to hold the bedpost, Madam. I, Crème Brulé, will make everything pairrrfect." He picked up the corset strings and tightened, starting at the bottom and lacing upwards.

Sami glanced over her shoulder. "Mademoiselle Brulé. You'd be more convincing if your towel hadn't fallen and your interest hadn't … um … risen."

"Pay no attention. I will place zee little man behind the curtain and finish theez job."

"Charlie, how can you make jokes? Everyone must be terrified."

Charlie slid the slim ivory tube skirt over her head. As her face reappeared, Charlie met her lips. Pushing him away, she sat at the dressing table and rolled her hair up.

"Shock, Sami. I was raised with a grim sense of humor."

She stared at his reflection. "Charlie, will you tell me about your present?

His mood darkened.

"It's a boline … a knife." His throat tightened. "Used for tasks—cutting herbs, removing bindings—activities deigned menial." He sat on the bed. "There are things I haven't told you. I thought that hellish time was behind me ... had nothing to do with us." He fought the rising bile. "Apparently, your house has decided there is no running."

She opened her mouth but he held up his hand. "I never wanted to discuss my family—the things I had to do—because it all seemed so melodramatic ... so farfetched."

Rising from the bed, he opened the wardrobe. "My family's involvement in the Magick arts reaches back generations." He stepped into the grey flannel pants and slipped on the starched white shirt. "Marriages are arranged ... always to highly talented women. Jessica is the strongest I've ever met."

"But Jess visited in our home every summer. Colby and I played with her and Anita. Why didn't we know?"

He kept his eyes averted. "She may not have known or shown any evidence. Being around the Ramhills may have brought it out in her. Magick is imbued in the atmosphere there. Damian met Jessica at a horse show in France. He hunted her out the moment he sensed her potential." He hurried to explain. "She does not practice a dark art. She can whistle up the winds. Haven't you noticed air always moves around her? Outside or in? Those are her windlings. They protect her ... tell her things ... especially Obadiah."

"Does he love her?"

Charlie's heart beat double sensing the possible return of his romantic wife. "I want to believe he does. She makes him laugh, an ability I thought he never had. They were happy when I left. He shared her passion for horses and supported her career."

Sami opened the powder, watching him in the mirror.

He pulled on suspenders and knotted his tie. "That he is displaying his controlling nature and his cruelty troubles me. These items from his collection disturb me even more."

"Charlie, I didn't arrange for them." She rose and approached him, reaching out. He shied from her. She edged behind him to the armoire picking up the cufflinks.

"I feel filthy talking about this. I do not want to frighten you."

He tucked in his shirt and buttoned his vest. "I disappointed my father. I would sick up whenever he tried to teach me. To him, following my mother's wisdom made me pathetic." A thick British accent laced his words, "I have one true son … Damian. You will never know power." His voice returned to normal. "The truth is I didn't want to. Music is where my passion lies." Charlie's fingers drummed against his thigh.

Sami pinched together his cuff, careful not to touch his skin, and worked the pearl cufflink through the buttonhole. She finished the second cuff. Slipping her arms into a golden lace blouse, she waited for him to work the small pearl buttons down the back. After a long moment, he leaned to kiss her neck and fumbled for the first button.

His halting rhythm pulled each word up from the dark well. "He would have had me strangled if he had doubted I was his son. I'm a dead ringer for him. Damian takes after our Grandfather … broad shoulders and heavier muscle mass. Father hated me but insisted I learn the subordinate ways. If I refused, he beat me or threatened my mother and my sisters. That thing." He pointed at the package. "It tied me to him and the path I couldn't accept. After he died, Damian tried to use the psychic connection to control me. That is why I left England."

He looked down, unable to meet her eyes reflected in the mirror. "Sami, I love you. You do see why I can't open it?"

She picked up her earrings. Speaking to the mirror, she said "I see why you don't want to. But you must use this gift for Niki's sake."

His face fell. Sami held out her locket. As he worked the clasp, she continued, steel in her voice. "It was brought to you to defend and protect our friends. I don't know how or when but you will when the time comes."

He picked up the box, his hands shaking. He unwound the ribbon and lifted the lid. Pulling back the tissue, he stared at the white bone-handled knife. He steeled himself for the remembered coldness, nearly dropping it when his fingers met warmth. Slipping it into the boot strap, he pulled his boot on and reached for the mate. He slathered his hands.

"We will stand together, you and me. If this brings trust back into our love then I deem the price reasonable." He looked her up and down. "Let me fix the hobble on your skirt. The style does become you, love."

He reached out toward the ivory fabric but pulled back his hands. Tiny blood spots welled in his palms. He wiped at them with his handkerchief. "I don't know if I've passed or failed this test since I am bleeding again, but it needs to stop." He looked at the ceiling. "Please?" The chandelier swung over his head.

Sami opened her arms, lifting her face to him.

He enfolded her and kissed her, his tension draining away when their lips touched.

"Let's hope Harry knows better than to boil the bacon." He swung her to his arm. "And we need to be with our friends."

CHAPTER 29

Niki's head throbbed, bile thick in his throat. Pain arced through him and he struggled between awareness and oblivion.

Where am I? Formulating the thought set his head spinning. Flexing his fingers, the burned flesh drowned him, pain and vertigo combining. Gagging, he blocked the sensation from his right hand.

Light flared red through his closed eyelids. A blow to the ribs knocked the wind from him dealing another agony. He curled into the fetal position, clutching his side.

"He's alive." A deep voice sounded above him. "Clean him up. Feed him the usual." The voice drew closer to him. Fingers grabbed his hair, snapping his head back. He felt the heat from the light. Released, his head dropped onto the stone floor.

"The pickings from the street must be slim to drag this in."

Cold water splashed over his face and shoulders setting off a tremor, once started, uncontrollable. He flinched, drawing his hands to his face.

"Stop!" The voice compelled obedience. An iron grip pulled his right wrist above his head and forced the burned fingers to uncurl. "Strange ... half a tarot card."

Pye? Niki shot out into the darkness enveloping him. *Pye?*

He swallowed hard, feeling the emptiness.

Kay? He reached out a mental touch.

"Stop!" The voice echoed in the chamber.

Hands grabbed him by the shirt front and pulled him upward. A backhand drove his head against the wall.

"Interesting. It seems this one has some talent. Where did you get this card?" Lord Edward Ramhill shook him. Niki hung limp in his captor's hands. "We'll find out." The voice hissed in his ear. "A little talent will heighten the demon's lust when your blood runs over my hands."

"Lord Ramhill." A new voice entered the room. "We found this young woman wandering the garden."

He dropped Niki and turned to inspect the disheveled young woman, twitching his nose at her soot-covered gown and robe. *Her skin is too clear and her nails too even for street trash.* He grabbed her chin between thumb and fingers, peering into her eyes. The emerald depths were empty, no awareness reflected back at him.

"What is wrong with her?"

"Sir, she has been like this since the grounds man found her." The footman hesitated. "But, my lord, she led us straight to this room."

Lord Ramhill grabbed her hand peeling the other half of the singed tarot card from her stiff fingers. "Well, well, it seems our two guests are somehow connected." He shoved her back toward his manservant. "Take her upstairs to Lady Ramhill's maid. Make her presentable then bring her to my study."

"My goodness, Edward but you have quite a party here." A lilting tenor voice interrupted the instructions.

"Nigel, go back to bed." Edward turned his back.

"But you often exhort me to be interested in the family affairs. I thought to take your advice. What charming young people. And what are those scraps in your hand?" Nigel pushed back the lock of dark hair on his forehead and reached for his older brother's hand.

Edward shoved the two pieces into his coat pocket.

Nigel shrugged and peered past Edward at Niki's still form. Blocked from approaching him, he turned to the young woman. He bent his knees to eye level and inspected her face. "Odd behavior, what. Is she in a trance? Or is it shock?"

Edward snorted, "Nigel, you are a wastrel and an idiot. It is six in the morning."

"I thought it early for such a fuss but I was curious. I will never get back to sleep. Are you certain there is not something I can do?"

"No!" Edward dismissed him with a wave.

"All right then. I will dress for the day. After all, there are several house parties in town and I wouldn't want to miss all the lovely food and scintillating company." He sidled to the doorway "Do keep me in mind if there is anything I should learn." He stepped out the door, "And would you mind lending me Westfield to tie my tie? I never seem to get it right."

"Out!" Edward commanded. "Westfield, tend to his hand. I want him alive for New Year's Eve. Dose him liberally." His footsteps rang in the stone hall.

Rough hands hoisted Niki from the floor. He tried to see Kay's face.

Kay! His plea echoed in the emptiness.

His stomach spasmed, chewing on despair. Cold water chilled him again. Heavy manacles snapped on his wrists. He welcomed the darkness.

CHAPTER 30

A loud knock echoed in the front hallway. Harry hurried to open the door. A dapper gentleman sporting a black Homburg hat and carrying an ornate walking stick smiled broadly at him.

"Good morning, Harry. Good to see you again. What has it been for you? More than five years, I wager."

"Good morning, Sir Nigel. It is good to see you, too." Harry bowed and invited the gentleman into the front hallway.

"The knighting isn't for quite a few years yet. I must remember to do more research before the little device earns me the Crown's attention." He handed Harry his hat and walking stick and pulled off his overcoat. "Good of you to remind me, though. Today, I must concentrate on dear Saminthea and my great nephew. Would you be so kind to ask the beautiful Mrs. Ramhill to speak with me?"

"At once, sir. Do take care. It is much for them to absorb." Lodging the hat, coat and walking stick on the hall tree, Harry paused. "Any word on Mr. Gordon?"

Nigel fidgeted with his sleeve. "Sadly, no."

Harry's leaden feet entered the kitchen. Sami arranged the serving tray, her eyes fever bright against her pale skin. He mumbled a prayer. Wiping her hands on a tea towel, she joined him in the doorway.

Harry bent close. "Madam, Mr. Nigel Ramhill is waiting for a private word with you. He is in the hallway." Harry held out his arm to support her.

Sami gnawed her lower lip over her hobbled progress. Nigel swept up her hand and applied a kiss. She studied familiar dark eyes behind thick glasses.

"Mrs. Ramhill, the pleasure is all mine." Nigel nodded to Harry. "Good show, Harry. You've fulfilled your charge admirably." The gangly young man admired Sami's attire. "Beautiful. Now, dear

Saminthea, I am your Uncle Nigel and I am pleased to meet you. Truly, actually, I am Charlie's great … two greats … uncle."

Sami maintained eye contact with him while trying to extricate her fingers from his grasp. He applied his lips once again then tucked her hand through his arm drawing her close. "We have some work to do. You and your all-together-quite-lovely house" he said in a loud resonant voice, "are under attack and you'll want to have your wits about you."

"What are you talking about?"

He peered over his glasses.

She blushed at the scrutiny. "Please, lower your voice a little. I have good hearing and, I assure you, my husband and our friends do, too.

"My dear girl!" He beamed at her. "You call them *your* friends, too! Well done! Your father worried the connection would be difficult without your Mother to teach you, but I assured him you would be quick, considering the lovely woman he married. You resemble her so much. Ah, I see you have the locket."

Sami's hand rose to her neck.

Harry appeared carrying a brandy snifter. "Madam, it would be wise to repair to the study." He offered the snifter to Nigel. Sami nodded and preceded Nigel down the hall.

"I say, marvelous outfit. Golden color offsets your lovely amber eyes."

"Thank you, Uncle Nigel. Please, won't you tell me what's going on?" She indicated the green leather wingback chair.

"I like the steel in them, so like your mother." Nigel cleared his throat. "My dear girl, I shall do my very best. I will rely upon you and Harry to keep me from becoming too muddled." He sat down heavily. Pushing up his glasses, his bright gaze drew inward for a moment.

Sami perched on the desk.

"Edward, the current Lord Ramhill, is quite bonkers. He is determined to control any and all magickal power in the region. Your father is rather a genius in that arena, you know."

Seeing her puzzled look, he continued, "No, I suppose you don't know, though I am surprised your foster father has not filled you in. But more to the point. After my mother died in a tragic accident, my father, the previous Lord Ramhill, became obsessed with your mother and pursued her relentlessly. When she married your father, he became hell bent on possessing her and her power. It is no coincidence he disappeared the same night she did."

"Where did they go?"

Nigel shrugged. "Unfortunately, though your mother is a strong witch, her real power is vested within these walls. He was completely blind to that fact. However, my brother is not."

He leaned closer. "The lust runs in the blood. Edward will be aware another mistress has entered this house. The fact that the spirit is back in this shell." Nigel removed his glasses and pulled out a large handkerchief. He cleaned the lens then meticulously refolded the cloth before tucking it into his pocket.

Sami bit her tongue, hoping he would continue without prompting

"Dear me, getting muddled again." he said. "I shall let my friends and family know a distant cousin has arrived with his American wife. I am the conservator for the house. Your party will be my guests. I have some ability to distract and confuse my sibling so you can rescue your friends."

He looked at his empty brandy snifter. "Dear me, there seems to be a continuing problem with evaporation."

"Harry, please." Sami rose. "Excuse me, Uncle Nigel but whatever else you have to say should be with Charlie present. Whatever we face, we face together."

"Good show, my dear girl." and "Harry, don't be so stingy" followed her from the study.

***

Charlie's momentum carried him to loom over Nigel. "Take off your coat. Be quick about it." Charlie said, his tone commanding.

"My dear fellow, it took me ages to subdue this tie. Are you certain it is necessary?"

"Do it. No more talk until I see your scar."

"Dear me, what scar? Where should it be located?" Nigel rose and absently pulled at his tie. "More importantly, when did I receive it?"

"Very funny." Charlie glared at him. "If you are Uncle Nigel, you'd remember you received a wound on the eve of 1911. Your exact words."

Nigel stood silent, digesting Charlie's statement. His coat hung off one shoulder. "I must protest, you see ..."

Charlie pulled back Nigel's sleeve, exposing unblemished flesh. "You've frightened my wife and tried to trick me. Get out!"

"Dear boy, I'm trying to tell you ..."

"GET OUT!" Charlie shouted, his hands clenching at his sides.

Nigel pulled up nose to nose with Charlie, looking over his glasses at him. "It's still 1910, you stupid git!"

"My God." Charlie shook his head. "I thought you were joking with me, Uncle Nigel. You said, 'If we ever meet in another place and time, ask me about my scar and demand I prove it'. I thought you were daft until now. It's too early. Bugger."

Jeff ran into the room, a coal poker in his hand. Mac hopped behind him, trying to get his boot on.

"Sami, should this gentleman be removed?" Jeff frowned at Nigel.

"Sami, are you crying? I'll kill him right here." Mac wiped the glistening tears from her cheek with his thumb.

Her arms wrapped tightly across her stomach, she burst out laughing. "No, no." she gasped. "This is all an odd misunderstanding." She hiccupped. "I can't breathe. This corset is too tight." She looked at the boot in Mac's hand and burst into laughter again. She fought for breath. "You both are so ferocious." She turned to Charlie, "I'm glad to know my darling husband is fallible."

He grimaced at her.

She turned away. "This is Charlie's uncle. We got off to a difficult start. Uncle Nigel, may I present Dr. Jeffry Conray and Mr. John MacIntyre?"

Jeff shook hands with Nigel while Mac pulled on the recalcitrant boot.

"Gentlemen, all is well. Breakfast is in the dining room." Harry stepped back to allow Sami's gladiators to precede him. "Shall we?"

Nigel looked elated. "See here, Harry. Are there kippers? Scotch eggs? Do you have the lovely new toasting devise?" He fumbled with his tie. "My poor tie. It will go into despair for it will not be its best again." Nigel's stomach growled.

Sami hid her smile behind her hand. "Uncle Nigel's right." She grasped Charlie's hand. "I'm hungry, too."

CHAPTER 31

Nigel headed straight to the sideboard. His plate filled to groaning in moments.

Sami stretched up to kiss Charlie's cheek. "Are all your relatives this quirky?" she whispered.

Charlie looked chagrined. "Yes … quite daft though I wish they were all as benign."

Tori entered the dining room. "Why in the world do all the clothes in my wardrobe require a corset?" She studied Nigel before coming to rest on the generously filled plate in his hand.

"A lovely outfit you are wearing, Miss Madison. You will set the pace for the fashion goddesses." Nigel set down the plate and grabbed her hand, kissing it loudly. Before Tori could respond, Colby and Jessica appeared in the doorway, arm in arm.

Glancing up, Nigel dropped Tori's hand to clutch his chest. "Great Gods! What visions! If I die now, I go with these images burned in my brain." Nigel grabbed Colby's hand. "You must be the ravishing beauty Carleton praises with such love. I willingly lay my heart at your feet, Miss Fairmont." He pulled her hand to his lips and looked longingly over his glasses.

"My father?" She glanced in Sami's direction. "But how do you know my father?"

"He was … er … is Gordon's dearest friend. For all time, you might say." Colby wrinkled her forehead. "Oh, my. You don't know about your Father's penchant for time travel? I am afraid I have spilled the beans as you Americans say."

"I do know my father's interests quite well. I'm quite certain your statement is pure fantasy. As to the beans, I'm more interested in eggs and sausage." She withdrew her hand.

At the sideboard, Jeff handed her a plate. Leaning down, his lips close to her ear, he whispered, "He did bring lovely color to your cheeks."

She elbowed him, hissing back. "It was trying to get into this infernal dress."

Jeff stepped back to look at her full length. He reached past her to snag the toast and, once again close to her ear, he murmured, "I think it would be more interesting getting you out of it." He ducked behind her and took a seat.

"And Jessica, you stunning creature, my great nephew is a lucky man indeed." Jessica did not smile. Avoiding his grab for her hand, she put the table between them.

"Please help yourself. Harry will bring fresh tea." Sami encouraged her friends.

Jeff raised an eyebrow at Colby when she set her plate on the table beside him. She did not look in his direction, paying close attention to her food. By stages, everyone settled. Nigel, having finished his portion, gazed with admiration at Tori's overflowing plate. He opened his mouth to speak.

Sami stopped him with a hand on his arm, "Nigel, Harry and I set the stage for our friends. They haven't had but a few moments to consider what we have told them." Nigel nodded.

Sami rose to stand beside Charlie. She placed her hand on his shoulder. "This is Charlie's great uncle, Nigel. He has information which may help us."

"I've been thinking about this," Chad interrupted. "This is a dream, isn't it? I mean, I'm having this …" he looked at his half empty plate, "delicious dream with fantastic people … but I'm going to wake up. Right?"

Colby shot Chad an angry glance. "Then we're all having the same dream."

"Hey, if you're in my dream, you'd say that." Chad looked hurt, glancing around the table for support, "Wouldn't she?"

Without looking up from his plate. Mac suggested, "Somebody pinch him."

Jessica and Chris simultaneously responded on each arm. Chad jumped, the affronted look on his face prompting laughter around the table.

Nigel cleared his throat. "There is a battle going on. My brother lusts for power which is leading him down the dark road. Your friends, Mr. Kaye and Dr. Kasavina will be victims in his quest."

Mac jumped in. "Where are Niki and Kay? How do you know them and others here?"

Nigel held out his cup for more tea. "Dear me, I hope I can keep my wits about me for this next bit. It was Charles."

Charlie looked at the young man who was to be his great uncle, his eyebrow raised in question.

"Charles, my boy. You described your friends perfectly. You come to visit and tell … er, … told me how all this turns out. But you don't remember because it hasn't happened yet."

Charlie put his hands to his head, shaking it.

"I am not delusional, I assure you." Nigel responded to the unspoken speculation. "To answer you, Mr. MacIntyre, I have seen them both and they are indeed in trouble." He peered through his thick spectacles at the assemblage.

"My brother is a thief and a murderer … worse than our father. He will steal your soul without hesitation. He will use Niki for sacrifice. To raise even higher-level demons." Nigel's genial face hardened with grim determination. "We need Niki alive."

He stared in his teacup for a moment, the room silent around him. "The world needs Niki alive." Draining the cup, he continued, "Are you at odds with him, dear Charles? I should think so. Since we Ramhills carry the essence of an enemy he vanquished years ago, it can't be very comfortable for you to have him under your roof. But still, you are mates. Shows great growth on both your parts."

Charlie tried to rise, anger blooming on his face. Sami's hand on his shoulder checked him. He glared at her. She looked down at him with fire in her eyes. He rubbed his palms together.

"I suppose climbing ramparts and storming walls is a crazy idea." Mac said.

"While I deeply appreciate your eagerness, I need to complete my story. They are at the manor." Nigel waved his hand. "I have devised a plan to get you in."

He stared at Sami. "We must introduce you to society, dear girl. Then you will invite Edward's new protégé to provide psychic readings for your amusement. By this time, Edward has Kay under his control and will use her talents to increase his standing in the spiritual community."

"Wait, Uncle Nigel," Tori drew his attention. "Are you saying Kay is psychic? Isn't that extra superstitious poppycock?"

Nigel chuckled. "After what has happened to you in this house, you question the existence of magick? My dear Miss Madison, she is quite powerful... as are many in this room."

Tori looked around the table at each face ending with Scotty. He shrugged slightly and rose, going for the tea pot. Her eyes followed him cross the room, her speculative stare inducing laughter among the group. She looked at her empty plate, her long, red hair hiding her face.

"Psychic readings and channeling, along with séances, are quite the rage these days." Nigel continued. "Edward uses demons to control people. In her condition, I doubt seriously she will be able to withstand. We don't know how much he has discovered about her or you, but assume he knows a great deal. In response to your invitation, he will send his son, Adrian, to accompany his property."

The young men bristled at the last word.

"Adrian will be easier to distract... to separate from her for a moment. You may be able to make contact ... to guide her back to herself." He looked doubtful.

"Nigel," Scotty leaned in. "If at a future time, Charlie tells you how this all turns out—I assume in the positive since we are all here—why don't you tell us when we can affect the rescue? We could translocate to that point in time."

Nigel reared back in his chair. "With your interest in time, young man, you know it does not have a linear flow. Only certain points are immutable … so to speak. Every other action can be changed by miniscule influences. If I told you when and where—and though I respect Foxie's abilities—we might arrive a moment too late."

He paused, looking at Charlie, "And there are things to be learned along the way." Flames rose in Charlie's eyes again, the firm hand still on his shoulder. Tears glistened in Sami's eyes, her face rigid.

"My dear, we must be ready. Edward performs his rituals during the dark moon." Nigel scanned their grim faces.

Silence shrouded the table.

"Nigel, how does getting his son here get us to the manor?" Scotty asked.

"Once young Adrian has been exposed to these lovely women," he beamed at each in turn. "He will extol your virtues to his father and it will heighten Edward's interest. He knows Foxie is picky about visitors. She has never let him in." Nigel guffawed. "Since you are a house party, all must be included in the invitation. Just the way things are done."

"Foxie?" Colby said. The chandelier over the table rattled, swinging in a slow circle.

"Yes, Miss Fairmont." Nigel chuckled and pointed at the chandelier. "Gordon's nickname for her. She slammed doors in his face for over a month. I explained to her one evening that it was a future term for a sexy woman. She seems to have accepted it."

Puzzlement on Colby's face prompted him to continue. "Did you notice the sign at the entrance?"

Colby shook her head.

"The estate is dubbed Foxhaven." He looked at Sami. "Your great, great grandmother frustrated my ancestors. She refused to allow the hunt on her property. It is said there were twenty or more fox families here at one time. They are very astute."

Mac brought the conversation back to the issue at hand. "How long do we have?"

"We have two days, dear boy. Today is December twenty ninth."

"What happened to Christmas?" Chad burst out.

Scotty patted him on the shoulder. "Time flows in strange ways. We lost seven days in transit."

Mac rolled a sausage bit into a ball. "I need to see the manor."

Jessica spoke for the first time. "Mac, I'll show you the estate from the Downs." She looked around the room. "This all sounds so bizarre. I agree with Chad except this is a nightmare and I'm hoping to wake up."

Chad reached out, his fingers poised to pinch.

She slapped his hand away. "I'll offer any assistance." Her jaw tightened. "But I will not be seen on the manor grounds nor meet any Ramhills from this time."

Mac searched under the table, ready to offer the ball to Pyewacket. "Hey, where's Pye?"

CHAPTER 32

Snarling and barking ripped the air. A heavy body slammed against the back door. The noise propelled Scotty toward the kitchen. Harry followed. Before the others could move, a large grey-gold dog burst through the dining room door. Blood sprayed from a rip in her shoulder. She leapt toward Sami, dragging Scotty, arms around her chest.

Mac lunged to intercept the beast but tangled with Charlie rising from his chair.

The dog pulled up short. Her sudden stop toppled Scotty to the floor. She stared at Sami. The dog quivered, whimpering, a black rag hanging from her mouth.

Harry raced in, a broom held high and one pant leg flecked with slobber and blood. He brandished the broom, "I've beaten off the other two but this one got by me. Let me at you, you hell hound."

Sami held up her hand, the air in the room thickening, holding all in place. Sami inched out her open palms to the beast. The huge jaws opened and released the singed fur into her hands. The dog shuddered and sank to the floor, the long pink tongue lolling.

Sami gasped. She clutched her bundle, staining her dress with soot and blood.

"Pyewacket." She looked up at Jeff, tears springing to her eyes. He stepped past the hound, holding his hands over the cat.

"Mac, get the drum. Sami, come with me. Charlie, I need you to keep everyone out." Jeff turned Sami by the elbow.

"My dear boy, would you mind if I join you? I wouldn't want to miss this chance. I assure you I—" Nigel rose to join them.

"There isn't time to argue. Anyone who comes into the parlor has to be absolutely silent. Not a sound." Jeff snapped back, his eyes cold.

He pushed Sami toward the door. "You need to sit on the floor and hold Pye."

"Charlie." Sami called back over her shoulder. Charlie followed her. Reaching the hearth, she said. "Cut this damn skirt, I can hardly sit on a chair. Let alone on the floor."

Charlie reached into his boot and pulled the boline from its sheath.

"Oh, my dear, your lovely dress—." Nigel started.

"Be quiet, Uncle Nigel." Sami snapped, setting him back a step. She didn't pause, "Charlie, please, just cut straight down."

Charlie grabbed the seam in the skirt and inserted the boline. The blade parted the material to the hem with little effort. Sami sank to the floor, her white pantalooned thigh showing through the slit. She held Pyewacket close whispering in his ear. He lay unresponsive in her arms. Her tears glistened on his bedraggled fur.

"Sami," Jeff bent close to her. "Try to synchronize his heart beat with yours. Hold him close. When I come to you, turn him belly up so I can get to his chest. Okay?"

Encouraged by her crisp nod, he addressed the group. "Normally this work is done at night. Chad, pull the curtains. Darken the room. No one moves until this is over. If you have a problem with that, leave now."

No one moved or said a word.

Softening, he said, "I'm afraid there won't be much to see, Uncle Nigel."

Nigel started, "Oh, don't think anything—."

Scotty clamped an iron hand on his shoulder, forcing him into a chair.

"Mac, point to the wind rose … where it will be."

Mac surveyed the room for a moment then pointed to a spot on the floor. Jeff knelt then rolled down onto his back over the spot where the wind rose inlay would be. He gasped, feeling the energy vortex drag at his heart chakra. Mac beat a quick steady rhythm on the drum. Laying his arm across his eyes, Jeff pushed into the darkness and shed his body.

His chest rose in deep inhalation. He framed his prayers to the four directions and asked forbearance for the haste. The canyon cleft where he had nearly frozen to death swam before his eyes. The cold wind cut through his light shirt. A whirlwind rose from the ground, swirled around him and lifted into the sky. He grabbed the vapor tail and willed himself into the starlit sky.

***

Sitting on the loveseat beside Jessica, Colby watched Jeff's breathing slow and the tension drained from his body. Her vision narrowed, darkening down to a pinpoint focus on his chest's rise and fall. Shimmering light drew up from him and rose toward the ceiling. Without thought, she reached, feeling herself jerked from her seat. Turning, she saw her body slumping over. Jessica grabbed her by the shoulders and pulled her back against the loveseat. Jessica shook her head when Tori and Scotty rose from their seats. They settled down.

Jumping up and reaching out, *oh, my god, do I see paws?* Colby frantically swiped at Jeff's leg, sinking claws into his heavy canvas pants. Bright red blood soaked through the cloth.

***

Jeff felt the sting and the tug. His heart skipped a beat, preparing to battle his way free. Dipping his head, he looked into yellowish-brown eyes of the bobcat clinging to his leg.

> *I'd have preferred to introduce you to this more gradually but now you're here, hang on tight.*

Her front claws dug in a little deeper and she scrambled for purchase with her hind claws. The muscles in Jeff's calf tightened but he didn't speak to her again.

Willing the whirlwind higher, he broke through a cloud layer and rose toward a second. A green vista stretched out before them. Jeff dropped to the ground, the bobcat releasing his leg and twisting in air to land on her feet. Jeff squatted down and held out a hand to her.

A snarl rose to her lips, ruff rising.

He settled back on his heels and looked at her for a long moment. He felt her confusion.

Colby, I don't have much time to help Pyewacket. You have to keep up. If we're separated, I'll have to make another trip to find you.

He planted a kiss on her tan nose.

He stood, drew a deep breath and focused on Pyewacket's essence—not the fur or eyes but the feel, the aura. The double terminated crystal appeared in his hand. He gripped it sending thanks to Foxie. Holding the construct in his mind and his heart, he cast out, waiting motionless. The crystal lit up, the light pouring across the distance.

There, he pointed to a valley across the plain.

But that's miles away. Colby stood on hind paws, staring at the horizon.

Jeff ran across the wild grass. She took off after him, her paws skimming the ground. She stumbled, rolling and scrambling back to her paws. She leapt forward. He glanced back at her.

Nearing the entrance to the gulley, Jeff slowed to a walk. A small stream ran along the bottom. The sides became steeper. He descended into the shaded darkness. Mosquitoes whined in the thick warm air. A splash alerted him to the bobcat's slip into the stream. He chuckled feeling the vibrations when she shook the water from her paws.

This will take some explaining. His fear for her rose in his throat. His heart skipped a beat fighting the distraction.

He stopped, reaching out to recapture Pyewacket's essence. He sent out another call, this time targeted down the cut. He moved along the gully hearing the water spirit singing. He pulled aside the heavy undergrowth, leaving a blood price on the thorny bush. A runnel poured out the rock face. Dropping to his knees, he crawled into the darkness.

The small tunnel's rocky sides scraped at his shoulders. He inched along, pulling with his hands. The tunnel twisted then opened outward. A rock chimney spread light across the narrow cave. A small muddy figure huddled far from the sunlight.

Pyewacket? Jeff sent out the inquiry. *Pye?*

The figure cringed back. Jeff focused, searching the boy's refined features, his chocolate skin. Large black eyes stared from under unruly black hair.

Let's go home. Jeff edged closer reaching out a hand, holding his breath.

No. It hurts too much. The boy pulled back into the crevice covering his face. Angry burns striped his hands and arms.

Please, Pye. Niki needs you.

Jeff sent out all the love he felt for the cat and now the boy spirit he'd discovered within him.

We need you.

He waited, praying, the crystal warming in his hand. He felt the bobcat ease up at his side. A deep rumbling echoed through the cave. The boy looked up, bursting into tears, his eyes locked on her burnished fur. He tentatively held out his arms.

I'm afraid.

Jeff pulled the boy to him.

We'll be with you.

The boy snuggled into his arms, burying his face into Jeff's shoulder. He shifted him to his back, arms around his neck and legs around his waist. He hoisted himself into the rock chimney swinging his leg over the edge.

Colby, go back out the way you came and wait for me.

Reaching the top, he pulled Pyewacket into his arms and slid down the cliff face. He searched for the bobcat. She scrambled out the cave entrance, swinging her head in all directions, her claws splashing through the water. She veered to the right. Jeff grabbed her by the scruff and hoisted her kitten-style into Pyewacket's arms. The boy wrapped around her, crying into her fur. She curled into a small ball and stayed still. Jeff ran across the plain. The drum beat again, much faster, pulled him along.

He tucked them both in tight to his chest and plummeted through the cloud layers toward the earth. Yards above the ground, he spread his wings and brought them to a jarring landing.

> *Colby, get back on your own or wait for me here. Just listen to the drum and reach out with your heart. Can you do this?*

He shook with fear for her.

***

Jeff rolled from his supine position on the parlor floor to his knees, his hands clutched tightly to his chest. Opening his eyes, he nodded at Sami. She turned Pyewacket onto his back. He cupped his hands over Pyewacket's chest and, drawing a deep breath, blew through his hands. He repeated the gesture on Pyewacket's head opening his hands and holding them in place. Head down, he filled his lungs, exhaled and stilled his rapid heartbeat.

Mac finished with four final quick bursts. "Coffee," he said to Harry.

Jeff sat back on the floor. "And chocolate. Please." His head snapped up and he scanned the room for Colby, having forgotten where she sat. Her beautiful brown eyes gazed back at him. Puzzlement shone in them. He lay back on the floor, staring up at the ceiling.

Sami sat perfectly still holding Pyewacket in her arms. He stretched his paws and uncurled his back. He opened one eye. A pitiful meow then a tiny vibration in his throat brought tears to her eyes.

"He needs a bath and warm milk." Jeff did not move.

"Are you okay?" She looked at his ashen face.

"Just need a little time."

Harry appeared in the door with two steaming mugs in his hands. Jeff accepted the offered mug. Inhaling the fumes, he looked up at Harry.

"Mocha. Harry, I think I love you."

The tension broken, everyone laughed, stretching and moving about the room.

Leaning towards the loveseat, he handed the mug to Jessica who held it to Colby's lips. She sipped once, twice. Jessica passed the mug back.

Charlie hoisted Sami to her feet. He steadied her before she hurried from the parlor.

Nigel jumped up. "I say, amazing. The drum, the energy. Exhilarating. I hope you will tell me all about this. I want to know what happened, why the cat is getting better so quickly … I have many questions." .

"Uncle Nigel, why don't we sketch the manor's layout?" Scotty distracted him. "We will need butcher's paper and the dining room table." Scotty escorted Nigel from the room.

CHAPTER 33

Edward

Damian contemplated the torn tarot card lying beside his own undamaged card. Identical images stared back at him. He fingered one half, a prickling in his fingers. *A summoning spell.* He grimaced. *But who?*

He rose from the desk and paced the study scanning the shelves, noting each book, each arcane item. Everything sat in its proper place.

"My Lord, the young woman." Westfield, his steward, escorted Kay into the room. She stared straight ahead. "She has quite unsettled the maids. She called each by name giving intimate details. They call her a witch."

"Stupid twits. Buy their silence. No, on second thought, don't. Let them talk … tell their friends about my new ward. It will give everyone something to ponder." He propelled her to stand in the pentagram inscribed on the floor. She remained standing where he placed her.

"You may go." Westfield bowed and backed out, sweat glistening on his face. "See I am not disturbed," Edward ordered.

He placed candles at the points of the pentagram. Pulling a black-handled knife from his boot, he pricked his finger. Circling her three times winder shins, he inscribed a circle with blood drops. He stepped away. His bound victims' terrified stares usually filled him with power. Her impassive state unnerved him. Anger rose. He would not be unmanned.

He uttered the first words. Wind poured into the circle, lifting her hair and swirling around her face. Smoke rose from the markings on the floor. Red sparks burst from her breast, quickly lost in the dense smoke. Edward put his hand out. He pulled himself up before his fingertips broke the circle's outer perimeter. He exhaled, shaking at his near error which would have set the demon free.

CHAPTER 34

Chris stood in the kitchen door. He winced at the angry burns striping Pyewacket's legs and head.

Sami held Pyewacket in the sink trying to wash the bedraggled fur. Pyewacket mewed, struggling.

"Pye," Sami whispered. "I'm trying to help you. Please don't fight me." Her hands shook.

Chris stepped up behind her. "I've good luck working with the wee ones." Sami wiped the tears from her cheeks with her hand, leaving a sooty streak.

"Harry, if you would give me a towel and warm milk...perhaps some soft cheese...brie, if you have it." Chris motioned Sami to lift Pyewacket from the sink. He folded the towel and slid it into the bottom. She set Pyewacket down onto the towel. His claws grabbed the rough fabric freezing in position.

Chris nodded at the mud and slime festooning her bodice and her white pantaloons showing through the slit in the gold silk skirt. "I like the way you approach your wardrobe. If I could find someone who isn't so concerned with how things are done, rather than getting things done. Well, life would be more comfortable all the way around. Not that you don't always look wonderful, you do." He looked at her tear-streaked face. "Ah, I'm fallin' down a slippery slope, now aren't I?"

"Chris, that's more than you've ever said to me." She wiped Pyewacket's tail from hip to tip. "I wasn't sure you liked me."

"I leave the talking to Scotty."

He pulled the brie into small pieces and rubbed one between his finger and thumb until it was warm. "Here now, Pyewacket, I know this is your favorite." He held his finger with the cheese against the cat's muzzle. "You can have little nibblies off my finger if you'll allow

Miss Sami to clean your lovely fur." Pyewacket mewed. Sami rubbed the washcloth across his back, his tense muscles relaxing.

"See?" Chris said, smiling at Sami, "The towel helps him to stay in place."

He jumped, pulling his hand back. "Pye, I want to be able to play with all ten digits, my friend."

Pyewacket's forlorn meow tore at his heart.

"We'll find him, laddie, don't you fret. You'll soon be fit for the rescue team."

Sami continued stroking with the warm cloth rinsing the dirt from the cloth between swipes.

"Have you a dropper, Harry?" Chris' voice rumbled, almost a purr itself.

Harry handed it to him.

Chris filled the dropper with warm milk and squeezed it into Pyewacket's cheek pouch, waiting for him swallow. "Now you need some fluid and if I know Mac, I'm quite certain, he'll be hunting over the entire city for sardines or anchovies for you. You know how he hates anchovies, so let's make him get them for you,"

A shaky purr sounded.

"Why isn't he's talking?" Sami asked.

"He's frightened." He spoke without taking his eyes from the shivering cat. "He'll be saucy again soon thanks to your loving hands. I suspect only the hell hounds themselves could chase him from Niki. By the way, where is the great beastie?"

"Scotty took her to Charlie's study. She saved Pyewacket, didn't she?"

"No doubt about it. I'd say from the way she bled, she ran from the pack Harry vanquished. She'll be bonding to you if you're not quick about casting her out." He chuckled at Sami's doubting look.

"She'll protect you with her life. It's in the Lurcher's nature." Chris fed Pyewacket the last brie bit. The cat leaned against Sami's hands. She bundled him in a warm towel, stroking his head.

Chris wiped his hands. "I'm going to need a little sandpaper rubbed on my finger before I put brie in my mouth. It won't feel right without it."

Sami laughed, nudging him with her shoulder.

A good sign. "Let me know if you need a break caring for the beastie. I'm good at taking cat naps. We both know how to curl up in small places and not be noticed."

"I'll keep him with me for now." Sami held Pyewacket, counting his heart beats.

"Then I'll change this wet shirt." He disappeared into the stairwell.

CHAPTER 35

J eff wiped his face with his sleeve. He sipped the mocha and leaned his head back against the loveseat, eyes closed. Mac hovered at the door.

Jessica touched Colby's arm and raised an eyebrow. Colby mouthed she was okay. Jessica rose, caught Mac's eye and nodded toward the door. Mac shook his head emphatically.

"Mac, go ahead." Jeff spoke without opening his eyes. "I need to talk with Colby. Will you check on Pye?" He felt Mac nod.

Mac offered Jessica his arm. The parlor doors shut behind them.

"He's very protective." Colby's soft voice caressed his ear.

"It's his nature. I'd lay down my life for him, too." His words lay heavy in the air. Colby remained silent, filtering through her chaotic thoughts. She leaned her head in her hands. The room spun.

"Breathe." Jeff said. She took a deep breath. The rotation slowed. She felt him take her hand and wrap it around the lukewarm mug. She tightened her grip and he slid back to the floor sitting beside her knees, back against the cushioned seat. His body warmed her leg. Opening her eyes, she glanced down at him and reached to touch his hair. He leaned his head against her leg and sighed.

"Colby, we need to talk about what happened." She strained to hear his soft words.

Clenching her jaw, she waited to be chastised ... *not that I understand at all what I did, but I hate to be scolded.* "I'm sorry, I didn't mean to cause a problem ... I just ... " She didn't know what she just anything. "I'm okay. Don't worry about—"

"Colby, I need you to listen for a moment."

She held her breath, waiting.

"Do you feel like yourself. Like any part might be missing?"

A quick response rose in her mind but she caught herself. *He's not going to scold me. He's asking me to check how I feel.* She thought about it for a moment. "I feel lightheaded though the mocha is helping. But I have questions."

He chuckled, shifting to face her, his arm laid across the loveseat cushion, hand resting on her thigh.

"Sounds more like the Colby I know and love." He grinned at her.

A flip retort sprang to her lips but her tongue refused to move. She wanted to believe his words. Color rose in her cheeks.

"I'll gladly answer any question I can but what happened just now is a sacred trust—a bond with Pyewacket— and we shouldn't discuss it with anyone. Not without his permission … not even Niki."

"Permission from the cat?" She stared at him. "You mean to tell me that was real, the cave, the boy …" Jeff's spirit image swam in her head. "The wings?"

"And the bobcat," he added.

Her heart beat against her chest. "Pyewacket talks to you?" Her words rushed on. "I know there are weird things going on. I feel like— or maybe I'm praying—Chad is right. This is the strangest dream I've ever had. But I know everything feels real. And, at this moment, terrifying."

Jeff met her eyes, his hand heavier on her thigh. "It's real. We're here and Pyewacket is hurt … and all the horrid rest. Breathe."

She took a deep, gasping breath, her lungs on fire.

"Why am I forgetting to breathe?" Her words rasped through her tight muscles.

Jeff chuckled, "You aren't forgetting. Your breaths are very shallow. That's normal, but add struggling with conflicting emotions, it all adds up to being lightheaded … and feeling more anxious than you actually are."

"God, you sound like my psychology professors." Her face twisted in distaste.

He laughed out loud, full and resonant, reassuring her. "Nailed me. I snuck in all the psychology courses I could and still complete an engineering major. My advisor told me roads and oil wells don't have personalities. Can't be psychoanalyzed. I happen to disagree." He shifted to grab a pillow, tucking it behind his back.

"Colby, Pyewacket communicates telepathically. You may not be gifted that way. Or you haven't been listening. Don't be surprised if he talks to you now. After what you did."

Here it comes. She tensed again. His hand closed on her knee, startling her.

"I couldn't have convinced him in time. Your purr did the trick. A brilliant move."

She stared at him. *Is he saying I helped?*

"I'm proud you found your way back on your own. Courageous. I'd have come back for you. Don't doubt it."

Oh, my god, she thought, *he's talking like it was real.* She looked down at his leg stretched across her feet. "Jeff, you're bleeding."

He pulled up his right pant leg. Three-inch bloody claw marks blossomed on his calf. "My fatal flaw. I manifest in this world what happens in the other."

She tried to rise, "I'll get some bandages and iodine—"

He grabbed her hand. "They're not deep and they'll go away."

A light knock sounded on the parlor door. "Come in," Jeff called.

Harry stuck his head through the opening. "A refill on the mocha, sir?" His tray held two fresh mugs, steaming in the light.

"Thank you, Harry. Would you mind opening the drapes?"

"Of course, sir. The message from the kitchen is everything is going well. Mr. MacIntyre is walking with Lady—er Miss Hamilton." Harry let in the early afternoon sun. "Is there anything else, sir?"

"Thank you, no. Colby and I'll step out for air in a few moments, too."

"Very good, sir." He picked up the small drum from the table. "I will return this to the shelf in the study."

Colby focused on the hot mug. Two more sips. Questions nipped at her mind. When Harry disappeared through the door, she burst out, "The little boy. Who was … is he?"

Jeff looked at her sharply then softened his gaze. "That's how Pyewacket chose to manifest his soul."

Colby chewed on that, pausing, unsure exactly what to ask.

"When someone is seriously hurt, physically or emotionally, the soul may decide it can't withstand the pain. It, or part, leaves the body for the other realities." He chuckled. "According to my beliefs, there is an underworld and an upper world surrounding the middle world in which we live. When the soul leaves the body, it goes to the other world—or stays in this world—like a ghost. Usually, it's only a part and the person feels disconnected from life. Everything is diminished and illness may follow. My people believe a healer can retrieve the pieces, bringing the person back to health." He paused, studying her face.

She nodded for him to go on.

"The trauma to Pye caused part of his soul to leave … to hide. Fortunately, he didn't go very far. He knew coming back would be painful. He was reluctant. But you reminded him who he is, here and now. For Niki's sake, he's willing to suffer it."

"Jeff, I see the scratches and I know what I felt but you looked the same to me … except for the wings there at the end. Why did I … why didn't I?" Colby wrinkled her forehead.

"You weren't exactly following protocol." He patted her knee. "You haven't been trained but your spirit hitched a ride." He looked at his leg "Your power animal jumped in to protect you, inducing the shape change. Again, I'm impressed." He smiled at her and she felt her cheeks warm.

"Okay." He stretched long arms above his head and arched his back. "Time to go see the patient then fresh air." He rolled toward her placing a hand on either side of her and pushing himself up. His face even with hers, he brushed her lips. "Next time, just tell me you want to go."

He stood and offered her his hand. She considered refusing but the contact was too enticing. She rose, pausing a moment to assure herself the room remained still. She wrapped her arms around his neck and kissed him. The room spun again, all thoughts slipping from her mind.

CHAPTER 36

Chris rounded the corner into the upstairs hall. A dark shape crouched at the door to his room. He stopped. The shape dropped heavily to the floor with a whine. He took a step, his eyes becoming accustom to the dimness. *Sami said she was in the study.*

Another whine. His heart broke from the pain buried in it.

The gash on her right shoulder oozed blood. Her nostrils flared, sniffing the air. The long tail beat against the floor while the shaggy body lay motionless.

"Ahh, lass. It's a bad day when the boys beat up on you. They must have desperately wanted that cat."

She whined again, raising her head.

He stretched out his hand for her inspection. "It seems to be my day to rescue the ladies." She nosed his hand then dropped her head back to the hardwood floor.

"Lady, indeed." Scotty's voice startled Chris. "I wondered where I would find her." Scotty carried a basin, towels draped over his forearm. "I was going to see if I could clean her up … even though she hasn't been very friendly towards me. Seems you've made progress with her, though."

Chris smiled, remembering similar beasts in the MacMillan household. His adopted father praised his way with animals. That won him some respite from the jibes and pranks played by Scotty's brothers. "I'm surprised she would refuse your hand."

Scotty shrugged. "Sometimes, they are single-minded about who is to be master." Scotty stepped over the dog and shouldered open the door. He deposited the basin and towels on the floor by the fireplace. Before either man could reach for her, the lurcher hoisted herself to her feet. She limped into the room and collapsed on the hearth.

"Brave heart in this one." Chris knelt by her and soaked the cloth in the warm water. He laid it over the matted fur.

"Harry said the dogs at the door were mastiffs. Three … bred for fighting. She must be fast to have escaped them." Scotty stroked the fur behind her ears.

Chris lifted the cloth and probed the edges around the wound. Her muscles ripple across her shoulder but she remained still.

"She'll need stitches." Scotty rose, stepping to the door.

"Aye." Chris rinsed the cloth and washed down her flank.

"I'll see what I can find." Scotty shut the door.

Chris hummed as he washed her muzzle and ears. He reached the tune's end. She raised her head and whined, looking at him, one ear cocked.

"You like the discordant noise I'm making, do you? Let me see if I have my ocarina." He pulled the small instrument from his pocket. "I'll find a tune t'will soothe you."

She tapped her tail to his lilting melody. Contentment washed over him. He didn't stop when he heard the door open. A warm hand touched his shoulder, Sami's lavender perfume reaching his nose.

"Pye's sound asleep in Jeff's arms." She laughed.

He looked up at her, her closeness bringing him peace. *She's still wearing the ruined dress*, he noted. *If I'd met her first…*

She settled to her knees and stroked the rough fur.

Chris finished his tune. "Sami, she needs stitchin' along the line. It might heal on its own but a few stitches will help it heal sooner. I don't know if she'll hold still for it and she's got mighty teeth. Are you sure Scotty shouldn't help me?"

Sami looked at him, her amber eyes shining. "Chris, I need to be useful here." She pulled out a strand and threaded the needle.

Chris pointed to the spots where stitches should go. "Sami, I'll do it—"

"No, you can keep her calm. Play for her." Chris measured the determination in her eyes. He reached deep in his memory. Sweet notes swirled around the room. The melody mourned yet rose with hope, crying and laughing at once. He looked down into the brown eyes marveling at the courage and devotion within. The dog held her head still against the floor, her paws twitching as Sami worked the needle through the flesh.

"Done." Sami said. "What do you think? Should I have embroidered your name in it?" Chris's startled expression brought a smile to her face. "After all, she dragged herself up the stairs to your room, didn't she?"

Sami rose and retrieved a quilt from the chest. Draping it over the dog, she rubbed the huge ears eliciting a moan close to a purr. "What will you call her?"

"Maeve…after the warrior queen." Chris fought hard then surrendered to a jaw-cracking yawn.

"It seems more than one needs a nap. Why don't you lie down and keep Maeve company?"

Chris kicked off his boots and laid on the bed. His eyes closed before his head found the pillow.

***

Sami unfolded the blanket, spreading it over him. She stood for a moment looking at him. She had spent the least time with Chris when the band called Foxhaven home. Around him, she was overcome by a lost feeling. *Don't be silly, he's a full-grown man. And he's so calming to the animals. Takes confidence.* Soft snoring rose from both man and beast. She pulled the door closed.

***

The lock's click roused Chris. He stretched and pulled the blanket up under his chin, settling back down. A groan and rustling cloth alerted him. He fought his heavy eyelids to check on Maeve. Before he mustered the strength to rise, the mattress edge sank under a weight. Maeve hauled herself up and flopped beside him, her large head across his arm.

"Sami won't appreciate your blood on her counterpane," he mumbled. "All hells, what am I saying? Sami won't care." He curled over, tucking the other arm around Maeve's chest.

She heaved a sigh.

CHAPTER 37

Tori set the platter on the table. "Gentlemen, we need the dining table. It's always good to have energy to deal with whatever comes down the old road."

Scotty snatched the maps out from under the dish and jollied them into a stack.

Tori removed her apron. "Mac, please bring in the soup tureen. I swear it's bigger than Harry himself. Wouldn't do for the dear man to drown."

Sami carried plates and silverware, pushing the door with her hip. Tori grimaced, observing the pale green silk gown, the lace inset highlighting Sami's ivory skin.

"Sami, what a beautiful dress." Tori picked up a sandwich and nibbled on it. "How's Pye doin', sweetie?"

"He's bathed and snuggled in Jeff's arms. Scotty, would you take Jeff and Colby a plate and coffee? They're back in the parlor."

The plate filled, Tori helped him balance two cups on the edge.

Mac carried in the ornate tureen "I said it to Scotty, I'll say it again. I don't see why we can't just kill him."

Charlie stood in the doorway. "Because he's my bloody great grandfather." He stared at Mac. "If I thought it would do any good, I'd kill him myself. The very act would tie me to his fate … creating someone you'd have to fight against, not stand beside. A circumstance I'd rather avoid." He sat down beside Jessica. "I know I sound paranoid. It doesn't mean I'm wrong."

"Charlie's right to be cautious." She looked at Mac. "Lord Edward is my husband's progenitor as well, Mac."

Nigel patted Sami's hand. "My assignment will be to deliver your letter, Sami. While I wait, I will do justice to the pastry." He patted her hand. "I will need to dress for dinner and return for you. It would be best if my distant cousin and his American bride were seen in public. I have several invitations for parties this evening. It is the holiday season after all." He chuckled. "And I am a bit in demand."

Concern flashed across Sami's face.

"My dear girl, I promise only one stop and I will have you and Charlie safely back here." His voice dropped to a dramatic whisper, "Knowing the murmurings amongst the house staff, rumors will already by making the rounds. I want to know what is being said."

***

Sami rose, heading for the study with Charlie close on her heels.

"Are you sure about this?' Charlie closed the study door.

Sami sat in the leather desk chair. "Charlie, we don't have a better plan." She didn't look at him. "I'll write the letter. Please, dear, make sure Jeff and Pyewacket are all right. I think Chris and Maeve will sleep the afternoon away."

He stood with his hand on her shoulder, watching her formulate the salutation to his great grandsire. Cold water poured down his spine, his hand shaking. Sami placed her hand over his. "You don't need to hover over me. A walk would do you good. Get some air." She returned to her composition, her tongue caught between her teeth.

He kissed her neck and left her to the task.

CHAPTER 38

Chad stepped out on the porch, seeking quiet. *What can I do to help? To save my future manager. They've welcomed me so far.* He shrugged, dismissing his growing feelings of uncertainty.

The umbral winter landscape matched his thoughts, charcoal branches etched with dark pine accents and the pearlescent grey clouds drifting across navy winter sky obscuring the weak winter sun. Black slashes dove and wheeled in the sky. Ravens, in a large unkindness, exploded above the stables. They circled the cupola, screeing and cawing, issuing battle orders then countermanding them. The dangerous aerial display reignited his anxiety.

We need protection. Wish Uncle Bernie were here. He settled his brown fedora further down on his forehead and hunched his shoulders against the chill wind. *He'd know what to do.*

A great she-raven broke away from the tumult, diving across the drive. Chad's head snapped up at the movement, a black feather drifting in his peripheral vision. Leaning over the railing, he snagged the feather from the breeze. He overbalanced, arms waving to recover. He tucked the feather in the worn leather hatband.

Thanks, pretty lady. Hitching one leg up on the railing, he cupped his harmonica. A blues riff in counterpoint to the cacophony rolled off the porch.

He studied the ravens. *Ravens are a family group. How do you protect your family?* He knit together threads to form a song with every note in and the shuddering breathy note wheezing out.

> Protection I seek on this cold misty morning
> The raven's battle cry rakes me without warning
> Helpless against the ebony gaze, echoing heartless rage
> Filled with great fright, I yearn to wing through time's page.

Chad played to the wheeling birds, his eyes drawn to the she-raven flying solo. *So lost, dear one.* The plaintive notes wandered through the air for several minutes then faded away. He banged the harmonica on his hand and returned it to his pocket. A motion in the field caught his eye. A figure in a gray Macintosh headed toward the trees.

Chad wanted to call out to Charlie but hesitated. Charlie bent to gather sticks from the ground, putting them in a canvas bag on his shoulder. He dipped and straightened several times before disappearing into the shadows. Chad's gaze lengthened beyond the trees tracking the disappearing ravens. Each strong wing beat accelerated the dizziness, forcing him to grip the railing.

The kitchen door opened. Chad nodded to Harry. "I hope I didn't disturb your peace."

"Not at all, young sir. I find the mouth organ to be a worthy musical tool. It moans and cries, mimicking the human voice." He held out a steaming cup. "I understand you have a decided preference for coffee. The clouds are bringing a chill."

Chad wrapped cold fingers around the mug. *Jeez. When am I going to learn to come in?*

"You seem deep in dark thought. I have a good ear if you wish to talk." Harry held the door open inviting Chad into the warmth. "Did you have sufficient at luncheon? If not, I have the one cupcake Mr. MacIntyre didna find."

Chad accepted the plate and sank into a kitchen chair. Peeling the icing off the top and setting it aside, he bit into the cake.

"Harry," Chad started. "It's amazing what Jeff did and Chris has a way with the animals." Another bite disappeared. "Mac and Scotty are ready to mount a military campaign. What can I do?"

"Perhaps you should consider your Yule gift." Harry pointed to the box on the counter.

Chad stared at it. "How did it get here? I left it in my room."

Harry shrugged. He handed him the box, sweeping away the plate with the icing.

Chad laid out each item, red strings, engraver's tools, pen nibs and a parchment sheet. "Harry, talk me through this. I don't want to misuse the gift.

"There is power in the spoken word." Harry's voice calmed Chad's turmoil.

Okay, things might be weird but at least I have something concrete in my hands. He fingered the fine yarn.

"Harry, are you familiar with Rachel's tomb? She's the matriarch who embodies compassion and selflessness." Chad wound the string around his finger. "To symbolize her Holy light, red string is wrapped around her tomb then cut into lengths." He looked at Harry. "It's a segula … a protective charm. The string is wound around the left wrist and tied with seven knots. Energy, good or bad, enters through the left side. The charm prevents the negative energy from getting through." Chad paused. "Do you believe we are under attack from the Droch shuil … the evil eye?"

"Son, what we're facing is most certainly evil."

Chad shook his head, clearing his thoughts. "Harry, Sami has moments when the energy in her is strong. But she also seems so fragile. It makes my heart ache."

Harry nodded, the affection for his mistress clear on his face.

"By providing this binding to the people I care about, they'll be shielded the best way I know." He slid his chair around to face Harry and held out a string. "These may not have been around Rachel's tomb but I choose to believe it has been blessed. The intention is what's most important. Harry, may I tie this for you?"

Harry stuck out his left arm.

Chad's hands shook. He tied the first knot, careful to leave a space between the string and the flesh. "My Uncle Bernie would describe your responsibility to help maintain the positive energy. You need to stay clean … no gossip, unkind words, or vengeful thoughts." He ticked off the list. "These actions will break down the charm."

Harry nodded.

"We're bound together in compassion and friendship. Though I haven't seen it written, I believe the seven knots represent the seven traits that help one find life's mysteries." Chad paused, flexing his fingers.

"Tell me about the seven traits." Harry kept his hand still.

Chad reached into his heart. "The first is Chesed ... kindness." Chad looked around the table. He didn't remember finishing the icing but guessed he had. He rose. "Do you want a cookie or some coffee? A sweet right now would be a kindness. This is hungry work ... all this thinking."

Chad filled the kettle. He pulled open the cabinet door and spotted chocolates on the top shelf. Reaching for the box, he glanced out the window. *How dark the clouds are.* He shivered.

Returning to his seat, he saw the plate with crumbs and the missing icing. Glancing at Harry who looked the other direction, he chuckled. *Okay, old man, one for you.* Chad scooped up the icing and popped it in his mouth. He pushed the chocolates toward Harry. "Want one?" He smiled to see Harry shake with the effort to stop laughing.

He picked up the ends. The old man's warm gaze washed over him.

"The rest are vigor, compassion, endurance, humility, connection and dignity." Chad tied one knot for each word. With the last knot secured, he clasped Harry's hand. "I'm striving for them but, in all humility, Harry, I feel you already embody these characteristics." He lowered his head and shut his eyes then whispered words strange to Harry's ear. "There, it's done. A prayer to seal it."

Chad rose and poured the boiling water over the coffee grounds. Then he filled the teacup for Harry. He set the cups down and slouched into the chair. Feeling eyes upon him, he looked up.

Jeff stood in the doorway.

"How much did you hear?"

"Enough. I'm in." Jeff stretched, placing his palms on the lintel and arching his back. He snagged Chad's cup, drained it and refilled it placing it back on the table. "If something can help us stay clean on this path, I'm in favor."

"Harry, will you tie for me?" Chad stuck out his arm.

Harry nodded, "Of a certain, lad. You do me honor. If you don't mind, I'll be adding a wee bit from my heritage. I don't think Miss Rachel will mind. The Celtic knots speak to interconnectedness. Some believe the twists and turns confuse the evil spirits." He tied a complex knot. "This one is the shield knot … with my own twist."

Harry looked into Chad's eyes and spoke. The cadence rippled up Chad's arm and swirled through him echoing comfort and peace.

"Harry, I'll tie the string for Jeff if you will guide me through those knots. It looks different upside down."

Jeff pulled back his linen cuff. An intricate braiding—black, red, green and blue—circled his wrist. Two garnet beads hung on the ends.

Chad hesitated.

"My sister." Jeff ran his fingers along the bracelet. "She's learning the medicine ways from our grandmother. The colors represent the four directions." Jeff held out his wrist. "All ways are to be respected."

With a false start or two and Harry's gentle correction, Chad absorbed the pattern. He repeated the blessing.

***

The back door swung open, frigid wind slamming it against the wall. Charlie stood at the door, holding a heavy sack filled with kindling.

"What are you doing?" His voice shook. Jeff took the bag from him and set it aside. Harry peeled off Charlie's coat.

"I've had the worst nightmare within the worst nightmare." The tremor in Charlie's voice matched his shivering. His eyes roamed wildly around the room.

Jeff took Charlie by the shoulders and steered him to a vacant chair. Charlie wrung his hands, staring at them with fixed gaze.

"Charlie." Jeff placed his hand over Charlie's, arresting their motion. "Talk to me."

For a long moment, Charlie stared into Jeff's dark eyes then drew a deep breath, his shivering abating.

"The weather darkened, becoming more dreary right before my eyes. But since Sami was so adamant I needed the walk—besides, we need kindling—it seemed worth braving the weather. I wandered into the forest. In the darkness, I thought about the twists and turns I learned in the family manor years away. I heard my father's hectoring tones."

Charlie rose and assumed a puffed out bullying posture. "There are many different mazes, Charles. Some are unicursal. No branches. Being the Ramhills are a magia family with a long, long history…" He swung around, looking sharply into Jeff's face. "Are you paying attention?"

Charlie's terror at his father's badgering ran through his body.

"We…" He stressed the word with pride. "… have a labyrinth to rival Thebes." His voice boiled out, low and ominous. "Complicated … to keep the dragon in. He gets very hungry." His eyes focused on the unseen target. "Walk it right or I will need another son." His shoulders slumped. "I could see every leaf and remember the boxwood stench."

He paced the kitchen. "Take five steps to the left, then a sharp bend under the arching rise and back straight to the beginning again."

He staggered … bending, twisting, beating on the floor.

"Do you think he's having a breakdown?" Chad stared at Charlie.

"No." Jeff said. "He's remembering something important."

Charlie fell to his knees, covering his ears with his hands. "Stop! Stop your humming!" Charlie ranted with the rhythms bred in his bones. "Home to the left. Hide in the caves until the Magus comes. I'll eat his bones." He froze.

Jeff gestured to Chad and they lifted Charlie onto a chair.

"Charlie." Harry placed his hands on Charlie's shoulders. "We're here to help, lad. Place your trust in this new friend." He winked at Chad. "He wishes to help protect us all."

"What?" Charlie looked around.

"Chad, explain the string while I tie the knots." Jeff placed Charlie's wrist in the first loop.

"I don't see how something this simple can do any good." Charlie's head moved from side to side.

Jeff raised his eyes from the string. "Even if you choose not to believe, someone else in this house will. If you asked me to wear chicken feet around my neck, a copper pot on my head, and stand in my guitar case, I'd do it … if someone in this house believed it would help."

Harry snorted, his sides shaking.

"When Sami walks through the door, Harry will offer this to her and I will find Mac and the rest. If you care about us, you'll play along."

Charlie stared at his wrist and sat still while Jeff returned to the knots. He half listened to Chad's explanation.

"Damn you, Jeff." Charlie hunched his shoulders. Jeff concentrated on the knots, not responding. "You always know the buttons to push. I'll do anything to protect Sami. All I want is a strong drink and my drums." He fidgeted in the chair. "No, that's not all. I want Kay back for Sami. Damn it, I want Niki back here, too. I want my family home."

The last knot tied, Jeff whispered a soft *Ah ho*. Silence filled the kitchen. Chad laid out the remaining strings.

Charlie jumped up. "I need to find Sami." He hurried into the front hall.

"Don't worry, Chad." Jeff rose. "He'll come through for her."

"You playing oracle now, too?" Chad tugged at the string on his wrist.

"No. Just trusting the Charlie I believe in."

CHAPTER 39

Chris swung around the corner into the parlor. Jeff sat cross-legged on the hearth, Pyewacket in his lap. Jeff shredded a small white fish and fed the cat. Chris smiled to see Pyewacket nibbling greedily and washing Jeff's palm, requesting more. Maeve shouldered past him, settling on the hearth, a nose length away from the pair. Without looking, Jeff flipped a morsel in her direction. She snatched it from the air, returning her chin to the floor between her paws. Her eyebrows twitched watching Jeff's slow movements.

"Chris, sleepy head, want something?" Mac handed highball glasses to Colby and Charlie.

Chris' stomach rumbled. "Not until I've eaten. I must have slept through lunch." A brisk knocking at the front door startled him and he moved away to stand by the Christmas tree. *Where is the little owl?* The branch was empty.

"Good evening, Harry." Nigel's voice echoed through the hall. A moment spent removing hat, coat and gloves, he appeared in the parlor door. Mac met him with the brandy snifter.

"Very good, and my thanks. Even with the sunshine, it is cold as a witch's ti …" he paused looking at the young women. "That is to say, brandy is welcome to a freezing man. Cheers!" They all raised a glass to toast Nigel's exuberance.

Nigel dropped onto the loveseat. "I do expect my brother will find your letter intriguing. He will want to know how, having just arrived, you have such a good grapevine established." He peered at her, studying her pale beauty. "I have found the perfect dinner party for tonight."

Sami grimaced, looking down at her hands. He took them into his own.

"I won't leave you alone for a moment." He nodded to the others in the room. "I do apologize I could not obtain invitations for all but it is important you two be seen by the right people."

Sami pulled her hand away from his grasp. "Uncle Nigel, is this necessary?"

"My dear, we must establish you and Charles in town. We don't have much time. Mrs. Stanton-Smith is entertaining. Everyone who matters will be in attendance. Her daughter is home from the conservatory in Paris. She is such an angel with her music." He smiled, a wistful look in his eyes. "And it will be a chance for you to meet my dear brother … if he attends. He often demurs at the last moment leaving my poor sister-in-law to make his excuses." He saw fear rising in her eyes and hurried on brightly, "You will like Genevieve. She is very kind … not to mention beautiful." His face lit up. "I won't expect you to stay long. We can point out you are newly arrived from America."

Sami rose. "Then I'll change."

Charlie glared at Nigel.

"Charles, I wouldn't ask this but I'm convinced it is necessary."

Charlie didn't respond.

"I feel terrible." Nigel said. He peeled off his glasses, pulling a clean handkerchief from his pocket. He absently rubbed at the lens. His next words died unspoken when Charlie stalked out the parlor door. Nigel trailed along behind.

***

Jeff listened to the interchange, observing the tension in Sami's shoulders and the heaviness to Charlie's tread. He glanced at Colby. He stepped behind the loveseat and leaned close to her ear. "Colby."

She looked up at him, her eyes reflecting the firelight. She waited for him to continue. "How tired are you? I had a long nap this afternoon."

His concentration shifted from Colby to the cat still nested in his arms. He held his palm above the raw wound. Warmth spread across

Pyewacket. The cat stretched and curled into sleep. Jeff closed his eyes. After three long breathes, he withdrew his hand.

Colby seized it in her own turning the palm up. "How do you do that?" She looked up at him. "I can feel the warmth, hotter than body temperature." She blushed, releasing his hand.

"Wait until you meet my grandfather."

She glanced back up at him.

"Ma claims he can boil water between his hands." He trailed his fingers along her neck. "I think Sami needs us along tonight. Are you up for it?"

Colby nodded.

"Do you wish help dressing?" Jessica stood. "I'll check in on Sami, too."

"Here, Jeff," Chris spoke from the floor where he lay curled up with Maeve. "Give me the wee kitten. He'll be safe with us." Maeve's tail thumped against the wooden floor. Chris settled Pyewacket against Maeve's chest. She drew her long tongue along his back. Pyewacket stretched in response. Chris laid back, his arm across Maeve's flank.

Jeff walked the two into the hallway. He heard Charlie's voice in the study, the tone heated.

"Uncle Nigel, I won't put Sami at risk."

"My dear boy, to be invited to the manor for New Year's, you have to be an item. Sami has to intrigue him. My words just don't carry enough..." He shrugged. "Any weight with him."

Jeff cleared his throat. Both men turned towards the sound, Charlie's eyes narrowed, suspicion written on his face. He grabbed the brandy snifter from the desk.

"Charlie, Colby and I will accompany you tonight." Jeff looked in Nigel's direction.

Nigel brightened then cringed at Charlie's dark scowl. He fidgeted.

Jeff stood motionless.

"I don't think that is a good idea." Charlie shot Nigel a withering look to silence his protest. "Jeff, the more we are about, the more opportunity to make a mistake." He looked out the study window at the dark night.

"Charlie, I agree with your caution but you can't do this alone. We can't hole up in the house and wait for a miracle." Jeff leaned against the doorframe. He waited for his words to settle into Charlie's thoughts. "We can assure Sami will have company. You alone might be separated from her." He considered his next statement. "Colby needs a way to help her sister."

Charlie lifted the snifter to his lips, finishing it in one gulp. "I suppose we should dress. Uncle Nigel, we will meet you in an hour." He laughed at Nigel's astonished face. "Uncle Nigel, if you expected a long argument then you don't know Jeff." He clapped Nigel on the back. "When he chooses to venture an opinion, he always wins!"

Jeff chuckled and followed Charlie to the stairs.

CHAPTER 40

Harry draped the heavy velvet cape over Sami's shoulders. The golden striped dress accentuated her elegant figure. Lemon scent rose from her hair held up by the jeweled combs she found in her mother's chest. A gift, he remembered, from Mr. Gordon on their first anniversary. His heart leapt into his throat. *Her mother's porcelain beauty with her father's golden coloring. What a lovely combination.*

Sami threw herself into his arms. "Harry." His heavy woolen coat muffled her voice. "I'm sorry to ask you to go out in the cold."

"No, lass. I know the people here. 'Tis a good opportunity for me to hear what's being said below the stairs ... where the real information is." He hugged her. "I was thinkin' how proud your parents would be."

Her eyes glistened.

"Now, now, danne be doing that ... it will ruin your makeup." He caught the first tear on his finger tip and held it up to the light. "These are too precious to waste."

Sami hugged him tighter. Voices from the upstairs hallway signaled Colby and Jeff's arrival with Charlie close behind. Jessica walked with him to the landing at the top.

"Now, Sami, this isn't proper behavior between a butler and his mistress so you have to act a little more aloof." She looked at him with all seriousness, her eyes wide. "And, if anything is said about my working for you, I left England for America for a position with your father."

"Yes, I'll remember." She pulled herself up and held her head erect.

Harry retrieved a wrap for Colby and overcoats for the gentlemen with his thoughts still on Sami. *This is so hard for her, so unlike her mother. She was the first to accept an invitation and lit up the room. Her spirit is in her if she can find it.*

Charlie fumbled with his cufflinks.

Sami held out her hand for the second cufflink when he hit the last step and inserted it. "Charlie, you're shaking." She straightened his tie, placing a light kiss on his lips.

"Yes, my dear, I am." Charlie shrugged. "You look magnificent. Your dress sets off the gold in your eyes and ...." He reached for her hand pulling it to his lips, "its lines accentuate your lovely figure. I am so pleased to see the amber ring on your finger."

"Sir?" Harry held out Charlie's coat.

Charlie slipped his arms into the waiting sleeves. "Thank you, Harry." Charlie offered Sami his arm. They stepped out. Mac maneuvered the carriage to the front step. He sprang from the seat and opened the side door. Charlie assisted Sami up the step, the train folded over her arm revealing ankle and calf. She settled into the seat. Jeff helped Colby climb into the carriage to sit opposite Sami. The two men eased into their places.

Harry clucked the horses into motion. "Miss Jessica." Harry's voice carried in the wind. "Keep the other scallywags under control, will you?"

The carriage disappeared into the winter's evening.

***

Under the windswept sky, the manor of Stanton-Smythes glowed bright. Men in dark green livery sprang to take the horses' leads and to open carriage doors. Elegant couples descended and hurried into the warm vestibule.

Colby leaned over Jeff to gaze at the glittering candles in every window. "This would be so lovely if there were snow."

"You haven't spent much time in these drafty old houses. Winter is to be endured here and the spring time blessed." Charlie stared out the window.

Colby reached across to take Sami's hand, cold in her rabbit-skin gloves. "How did you get mixed up with this cad? I doubt there's a romantic bone in his body!"

Charlie pulled Sami tight to his side. "Sorry, Colby. I will try and be more sensitive." He remarked, sarcasm dripping.

The carriage lurched to a stop. The door swung open, a cold blast stealing away the accumulated body heat. Jeff jumped to the ground. Before the footman could assist, he reached up and lifted Colby, his hands spanning her waist. She laughed, flying through the air with her hands on his shoulders. He aimed her descent to land on the first step, away from the mud.

Charlie swung out, reaching back to help Sami. Her face pale, she whispered, "Please, don't do that to me. I might throw up."

Charlie choked back his laughter, realizing she was not joking. He held her hand and helped her step to the ground. She leaned against him, her breathing shallow.

I am going to kill Uncle Nigel. He bowed his head and recanted, aware his Uncle understood the situation better than anyone else. He tucked Sami's hand under his arm, and mounted the steps to the open door.

Inside, maids in black dresses and white starched aprons wove around the entering guests. Two accepted Colby's cape and Jeff's coat. Charlie lifted the heavy cape from Sami's shoulders marveling at its weight. He leaned close to her ear, trying to make her smile. "No wonder you are weak in the knees. This thing is heavy."

"Ladies." Uncle Nigel appeared in the swirling crowd. "Aren't you fetching!" He studied each one in turn. "Sami, you are a vision… such loveliness." He kissed her cheek.

Turning to Colby, he raised his voice over the din, "Miss Fairmont, your blue gown is becoming with the high color in your fair cheeks. And the cut is magnificent. The drape highlights your lovely figure."

Colby dropped a curtsey to Nigel. She stared deeply into Nigel's eyes. Her actions were rewarded by his ready laugh. He handed her up and swirled her onto his arm. Looking back over his shoulder, he remarked, "I say, dear boy, I have charmed your lady away … at least for the next few minutes." He proceeded to the door and paused behind the couple next to be announced. Jeff bowed Charlie and Sami ahead.

Candles placed in every conceivable nook suffused the salon with soft light. A barrel-sized Yule log blazed in the fireplace. Fresh evergreen garlands graced the walls and glittered with crystal ornaments. Susurration filled the room. Couples greeted friends, the silk, velvet and brocade garments swishing, counterpointing the genteel voices.

Nigel navigated the crowd and stopped before a tall woman dressed in deep burgundy velvet, her creamy skin offset by a large ruby necklace set in heavy gold filigree. Her face lit into a wide smile. She extended her diamond-laden hand to him. Nigel brought it to his lips.

"Nigel, I am so glad you could join us." Sweeping her gaze from Colby to Charlie and Sami, her warm voice encompassed them all. "I am delighted you sent word regarding your guests. I will always make room for your friends."

"Constance, I wish to introduce Charles Ramhill and his American bride, Saminthea. And this lovely young thing," he nodded to Colby, "is her sister, Colby Fairmont."

He looked around for Jeff who, upon stepping singly into the room had been corralled by two young women. One dressed in light green brocade with upswept auburn hair clung to his right arm and the other, blonde and dressed in an oriental patterned silk edged in pale pink fringe, held his left.

"Oh, dear." Nigel fidgeted. "Please excuse me for a moment while I extricate the last member from his predicament." Nigel wove his way back through the clustered guests.

"It is a pleasure to meet you, Charles. Forgive my familiarity but Nigel does tend to instill his disregard for decorum in us." Constance smiled at him then examined Sami. "May I offer you wine? I hazard a personal comment that you are not well."

Sami drew a deep breath. "Thank you, Mrs. Stanton-Smythe. I am not a good traveler."

"Please call me Constance." Constance scanned the crowded room. She waved for the servant circulating with tall crystal glasses filled with wheat-colored wine on a silver tray. The young man danced through the assembly. Constance retrieved two glasses, holding one out to Sami.

"Here, this is a fine vintage, light and crisp. It will help settle your stomach. My Edgar travels the continent to maintain the wine cellar."

"It's very good." Sami replied after a sip. "This will bring back my appetite."

"Delightful. Nigel tells me you are Gordon's niece. You're coloring favors your uncle."

"You know my … uncle?" Sami asked.

"I do. Your aunt and I share an interest in art … particularly the American artists." She swept her hand indicating the salon's walls. "You can't see them in this dim light but I have several works from the Hudson River School … the second generation. And I love the depictions of the American West. Do you have an interest in art?"

"Yes." Color returned to Sami's face. "I studied art … the Hudson River School including Remington and Caitlin."

"Are the sunsets so dramatic or are they exaggerated?"

"I accompanied my father on a trip to the West. Every sunset in these paintings is possible. Each morning was a delight." She sipped the aperitif. "Forgive me for being forward but do you know what happened to my aunt and uncle?"

"A tragedy and a mystery. I attended the twins' delivery. Then a week later, the detectives are turning the countryside upside down looking them. Gordon disappeared which prompted dire rumors." She looked at Charlie. "Edward Ramhill was the last to see Gordon. Even their butler left the country. You can imagine the fantastic explanations and accusations." She cupped Sami's face in her hand. "But I am distressing you."

"I'm quite anxious for any news."

"My dear, if I hear even a whisper, I will share it with you." Constance looked at the next arrival. "Excuse me but I must see to my other guests. Dinner will be announced in a moment."

Charlie leaned close. "Are you all right?"

"Yes." She rose on tiptoe to kiss his cheek. "I'm sad she didn't know more but I'm feeling better."

The butler announced Lord and Lady Ramhill. Charlie spun around, alert to the parties at the door.

"Sami, that's my great grandmother."

Crystalline laughter echoed above the steady conversation.

"I've often looked at her portrait and wondered about her. Her face was so kind." His voice trailed off.

Constance greeted Genevieve Ramhill and shared a moment together. Constance directed her attention to them. Her deep green gaze assessed the group landing on Sami last. Sami looked for Colby, trying to avoid eye contact with Lady Ramhill. Colby stared at Nigel trying to extricate Jeff from the two young women who held him prisoner. The conversation contained much laughter and easy banter.

"Colby" Sami touched her sister on the arm.

"What?" Colby turned to Sami.

Sami edged around forcing Colby to turn away from the scene.

"I'm sorry. I don't know what's gotten into me. If he wants to flirt with other women, well, there isn't anything I can say about it." Colby wrung her handkerchief.

"When this is over, you can sort out your feelings." Sami hugged her. "Do you see the tall dark-haired man at the door?"

Colby craned her neck to see.

"That's Lord Ramhill. There's definitely a family resemblance, don't you think?"

Colby studied Lord Ramhill's face, the sharp plains and aquiline nose. A hand settled on her waist. She turned, staring into Jeff's eyes.

"Waylaid for a minute and you're staring at another man." He kissed her ear. Colby thrust her elbow into his midsection.

After a moment's delay, he said, "Oomph".

Sami burst out laughing at the two. She glanced at Charlie's face, his gaze on the approaching women.

Constance drew Lady Ramhill to her side. "Genevieve, may I present Saminthea Ramhill ... and Charles Ramhill. By your brother-in-law's calculations, your second cousin by marriage so many times removed." She laughed. "Saminthea is Gordon's niece."

Charlie kissed Genevieve's hand. Withdrawing her fingers from his grasp, she spoke to Sami. "It is a pleasure to meet you. Your aunt and uncle are good friends. I didn't know Gordon had any siblings. He is a private man. I am pleased you found your way into the Ramhill family."

"Lady Ramhill, my wife and I are most grateful to Nigel for his hospitality." Charlie fell into his social training.

"Nigel is a dear soul." Genevieve glanced at her brother-in-law. "How long will your party be in England?"

"We are uncertain. Two friends have been waylaid and we anxiously await their arrival."

Sami tapped him on the arm and leaned her head in Colby's direction.

"Please let me present Colby Fairmont, my wife's sister. And my good friend, Jeffry Conray from Texas."

The butler drew open the dining room door and announced dinner.

"My dear." A deep voice near Colby's shoulder startled her and she stepped sideways into Jeff. Edward Ramhill nodded to his wife. "Shall we go in to dinner?"

"Edward," Genevieve held out her hand to him. "Please meet Charles and Saminthea Ramhill."

He glanced at Charlie then focused on Sami. "The distant relatives Nigel has been prattling on about? I am pleased we have relatives wise enough to sweep the beauty from the colonies back to Britain where it belongs." He took Sami's hand and drew her closer. Lifting her hand to his lips, he forced her to shift to her toes. The color rose in Sami's face.

"For once, Nigel's story suffered from understatement. You are far lovelier than he described." He allowed her to settle back to her feet and tucked her arm under his, "I believe Saminthea requires guidance to her place at the table and I am always happy to serve." He pulled Sami into the moving tide.

Lady Ramhill motioned for Charlie's arm. "Charles, I am inconvenienced since my husband is captivated by your wife." She chuckled at the deep scowl on Charlie's face. "Don't worry. I will assure he returns her when dinner is completed."

Charlie escorted her to her seat and found his own beside her.

CHAPTER 41

E dward pulled back the chair, moving it into place as she sat. "How fortunate you will be my dinner companion." He looked down at her, appraising the curve of her neck as she tilted her head to look up at him. He walked away to speak with other guests before returning to his seat.

Sami studied the Haviland-Limoges plates. *Art Nouveau. She* admired the rich colors. *She truly is an Americanophil*. A hand enveloped her own under the table. She jumped, her breath held in her chest. Jeff squeezed and settled into his own chair. He half rose as Lord Ramhill appeared on Sami's other side but Edward waved him back into his seat.

Edward addressed Constance. "My dear, a lovely setting as usual. It will be delightful to hear Estelle play.

"Thank you. And there is a surprise. Adrian has been working on a duet with her. It is Estelle's gift to you and Genevieve. Adrian has been most attentive."

Edward drummed his fingers on the linen table cloth waiting for his wineglass to be filled. He glanced down the table at Adrian. His son engaged the doe-eyed Estelle in conversation.

Sami could feel the irritation rolling off him. She focused on her place setting.

A waiter set down a bowl containing a steaming soup. Sami relished the Scotch broth, placing her fingers around the bowl for warmth. She looked up at Colby to find her staring beyond her. Sami smiled at her and scooped up another spoonful. Colby shifted her eyes sharply to Sami's left.

Sami glanced to find Edward near her. She dropped the spoon sending droplets across the table. She dabbed at the stain with her napkin. A flush crawled up her neck at Edward's chuckle at her discomfort.

"My dear." He leaned, bringing his lips close to her ear. She felt his breath as he spoke. "I did not mean to startle you. As lovely as you are, I would think you familiar with admiring stares."

A maid appeared to gather the wet napkin and offer a fresh one. Sami looked at Jeff, the tension evident in his posture. She shook her head slightly.

He nodded, returning his attention to the young woman on his right.

"Lord Ramhill, my husband will be gratified his family approves." She avoided his eyes, busying herself with placing the fresh napkin on her lap.

"Indeed." Edward drew back, signaling the waiter he was done, his soup untouched. "The family connection is a mystery to me. I am not aware Charles is on the family tree but that bookkeeping is Nigel's passion. However, I would like to explore it in more depth … with you."

Before he could go on, Constance drew his attention asking his opinion on the current actions before the House of Lords. He turned to respond.

Sami looked down the table where Charlie and Lady Ramhill spoke in quiet tones. *What could they be discussing?* She worried the napkin then clasped her hands tightly. *Stop*, she shouted at herself. *For God's sake, she's his great grandmother*. The thought overwhelmed her, the blood draining from her face as the dinner noise roared around her.

She willed the tension to drain away.

"America? My God, do you get to the symphony?" A loud voice sounded from across the table.

Colby nodded, paying attention to her plate.

"You must have heard the French cellist who crossed the Pond to play with the New York Symphony Society." The portly gentleman gesticulated with his spoon. "He is a genius … such technique." He looked into Colby's face. "Of course, you know him."

"I know his work." She nodded. "Though he does not compare to Modest Altschuler ... the Russian Symphony Orchestra of New York. He is rumored to be recording on the gramophone."

Her companion looked at her. His spoon hung in midair.

Sami caught Colby's eye and tipped her head in appreciation. Colby smiled back at her, eyes alight.

"Of course, he has gone off to some great adventure." A gruff voice startled Sami. She looked down the table at a portly gentleman with an impressive mustache. Nigel leaned in, talking over the woman next to him.

"Now, Arthur, surely you don't believe Gordon is searching for the Lost World. I heard your conversation last New Year's Eve but ..."

"Nigel, old man, certainly he is. Dinosaurs. A plateau in South America. Don't you remember he wanted a live pterodactyl?" He leaned back with a bellicose laugh, drawing a blistering look from Constance. "Constance, please. You have laughed at his expense yourself."

"Perhaps, Arthur, but not publicly and not with his niece in attendance." She kept her voice soft but heated. She tilted her head in Sami's direction.

He startled when he saw the amber eyes on him. "My apologies, I was not aware you are a relation. I conjecture he is off adventuring. I hope he will write a marvelous book one day. It will put my poor Sherlock's adventures to shame!" He laughed again then his eyes softened towards her, waiting for a response.

Sami found herself at a loss for words. *One heartbeat, two heartbeats, three*, she counted. His eyes remained upon her. She willed her voice steady. "No offense taken, sir, but would he go off after my aunt's kidnapping?"

Sir Conan Doyle glanced around the table, clearly warming to the subject. "Well, now that you ask, I do have a theory. I think ..."

"Arthur, this conversation is not appropriate for the dinner table. Please reserve it for brandy and cigars with your cronies." Constance glared at him. The portly gentleman coughed, winking at Sami.

"Sir Arthur," Jeff's voice broke the silence. "Your character, Holmes, would fit well into the American West. He's dedicated to noble purposes while he finds breaking the law sometimes necessary. We, too, believe in preserving family … or a woman's virtue." Jeff lifted his wineglass and tipped it in tribute to Conan Doyle.

The portly gentleman lifted his own glass, drained it and held it up for the servers to refill. "Young man, you do me honor. It would seem you have read my poor scribings."

"I have read your stories and eagerly await another adventure."

Sir Conan Doyle beamed.

Though she had only sampled each delicacy, Sami felt relief when the last course arrived on the table. From consommé to caviar, Quaille Veronique to galantines, the meal was rich and sumptuous. Lemon trifle with billowing cream and sponge cake covered in lemon and orange curd graced the last plate. Almonds and crystallized violets glittered in the flickering candlelight.

She glanced at Charlie a to see him engaged in conversation with a stunning woman dressed in scarlet and gold brocade. His face gleamed responding to her soft-spoken comments. She caught the names Walter De la Mare and William Conrad. She shrank inside at the thought she had spent little time exploring Charlie's interests beyond his music … that was a safe conversation often needing few words as he entertained her. *How little I really know him.*

Her hand shook as she set down her spoon, her interest in the delicacy lost. She put her hands in her lap. Jeff's warm palm settled on her cold fingers.

She heard his conversation with the gentleman to Colby's right.

"…Madam Blavatsky wrote in *Voice of the Silence*, and I quote, sir, 'in order to become the Knower of all self, thou hast first of self to be known.' That requires a significant commitment to reflecting on one's own strengths and foibles."

"Egad, man," A skeletally thin gentleman stared at him. "Edward, what do you think regarding this young man's grasp … considering his American upbringing?" He looked at Edward.

Edward deposited his napkin on his untouched dessert. "The ability to quote her writings does not represent understanding. The proof is in the practice … not so simple or easily achieved by the uninitiated."

Jeff leaned over the table to face him. "Lord Ramhill, well said. To truly appreciate the brilliance in her words takes searching with a pure heart. Over many years. Grace to which we all aspire."

Edward's face betrayed his ire. Crinoline rustled beside him stopping his retort.

**

Standing, Constance nodded to her husband. He offered his arm to Genevieve. "Ladies and gentlemen, entertainment will be in the salon."

The gentlemen escorted the ladies to chairs arranged around the baby grand piano. Constance remained in the doorway, assisting Estelle in pinning her long sleeves. She felt tears forming. Her daughter entered the salon to sit before the piano.

Genevieve stepped up beside Constance. "Estelle is radiant tonight."

"Genevieve, it is so hard to watch her grow up." Constance placed her hand on her friend's arm. "What are your thoughts on Saminthea?"

Genevieve's voice remained low. "She has Serena's aura markers. The name is an interesting coincidence. But how is she here … now as a young adult? She would be turning five."

Constance nodded. "I fear Edward is involved somehow. Charles exhibits too much resemblance to be a 'cousin' too far removed."

Genevieve looked into her coven sister's eyes. "If she is Serena's, where is the boy?" Constance had no answer.

**

Charlie fidgeted in his chair, beating a tattoo on his leg. Glancing in his direction, Sami tried to take his hand but he eluded her. She took a breath trying to slow her heart. The melodic piano music soothed her and she closed her eyes.

The first piece ended to an enthusiastic response. During the applause, Sami captured Charlie's hand. He looked at her, forcing a smile which did not reach his eyes. Holding her hand, he turned his attention back to the piano as Adrian joined Estelle. They launched into a spirited rondo.

Genevieve motioned to Nigel. "Take them straight home, Nigel. I don't want Edward harassing her any more tonight." She laid her hand on his arm. "And come talk with me tomorrow."

CHAPTER 42

Sami laid her head on Charlie's shoulder, drifting with the swaying carriage. She worried about Harry, riding in the wind and cold. He assured her he was fine, but she felt better knowing he had accepted a lap robe. She didn't mind being a little cold and she could snuggle closer to Charlie.

Colby shivered under the blanket. Jeff laid his arm across her shoulders and pulled her tight against him. Sami waited for Colby to push him away, smiling to herself when Colby relaxed and put her head on Jeff's chest.

"Don't you ever get cold?" she murmured to him.

"Not since the night I almost froze to death in the mountains." He kissed her forehead and, laying his head back, shut his eyes.

Jangling bridles woke Sami. The light from the open front door shone across the drive. Charlie swung down from the carriage. Sami reached for his hand and he pulled her to him. Gathering her into his arms, he carried her up the steps.

Colby poked her head from the carriage.

"Can't be outdone by a bloody Englishman." Jeff wrapped his arms around her legs. She overbalanced, falling across his shoulder. He marched up the front steps.

"Here, buddy," Mac's voice rose over Colby's protests to be put down. "Let me help with that heifer." Jeff rolled Colby into Mac's waiting arms, tangling all three in her cape.

Mac gave Colby a squeeze and hefted her into the air. His arms dropped away. She squealed, the sound dying when Scotty caught her. She grasped his neck.

"Stop it." Colby gasped for air. She squirmed in his arms. Scotty set her upright, holding her until she steadied. "You're very kind, Scotty." she whispered.

"Mac, stop," Charlie protested as Mac scooped Sami away from him.

"Aww, let me have my baby girl," He swung her in a circle. Sami buried her head against his chest. "See? I know how to make her happy."

"Mac, she's tired," Charlie protested. "I'm taking her up to change."

"Not if I get her there first," Mac mounted the steps two at a time. Sami's laughter drifted in his wake.

***

"Charlie," Jessica spoke from the parlor door, "Come sit with us for a moment. We'd like to know how the evening unfolded." She held out a snifter to him. Charlie looked from her to the landing then shrugged off his coat.

Jeff joined them, settling on the floor by Chad's chair and throwing his tuxedo jacket over the arm. Chad handed him an acoustic guitar, picked up his own, launching into a capriccio. Jeff listened for a moment, studying Chad's fingering then joined in. The notes sounded in synchrony, the two guitars blending in harmonics.

"You know this piece?" Chad asked.

Jeff answered without looking up, "Yes, Legnani, isn't it?"

Chad chuckled. "On target."

Charlie drew a deep breath then exhaled. The music wrapped around his soul unraveling the knotted worry. He assessed the Yule log. He felt Jessica searching his face, her eyes dark with concern.

"Jess, I met my great grandmother tonight." He took her hand. "You know, Genevieve. Her portrait hangs on the landing. When I was little, I would sneak down at night. I could tell her anything and her smile soothed me. I know it was just the light and shadows." He let go of her fingers. "Silly, isn't?"

Before she could respond, he went on, "She is everything I imagined … gracious … kind. Her eyes pull at my soul. I wanted just to hear her voice. I abandoned Sami." He looked down, picking at the buttons on his shirt. "Thank goodness Jeff insisted they come along. I feel terrible."

"Charlie, don't be so hard on yourself. We're all off balance." Jessica lifted the empty snifter from his hand, pouring another splash. Charlie cupped the snifter, warming it. He looked around the room, studying each friend in turn.

Jessica held a snifter down for Jeff. He mouthed "Bourbon." She nodded. In a moment, she handed him a lowball. He motioned for Chad to play again. Chad launched into *Allegro Moderato* by Dionisia Aguado. The spirited music conjured the Spanish court.

Tori pushed the tea cart into the room, laden with mugs filled with hot chocolate and a platter of sugar cookies. Maeve bounded in, a large stick in her mouth. Scotty and Chris followed, each carrying firewood. The dog tossed the stick into the fire, barking. She settled at Scotty's hand signal, flopping across Jeff's legs. The room filled with crackling sound.

Mac returned, escorting Colby and Sami, one on each arm. Colby shimmered in a royal blue chiffon tea gown edged at neck and wrists with small white shells. The shells rattled softly as she moved. Charlie's eyes traveled up and down Sami's coral satin gown trimmed with eggshell lace.

My god, she is beautiful. He loved her in his shirts and leggings she so favored. *But in these clothes, she is breathtaking.* He opened his arms to her and she folded into his lap.

Tori picked up a mug, poured Jeff's bourbon into it, and backed into a wing chair. Scotty leaned over the back to kiss her hair. Pouring Scotch whiskey into his glass, he settled on the hearth. His arm resting on his knees, he gazed into the fire. Maeve groaned and stretched, pushing her rear paws against Scotty's leg.

The fire flickered and flared as a cold breeze ran through the room from the open front door.

"Well met, Harry." Nigel's bright voice echoed in the front hallway. "It is a foul night out." Nigel appeared from the foyer "Do I smell cocoa?"

Jessica held out a mug to him.

"Dear lady, what a charming offer but does it have a little John Barleycorn in it?" Jessica poured brandy into the mug. Nigel sank onto the loveseat next to Mac. "Ahhhhh, that is bracing."

Jeff picked up the guitar again. His fingers ran over the strings. Chad sat out, his eyes closed.

Harry carried a small furry bundle into the room and passed it to Scotty who tucked the cat in his lap where the fire's warmth would reach him. The last notes blended with a loud rumble from Pyewacket.

"I say, this is a congenial group," Nigel ventured. Looking at Charlie, he went on. "Genevieve was impressed with you, my boy. And …" He looked at Jeff, "Edward was definitely intrigued by your quotations from Madam Blavatsky. You are a surprise, young man."

All eyes turned on Jeff. He shrugged.

"It's his mom's fault." Mac guffawed, startling the group. "She has high falutin ideas … expected Jeff and me to read everything she left on our beds. I remember that piece. Odd stuff if you ask me. I'd guess the passage was something about give up self to nonself, being to nonbeing and then thou canst repose between the wings of the Great Bird."

Colby chimed in, "That was exactly the quote."

Jeff's baritone voice continued. "'Aye, sweet is rest between the wings of that which is not born nor dies, but the AUM throughout eternal age.'"

The silence was broken by the crackling fire and Pyewacket's small motor.

"I'm confused," Colby addressed Nigel. "It sounds like she was a positive force in the psychic world. If Lord Ramhill is a follower, how did he fall off the path?"

"Power, my dear," Nigel sipped then sighed. "Edward also knows Aleister Crowley. He has studied his book, *The Goetia.*"

"*The Lesser Key of Solomon*. But that's black magia." Chad looked at the puzzled faces. "Magia … or magic. It's a grimoire supposedly written by King Solomon but it didn't show up until the 17th century. It associates the 72 names of G-d with 72 demons."

"Quite right." Nigel chimed in. "King Solomon is reported to have summoned the demons and imprisoned them in a bronze vessel. I am quite certain Edward is functioning under the illusion if he can summon the demons, he can gain power over them and, through them, obtain everything he wants."

"It's nightmares for me after this conversation," Tori shifted, putting her empty mug on the floor. "He'd kill Niki to summon a demon? What about Lady Ramhill? Why doesn't she do something about it?"

"First, my dear, he already commands the lesser imps. It is rumored he has tried a greater demon and is convinced he failed because the sacrifice was not worthy. I don't know how he determined that but I am certain he will keep trying. While Genevieve is not without her own talents, she will need help to stop him. The Ramhill family practices perverse eugenics. The Ladies Ramhill are chosen as much for their special abilities as for their worldly qualities."

"Harry," Nigel looked around for him. "What did you discover below the stairs?"

"Sir, there is speculation about Lord Ramhill's new protégé. Lady Ramhill's maids were called to help a young woman found on the grounds." He looked around the room. "She thanked each by name then told them each something personal which she could not have known. The word is spreading regarding her apparent abilities."

"There was some behind the hands conversation as everyone was leaving tonight." Nigel's grin faded, "And the silly auto wouldn't start." Nigel stared into his cocoa.

Jeff rolled Maeve into Chris' lap and pulled himself up from the floor. Stretching, he grabbed the empty glass from the table and refilled it. "This time, it's going to stay in my hand." Tori laughed at him, holding out her hand. He relinquished it to her and poured another. He clinked glasses with her.

"Harry, is there more to tell? It's well past midnight." Jeff leaned against the doorframe.

"A little, sir." Harry looked at Mac, "In case storming the walls becomes necessary, I found out Miss Kasavina is being kept in a chamber on the third floor in the tower hall. Anna Simpson has been assigned to assist her. Though the house staff lives at the manor house, I may be able to find out more through her mother."

Sami pushed away from Charlie's arms. "I'm off to bed." She rose and looked around the room. "Thank you all. I pray the morning will bring better news."

Chad picked up his guitar. He strummed, humming the melody line. Charlie followed Chad's fingering, running the notes through his mind seeking the name and artist.

Sami felt his attention drift away from her. She leaned to his ear, "Stay and enjoy the music, darling." She kissed his cheek. She lifted the long skirt and edged past Chad. Jeff offered her his arm and they ascended the stairs. Mac picked up Jeff's discarded guitar filling the room with a soft melody from the bayous.

Jessica's shadow flickered across Colby's vision, the firelight behind her. She blinked, waking from her reverie.

Jessica handed Colby a snifter. "I don't think sugar cookies will go with this but they do smell good. Tori drove Harry to distraction. She works as fast as she talks and leaves destruction behind her."

Colby yawned, her eyes large and luminous.

"Colby, I will go up with you."

"Jess, I can't fit all the pieces in my head together. And every time it seems right, my heart aches and distracts me." She finished the cognac. "I'm seeing things ... places, people ... that might be important but I don't know what it means."

Jessica pulled Colby to her feet. "At this late hour, nothing is going to make sense. A good night's sleep, a brisk walk in the morning then we'll talk about the things in your head."

Colby yawned again, cracking her jaw. Arm in arm, the two women left the parlor.

The soft music carried them up the stairs and into their dreams.

CHAPTER 43

December 30th

Mac stretched his legs across the horse-drawn cab and pulled his ten-gallon hat lower. "Perfect morning for a ride in the country."

"Never mind this poor working-class stiff. I'm just fine." Chris shouted from above the cab, jiggling the reins.

Jessica studied the passing countryside. A cool breeze blew her hair around her face.

"If you'd like to continue the bass lesson, you should sit a little closer." Mac patted the seat beside him.

"Mac, there's no excuse for my behavior the other night." She did not look at him.

"I was hoping you'd tell me I'm irresistible, especially when I'm sweaty," Mac quipped.

She turned to face him, "Mac, it's not that—"

"Jess, relax. I love to flirt with beautiful women but I know I'm not in your league." He scanned the horizon. "What a privilege to see this beautiful land in pristine condition. I realize there's pollution already but so little development."

Jessica looked around. "You're right. Now, there's houses all over this meadow."

The cab slowed to a stop. The carriage rocked under Chris's weight as he descended. Landing on the ground, he held out his hand to Jessica. Mac remained still.

Chris stared at him. "Have you become landed gentry that you need to step on my back?"

Mac swung to the ground. "Yeah, yeah. I know it's all a nefarious plot to make me feel guilty so I'll drive home and you can plant your lecherous hands on the fair Lady Jess."

Chris scowled at him.

"Mac." Jessica drew his attention to the overlook. "The manor house is edged by stone walls along the south and west. You can see the North Sea to the east. The border on the north is a hedgerow with stone breakers at odd intervals. The wildness beyond is for hunting."

Mac studied the estate. The large Georgian manor sat halfway between the heavy iron gates and the cliffs. A stable, and a more recent construction, stood several feet behind the house. On the northeast, a formal garden spread outward from the house to a hedgerow labyrinth.

Despite the cold blustery day, a wind with summer scents blew gently around Jess. She stared at the manor house. "In our time, the tower behind the house is gone. We never go into the labyrinth."

"The ley lines are twisted." Mac's voice shook, his fists held at his side.

Jessica laid her hand on Mac's shoulder, feeling the agitation in his aura. "Show me." She closed her eyes melding her energy with his. Dark inky lines surrounded the house extending from the black brambles forming the labyrinth.

"I thought ley lines run straight." Her breath tickled his ear.

"They've been perverted." He whirled to face them. "That takes blood sacrifice." Sweat stood out on his forehead. "I was in a place like that once. I got out. My friend didn't. I'm not going to lose any more."

Chris nodded, clapping him on the shoulder. "Let's start planning then. See if you can find any weaknesses in the building. Every place has them. If we're to get them out, we'll need a major distraction. Something that will satisfy Tori's desire for chaos." He chuckled.

"You're right." Mac pulled out his inclinometer and a sketch pad. The manor's image took shape in short, decisive strokes. "I need a better look at the foundation. Have to get closer." He tucked the sketchpad away.

"Mac, you'll give us away." Jessica grabbed his arm.

"Pretty lady, study the winds and think about lightning, will you? The tower has me intrigued." He ran a finger down her nose and grinned at her. "Trust me."

He mounted the carriage. "I'll be back within an hour." Mac shook the reins setting the horse in motion.

"Mac, hold on." Jessica grabbed the bridle. "Remember, that's my home you're planning to destroy."

Mac clucked to the horse, urging him into a fast trot.

CHAPTER 44

Edward sipped his tea, considering the strained look on his man's face. Westfield's demeanor had changed overnight … in a manner Lord Ramhill could not identify. *Has Genevieve been meddling?* The thought nagged him but the young man in the smuggler's cell interested him more.

"Westfield, bring him up."

Westfield bowed and tripped the hidden latch to the stairway inside the tower wall. He descended into the darkness, his tread heavy on the stone steps. The staff caring for young man reported strange events. He refused to eat, uncommon for the normal riffraff prey. The rats leave him alone. An owl appeared on the tower. It stared at the servants through the day and would not be scared away.

"What his Lordship wants, his Lordship gets," he mumbled, pulling back the bar. The heavy wooden door swung outward. Westfield stepped into the empty cell. He drew breath to yell for the steward. Niki dropped on him from above, riding him to the ground. Straddling the larger man, Niki grabbed Westfield's hair, pushing his face into the stone.

"I wouldn't if you wish to save your sister." Westfield lay still.

Niki paused. Shifting his knee on Westfield's back, he bore down with all his weight.

"Explain."

"She is under his Lordship's control. He is cruel when crossed."

"How do you know she's my sister?"

"The Lordship has his ways. She had no choice but to answer his questions. He will send down a small army if I do not reappear. His Lordship requires punctuality."

Niki rolled off and stepped back.

Westfield rose to his full height and dusted his coat. He rubbed his wrist easing the pain from the fall. His shoulders filled the doorway, cutting off any exit.

"If you will please place your hands together," Westfield's voice remained polite. "I must at least make the pretense you are restrained."

Before Niki could move, Westfield held both wrists in one large hand and slipped on a silk cord. Niki pulled back, the cord cutting into his wrists.

"I wouldn't, sir." Westfield loosened the cords, securing the ends.

"I bet you catch snakes." Niki flexed his fingers.

"I spent my youth in India. The house boy taught me a few tricks. If you would, sir." Westfield indicated the doorway.

Niki gave him a half bow and entered the long stone hallway. The hallway ended at a heavy wooden door, opening into the dim cellar.

To the left, wooden crates and burlap sacks filled the large space. To the right, a wooden lattice divided the provisions from the wine cellar. Wine racks ran off into the darkness. Westfield placed a hand on Niki's shoulder and guided him to the right. He unlocked the grilled door in the lattice wall.

"Lord Ramhill enjoys excellent wine. This is the finest collection in England including Buckingham Palace." Westfield surveyed the bottles with pride.

"Is he the connoisseur, or are you?" Niki looked up at him.

Westfield fixed a stern eye on him. "His lordship is the master in all things here. You would do well to remember."

"I doubt I will have long to worry about it."

"I regret so but one does what one must." Westfield nudged him farther into the gloom, continuing to a stone wall. Moving a stone on the top edge, the wall slid aside.

"Interesting." Niki peered into the dark stairway.

"What I find interesting is how you managed to free yourself from the chains. But having seen Mr. Houdini's escapades, I know the impossible can be possible for the correct individual."

***

Several steps upward, a panel slid aside filling the stairway with bright light. Niki shielded his eyes with his hands. Westfield steered him to stand in the pentagram carved into the floor, scorch marks radiating from the points.

He kept his hands over his face, allowing his senses to expand. The walls bristled with dark power. He sensed another presence, a youth … his energy in turmoil. Niki's questing brushed against sharp spikes and stinging energy throughout the room. He pulled back.

Imps on the shelves, over the door and the windows. He shut down his probing, waiting for their alarm. Rustling in the corners, calculated to frighten him he was certain, reached his ears. He shivered.

"Ahh, I see. You are sensitive to my pets. I require answers. We can do this the easy way … or the hard way." Edward sat in a chair beside the fireplace. Kay knelt motionless at his side, her long auburn hair hanging down over her face. He rose. "As you can see." He grabbed Kay by the hair raising her face. "I have a trump. Her welfare depends on your answers."

Niki remained with his face covered.

"Take your hands down, boy!" Edward took a step towards him.

Niki dropped his hands.

Edward stepped closer, grabbing him by the chin and raising his face to the light. "You are younger than I thought. The question is what are you?" He turned his back on Niki. "Why would she risk herself for you? Personal survival is the code in the streets." He stood next to Kay.

"Who are you?" he demanded.

"What, me, gov'ner," Niki affected a street accent. "I'm no one, sir. Just a goniff and pimp for the girl. She may be my sister but she's my meal ticket, your lordship."

"Interesting." Edward ran his hand along Kay's jaw and across her collar bone. "Then you won't mind if I sample the wares." He placed his hand under her chin and drew her to her feet. Pulling her head back, he kissed her, biting her lip. Blood ran down her chin.

Niki fought his anger, desperately trying to stop any projection the imps might sense. Edward released her. Niki reached out to her but she remained motionless, his call finding no response. Red glinted on her throat where blood dripped.

Morrigan. S*he's wearing that damn necklace. No wonder he got the demon into her.*

"Adrian, it is time you assisted in the preparations." Edward spoke to the young man standing in the shadows. "Set the candles."

Adrian placed tall black candles at the points, staying away from the circle's edge.

His resemblance to Charlie startled Niki. The same grey eyes … lighter hair. Niki felt a tentative probe slide along his defenses and traced it back to Adrian. He repulsed the contact sending a mild shock along the tendril. Adrian stiffened, looking Niki in the eye. He dipped his head a fraction, hiding the smirk on his face. He stepped back, his task complete.

Lord Ramhill assessed the placement. He spoke a guttural word and the candles flamed to life. Dark smoke poured out forming a circle around the pentagram. "I will have correct answers. The outcome is inevitable, boy."

Niki felt a presence crawling up with the smoke. It sank long claws into his thigh, climbing to his shoulder. The room disappeared, lost in the smoke enshrouding him. The demon pressed himself between Niki's shoulder blades, melting into him. A cold fog wrapped around his consciousness. It gloated. He waited until the demon settled within his chest. He reached out, catching it about the throat.

The demon struggled, thrashing, claws flying.

I know your name. You will not betray me.

He knows my name. The demon spat at him. *"Or I wouldn't be here, you mongoose spawn. He controls me ... not you."*

He knows your working name and keeps you from home, Asbalam. He felt the demon cringe. *"I know the name your father cursed you with, Obranim."*

The demon convulsed, clawing at the grip around his neck.

How? Who? Fiery eyes promised eternal punishment. The demon writhed, clawing at Niki's chest.

Sit. Niki hissed at him.

Niki opened his eyes. The smoke dissipated, running in swirling tails across the ceiling. Edward studied him from beyond the circle.

"Drop your act. Your sister is both articulate and educated." He picked up a small bone and tapped it against the desk. The noise set the imps scratching sharp claws on the woodwork.

"Tell me who you are."

"Not much to tell. Just passing through." Niki responded, dropping the street accent.

Edward tapped the bone twice on the desk. The demon in Niki's mind cringed alerting him a response was expected. Niki shuddered, raising his hands to cover his face. Edward nodded.

"Let's try again." He grabbed Kay's wrist pulling her back to her knees at his side. His fingers ran through her silky hair. "Are you from London?"

"No." Niki replied.

"Is your family from England?"

"No." Niki repeated.

"Explain." Edward demanded.

"My father's from the Ukraine and my mother is Irish."

"Very good. You have given the same answers." Edward stared at him.

Small clawed feet skittered on the shelves breaking the silence. Niki tried not to glance their way.

"Do you possess psychic abilities?"

What has Kay told him? He felt Adrian shift in the shadows. "Yes."

"Do you have family or anyone in England?" Edward's voice filled with menace.

Niki allowed despair into his voice. "No."

Edward smiled. He forced Kay's chin up establishing eye contact. "Is he telling the truth?" She nodded. He released her. He tapped the bone again … on the tarot card's burnt halves.

"How did you get here last night?"

"I don't know how I got here. It was not by choice." Niki put a little whine in his tone reinforcing his apparent youth.

"Your answer also corresponds but unfortunately for you, it is not one I accept. How did you get here?" Edward leaned across the desk.

"I don't know." Niki answered. "One minute I was sitting in the kitchen and the next, I was in the cell."

Edward's face clouded over.

Holding out his burned hand, Niki continued, "It was not without pain."

Edward stared at him. A slight nod. "A summoning." He picked up the two pieces, one in each hand. "How did you get this?"

"It was a gift." Niki looked Edward in the eye.

"From whom?" He stepped toward Niki, his face reddening.

"I don't know." Niki maintained eye contact. The demon leapt to escape. Niki shifted his attention inward, smacking the demon down. *No, you don't.* The demon curled into a ball.

Niki returned his awareness to him, too late to dodge the backhand blow. He staggered, stepping over the inscribed circle. Edward grabbed him by both arms and shook him.

"I will ask you one more time." He spoke through gritted teeth. "I painted this card. You had half the card, the other half in her hand. But my card is still in my deck." He pulled Niki closer. "How did you get this card?"

Niki repeated his answer, "I don't know."

Edward drew back his hand and Niki reflexively covered his face. He heard Edward chuckle, the sound chilling him. He lowered his hands.

"It seems you are used to a blow or two." Edward released him. He stepped around the desk once again drawing Kay up close to him. He kissed her bloody lips, running his tongue down her chin. He backhanded her, sending her to the floor. Niki stepped forward, restrained by Westfield's hand on his shoulder.

Edward sat in his chair. "I will have answers. I will find—and I will kill—the individual who dared to enter this room. And you will help me find the guilty party or I will find interesting ways to take out my frustration on…" He extended a hand to Kay. She placed her fingers in his palm. "As you can see, my control over her is absolute. She will deny me nothing." He swung his chair to gaze out the window.

"Westfield, take him back." Westfield guided Niki toward the hidden stair. Niki noticed Adrian slip out the hall door.

"Then return the lady to her chamber. And, Westfield … next time, do not be so careless."

Westfield's hand tightened on Niki's shoulder. "Yes, my lord." He pushed Niki into the dark stairwell.

CHAPTER 45

Jessica pointed to the horse-drawn cab disappearing down the winding road. "Does he always go charging off?"

Chris nodded. "The man is larger than life in all ways. He canna stand to see anyone mistreated, more so those he cares about. And he wasn't pleased with the idea Chad would get a look at the place first."

Jessica opened the picnic basket. "Mac doesn't look like a grocer's boy." She spread out the woolen blanket. "I hope Chad doesn't run into trouble with Pye in the box." She handed him a biscuit. Chris snorted. Jessica shook her head at him. "Don't say it."

"But, my dear Lady Jessica, I've always wondered who let the cat out!"

Jessica sighed. "I wonder how long a transformation spell would work on you. I may have to practice soon. I'm thinking you'd be an adorable ferret."

"Now, lass, you wouldn't."

She didn't answer. Chris studied his hands, checking for fur. Jessica scanned the sky. Tension lined her eyes. Chris fidgeted with the biscuit, making crumbs for the small birds moving in the scrub.

"You can increase my strength with your skill." She continued to stare at a cloud west of the manor. "See that cloud? Play your ocarina."

Chris palmed the instrument. He studied the cloud.

"Call to it. Use the gentle coaxing manner you do with animals. Seduce it with your song." Her silken voice caressed his ear. "Your wildness and love for our friends may be the saving grace."

He glanced at her, sweating under her intense gaze. "I hate storms," he whispered.

She considered him for a long moment. He fidgeted, concerned she would dismiss him from her plans. He pulled out the ocarina, seeking a questing tune.

The cloud drifted closer. *That's just normal*, he thought. Black ravens burst from the woods beyond the manor, their cries strafing the sky. Jessica uttered several sibilant syllables, raising the hair on his neck. The cloud darkened, roiling upward above the labyrinth, the horizon greying behind it.

Exhilaration swept through him. He stood, planting his feet, breathing deeply and changing the tune. The dark clouds, the wind, sharp claws flashed through his mind igniting his fear. *Not this time*, he shouted at himself. *If evil abides there, let's tickle its toes.*

Lightning crackled through the sky, meeting the earth within the labyrinth. Black stones exploded upward, raining down on the garden. Darkness rose from the ground, grasping at the sky. Thunder deafened him, his music sounding in his head.

Chris let out a whoop, dancing in place. Turning to Jessica, his laughter died. She swayed, face ashen. He followed her gaze. An oily mist rose from the labyrinth. It boiled over the shrubbery walls, slinking, sliding toward the manor house.

Jessica uttered a wild cry, the wind swirling around her, knocking Chris to his knees. She swept her arm in a wide circle, gathering the windlings and thrusting them toward the manor. The mist coalesced, ice crystals glinting in the scattered sunlight. The winds swept the mist around the inky mass, tugging it away from the manor, the tornado gathering up dirt. The wind flung the darkness over the cliff into the ocean below.

***

Mac slowed the cab before the carved oak doors. A groom appeared from around the corner, skidding and grabbing the gelding's harness. Mac leapt from the seat.

"I won't be long, lad. Keep him steady." He pulled off his hat and lifted the heavy brass knocker.

"Yes, milord?" A maid in a white cap peeked around the door.

"Miss?" Mac smiled at her and applied his best soft drawl. "I'm a visitor in England. I saw the manor from the Downs." He leaned close to the young woman and continued, "I'm an architect and I have some concerns about the tower back there." He edged into the foyer. "I'd like to tour the manor. I'll wait while you inquire. Thank you."

Wide-eyed, she curtseyed and scurried up the stairs.

Mac studied the wide hall, the doors leading off to the library on the left, a lady's study on the right. Hallways disappeared on both sides of the stairway. He moved to the left. The light from the ballroom windows glinted across the polished floors.

Rustling silk drew his attention. A petite woman with vivid blue eyes descended. Her high, white collar, redolent with lace, highlighted her dark hair.

Dowdy but deliberately so. He admired her high cheek bones and strong jaw line.

She smiled at him, her blue eyes dancing. "You have me at a disadvantage, sir. My new maid did not request a card."

"My apologies, ma'am. I'm visiting from America and don't have a card. And in my haste, I did not give her my name. I'm John B. MacIntyre, ma'am. There is a structural element I noticed in your home when I was up on the Downs. Ha ha," Mac guffawed. "I bet you get that a lot." He shuffled his feet, trying to look abashed at his feeble attempt at humor.

Genevieve's eyes danced, observing him closely. She proceeded him into the parlor and sat by a small table, spreading her skirts. Mac perched on the chair opposite, running the hat rim through his hands.

"I was startled to see such a classic architectural mistake. I'm concerned for your safety, ma'am. See the crack in the wall over there?" Mac gestured to the wall adjoining the ballroom.

"My dear sir, it is quite rude to discuss one's failings so pointedly this early in an acquaintance." The maid returned with a tea service. Genevieve poured. "Would you care for milk or sugar in your tea?"

"No, thank you, ma'am." He accepted the cup. "I wouldn't hurt your feelings for the world, ma'am but I have read so much about this fault. I'd feel terrible if I didn't explain what could happen."

"Proceed." She lifted the cup to her lips and looked at him over the edge. Her long eyelashes and the artful color on her eyelids captivated him.

"Well, this whole area is built on limestone and chalk. Are there caves leading down to the water?"

"If you know this area, then you are aware this is a smuggler's haven. Precisely what do you wish to know?"

Phew. Mac took a deep breath. *Good thing I'm telling her the truth. Guile won't hold much water here.* "I'm concerned your tower room might collapse. The cracks indicate a serious flaw in the foundation. I can execute some drawings which will explain the problem and a possible solution. You'll want to speak to your own people but when I go home to Louisiana, I'd have bragging rights if I could say I saved a noble's home. Though, I must admit, my clients have greater fondness for the French."

She laughed out loud, a genuine laugh. It washed over Mac wiping away any dowdy image. Her aura sparkled. He could be locked in conversation with her for eternity and wouldn't mind a bit.

"Mr. MacIntyre, you are most amusing. What brings you to England?"

"My friend, Charlie, is always going on about his relatives. We're staying at Foxhaven. A couple friends and I wanted some fresh air so we rode out on the Downs. Magnificent view. But then I noticed the slight lean to the tower. Well, here I am, ma'am."

"Nigel never ceases to amaze me with the family members he dredges up. I met Charles and his wife last evening. I am told she is Gordon's niece."

Mac nodded in response. She rose. Mac launched to his feet.

"I cannot deny a request from Nigel's friends. You may examine the rooms on this floor and the foundations around the outside. But my husband is engaged in his study upstairs and you may not disturb him." She pulled on the bell cord. "We are having a small event on New Year's Eve. I will look forward to hearing your findings then. Will that give you enough time?"

Mac nodded.

"Very well." A pretty snub-nosed maid entered the room.

"My Gawd, they grow them big in the Colonies, don't they now?" She curtseyed and blushed, lowering her eyes. She sank into a deeper curtsey and remained.

"Anna, that is quite enough." Genevieve raised an eyebrow at the girl. "Anna is new and requires an additional lesson or two in propriety." She commanded the young woman's attention. "Anna, escort Mr. MacIntyre through the downstairs rooms and around the perimeter. Do not disturb his Lordship." She addressed Mac. "Do not disappoint me and try to make away with the silverware ..." She glanced at Anna, "or the maid."

She offered Mac her hand. He wished for a century or two to appreciate this woman. Lady Ramhill left the room. Anna glanced at Mac, the color still high on her cheeks.

"Ma'am, we may be big in America, but nothing can beat a beautiful English rose." He held out his hand to help her rise. She shot to her feet, avoiding his touch.

"Do you want to start in the ballroom?" She studied his face but kept her distance.

"Anywhere the tower attaches to the original manor house." He followed her into the foyer.

"It's on the first floor, sir." She skipped a step to keep up with his long stride. "The tower was added about ten years ago, under orders by the old Lord Ramhill. My Da was a workman. He's a stone mason."

Mac stopped at the doorway to the ballroom. The older building opened to meet the tower, cracks around the doorframe indicating settling.

"Anna, what's on the floors above?"

"The next floor is Lord Ramhill's study. We're not allowed in there even to clean. Mister Westfield sees to it himself." Her cheek dimpled when she mentioned Westfield. She dropped her voice to a whisper and pulled his sleeve to make him bend down. "And the next floor has two bedchambers ... for his Lordship's special guests. If you know what I mean."

Mac chuckled remembering the nobility's foibles were the soap opera for those below the stairs. Anna danced before him telling tales. They descended through the kitchen to the rear door. Curious eyes followed him, the kitchen staff clanging pots, orders shouted in a harsh male voice with a French accent.

Mac settled his hat against the bright sunlight. He estimated the distance from the house to the stables and the garage. Then he followed the foundation to the tower's base. The large stones were well mounted and mortared.

"Young lady, tell your father he does excellent work. These stones are firmly set and mortar has weathered well. It's a shame the ground is shifting." He pointed to a finger-wide crack running vertically up the wall near the joining.

"No, sir." She lowered her voice. "It's them spirits trying to get out." She glanced at the grooms milling around the stable door.

"What?" Mac looked at her.

"I hear them cry at night. I'm not crazy. Story is the old Lord Ramhill caught them trying to use the smuggler's caves. Hear tell, he put them to better use. They're buried down there ... holding up the walls."

Mac placed a hand on the stone. Cold fingers ran down his back. His eyes unfocused, seeing the minor ley lines curving away from the tower and blood along the foundation. He shook himself, gnashing his teeth.

"Stars and garters, sir, I didn't mean to upset you." Anna peered up into his face. "I'm sorry. Me mum says I'll get myself in trouble with my wild talk."

Mac pulled free from the stone face, continuing his circuit around the base, the labyrinth appearing ahead. "Have you ever been in there?"

"Oh, no, sir. Lord Ramhill don't allow anyone in there. He says it is because you'd get lost forever. And it's guarded by those hellhounds." She shivered. "They're enough to scare a body good."

Mac scanned the labyrinth, assessing the size. *Large enough to contain several layers before opening to the core. Tricky business without the key configuration.* He'd solved several labyrinths and mazes with a hand-on-the-wall approach but some were constructed to foil that strategy.

Wind lifted his hat. Clamping it back on his head, he glanced upward. A cloud boiled above them, growing darker. Static raised the hair on his neck.

Grabbing Anna, he pinned her against the wall, his back to the labyrinth. Crackling tore through the air. Ozone burned his nose. Anna's fine red hair danced around her face. Her wide green eyes stared at him. She twisted gamely around him trying to see.

"Gawh, where'd that come from?" She pointed a shaking hand at the labyrinth. A black mist rose from the center. The foulness touched Mac's skin, acrid bile filling his throat.

The windlings flashed around the tower, swirling in a funnel cloud. The two masses contorted around each other. Dust stung Mac's eyes. Ice crystals danced in the air, the light draining the energy from the black mist pushing it over the cliffs.

Mac grabbed Anna's hand, pulling her away. At the kitchen door, he let her go. He swept his hat from his head and bowed, bringing his lips close to her ear. "Be careful, little miss. Avoid his Lordship's notice. Thank you for your help."

He ran to the waiting cab. He waved his hat at her and set the horse trotting down the driveway.

CHAPTER 46

The explosion rent the air, shaking dust from the ceiling above the stairs. Edward staggered. He grasped the wooden banister, coughing, spitting blood on the floor.

"We'll see about this." He raised his head. Dizziness washed over him. "Westfield, bring the girl back to the study. And my son!" He staggered against the door frame.

He waved off Westfield's hand. "I don't need your help."

I will not be stopped any longer. I will possess that house.

***

"We did it!" Chris' face lit up, his eyes gleaming. His head snapped back from her slap.

"Don't ever do that again!" Jessica glared at him.

"Do what, lass?" Chris worked his jaw.

"Take over. Take charge … like all the men I know." Her eyes glistened with unshed tears.

"Now, I was just doin' what you asked."

"And more." Jessica sank to the ground, her dark hair writhing. After a moment, she shuddered and looked up at Chris. "Chris, I didn't explain what we were doing. But lightning was not what I expected."

"What did you want?" Chris squatted beside her.

"Just to find out if we could work together."

Chris laughed. "It looks like it worked."

"But we've warned him there are powers out here… and people after him." She rose, dusting off her skirt. "It's my fault. I should have worked with you differently."

"How did you learn?" Chris followed her to the edge.

"By making stupid mistakes." She gathered up the basket and blankets. "Like we just did."

The harness' jangle alerted them to Mac's return. He waved his hat above his head, whooping wildly.

***

Nigel strolled into the ornate library, hoping for a little good luck. His eyes found the labyrinth through the window, the remembered lightning and the forbidding miasma draining his courage. *I would rather sink into that chair and shake for several hours. Perhaps days. But the young ones need the map.*

He straightened his shoulders and glanced around to assure he was alone. He reached for the pull on the corner cabinet.

"Nigel, dear, I assume you will be visiting with our relatives."

Nigel jumped, shaken to be surprised.

Genevieve straightened his tie, the small gesture calming his racing heart. "What do you know about the sudden storm?"

"A freak occurrence, I am certain. Nothing to worry about." Nigel took out his handkerchief and wiped his face.

Genevieve cocked her head, studying him. "Nigel, you are a lousy liar. I tasted magic, wind magic. Is there one in their party with that talent?"

"Genevieve, I do not wish to lie to you again." Nigel took her hand, pulling it to his lips.

Genevieve laughed. "You are playing with fire but you know that. Do be careful." She pulled her hand away and retrieved a vanilla linen envelope from her pocket. "I enjoyed meeting young Charles and his wife. Will you take the invitation to the New Year's party?" She looked up at him, her blue eyes dancing in the light. "That was your goal, wasn't it?"

"Genevieve, the only smart thing my brother has ever done was marry you. You are clever, beautiful … dazzling. And might I add," he stepped back to look her up and down, "your outfit today is a smasher. What say you, we run off together. Leave all this nonsense? We could create great mischief." Nigel presented his most beguiling gaze.

Genevieve burst out laughing.

"Nigel, you make the sun appear through the storm clouds." Her face darkened. "Gather what you must and be gone." Genevieve paused at the door. "Try the new automobile. It might amuse your guests."

Nigel fumbled through the maps and drawings, glancing repeatedly at the doorway. Finding the one he sought, he tucked it under his coat and hurried out the front door.

***

Edward looked out on the labyrinth from the study window, his arm draped across Kay's shoulders. "My dear, you will be well cared for, I assure you. We will spend much time together."

Westfield opened the door, waving Adrian into the study. Adrian stepped a short distance into the room. Edward turned.

"Westfield, you will accompany Adrian this afternoon. I was not intending to honor this request but Nigel's loose tongue has provided a unique chance to assess Foxhaven." He fingered the fine cream paper. Sami's eyes rose in his mind. He smiled at the fearful scent his touch had evoked. "I must devise the appropriate thanks for the young woman who is unlocking the door." Edward wove his fingers through Kay's hair pulling her head back. A moan escaped Kay's lips.

"Ah, you like that, do you, little demon." He kissed her roughly, leaving her lips bruised. He motioned to Adrian. "Come here, boy. Have a taste. Demon possession imparts a smoky flavor."

Adrian stumbled toward the desk.

"What are you waiting for? About time you weren't a whey-faced virgin." He chuckled at the flush on his son's face. "I thought so. Not even a kiss from that doe-eyed girl." Edward laughed.

"It would not be proper, Father." Adrian protested.

"Proper? Who cares what is proper? As my son, you shouldn't." He shoved Kay at Adrian. He caught her, tripping backward. The rapid growth in his fifteenth year stole any grace.

"Kiss her, you damn fool." Edward glared at him. "You will be lord here after me. Time you behave like one. You can do better than that stupid girl who slaughters the piano."

Adrian tightened his hold on Kay. She leaned into his chest, burying her face against his neck. "But you said she would be an appropriate wife. Her breeding."

"Of course, her breeding. Adrian, you will learn breeding is all that she will be good for. Wed her, bed her, and produce an heir." He sneered at the boy. "But for pleasure, you must look elsewhere. Good breeding is not satisfying in the bedchamber."

Kay's breath fanned his neck. His heart rate climbed.

"She is willing."

The blood drain from Adrian's face.

"Or I should say, the demon is."

"You haven't done this with the others. Why her?" Adrian fidgeted, his hand behind his back.

"This one is different," Edward circled the two, running his hand down Kay's back. Adrian shifted, keeping her between them.

"I do miss the struggle. It imparts a different quality but I don't want this one hurt. She is too valuable." Edward returned to the desk, picking up the boline knife. "It is time you entered your training." He held the knife out in his hand. "And I don't mean your Mother's insipid magick." He pulled the blade from the sheath, flipping it over and presenting the handle. "Take it."

"What for?" Adrian pulled back a step. His father grabbed his hand and slapped the cold, bone handle into his grip.

"Don't question me, boy. Do what you are told. Cut her on the wrist. Taste her blood."

Adrian grasped the knife. His hand shook. He lifted Kay's arm, pulling back the dark sleeve. He stared at the blue veins running under the skin. "I am sorry," he murmured drawing the blade across her wrist.

Edward grabbed Kay's wrist, forcing it against Adrian's mouth, smearing blood on his lips. "Go on. I don't have all day. Now, kiss her."

Adrian leaned down touching his lips to hers. She slipped her arms around his neck and kissed him hungrily. Pulling away, he stared at her dead eyes.

"She will obey you and perform for Nigel's guests." He grabbed Kay by the shoulders pushing her away from Adrian. Once again, he chuckled at his son's obvious growing discomfort. "Observe those people, Adrian. Get their measure. I must know who they are. And what they may be." He paced to the window, staring out at the bright daylight. "Find a way I can possess that house."

He paced across the room. "If you care to share this wealth with me, then you must prove yourself worthy. You are dismissed to dress. She will be waiting downstairs in your mother's study."

Adrian stumbled out the door.

Grabbing Kay's arm, Edward looked into her eyes. He rubbed his thumb over the smeared blood on her wrist. "Mrs. Ramhill interests me deeply." He pulled her head back, snarling into her face. "Don't fail me."

CHAPTER 47

Chad sat on the wagon seat next to the grocer's boy. He tried to keep the box in his lap from bouncing, leaning on it to rub his hands against the cold. Grey overcast skies filtered the afternoon sun. He glanced at the emaciated youth beside him. The box shifted and he tightened his grip.

The cart pulled up the long driveway, stones crunching under the team's hooves. It rumbled to a stop behind the house. A tall man dressed in an elegant black long coat stood in the kitchen door.

"Becker, you are late." His face was stern.

"It's just after noon time, Mr. Westfield." He cringed not meeting Westfield's eye. "And me Da broke his leg and I 'ad to find this help, sir. But we've got everything, sir."

Westfield looked Chad over. "Well, at least you found an able-bodied assistant." He addressed the scrawny man dressed all in white beside him. "Chef Gibard, I will leave them to you."

The chef waved his hands this way and that at the wagon backing up to the cellar doors.

"Not that I haven't done this every week for the last four years." Becker muttered under his breath. "What's so blinkin' important you'd carry that box up here?"

"Eggs from Mr. Harry."

The wagon jerked to a stop.

"Drop 'em off and come help me with the barrels."

Chad dove into the cellar. He paused waiting for his eyes to adjust to the dimness. Setting the box in a far corner, he loosened the top. "Okay, Pye. Be sure to wait until it's quiet."

A soft mrrrwww answered him.

"Good luck … and be careful."

Chad hefted the barrels, grunting with the weight. They carried fifty-pound flour sacks, and boxes filled with fresh vegetables. Out from under Westfield's watchful eye, the small chef talked rapid fire, describing each epicurean delight planned for the Ramhill's New Year's Eve event. He regaled them with descriptions from past years.

"This year must top them all."

Chad ground his teeth. *All this for one party. It'd feed half the town for a month.*

The inventory completed, Becker slipped an apple in one pocket and a potato in the other. Chad kept his expression bland and followed him out. They hauled the bulkhead doors closed, the little man rattling the lock to assure security.

Becker shook the reins, the draft horses hauling the cart into motion, forcing Chad to swing up on the run. They rode in silence along the driveway. Beyond the gate, Chad pulled two tins, sardines and crackers from his pockets. He set them on the seat. Becker stared at him.

"Thought these'd go well with your apple."

The boxes disappeared under the wooden seat. "Me Da's fair partial to sardines." He didn't take his eyes from the road. "Haven't had any since his accident, him not workin' and all."

They fell into silence for a few more moments. Chad murmured a prayer for Pyewacket… and for Kay. *Damn but I want to talk with her again.*

Becker cleared his throat. "Thanks, mate. Mister Harry's friend are always Da's. You pulled yur weight."

Chad smiled. He swung off the seat, landing in the dust. Raising his hand, he shouted, "Thanks for the ride. I'll get back on my own."

Becker shook his head. *Crazy Yanks.*

***

Pyewacket crouched in the box, his tail twitching against the sides. The doors closed with a heavy thunk. He waited, straining his ears for any sound. He relaxed his shoulder muscles when he heard the skittering, small claws on the stone floor. His nose twitched at the rodent scent.

He nudged the box lid aside, scanning the aisle. Leaping from the box, he surprised the rat. Chittering in protest, it disappeared under the sacks. Pyewacket's attention fixated on the disappearing tail. He wrestled with the urge to give chase.

He followed Niki's scent to the rough oak door. He hooked a claw under the edge but it wouldn't move. Jumping to snag the latch, it gave under his weight but the door remained closed. He backed into the narrow space between two boxes, frustration gnawing at him.

Niki, Pyewacket sent out.

Imps! Rat!

The response raised his fur from head to tail tip. Pyewacket arched his back and hissed. Feeling eyes on him, he settled belly flat and froze. The watchers lost interest, their scrutiny no longer brushing his fur the wrong direction.

One muscle at a time, he crawled around the crate, searching. He sniffed at a crack in the wall close to the door. His whiskers brushed against the damp walls. *Too narrow. But Niki's in there somewhere.* He shivered, wishing for Jeff. *What would he do?* Pyewacket mewed.

A small, black nose appeared from the inky darkness. Shivering, the brown rat tentatively approached her natural predator. She stopped at the edge and crouched, licking her paws to wash her ears.

Pyewacket remained still. *That's the same way I do it.* His ears itched. Niki talked to all the animals but Pyewacket was certain only the felines could carry on a decent conversation. *Maybe ... just maybe.*

Do you know where he is?

Pyewacket kept his thought pointed, looking into the black eyes. He built Niki's image. The rat chattered, running into the tunnel.

Wait! Come back!

The black nose poked from the hole, whiskers twitching. In her eyes, Pyewacket saw a shadowed figure … his head in his hands.

Niki! Pyewacket scrambled to keep control.

She bounded backward beyond his reach.

Madame Rat! Pyewacket begged. *Please take me with you.*

The rat sat up straight, staring at him. She nodded her head.

Pyewacket remembered flying through the clouds in Jeff's arms. He took a deep breath, closed his eyes and reached out to her. A deep drumming sound filled his ears, vibrating through his body.

That's it, Pye, Jeff's voice sound close.

Pyewacket startled, scanning the darkness.

The imps aren't used to spirit walkers.

Pyewacket felt Jeff's presence in the room.

Why didn't we reach him this way in the first place? Pyewacket took a deep breath.

If he wasn't expecting us, we might not be able to get his attention. And he needs contact with you. Even in another form. Go on. I'll be close behind.

Pyewacket sent a spirit paw toward the rat. The rat shivered but held still. Pyewacket settled in behind her eyes, touching the small rodent brain. *Wow, she's all nose,* he startled at the overwhelming scents, cheese, apples, eggs. The rat's stomach growled. *And hunger … oh, the hunger.*

Pye, keep on task. Jeff touched him again refocusing him.

The rat navigated the narrow cleft and ran toward the hand that fed her.

Leave it to Niki to share his dinner with a rat, Pyewacket mused remembering his first meal with Niki. There hadn't been enough for Niki but he had given the kitten all Pyewacket could hold.

The rat burst into the small cell. Niki held out his hand. She climbed onto his palm, up his arm to perch on his shoulder. Pyewacket took charge, rubbing against Niki's cheek, trying to purr.

Jeff's shadowed image appeared by the door.

Pye, not much time.

They're coming for you, Niki. Everyone. Well, except Jess who's worried about her energies being here before they are supposed to be ... and Chris who'll protect Jess. Everyone else is invited to the ball. They'll get you out.

Pye. I can't leave without Kay.

They won't leave her behind.

Pyewacket rubbed back and forth turning in a circle on Niki's shoulder.

Can't I stay?

Too dangerous. His mental tone softened. *I couldn't feel you for so long. I dreamt you were flying and Jeff had wings.*

Pyewacket chuckled.

He saved me, Nik. He came after me in the darkness.

Jeff beckoned to him.

I've got to go.

The door swung open. Rat instincts grabbed control. She scrambled off Niki's shoulder, tail disappearing into the crack.

The rat careened between Pyewacket's outstretched paws. Pyewacket crashed into his own body, his head throbbing.

Pye. Jeff's voice caressed him, the pain abating with the touch. *You have to find a way out. Chad is at the back wall.*

Jeff's presence receded, leaving a frightening void.

Pyewacket prowled the cellar, his eyes round in the gloom. He pounced, landing front claws extended on a wiggling brown body. Flashing fangs pinned the squirming mass. He trapped the small male rat. It cringed, shivering.

Wait, this might be someone important to her. Smells like her. Pyewacket harrumphed, withdrawing his claws. He remained frozen. Pyewacket nudged him with his nose. The rat ran under the divider to the wine cellar.

Pyewacket's ears twitched at a sound, rustling cloth and paw steps vibrating the silence. He waited, his hind quarters quivering. A pink nose came into sight. The mouse ventured out, climbing the rough burlap sack.

In a blur, it dangled from Pyewacket's mouth. He murmured sorry and bit down. He laid the mouse's body between his front paws and settled down to wait.

Footsteps echoed in the stairwell. He scooped up the carcass and bounded to the stairs. Petite feet in black boots descended, hesitating on each step.

"I hate going down here. There's always skittering in the corners and I feel eyes on me." A female voice complained.

"Get a move on, Amelia. The quicker we get the things, the sooner you be back upstairs." Her companion replied.

Amelia's foot hit the cellar floor. Pyewacket rubbed against her leg. An unearthly shriek echoed through the cellar. Dropping the lantern, she bowled back up the stairs, knocking her companion flat on the steps.

Oops, perhaps that was the wrong approach. Pyewacket stepped around the spilled lantern oil. He waited.

"Anna," a matronly voice called from above. "What's all this bobbery? Is there a bogey in the cellar or is Amelia barmy?"

"Mrs. Mallory, I don't know. She screamed, dropped the lantern and landed me on me bum." Anna yelled. "I'll have a look." She rose, dusting her woolen skirt and picked up the lantern. Pyewacket sat very still, his eyes wide.

"Well?" Mrs. Mallory demanded, an edge creeping into her voice, "Find anything? Should I send Rogers?"

"No, ma'am. The lantern is out and there's oil all over the floor. I'll need hot water to clean it up."

"No, you won't. I'll be sending Miss Afraid-of-the-Dark to do it. Just get what you were sent for."

"Yes, ma'am." Anna set about gathering the requested items. She spotted Pyewacket. He nosed the mouse towards her, a rumbling in his throat. "Mrs. Mallory, I've found the bugger. It's a cat … looks to be a good mouser, too." She picked the mouse up by the tail. "You've worked for your supper, I see."

Pyewacket wove a figure eight around her leg, purring.

"Proud one, ain't ya. Mayhap a reward be possible." She scooped him into her arms. He rubbed his face against the white apron. Anna carried him up. Noise assailed them from all directions, preparations for the evening meal continuing.

"Here's the little demon what scared Amelia." She displayed Pyewacket and the mouse. "The mighty hunter and his prize!"

"Anna, take that mangy beast from my kitchen this minute." Gibard brandished a large knife at her.

She ducked from his swing. "But he's been hurt. See the burns. Just a little bite before he goes. Look how scrawny he is."

"Let him eat his catch." He glowered at her. "Throw him out."

Anna swept past the long counter filled with open containers. She dipped her hand into one tin, hiding her movement. Before she reached the door, Mrs. Malloy caught her upper arm in an iron grip.

She hissed in Anna's ear. "You best be careful the words you choose, Missy. Demons are very real in this house. Don't be flip about it. Put the cat outside."

"But, ma'am," Anna tried to curtsey, the strong fingers on her arm holding her up. "The dogs. Those brutes will tear him apart for fun. Let me run him to the gate."

"You need to care for your own skin, not a blinkin' cat!" She shook her. "You'll not be long for this household. Do what you like. But if he …" she jerked her head toward the chef "notices you gone, I'll not stand up for ye. The whole matter will go to Mister Westfield."

Anna pulled away, sprinting across the yard. A groom walked from the stable followed by two wolfhounds. The dogs perked up their ears, tracking her running form. "Uh oh." She slowed. "Won't do to have those lads give chase. Walk, ninny, walk." Pyewacket felt her heart pounding. "His Lordship keeps that beastie pack. They kill anything they catch."

Pyewacket noted the vitriol in her voice. The distance from the house to the wall was farther than he'd hoped. *Would have taken me hours.* He shivered, wishing Maeve was there but glad she wasn't.

He strained to look around. He twisted so far, she tightened her grip on him.

Anna headed for the closest wall. The barking dogs drew nearer. The wall ran straight and unbroken for several yards. Anna plowed into the undergrowth along the wall. "We're almost there." She stopped by a grate in the stone.

"This is the best I can do. Stay away. It isn't safe." She kissed him on the nose and pushed him through the bars. Strong hands reached from the other side and pulled him into an embrace.

"Thank you, Miss. I pray you don't get into trouble for us." Chad looked through the grate into her brown eyes. Her smile lit up the gloom. The hounds gave voice, approaching.

"Give him good care. He's got a lion's heart, that one." She held out the morsel she'd stolen. Chad snagged it. Anna walked back toward the house, her fists held at her side.

Chad tucked Pyewacket into his coat. Hugging the shivering cat, he moved through the meadow growth toward the road. Pyewacket burrowed deeper in Chad's arms.

CHAPTER 48

Mac shifted on the hard kitchen chair. The ride home had been chilly with Jessica maintaining a stony silence. *Whatever is bugging Jess will be okay somehow.* He glanced sideways at her. He stared into his coffee, looking for words.

Before he could speak, she faced him, lips white, dark eyes swirling. "I'm not in the mood to be chatty." She stared back into her tea.

Mac sensed Nigel's eyes on him. Nigel wrinkled his brow eliciting a shrug from Mac. Nigel settled into the chair on the Jessica's other side and refilled her cup without comment. He placed the maps on the table and pushed them towards Mac.

Tori cocked her head, meeting Mac's eye, "Mac, you're are gonna bust wide open if we don't start with you."

Mac reached out to touch Jessica's hand. She pulled away from him. "The lightning striking the altar was a good thing."

He looked at the astonished faces around the table. "It caught me off guard, too. I was at the tower's base and glad for the small shelter it provided. I still taste ozone. But I saw four spirits released. We're talking deep soul chains tying them. They couldn't have been freed any other way, Jessica."

"Sounds fantastic to me," Tori broke in. "And if you do it again, I'll congratulate you again." She met Jessica's stony glare. Her tone changed, solicitous and concerned. "I wouldn't expect you to flinch from anything."

"Shut up, Tori." Jessica snapped. "You don't know anything about it. You don't know me well enough to judge." Wind chilled the air, stirring the papers.

Nigel patted Sami's hand. "My dear, I think we all need reinvigoration. Brandy, whiskey, biscuits." He looked hopeful.

She nodded to Harry.

"Now," Nigel peered over his glasses at Mac. "The dragon's ire has been raised. Edward will be looking for you." He looked at each one.

Mac shuddered. "Human bones were placed under the foundation." The words out, he opened his eyes and looked at Nigel. "Were you aware, Nigel?" Mac's shoulders relaxed when he saw the shock on Nigel's face.

"A conjure man, my father." Mac's voice held no pride. "He could summon spirits. But he strayed from the Santeria paths." He'd never shared this with his adopted family.

"Mac, what did you see?" Sami's voice trembled.

"I saw the bloody pathway in the maze." He paused, feeling Jeff's reassuring presence in his mind. "There's a natural fault line that runs under the manor." He spread the maps out on the table. "The tower is already unstable. With Jess' help, we can weaken it further. The lower wall will collapse and create a distraction."

"Nigel, how much time do we have?" Scotty asked. He handed around the silverware.

"The sacrifice will be on the dark of the moon … New Year's Eve." Silence thundered in the room.

Mac pulled the sketches from his coat pocket. Chris and Scotty leaned in.

"Mac, show me where the strike should be. Harry, the footman said there'd be fireworks?" Chris glanced at Harry.

"Yes, and he was quite amazed his Lordship listened to Nigel and purchased a fire containment system." He handed a bowl to Nigel. "Your love of gadgets may do some good."

"I'd bet the fireworks are stored in the garage." Chad said. "I doubt they'd be in the cellar. Just food stuffs … sacks and baskets and the wine racks. There was a girl—"

"Anna." All eyes turned on Jeff. He rubbed Pyewacket's head. "She carried him to the wall … afraid the dogs would hurt him." Jeff stroked the cat. "He's worried she'll be in trouble. There are imps everywhere in the house. Niki's injured."

"How badly?" Charlie broke in, a sharp tone in his voice.

Jeff paused for a long moment. "There are burns on his hand and he's been beaten."

Charlie sucked air through his teeth. He shook, his hand a tight fist on the table.

"At least, Niki knows we're here. He said Kay's possessed." Pyewacket stretched, muscles quivering.

"Mac, the fireworks would be a good target, too." Scott pulled the conversation back to the moment. "Jess, how many lightning strikes can you generate in succession?" Scotty ignored her pale visage, his tone gentle.

She met his gaze without smiling. "I don't call lightning. At least, I didn't before working with Chris. Two. Maybe three." Chris stared at her.

Scotty went on. "Mac, did you see anything that will help if we have to go into the labyrinth?"

"It's a true labyrinth, not an affectation. I'd like a bulldozer."

"Uncle Nigel, do you know the way?" Charlie accepted a bowl from Harry's hand.

Nigel shook his head. "It is a closely guarded secret passed to the first-born son. Been that way since it was built in my great grandfather's time. Some folderol about keeping the dragon contained."

"Dragon?" Sami stared at him, her eyes wide.

"Not a literal one, my dear. Rather the Ramhill temper or now, the dark leanings with all this congress with demons." Nigel held up his bowl for another helping.

CHAPTER 49

Edward stood in the doorway staring at his wife. She wore styles beyond their fashionable heyday and cloaked her glittering intelligence behind lowered lashes and a demure expression. He cleared his throat compelling her to look up from the desk. The silence lengthened.

"What is it, Edward? I have a meeting to attend and must finish my notes."

"I've given instructions to your son. This one is in your care until he is ready. Adrian will accompany her to entertain Nigel's friends." He swept his gaze across her desk, irritated he did not know what meeting she was attending.

She shuffled the papers, tidying the desk, an action he knew was calculated to irritate him further.

"I am going to my club. I expect high tea upon my return."

Genevieve rose and took the young woman by the elbow, guiding her to a chair. "Here." She patted Kay's hand, propelling her to sit.

She returned to Edward and straightened his tie. His disdain for her dithering burned his throat.

"Edward, this must stop. You've frightened the staff..." she touched his lip as it drew back in a sneer, "and are alarming me with your activities."

He slapped her hand away from his face.

She paced to the settee and back. The rustling silk and crinoline combined with her fragrance still aroused him. Facing him, her eyes flared with the wild light that had marked her for his marriage bed but had settled into the patient acceptance he despised. She wrung her hands. He grimaced at her anxiety, weakness in his book. She approached him again, placing her hands firmly around his face. "I have already arranged with Monsieur Gibard for a high tea this afternoon. I urge you to reclaim the fine manners you used to display."

He tried to turn his face away from her, his anger rising at her presumption.

"Do not demonstrate your anger with me." She maintained her hold on him, surprising him.

She moved to embrace him but he shrugged away. "Mind how you behave publicly. We do not need censor. It would harm Adrian's entrance."

He reluctantly acknowledged her wisdom. He could not afford to damage his heir's future reputation.

"You may leave your plaything here with me."

"Fine." He turned toward the door. "You are well suited to be a nursemaid since you've proven a limited brood mare." The door slammed behind him.

Genevieve shrugged off his anger. She raised Kay's face. The blankness in her eyes pulled at Genevieve's heart. *This one is very different. I have never seen such emptiness ... or such unthinking obedience. Either he is calling stronger demons or something traumatic brought her here. If it is a stronger demon, he will destroy himself.*

"I hoped to see you alone." Genevieve reached for the teacup on her desk, bringing the warm brew to Kay's lips. "This will loosen the hold on you." Kay accepted a small sip. Genevieve encouraged her to drink, filling the cup again.

"Madam, the young sir is ready." Westfield's tall body loomed over the women, his face impassive. He took the tea cup from Lady Ramhill and set it on the desk. Taking her gently by the arm, he led Kay from the room.

Genevieve followed, smiling at Adrian. "You look charming. How lovely to give her a corsage. One of your orchids, isn't it, darling?" She peeled the flower and pin from his fingers. "Here, let me. You should not risk pricking your finger."

She unbuttoned Kay's high collar, reaching inside to position the corsage, securing it with the long pin. Genevieve felt the heat from her son's gaze on Kay's exposed collar bone. She worked the small buttons and ran her fingers along the black silk cord around Kay's neck. Blocking her son's gaze, she studied the amulet, allowing it to drop back. "There, you look lovely."

Adrian took Kay's arm, leading her down the stairs.

Genevieve remained at the top. *The girl is strong but she drank so little tea.* She reflected on her son's discourtesy. *Yes, my husband's bad manners are affecting everyone.*

***

Colby peeked out the front parlor window. "They're here!" Adrian descended from the coach. He held out his hand to assist Kay from the carriage. *Kay looks drawn.* Her breath came in ragged gasps. *How will Sami carry this off?* The Reynard turned and nipped the tail of Adrian's long coat. Adrian jumped aside, stumbling on the first step. Colby chuckled and turned away from the window.

Tori descended the stairs in the newest fashion from France. The shimmering fabric clung to her body, unrestrained by a corset. Soft pleats flowed to the floor, bright colors dazzled the eye. Colby muttered a curse at Tori's daring and apparent comfort. Looking away, she poured tea, avoiding looking into the cup.

Harry opened the front door. Adrian shrugged off his coat and let it fall. He glowered at Westfield who removed Kay's cape.

Tori floated down the last few steps and extended her gloved hand to Kay. "It's a pleasure to meet you."

Kay's eyes remained downcast.

Adrian's face darkened. He stepped between them. Tori smiled at him, "And are you young Lord Ramhill?" Her soft Southern drawl festooned every word. "I am Victoria Madison ... the Charleston Madisons."

Tori stepped around Adrian and reached again for Kay. Westfield tucked Kay's hand through his arm and guided her to a chair by the window. At a soft word in her ear, she sat looking up at him.

"Thank you." she said. "Anna is very lucky."

Westfield frowned before his face returned to a stony façade.

Colby heard Scotty whisper to Jeff. "Watch Kay. I don't think she's under as deep control as Adrian's man expected. She just surprised him."

Jeff nodded. He set his glass on the mantelpiece. Chad poked at the fire.

"Madam, I insist on seeing Mrs. Ramhill. It is she who requested this visit." Adrian drew himself up, raising his chin and peering down at her.

Tori patted him on the arm. "Mrs. Ramhill will be along shortly. There are so many things that intrigue me." She ran a finger along his jaw. "I always confuse British royalty. Are you a Lord or do you just use that title because you're the heir? You are cute. Your Uncle Nigel mentioned you would be interested in the conservatory."

Adrian's scowl deepened. He attempted to step away from Tori but she snagged his arm, pulling him past the parlor door towards the conservatory.

"We have a moment. You must see what I've found. It's such a surprise to find roses blooming now. My sweet Mama was quite inventive in propagation." Tori's pace to the conservatory matched her speech. "But even she would be surprised."

Adrian tried to disengage her from his arm, his face frantic. Colby choked back her amusement, close to losing control when she saw Scotty hold his sides.

"Excuse me, madam." Adrian pivoted turning her back toward the parlor. "I must see to my charge. My father was very specific regarding her welfare. I insist Mrs. Ramhill be sought immediately."

Tori's red lips quivered.

Colby looked away from the scene. *If she produces tears, I'll choke to death.*

A quaver in her voice, Tori plunged onward, "Mrs. Ramhill and her husband are in conference … something about her Uncle."

Adrian stared at her. Colby noted the sudden increase in attention.

"They send their apologies." Tori wove both hands around Adrian's arm. "Now, I heard your mother is a fabulous hostess. Are you allowed to attend all the soirees?"

Adrian opened his mouth but he failed to find an opening.

"Or is life too busy just going to … Eton … is that right? Your Uncle's so proud, he's ready to burst his buttons." Arriving once again at the parlor door, she looked around.

Westfield stood behind Kay, her chair separated from the others. Scotty and Jeff leaned against the fireplace while Chad stood by the window.

Colby lifted the tea pot from the butler's table and poured a cup. She held it out to Adrian who conducted Tori to the loveseat and removed her hand from his arm.

"Are all American women quite as … talkative as you? Your husband must be quite exhausted by day's end." With a half bow, he accepted the cup.

Tori looked around, her eyes wide. "What? You're all ready and there's no time for the conservatory? Oh, I don't mean to be such an addle-pated, silly thang. I'm just so excited to have a true psychic in our midst."

Jeff placed a firm hand on Tori's shoulder, ending her torrent.

***

Sami entered, Nigel and Charlie on either side.

Adrian froze, tea untasted. He stared at her, mesmerized by the golden curls framing her face. Her ivory gown flowed gently across her petite figure highlighting the porcelain sheen of her face and shoulders. His eyes travelled to the swell of pale breasts. Diaphanous fabric hung from her arms, the sleeves wrapped with gold cord in Grecian style leaving more flesh uncovered than within the sleeve. Adrian glanced from her warm golden beauty to Kay's dark sultry coloring. Now he understood his father's affairs. *Who could choose a favorite? Even the redhead would be a conquest ... with a gag.*

"Adrian." Nigel greeted his nephew. "Isn't this jolly?" Turning to Westfield, he spoke firmly, "Westfield, I assure young Adrian's safe from all but ..." he bowed in Tori's direction, "perhaps Miss Madison." He winked at her. "Rogers is in back having a lovely spot of tea with Harry. We'll ring if you are needed."

Westfield shook his head.

Nigel cut him off with a wave. "I insist. I know my brother runs you ragged." He placed a hand on Westfield's shoulder and directed him toward the kitchen. Westfield hesitated, looking at Adrian.

Adrian nodded. *Good. Now I am free to choose what I report. You do have your uses, don't you, old man.*

"There's a good fellow." Nigel returned, his smile broadening. "Adrian, I wish to introduce you to your fourth cousin twice removed, Charles Ramhill. He was smart enough to travel across the Pond and find this stinking rich heiress."

Adrian choked on his uncle's comment, hurriedly setting down the tea cup. Patting Adrian on the back, Nigel continued, "Charles is quite remarkable in his genealogical research. You know how dotty I am on the subject."

Adrian bit back a sharp retort as he stepped past his uncle to face Sami.

"Forgive Uncle Nigel. He does get involved in things. You may have noticed." Adrian lifted Sami's hand, silk against his lips. He lingered a moment, staring into her golden-flecked eyes. *She is the key,* he thought, *not some artifact. My father be damned. He won't have her.*

Adrian lowered her hand maintaining his grasp.

"Cousin Adrian, welcome." Charlie smiled at Adrian's glare.

"Make no assumptions regarding our shared blood until my father concurs. Madame Blavatsky counseled him to beware of relatives unknown." He returned his gaze to Sami. "Mrs. Ramhill, your lovely face is quite reminiscent of a Tarot card my father painted." He grasped her chin, thrilled by his presumption, "The High Priestess. Your face is more delicate—"

"You will refrain from touching my wife, dear cousin." Charlie took a half step in his direction. Sami turned her head, pulling her chin from Adrian's grasp. She shook her head at Charlie.

He unclenched his fist and gestured in Kay's direction, "We are gathered to be amazed by your Father's protégé. What messages do you have for us, Miss?"

Kay did not respond, her eyes on her folded hands.

Adrian gave Charlie a smug look. Adrian pulled Sami by her captured hand. "May I introduce you?"

Charlie's face grew darker.

"Please greet your hostess."

Kay met Sami's gaze with a brittle stare, no recognition on her face.

"Welcome and thank you for sharing your gift with us." Sami murmured, her face ashen.

Pyewacket slipped under Colby's skirt. She jumped, losing her grip on the saucer. The tea cup shattered drawing everyone's attention.

Cursing under her breath, she addressed Adrian. "My sister and I haven't been well since the voyage as evidenced by my clumsiness." She took Sami by the arm pulling her to the loveseat. Charlie sat beside her.

Jeff gathered the porcelain pieces from the rug. The broken fragments in one hand, he offered his other to Adrian. "I'm Jeff Conray. We appreciate your Uncle's hospitality."

His soft drawl confused Adrian for a moment, his face reflecting his concentration on the words.

"If you'll excuse me, I'll take these out." Jeff nodded toward the door.

Adrian felt the large hand pulled from his fingers leaving behind a peaceful warmth. He shook himself, wary he was showing a weakness yet unable to shed the effect.

Jeff walked between Adrian and Kay. He stopped and spoke to her too softly for Adrian to make out the words and, though he wished to interrupt the contact, the lassitude prevented him. To his relief, Kay did not respond except to follow Jeff's exit with her eyes.

Adrian felt control returning to his body. *I need to know more about him, too. She must touch him.*

The silence stretched on and Adrian felt eyes on him. He took control again. He lifted Kay's face to look into her eyes. A palatable tension flared in the room but he didn't turn to look at the others. *Interesting.* He took note.

"What do you need for the readings?" Adrian asked Kay.

"An object ..." Kay's voice held no inflection, "something of personal value."

He surveyed the others in the room. "Would anyone offer an object ... a brooch or locket?" He looked at Sami. She cupped the locket around her neck in her hands.

Scotty stepped up "Here is my ring." Adrian pulled out a silk handkerchief and reached for the ring.

Scotty sidestepped around him, going to one knee before Kay. "Tell me something about myself." He extended his hand. She took the ring, her fingertips brushing his.

"You are a guardian," Kay's hand shook. Scotty laid his hand over hers. She hesitated, raising her eyes. "You hoped to be a pilot but have a paralyzed muscle in your right eye ... the result of an injury. You were fighting a—." He squeezed her hand and she stopped.

Adrian moved to break the contact but Jeff returned and held him back, a hand on his shoulder.

"You are ineligible for the service. But you have built a hang glider."

Adrian looked at Scotty, his face reflecting his confusion at the unfamiliar words.

"She is correct. I am fascinated by flying … in fact, I was in Dover when Louis Blériot landed from France." His eyes gleamed. "Blériot was the first man to pilot a plane over the Channel. The hang glider is a dotty thing. My mother is concerned for my sanity." He smiled at Kay. "You have exposed my obsession."

Adrian edged closer. She did not acknowledge him, looking at Scotty. "Where her heart is at risk, she is not as confident as she presents." Adrian looked at each woman's face, settling on Tori's.

Scotty did not glance in Tori's direction. Kay held out the ring.

Tori's face went from pale to bright red. She sat perfectly still not meeting anyone's eye.

Harry broke the moment as he wheeled in a tea cart with sandwiches and pastries, blocking Adrian's view. Scotty lifted the ring from Kay's palm and kissed her forehead. Her acrid sweat burned his lips.

"Not much longer," he whispered.

***

Red flashed on Kay's chest, startling Chad. *Must be light from the window,* he thought. He looked away, hoping his peripheral vision would be more acute. The flash did not repeat.

Jeff filled a plate with delicacies. He touched Tori's shoulder and passed the plate to her. Setting the plate down, she looked up at him. Leaning down, he kissed her on the cheek, running his hand down her arm.

Pretty astute, big man, Chad thought. *Throw the little bastard off.*

Adrian observed the interaction, puzzlement flashing across his face.

"Perhaps, one of the ladies?" Adrian held out his hand to Sami. "The hostess should have the opportunity for otherworldly wisdom. I am certain she can identify your heart's desire."

"Thank you, but I have my heart's desire." She entwined her fingers in Charlie's. "My sister is interested in her future."

Colby rose from the loveseat. She focused on Kay, unwilling to catch Jeff's eye.

"Do you have a small object you carry on your person? A ring or a pin … something you value or a gift from someone who loves you?" Adrian smiled at Colby but failed to cover his irritation at Sami's refusal.

Colby pulled off her graduation ring. Though deemed safe by the group, she wondered after Kay's words to Scotty. She held out the gold band set with sapphires and diamonds. He accepted the ring with the handkerchief, admiring it.

With a dramatic flourish, he presented it to Kay. She reached to take it, her hand hovering over the ring. She stopped, turning her head toward Chad.

Chad stared out the window, lost in his thoughts. *It's her voice, the way she tilts her head ... even the way her eyebrow rises. The body responses are intact but the essential Kay is gone. Dead?* He wondered. *Jeff believes the soul's departure leaves the body in mortal danger. Can souls be lost and still leave the body responding? Could this be possession by a dybbuk? If her soul is gone, where is it?*

Chad shifted on his feet. *That cocky bastard, a blue-eyed raptor or an English Cossack.* He pulled at his collar. *How am I supposed to figure things out when I can't swallow?* He looked around to find everyone staring at him.

"What?" Chad asked.

"You are too noisy." Adrian spoke to Chad. "She cannot continue if you persist in projecting your thoughts. She also said you are correct in your assessment of me." Adrian glared at him. "I would be most curious to hear what that might be."

"Did she tell you this psychically?" Chad curled his lip.

"Everyone heard her distinctly. Please focus your attention. You might learn something beyond the ordinary." Adrian turned away from Chad. "Or are you frightened it might shake your reality?"

I'd like to shake the shit out of you, you little snot. Chad glared back at him.

Kay laughed, the raven's red eye catching Chad's attention.

This is worse than I imagined. I do need to shut up.

"I meant no disrespect, ma'am. I will take my thoughts elsewhere." Chad crossed the room. "Maybe smoke a cigar on the porch if I might have the lady's permission?" He nodded to Sami.

"Colby brought Havana cigars. I'm certain Harry will find them."

Chad brushed past Adrian. His heavy tread echoed in the hall.

Kay spoke, startling Colby. "Oracle." She looked into Colby's eyes. "Be careful to listen to your heart despite the interference of others. If you don't, you will live only in your body … never realizing your spirit." She paused for a moment searching Colby's face. "Choose your family."

Adrian's eyebrows shot up as Colby choked. "This has meaning for you, Madam?" he inquired.

She whipped around to face him, the scent of lemon and sage swirling around her. "It's Miss," each word ice-laden, "and it's not your business. You've been impertinent and haughty. I don't care if you're English nobility. I find nothing noble in you. You're a boor and far too self-important for any well-bred man." She pushed past him, wrestling with the weight of her petticoats.

Sami stood, releasing Charlie's hand. "Please enjoy your tea. I must see to my sister." She stopped in front of Kay, extending her hand. Adrian held his breath. He wanted Kay to touch Sami … to tell him more regarding the ethereal Mrs. Ramhill.

Kay accepted Sami's hand and rose to look down at the younger woman.

Sami maintained the formal posture. "I apologize for my sister's behavior. She is overwrought by the unexplained absence of friends. I hope to see you again, soon."

Kay nodded but remained silent. Kay turned Sami's palm over and placed Colby's ring in her grasp. Leaning down, she whispered, "And they wish to rejoin you."

Sami's back stiffened. She looked at Kay's face but leaden eyes stared back at her.

Turning to Adrian, she said, "Please carry my appreciation to your father." She swept from the room.

***

Jeff picked up a bottle from the side table. "I hope no one will mind but I prefer something stronger than tea. Adrian," he addressed the young man who continued to stare after Sami. "Would you care for a Scotch whiskey?" Jeff held out a cut glass lowball with two fingers of the dark liquid.

Startled by the pleasant tone in Jeff's voice, he nodded and accepted the glass.

"I'll check on my wife and her sister." Charlie climbed the stairs two at a time.

"My goodness." Tori rose from the loveseat. "Now, Miss, while the menfolk are busy with their libations, why don't we investigate the conservatory?" Before Adrian could object, she pulled Kay from the parlor. Looking over her shoulder, she said, "Don't worry, Adrian, I won't talk her ear off or ask for free advice."

Adrian stared after them, uncertain how to respond to the impetuous redhead. Hearing a chuckle, he prepared to defend his honor.

"Don't mind Miss Madison," Scotty held his glass up in toast. "Here's to the ladies."

Adrian responded holding his glass high, his eyes sweeping the room. He approached the fire. "A lovely Yule log," he commented, placing his hand on the mantel. A shock ran up his arm and he flinched away. Aware Jeff watched him, he tried to be casual. "Will you be staying for the New Year?"

"Yes, but I'll return home shortly after … for family business." Jeff said.

"And you, Mr. MacMillan? Your accent confirms you are not from the Americas."

"No, my home is in the Grampian Mountains but I am helping Charles set up a business venture in New York." He handed Jeff his glass. "I will check on the ladies. Excuse me."

Adrian drained his glass, struggling with the burning liquid. "I will accompany you. I am negligent in her care by allowing Miss Madison to spirit her away." He set the glass on the mantel without touching the wood.

CHAPTER 50

Genevieve entered the kitchen. The maids curtseyed and the footmen bowed. She nodded to each, a smile on her face. Motioning to Anna, she said, "Clear the tea from my study." Dropping her voice, she added, "You are to finish the full cup left there and share the biscuits with your two friends." The young girl curtseyed.

She straightened to her full height and spoke to the chef. "Monsieur Gibard, I am aware there are issues in the cellar. I will ascertain the current conditions."

Monsieur Gibard wrinkled his pointy nose. "Madame, I assure you all is in good order—"

"The keys to the cellar." She held out her hand.

He pulled the keys from under his long white apron and dangled them from his scarred fingers. His dark eyes studied her as if to measure her resolve. "But, Madame, I must object, Lord Ramhill has not—"

"Lord Ramhill was disturbed that, as his chatelaine, I allowed the intrusion. He reminded me most firmly I am responsible for the manor." Silence rang through the kitchen. "I do not require assistance. This is my duty and I will see it properly discharged."

She pulled the keys from his bony fingers.

Turning on her heel, she descended the stairs. Soft squeaks and rustlings emanated from each corner. A chill ran down her spine as she located each imp. Her disgust soured her stomach. She unlocked the wine cellar door, ensuring the grate locked behind her.

Kneeling at the base of the farthest wall, she pulled an earthen bowl and a silk bag from her pocket. She sprinkled a pinch of herb mixture into the bowl. Sibilant words passed her soft lips, trailing silver light as her musical tones rose and fell. She blew over the mixture. A flame kindled, sending up smoky tendrils. She breathed in the smoke then blew it upwards.

The rustlings increased, the smoke growing thicker.

"I cannot release you." She spoke to the niches near the ceiling. "I can give you a few moments freedom." Genevieve's voice commanded obedience. This they understood. The imps scrambled to inhale the pungent fumes. They scattered, crawling across the ceiling to the windows.

She tripped the mechanism on the door and entered the narrow stone hallway. She touched each closed door until she found her goal. Placing her hand over the lock, she entreated it to open. The mechanism clicked. She set the bowl of burning herbs on the floor.

Stepping into the cell, she pushed the door closed. A soft word from her lips lit the candle stub on the shelf, shedding weak light. The young man sat in the corner with chin on his chest, an arm draped across a raised knee. His aura shimmered with pain. She waited in silence until he raised his head. His blue eyes swept her into open air on the wild winds above the cliffs. Her breath caught in her throat, diving through the mists at the bottom, the air rushing under her wings. The candle wavered, bringing her back to the moment.

Drawing a rattling breath, he struggled to rise. She stepped to help him, stopping a hands breath from touching his shoulder. Withdrawing her tingling fingers, she waited as he straightened and bowed awkwardly to her.

"Lady Ramhill, I'm pleased to make your acquaintance. Forgive my poor grace." He coughed, covering his mouth with his hand, blood staining his fingers.

His manners and educated speech reinforced her feelings he and his sister were not Edward's usual prey.

"Young man, will you allow me to ease your pain?" She sent a silent prayer as suspicion turned to resignation across his face. "You have been ill-treated."

He coughed again, leaning against the cold wall. She caught his arm as he sank to the floor.

"Madam, I am afraid my manners are overcome by a lack of constitution." He chuckled, fighting another coughing fit.

She held out a silver flask. "Drink this." She wrapped his fingers around it. The look of doubt on his face compelled her to open her aura, hoping he would feel her concern and her troubled heart.

He lifted the flask to his lips. The first sip induced more coughing.

"You have a stronger will than that." She clicked her tongue. "Drink the rest down." She placed her hand over his and tipped the flask into his mouth.

He struggled to swallow without coughing. Leaning his head back against the wall, his face relaxed and a flush of color replaced the pallor. She felt him nudge the demon in his chest, but the grizzled snout remained tucked under its tail.

"Most unique, madam. You're talented with elixirs." Niki whispered.

"You need not worry about listening ears. His pets are absent for a few moments. I assume you know about the one within." Niki nodded. She probed him a little deeper observing his reaction. "It holds little control over you."

Niki remained silent.

Genevieve fidgeted, pulling her thoughts together. *His eyes are too old for his youth.* "But you must have Edward convinced otherwise?"

Niki shrugged.

"Who are you?" she asked.

He shrugged again.

"It will not do to dissemble with me. I am here to help you." He shrugged again, this time with an air of apology. "I see." She chose another approach.

"I do not blame you for being suspicious." She settled on the floor, tucking her skirts around her legs. "My, but this floor is cold." She laughed. "What a vacuous statement! Young man, you have unsettled me." She drew a deep breath. Her lips formed soundless words. Warmth radiated through the stone floor.

"It won't last long." She apologized. "If you won't let me help you, at least tell me about your sister."

His pupils dilated.

"I know my husband controls several imps and a minor demon but to control her so thoroughly …" The words were distasteful in her mouth. "Given you are talented, I suspect she has ability beyond clairsentience."

Niki nodded.

She studied his face. "Either my husband has summoned a stronger demon than ever before … which frightens me for him." She fell silent, looking down at her hands, turning her gold wedding band. "Or your sister's soul is absent. I have seen the raven around her neck." She looked up, praying he would be willing to speak.

"Lady Ramhill, you compel me to honesty. I might blame it on that noxious concoction but I wish to trust you. The raven is dedicated to Morrigan." He smiled when she nodded. "I fear her soul is trapped within which means she is very aware of any torment he visits upon her but has no control to avoid it."

"I have given her a small—and better tasting—dose of my concoction."

He laughed.

"But his man is watchful. I do believe, though, even a small sip gave her back a level of self-control. Perhaps not a kindness."

"Anything you do to free her will put me in your debt." Niki's voice broke.

"A favor well worth my effort to earn."

"We have friends who will come for her."

She felt him open his aura to her, inviting a search for any duplicity or guile. The warm connection took her breath, calling back memories of the first years of her marriage. *How I miss the feel of another soul against mine*. She realized her vulnerability but—*if I pull away from him, he may no longer trust me.* She soothed him with her white light. He drew a ragged breath.

Skittering alerted her. "Tell me how I may contact your friends."

"I don't know where they are … and it wouldn't be safe if I did." He flexed his swollen fingers. "Your husband can be very persuasive. All I ask is you find a way to free my sister."

"I will try" she assured him. "How did you get here?"

"I will tell you what I can. I held an object of your husband's."

"The tarot card," she interjected.

"Yes," Niki continued. "I was holding it when I felt the summoning spell."

"But Edward doesn't perform that kind of magic."

"No, but his great grandson does. The card was taken from him."

She sucked in a breath.

"The card burst into flames. I called for Kay. That's when she reached out for me." He stretched his burned hand. "I suspect the house spirit moves through time. The summoning was thwarted … partially. Instead of landing at the Ramhill estate of my time, here I am."

"Foxhaven." She nodded. "My son has taken your sister there, parading her talents. Nigel is a sneaky devil."

"Then they will have seen her … perhaps they will understand the state she's in."

"I have met your friends and I know how to reach them." She rose, observing the tin tray untouched. "It appears I do not need to warn you that laudanum or other tinctures are in the food." She pulled a vial from her pocket, holding it out to him. "A drop on your tongue before the meal will neutralize the effects."

She swept from the room, the lock clicking behind her.

***

He shook out a drop. A bloom of lavender and deadly nightshade filled his mouth. His heart raced, thundering in his ears. Steadying his breathing, he called the rat. In the corner, a black nose poked from the crack. Holding out his hand, he waited for her to risk the open space. She scurried to him and rose on hind feet, placing front paws around his fingers.

Keep this safe for me, little one. Bring it back when I call.

She wrapped her teeth around the vial and hurried into the hole.

He pulled the discarded plate closer and brought the stale bread to his lips, the saliva flowing. Chewing the bite for a moment, he prayed to her skills.

CHAPTER 51

Chad entered the kitchen and the quiet conversation between the retainers ceased.

"My apologies for disturbing you. I'm going out to smoke." He addressed Harry, "Mrs. Ramhill indicated you've a good cigar."

"I will locate one for you, sir. Would you like a cup of tea to take with you?" Harry rose from the table.

"No, thank you." Chad retrieved his coat and hat from under the stairs. He grabbed four tea sandwiches, grinning at Westfield's disapproving stare.

Rain scent swirled in the wind. He settled his hat on his head. *Rain by nightfall*. The gray dusk light matched his mood. Raucous cries filled the skies.

Wonder if the ravens will dance today.

He felt for his harmonica coming up empty-handed. Grimacing, he hoisted up on the railing, dangling his legs over the edge. *How the hell did Kay get into this mess and where is her soul?* He would enjoy competing with Mac for Kay's attention, encouraged by the warmth in his heart chakra from her touch. Warmth missing from the woman inside.

He studied the ravens wheeling in the breeze. The she-raven folded her wings and plummeted earthward. Chad tracked the fall. The bird skimming the ground. She landed on the railing and rocked from foot to foot. The wind raised one feather on its head. Chad did not move.

The murder swooped to perch on the stable peak as if waiting.

The raven stood tall, cocked her head and aimed one black eye in Chad's direction.

Chad trilled at her. He reached out his hand, startling the bird. She hopped into the air, hung a moment then dropped back to the railing. Chad inched his hand along the rail, displaying the tea sandwich.

The raven turned her head one direction and then another.

"Are you hungry?" He placed a small piece on the railing as far as he could reach. She eyed the morsel then Chad. Chad fought the urge to look away. He whistled the remembered tune through his teeth. The raven edged a step closer, ducking its head toward the piece unable to quite reach it. A second step … a quick jab and the prize hung from her beak. Chad set out another piece, half the distance between them.

He murmured to her, "Come on, beautiful. You need to eat to keep up your strength." She grew bolder, taking less time measuring the distance between them. The second bite disappeared. Chad set out a piece next to him.

"What a fine winged seduction." He extended his heart energy toward the raven. "Longing looks and sandwiches. I've forgotten the intimacy in coaxing."

The third piece disappeared. The raven sat within his reach. He held out the next piece between thumb and forefinger. A long moment passed before the sharp beak snatched the bread from his hand, grazing his thumb. The last piece lay in his palm. He held it out.

"Come on."

She stood motionless, the wind lifting her feathers. He held his breath. She extended her wings, lifting and landing on his wrist. She dug her long claws into his coat sleeve. He gasped, feeling the heart energy he remembered. At his sound, she lifted from his wrist, flapping in place for a moment.

"Please come back, pretty lady."

She landed. Sharp tips pierced the fabric, tickling his skin. A thrill ran up his arm. She rocked back and forth then she cawed at him.

"Kay?" he whispered.

The raven bobbed its head, staring, unblinking.

"More?" He pinched off another piece of sandwich. His hand in range, she disregarded the sandwich, pulling instead at the red string.

"You approve of this precaution?"

The black head bobbed up and down.

Chad asked, "How can we help you?"

She hopped from his wrist. A wing beat landed her on his shoulder. She pecked his ear.

"Oww!" Chad steeled himself. "Okay, I deserve that. All you can do is yes or no, right?" A rolling purr sounded in his ear. "Come on back down where I can see you. I'll try not to be so lame."

She gave a dismissive caw but hopped back to the railing.

"May I?" he inquired. At her nod, he stroked her sleek back. His heart chakra warmed again.

"You're in there with her?" he whispered.

The raven bobbed.

"Do you need to be close to your body or can you stay with us until we can get the other part of you to safety?"

She nipped at his hand, drawing a bead of blood on the mound of his thumb.

"Hey! Watch the hand."

The raven hopped onto his arm and deposited a white dollop on his sleeve. She cawed dancing from foot to foot.

"Won't put up with my neurotic behavior?" He laughed, stroking her head again, sending warmth. "New Year's Eve. I don't know how we'll find you. Have you seen Niki?"

She bobbed.

"Is he hurt?"

She stretched out and cawed plaintively.

Before he thought, he blurted out, "How bad?"

Lightning struck his thumb. "Lame-O again. Sorry."

The door burst open behind him. The raven exploded into the air followed by the black wave from the stables. Rogers ran down the steps toward the stable.

Chad held the napkin to his bleeding thumb. *I guess the party's over.* The ravens' loud conversations faded into the gloom.

"My apologies," Harry stepped up beside him. "I am *en retard* with your cigar." He held out the Havana.

Rolling the cigar between his fingers, Chad noticed the cut tip. Harry struck a match and cupped the bright flame. Chad pulled the soothing smoke into his mouth

He felt Harry dab at the spot on his sleeve.

The door closed as the first drops of rain splattered on the railing. He turned his collar up against the wind lest it blow his thoughts away.

CHAPTER 52

Tori sank onto the kitchen chair. "My God, that was difficult." Jeff looked up from the floor plans spread across the table.

She picked up Jeff's glass and downed the last sip of whiskey. Jeff raised an eyebrow as she set the glass deliberately in front of him, her eyes wide. Jeff rose to refill the glass. "I never knew how much I would miss ice." She sighed.

Scotty patted her hand, "Poor baby."

Tori jerked her hand away as she rose. She stepped up behind Jeff. "At least, you were concerned for my feelings." Turning, he ran headlong into her.

She draped her arms around his neck, "Let's continue the conversation you started in the drawing room. Nice work distracting the little snot but there was a whole bunch left unsaid."

Scotty bit the inside of his cheek, the corners of his mouth twitching. Jeff's glance over Tori's shoulder displayed his desperation. Scotty shrugged his shoulders.

Harry pushed through the swinging door bumping Jeff's shoulder. "Sorry, sir," Harry said as he juggled the tea service. Jeff wrapped his arms around Tori, moving her aside, his hands encumbered by the full glasses.

Tori unwound from Jeff's arms and snatched a glass from his hand. With a glare, she disappeared up the back stairs. Jeff drained the remaining glass and poured another.

Scotty laughed. "Jeff, don't let Tori bother you. I suspect she lives to flirt."

"Scotty, I didn't mean to send her any kind of message in there."

"Jeff, don't worry. To be honest, I haven't felt this strongly about someone in a long time. If she feels the same way, it may scare her as much as it does me." He shuffled the sketches, staring at the circle indicating the tower. "Now isn't the time to be talking about it, anyway."

Jeff set a glass in front of him.

"Even though this tower is a more recent addition, there is probably an access from the upper floors to the cellar." "See?" Scotty pointed to the connecting wall. "It may not be exactly to scale but the inner wall is wider than necessary for a supporting wall." He pulled the next sheet to him. "The Lord would not want this too accurate in case his enemies got hold of the plans."

"So, if Lord Ramhill's study is on the second floor, he can come and go through the cellar?"

"Or through the caves. This area is riddled with them."

The cold wind lifted the papers sending them flying across the kitchen floor. Jessica pushed through the door with Maeve and Chris close behind. Rain drove over the threshold. She shouldered the door closed.

Chris dove at Maeve as she wound up to shake her wet fur. He wrestled her to the floor slipping in the pooling water. Harry appeared, his arms laden with towels, and dropped them on the struggling pair.

"Madam," he addressed Sami as she and Charlie joined the group. "Dinner is ready. However, be careful of the miscreants on the floor."

"Fill a plate and find a place to eat that suits you. We all need a moment of peace before we talk." She accepted a bowl from Harry, grabbed a piece of fresh bread and disappeared into the dining room.

Colby took the next bowl and set it in front of Jeff. She poured coffee.

He smiled at Colby. "Will you join me?"

Colby nodded.

"Mr. Mac, will you be staying in the kitchen or going to the main table?"

"I guess I'll stay …" Jessica caught his eye and nodded towards the dining room. "by this lady's side."

Mac took two bowls from Harry. Jessica picked up silverware and bread. Chris followed them with the tea pot. The conversation's soft susurration issued from the dining room. Harry set a large bowl on the floor. Maeve sat stone still until he signaled. She bounded across the kitchen, burying her snout in the bowl.

Scotty pushed back from the table. He rubbed Maeve soundly around the ears and neck. "Brought them back safely, did you, girl?" Maeve licked his face and sunk her snout into the bowl again. Scotty snatched a tray from the butler's pantry. He filled it with two bowls of stew and two cups of coffee then headed up the back stairs.

Jeff felt a soft pat on his leg. Scooting the chair back, he scooped Pyewacket into his lap. He fished a piece of beef from the stew and tore it into pieces, offering one to Pyewacket. He accepted the bite and settled into Jeff's lap. Jeff placed the remaining pieces along the edge of the table in front of him then picked up his spoon.

"I'd love to be a fly on the wall upstairs right now," Jeff said, amusement in his voice.

Colby looked from Pyewacket to Jeff's face. "Are you a voyeur or just nosy?"

Jeff paused before answering. The moment stretched out to several heart beats.

Discomfort in her voice, she said, "You're actually thinking about it."

He chuckled. A paw snagged a piece from the table's edge.

"You're terrible." She elbowed him in the side.

"And you're wonderful." He tore another piece of meat into shreds replacing the disappearing pieces.

Colby blushed, "I don't think so … after my scene in there. I just couldn't stand that child's haughty demeanor. The gall to have such an attitude toward another human being. So controlling." Anger crept into her voice.

"In this time, women were still considered possessions."

"I can't stand seeing her like that. We've got to do something. And soon." She picked up a spoon then tossed it into the bowl. "While Sami was in school in Paris, we visited one spring. Kay was a vibrant hostess. She even drew Mick out of his shell. Mick and Sami have so much in common with their shyness, and they aren't related ... after all. But he was actually telling jokes. Some of them too erudite for me but Kay seemed to appreciate his egghead sense of humor." She stopped, color blooming in her cheeks. "I'm rambling."

"No, you're showing your concern." Scooping Pyewacket onto the empty chair beside him, he rose, taking his empty cup with him.

"More coffee?" He reached for her cup.

"No, thank you" she said. "It's tea, anyway." Colby stared into her cup, shaking her head slightly from side to side.

"Colby, what it is?" Jeff sat in the chair next to her.

She looked up at him, blinking. "Jeff, I keep seeing things. You know what I mean?"

He nodded, maintaining eye contact. *Oh, Great Spirit, eyes I wish to fall into*, he thought. *Can she bear the burden of Seeing?*

"It's just fragments. Kay in a room with muslin curtains. Jessica with her hair streaming with water and blown by a strong wind. Chris shaking but standing in the lightning." She paused. Jeff waited in silence. "Niki lying on a slab of dark stone. An altar, I think, but now, I feel melodramatic."

"Colby, you're seeing possibilities. Kay named you Oracle. You just need time—and training—to be able to interpret the information."

"What if what I'm seeing is wrong or causes us to make a wrong decision?" Her voice dropped to a whisper. "What if I see something awful?"

He wrapped his arm around her. "We'll deal with it. You have to honor your gift." She leaned heavily against him for a moment then let out a shuddering breath.

The back door banged against the wall. Chad stumbled through the door, his teeth chattering, and water flowing off his coat. Jeff grabbed the tea towel and threw it at him. Chad caught the towel, snatching the sodden hat from his head. Water from his coat sprayed around him as he moved. Pyewacket arched and hissed, running through the dining room door as the force of the wind pushed it open.

"Chad, for heaven's sake! Won't you learn to come in from the cold?" Colby escaped behind Pyewacket. Jeff chuckled as he helped Chad peel off the heavy coat. He hung the coat over the chair and shoved the shaking man toward the back bedroom.

"Change." He ordered. Chad mumbled thanks. Jeff filled a mug of coffee, added whiskey and headed under the stairs.

"Sit," Jeff ordered. Chad stripped the white cotton shirt over his head and sat heavily on the edge of the bed. Shoving the coffee into his hands, Jeff grabbed a towel and roughly dried Chad's hair. He rubbed the towel down across Chad's shoulders and arms until the shivering stopped. "What were you doing out there?" Jeff inquired.

"I was walking." Chad's teeth chattered. "I didn't notice the cold until I was shivering so badly, it didn't make any difference." Chad arched his back, reminding Jeff of Pyewacket.

Jeff opened the press, retrieving a flannel shirt and pants. He tossed them to Chad and leaned back against the door frame, "What were you thinking about?"

Chad stopped, his hand on the buttons of his pants. "Do you believe someone can have her soul removed and still be alive … so to speak?" Jeff raised an eyebrow at him. "Okay. I know what you did for Pye but what about Kay?" Chad finished exchanging the wet wool trousers for a dry pair of denim waist overalls. "My god, the house heard me. I can't believe it." He danced a jig. "Where's my harmonica? I almost feel human again."

"Chad, I believe parts of souls can be lost or pushed out … but before today, I wouldn't have thought someone could keep functioning—at least on some level—without one entirely."

Chad picked up the flannel shirt, fingering the soft fabric. He caressed the wall. "I love you." He pulled the warm fabric around his chest and buttoned it. "I had a conversation with a raven on the back porch while His Junior Lordship was playing in the parlor. She's carrying Kay's soul, I know it." He stared at Jeff, waiting for him to object. "The necklace, the carved raven … it's around Kay's neck. It winked at me. Its eye is set with some type of red stone— "

"Garnet," Jeff interrupted. "The warrior stone."

"She's seen Niki. He's hurt but she couldn't tell me how bad." He straightened, shaking the strain from his shoulders. "We have to do something soon. If he finds out about the necklace, she could be …" he searched for words, "torn asunder."

CHAPTER 53

Scotty nudged the door open, watching Tori concentrate on her reading. She looked up, casually dropping her book on the side table. He recognized the cover. *The Art of War. Interesting reading.*

She rose, her look distant. "Stew? You brought stew as a peace token?"

"Chocolates and coffee as well."

She glared at him. "I'm not hungry." Tori tossed her head and paced in front of the window. Her stomach growled.

Scotty chuckled, coughing to hide his amusement.

Tori whirled on him. "Damn it! You don't play fair and I don't know you well enough to let you through my defenses this soon. You are a complete son of a gun, Scott Miles."

Scotty pushed the door closed with his foot, setting the tray on the dresser. He felt her anger growing at his lack of response and raised his eyes to her face.

Her eyes flashed. "I don't remember inviting you in and, to make matters worse, I know you're listening." Her voice dropped to a hurt whisper then climbed. "I thought we had something good happening." She whipped around, pulling back the curtains. Her back straightened.

He put his hands on her shoulders to turn her around. She shrugged him away.

"No! I don't want you to look at me right now. Just go away." Her voice shook. "Just get me back to my own time!"

Scotty pulled her back against him. He fingered aside her soft hair and ran his tongue down the back of her ear. He heard her intake of breath. He kissed her along the nape of her neck.

She struggled out of his grasp and, pushing him away, stomped to the center of the room.

"The woman I recruited to be my partner is now in mortal danger. I've built a fine business. I have powerful clients … even richer than those upstart Conrays." She stamped her foot. "Damn it, you're not taking me seriously."

She straightened, her posture imperious. "Do you think Kay Kasavina, a recognized authority on antiquities, would travel halfway around the world for a nothing person? Would I touch that filth of a child if I didn't think I could protect Sami from whatever vile thing is harming my partner? Doesn't anybody here understand subterfuge and strategy?" Tori's voice dropped to a quiet snarl. "No one is going to judge this Geechee girl!" She scrubbed at her eyes.

He stood still waiting for the next wave. Her gentle gasps to keep back the sobs broke the silence. He pulled her into his arms. She tensed. He held tighter. "Tori, if you've more to say, I'll listen. But if you are done, I will share my thoughts."

She paused, still in his arms.

"I am not sure what you've seen or heard—." Before he could continue, she once again pushed him away.

"I'll tell you exactly." She sneered at him, the fire in her eyes rekindled, "You had no reaction when Jeff kissed me." Scotty opened his mouth but she glared at him. "Then Kay says things about me … things you shouldn't know. It's just not fair."

"Tori, look at me." She remained with her head down. He waited.

She raised her head, pushing her hair back. He ached to kiss her but he stood with his arms at his side.

"So, there isn't anything here, is there? How could I be such a fool?" She dropped her head into her hands.

Scotty knelt in front of her, taking her hand. "Somewhere over the last three days, somewhere in the middle of all of this insanity, you've gotten under my skin. Yes, I've backed away from you. When I woke up in this wild situation, all I wanted to do was wrap you in one of those woolen capes and take you far away from this nightmare. Tori, I want more than a flirtation."

Tori opened her mouth but he held up his hand. "It's still my turn. I want to get to know you and let you know me. I haven't felt this way about anyone for a long time. I won't pretend I don't have baggage. I know the teasing and fooling around is to stave off the fear that threatens all of us."

"My turn?" she asked. He nodded.

"Okay, I get it. But why didn't you tell me this before? Why don't they trust me?" A hurt little girl looked through Tori's eyes.

"I'm going to give you an analytical answer. Remember, this is my observation. I haven't discussed you with anyone." He hastened on. "You come on large and in charge. Now, I know, Mac does the same thing, but he's a known entity. He's been with us for a while and he comes along with Jeff. Sometimes I think of my father's matched Percherons … two magnificent horses in perfect harmony."

Tori nodded, laughter in her eyes.

"So, you come in, a stranger—but with a connection to Kay— someone very important in Sami's life. That is a challenge in a way. I don't believe Sami sees it that way but I bet Colby might. I suspect Colby is so off balance with her sister's vulnerability, she will lash out at anyone's attempt to control the situation."

"I'm just trying to help. I can't stop the ideas bubbling up." Tori looked down, clenching her fingers. "What do I do?"

"Let Sami take the lead. She has to find the strength. We must get Niki and Kay out of this mess." He shook his head. "Use your pendulum. See if your ideas fit the path we need to walk."

Tori stood, her long dress dragging across his knees. She retrieved the crystal pendulum and returned to sit. The movement stirred thoughts of her long legs but he resisted reaching to stroke her calf through the luxurious fabric.

She held the gold chain between her thumb and forefinger, dangling the pendulum. It swung gently. She studied the refracted light. "I don't know how to use this."

"My mother finds lost things. My family is infamous for misplacing everything from homework to Dad's glasses. I'd swear it's how she always knows if we boys are lying." He grinned at her, earning a smile in return. "Hold the chain between the thumb and forefinger of your right hand. Let the pendulum hang about an inch above your left palm. Ask it to show you what the swing is for an affirmative."

She held out the pendulum over her palm. It hung perfectly still. "It's not working."

"Ask out loud."

"Okay, show me a yes." She hesitated, "Please?"

The pendulum swung back and forth lengthening the arc with each swing. Tori opened her mouth but Scotty shushed her. She held steady, watching. The arc changed to a circle and settled into a steady rhythm.

"I must be moving it but I don't feel it."

"Trust it, Tori. That's odd. The circle means no for my mother."

Tori's brow wrinkled.

"No, you aren't doing anything wrong. It's a personal thing. Now ask for a negative response."

"But won't it swing back and forth?" She fingered the crystal.

"Sure, but you're jumping ahead again. You have to set up a relationship with it. Go through the baby steps."

She held up the pendulum. "Please show me the swing pattern for no." The pendulum swung in a back and forth pattern, not changing.

"Thank you," she whispered.

Scotty smiled at her.

"So, it has to be a yes or no question?"

"At first. Mom dowses with it, too. The swing pattern is more complex."

The look on Tori's face demonstrated her confusion.

"See, if she misplaces an object, she asks the pendulum questions. Is it in the kitchen? Is it in the barn? It helps her remember. But if I lost something, she would walk through the house and it would pull her to the object."

Scotty rolled to his feet and retrieved the two bowls of stew. Tori continued to watch the pendulum swing. He filled a spoon. "Open."

He stuck the spoon in her mouth and, as she closed her lips, let go. She held it between her teeth for a moment and swatted at him with her free hand. He grinned, setting the bowl beside her on the bed. Retrieving the coffee mugs, he set her mug on the blanket chest and eased himself back to the floor.

Tori picked up the bowl, the pendulum in her lap.

"Do I always have to ask the questions out loud?" she asked between bites.

"I don't think so. You'll have to find out." Scotty ran the spoon around the empty bowl. The coffee cups were soon drained dry.

"Chocolates?" Tori questioned. Scotty rose to snag the sweets off the tray. He handed her two chocolates, stacked the empty bowls on the tray and popped one of his two in his mouth. She held out her hand for his last chocolate, her eyes big with pleading. Scotty placed the last chocolate in her palm. She bit it in half and offered the remaining half to him. He leaned down, placing his lips around the sweet, gently running his tongue over her fingertips.

Tori ran her fingers through Scotty's hair trailing her nails down his neck and under his chin. Warmth ran down his spine, taking away his breath. He wrapped his arm around her waist and cupped the back of her head with his free hand, easing her back onto the bed. Bending over her, he kissed her, drawing her lower lip between his teeth. She wrapped her arms around his neck, entwining her hands in his hair.

Tori arched her back and shifted her arms to reach around Scotty's chest, trying to pull him to the bed beside her. He resisted and lifted his lips away from hers. "That was a promissory note, but tonight, we'd better be part of the discussion down stairs."

Tori stuck out her lower lip. Scotty laughed out loud. He grasped her hands and pulled her up into his arms. She clung to him for a moment, then pulled away to straighten her dress. She coiled her hair back into a loose bun and picked up pins from the dressing table.

"You know, Miles, we'll make a pretty good team." When there was no response, she turned to find the bedroom empty. She grabbed the crystal pendulum and descended the stairs.

CHAPTER 54

Shadows danced across the parlor walls. Charlie stoked the fire. The Yule log burned low in the grate while the fresh wood flared.

Jessica settled on the loveseat and Chad pulled up a wingback chair.

"Chad," Tori swept in. "Can we put a slipknot on these strings? Our conversation about strategy… analyzing our opponent's weaknesses… is not a topic filled with compassion and love. I'm asking for rabbinical dispensation."

Sami laughed. "Oh, Lord, Tori, you and Kay will be good partners, leading each other down a wavy path. You're irrepressible and she is always ready for a new adventure."

Tori smiled, dropping into the empty wingback.

Charlie picked up a small marble cutting board and a cedar bough from the hearth. Kneeling at the coffee table, he pulled the boline from his boot, using it to shave the cedar. He glanced up, all eyes on him.

"If I'm going to honor Chad's traditions then I should use my skills, too. This is a process my Mum showed me. It will bring the sacred back … maybe buy some grace for Tori."

Tori glared at him until Scotty's chuckle responded to Charlie's humor.

Charlie tossed the cedar strips in the fire. He murmured several lilting words. Cedar's tangy scent infused a crisp edge to the energy. Mac inhaled deeply and ran his fingers through the Christmas pine, stirring the scents in the room.

Jeff settled on the hearth with Pyewacket in his lap. Colby moved over on the loveseat close to him. Lifting Sami to her feet, Charlie sat on the other loveseat and drew her into his lap, encircling her with his arms.

Mac stood. "We're all tired, homesick, and heartsick. But now we've got to focus on solutions." He fidgeted with the papers in his hands. "How did Kay look? What happened?"

Sami's face paled. "She looks well enough, not physically hurt but under someone's—or something's— control. I'm beginning to believe what Uncle Nigel said about demons."

"That horrid young man is demon spawn." Tori burst out. She pulled at the red string around her wrist. "I admit the whole afternoon shook me."

"Kay's in big trouble." Chad paused worrying his lower lip. "The pendant." Chad felt the raven's beak again. He shook himself free. "Her soul is in a raven ... somehow." Silence met his declaration. "Hey, I know it sounds weird. But what isn't right now? There's definitely a demon inside her and it's not only controlling her but turning up all that sex appeal she emits naturally."

Charlie nodded, looking a little sheepish until Jeff also acknowledged his statement with a rueful smile. Tori narrowed her eyes at Scotty who shrugged.

"Okay, okay," Colby burst out. "We get it. Go on, Chad."

"That energy is why I wanted to punch that little shit today ... being so controlling of her." Chad shrugged at Tori, her fingers still worrying the bracelet. "Tori, I don't think I'm in any position to judge anyone ... not with the way I behaved today. I'm surprised I wasn't strangled with my own red string."

The front door slammed opened. Mac and Jeff launched for the parlor door, skidding to a halt. Nigel peered at them through rain-covered glasses, the open door forgotten.

"Have I missed anything?" Removing his glasses and wiping them dry, he placed them on his nose. He jumped at their proximity. Jeff pushed the door closed against the wind. Mac helped Nigel struggle from his wet coat. "Did I startle you? My abject apologies."

"Uncle Nigel, you are forgiven ... evidenced by the fact that you are still standing." Mac laughed.

Nigel entered the parlor and accepted a snifter from Harry with a grateful smile.

"Uncle Nigel, Chad told us Kay's soul is in a raven." Sami patted the seat next to them.

"Outstanding!" Nigel grinned. "Never ran into a real soul transference before."

"Your enthusiasm aside, sir, I need to find a rabbi tomorrow. I think we can drive the demon out but I need the materials and the proper prayers." Chad stared at Nigel.

"I know just the man." Nigel beamed. "I will be glad to take you. I have wanted a chance to give the new automobile a good run. I bet I can get you there and back in a few hours."

"Chad, please tell us more about the raven." Jessica focused in on him.

"It sounds preposterous but she made it pretty clear."

"Chad, I don't doubt you." Jessica said. "Chris met up with a raven on the Downs this afternoon."

"Aye, and she seemed a bit too bright even for the smart birds they are." Chris said. "She flew off following the carriage coming here."

"She's seen Niki and says he's hurt …but couldn't tell me much more." He felt the tension rise, "Hey, try getting information with yes or no questions." He took a deep breath preparing for the reaction to the next statement. "And if the fairy tales are true, we don't have long. Three days. If she isn't restored in three days, she may not be able to return."

"But that is just in fairy tales." Charlie burst out.

"But even fairy tales contain a kernel of truth." Sami said. "That's what Kay would say if she were here." She sat up straighter in his lap. "It all comes to the New Year's. The final hour for Kay. Mac, what are you planning?"

"The grounds men have the dogs with them at all the times. So, the idea of sneaking out under the cover of the storm won't work."

"But won't it be chaotic if the tower falls?" Sami said. "Won't we be able to bring them out in the carriages?"

"If we get Niki from the labyrinth, it's a long way to the carriages." Mac commented. "Nigel, are you certain Edward will go out there on a cold night?"

"Absolutely, my dear boy. He always conducts his affairs in the labyrinth. He has no interest in the party goings on. He is just humoring Genevieve and keeping up appearances."

"We'll have to split up. One group to find Kay and the other to rescue Niki." Tori fingered the pendulum in her hand.

Sami rose from Charlie's lap and faced the group. "Okay, we split up. It's imperative to free Kay from the demon or she … it might raise an alarm. I imagine if we are all in hooded cloaks, we can get her out during the exodus from the house."

Chad nodded, his face dark. "If for some reason my idea about expelling the demon is wrong, we may have to find another way to subdue Kay … I mean the demon inside her."

"What about chloroform?" Nigel eyes gleamed. "I have access to a small amount. I have—ahem—friends who use the wonderful elixir to relieve pain. It will render her unconscious for a while." His face grew serious, "but you must be judicious. There are hazards."

"That will be interesting." Scotty said. "Mac, are you sure the wall will collapse?"

"If the lightning hits within the area I've described and the winds are directed against it, it will collapse. That should rattle the timbers in the ballroom … enough to evacuate the house."

Chris edged over to sit on the floor beside Jessica, patting her knee. She ruffled his hair. He let his tongue loll and panted, looking up at her. Maeve raised her head, sensing a game. She leapt to land both paws on Chris' shoulders sending the loveseat scooting backwards. Nigel and Harry roared watching Chris fight to escape the face washing.

Jessica snapped her fingers and signed. Maeve fell to her belly, on Chris' chest. He oophed rolling her off. Jessica held out a hand to help him upright.

Sami waited for the laughter to subside, hating to darken the mood again. "So, who will be in each group? Mac, you and Jeff should go after Niki. Uncle Nigel, will Mr. Westfield be with Lord Ramhill?"

Nigel nodded. "It is possible young Adrian may be included." He frowned, "He seems to have performed to his father's satisfaction this afternoon.

"Nigel, where will Kay be?"

"In a chamber on the third floor above the ballroom. I do not know which. I am not allowed up there. Anna is assigned to her. A pretty little redhead."

Pyewacket let out with a loud mrrowww. He placed both paws on Jeff's chest, rising to eye level. Pyewacket gave a guttural growl. "Pye says we have to bring her with us."

"I'd agree," Mac spoke up. "She escorted me around." He rubbed his face. "She has some psychic ability and, if she doesn't attract Lord Ramhill's attention for that, she's just too pretty to be safe."

"My goodness, what a tidy household ... Westfield, if he will agree, and Anna." Nigel flushed. He cleared his throat, "It occurs to me, I would be wise to change my residence for a while and I'd welcome them in my entourage. I've been thinking about some time in India or perhaps America. I will make arrangements once you are all off safely."

"Nigel," Sami patted his arm. "You must not take chances for us. You've done so much already. If you need to be leave now, I ..." she scanned the faces, "we'll all understand."

He placed his hand over hers and shook his head. "I will be fine."

Sami glanced at Tori. "You should stay in the ballroom... to distract the men." She smiled at her.

Tori nodded, color rising in her cheeks.

Pyewacket squirmed loose and ran out the parlor door.

Jessica's chuckle followed his tail. "He must be feeling better. Off for the evening prowl." Jeff brushed fur from his shirt.

"We'll take two carriages." She turned to Nigel. "Will Lord Ramhill keep the dogs up during the party, what with all the people coming and going?"

"That would be prudent." Nigel studied her over his glasses. "But my brother doesn't always see reason. If he is engaged in the labyrinth, he will order the dogs out."

"Then we have to prepare for them." Sami laid her hand on Charlie's shoulder, fatigue evident in her posture. He reached around and pulled her back into his lap.

Jeff leaned over to Colby. "Your job is to look into your crystal ball and tell us what we're forgetting."

"You believe I can, don't you?"

Jeff whispered. "Yes."

Colby swallowed hard then spoke up. "I do have one question. How are Jess and Chris going to know when to …" she searched for words, "scare up the storm?"

"Plan on midnight." Mac looked to Nigel. "We assume the fireworks are stored in the garage but where would you set them up for use?"

Nigel considered the question. "I would say behind the garage … closer to the cliff face."

"Nigel, do you think your brother will have Kay attend the party?" Jeff asked.

"I rather doubt it, dear boy. Edward will not expose her to his social crowd. An evident affair would endanger his standing." He held out his empty glass in his hand. "He will be attentive to Genevieve during the evening."

"Then Kay will be upstairs. We watch for Lord Ramhill to disappear from the ballroom then we slip off." Tori looked at Sami.

"He will signal Westfield to take Niki to the labyrinth. Then propose a toast to the New Year and escape amidst the champagne." Nigel shrugged, "If he becomes bored with the whole proceeding, he will offend Genevieve and leave early." Nigel stared into the swirling brandy. "He is easily bored these days. I just don't understand it, what with that beautiful woman in his life." Mac nodded.

"There we have it," Tori ventured. "We wait until Westfield leaves and watch Lord Ramhill." She looked at Sami and Colby, "We have to find a way to get upstairs."

Sami laughed and hid her face in Charlie's shoulder. He tried to draw his head away to see her face. "Okay, Sami, what is so funny?" Charlie tried in vain to tickle her through the stiff clothing.

"I have an idea how to create a good cover." Her smile brightened. "Let me talk it over with Colby."

Tori stood. "I, for one, want a good night's sleep. Tomorrow will be a long day."

Sami rose, running her fingers through Charlie's hair. "Tori's right. Come up before too long." He lifted her hand to his lips. She pulled away dragging her nails across his palm.

Colby shifted on the loveseat. Jeff rolled to his feet and offered her his hand. She rose and followed Sami. Standing by the piano, Mac picked out the melody to "Every Little Thing She Does Is Magic."

"Hey, Mac," Chad snorted, "Sting won't be born for another fifty years!" He grabbed up the acoustic guitar from the corner and launched into "Come, Josephine in My Flying Machine". Charlie pushed Mac from the keyboard and picked up the accompaniment. Mac took up the chorus in his rich, bass voice.

> Come Josephine in my flying machine
> Going up she goes!

***

Tori ran her fingertips along the ornate headboard. The moonlight shone in bursts through the drifting clouds, sending moonbeams dancing across the striped wallpaper. She lay still, listening to the music. Closing her eyes, the crystal pendulum glowed in her inner vision. It swung back and forth, reflecting hypnogogic sparkles. She took a deep breath preparing to sink into sleep but the image pulled at her. The pendulum drifted through the house, swinging, illuminating each room with purple light. The white ornaments on the Christmas tree reflected the light from the Yule log.

Light, Tori thought. *I can see the house through the pendulum.*

A black shadow slunk through the puddle of moonlight and jumped onto the white counterpane in the next room. Pyewacket pawed at the empty pillow. Niki's face flashed into her mind. The cat settled, tail tucked into curled smoke. His glittering eyes stared. With a shuddering sigh, he lowered his head and covered his nose with his tail.

A sob caught Tori unaware. *Don't worry, Pye, we'll get him out.*

She rolled on her side. Her fingers twitched as if scratching his ears.

The bed shook by her feet. Pyewacket flopped down, his back against her stomach. His rumbling vibration eased her to sleep.

CHAPTER 55

December 31st

The next morning dawned far too bright and early for Chad's taste. Nigel burst into his room, holding out a large mug. "Come now, dear boy, we must be on our way. I am not certain when your Rabbi will have visiting hours."

Chad grimaced at Nigel's enthusiasm but tried to be polite. "Please, sir, why don't you have your tea. I'll not keep you waiting long." Chad dreaded the chill floor. Nigel closed the door behind him.

Cold soles followed by splashing water cleared his head. *Depending on how long the round trip is, I pray I have enough time. Dear G-d, please don't let Nigel dawdle along the road.* He pulled on a heavy cable knit sweater. The soft wool caressed his neck. He patted the door frame murmuring, "Thank you. You have great taste in clothes."

Harry handed him a warm sandwich wrapped in brown paper. Chad opened the back door and bowed Nigel out. Nigel bounded off for the roadster.

The car growled to life. Chad settled onto the leather seat. Harry appeared at his door with goggles and a long muffler. He deposited the items in Chad's lap and tucked a small hamper in the back. "A ride with Mr. Nigel tends to be breezy and dusty. You will need these." Harry smiled at Chad. "And the hamper is lunch."

"Jeez, it's only twenty miles, isn't it?" Chad fumbled with the goggles.

Nigel pulled on his leather driving gloves. "That's right. I'll open this beauty up to her full thirty miles an hour if the roads are decent. Barring flat tires, we should be back by early afternoon!" Nigel beamed at Chad as the Silver Ghost leapt into gear and careened down the drive.

Chad's heart lurched. Turning to look back, he saw Harry doubled over, his laugh echoing in the distance. *Oh no, I am going to kill Niki when we save his butt. He has to be my manager after this.*

The car swung sharply onto the main road, two wheels in contact with the dirt. Chad scanned ahead, eyes sweeping left, right, left. A large shape stepped out from the overgrown bushes.

"Nigel! Look out for that cow!"

"Steady on! We'll be just fine." Nigel swerved, running right side tires into the ditch and out again. The startled animal bolted away. Nigel patted Chad on the arm. "You see, I've had practice." He peered through the goggles at Chad's face.

The car plunged toward the stone wall.

"Nigel! The road!" Chad shouted. "Watch the road!"

Harry held his sides against the suppressed laughter. *One can always count on Nigel to erase one's complacency with life.*

***

A few hours later, the roadster pulled into the drive. Nigel leapt out and strolled toward the kitchen. Chad remained seated, staring straight ahead. Nigel paused, turning around to find Chad motionless. He walked back to the car and patted Chad on the shoulder.

"Chad, boy. We have returned." Nigel's loud voice carried to the house. Harry appeared on the back porch.

Chad shuddered but remained seated. Nigel shrugged and, removing his goggles, crossed the driveway. His eyes gleamed. "By the gods, Harry, what a gorgeous day for a ride. We had a blinding good time, I'll tell you."

"Yes, sir. Will Mr. Chad be arriving soon?" Harry hide his smile recalling the hilarity below the stairs at the Ramhill manor. Nigel was beloved for his complete unawareness that brave men quailed when they went adventuring with him.

"I don't think he travels well. He is …" Nigel dropped his voice to a loud whisper, "a rather nervous sort. Always shouting, watch this, don't look at me, look at the road." Nigel sauntered off.

Chad emerged from the Silver Ghost, holding on to the car with one hand, carrying a small leather bag in the other. Reaching the steps, he grasped the railing, kissed the porch post and staggered up the steps. Harry opened the door, proffering steaming cocoa.

"Thank you, Harry." Chad whispered. "I'm going to bed. I'm going to sleep 'til I stop shaking. Harry, I thought you were my friend. Why did you let me go with that madman?"

"I needed a good laugh, sir." Harry smiled. Chad staggered down the hall, hysterical laughter emitting from his direction.

***

Within the hour, Chad roused from his uneasy sleep. He sat up, his head spinning with the rabbi's words, images swimming in his head. Running his fingers through his hair, the bangs dropped immediately back over one eye. He set out the iron medallions on the desk. Glancing at the door to assure it was closed, he pulled reading glasses from his jacket pocket. He concentrated on his notes, tracing the inscriptions with his fingers. Closing his eyes, he folded his hands over the papers, the medallions and the engraving tool. His prayers complete, he began.

The sky darkened, the light from the gaslight turning the walls yellow in the dusk. His hands shook until he laid the engraving tool against the metal. Then, trusting in the Fathers, each mark appeared, the exact width and depth required. His lips moved in silent prayer.

His neck itched. He glanced around and startled, dropped the tool. He snatched the glasses off, hiding them in his lap.

Scotty stood in the doorway.

"Is everyone trying to scare me today?" Chad scowled at him. "What? Jeez man. Knock or something next time." He muttered more under his breath.

Scotty chuckled, holding his hands up in mock surrender and juggling a large mug. "I did knock. Softly, then banged a few times.

Whistled when I came in." Scotty held out the mug. "Heard you had a tough morning. Harry's fixed a light meal for us before we dress for tonight." He studied the medallions, making no move to touch them.

Chad looked at the Scotsman. "I'd wager if you and I'd created this plan privately, there wouldn't be quite so many complications."

"Nor half as much potential for mischief, either." Scotty's smile grew broader. Chad laughed, sensing Tori stimulated Scotty's amusement.

"Here's what I've done. We know Westfield and Kay have been infested by a demon, right?"

Scotty nodded.

"We must assume Niki has been, too." He looked at Scotty for concurrence.

Scotty hesitated, piquing Chad's interest. "Niki is an odd one." Scotty studied Chad's face. "I'd be hard pressed to predict Niki's behavior."

Chad nodded, tucking the information away.

"Let's assume the worst. That makes three but I have six medallions. Of course," Chad let a little sarcasm into his voice, "I figured some jerky Scotsman might come in and make me slip on the last letter."

Scott looked sufficiently repentant to produce a chuckle. Chad rolled his shoulders, feeling the tension draining.

"What if one of us becomes possessed by his demons?"

Chad rose from the table and picked up the wooden box. "I took the clue from the different colored cords in my box." He drew the strings from the box and untangled them. "Five cords. Guess someone knew I'd zig when I should have zagged. We're covered for one emergency in the labyrinth and one in the house." He tossed two cords to Scotty. "Let's get them finished."

Scotty reached for the first medallion, looking at Chad for permission. Receiving a nod, he fed the cord through the ring allowing it to swing free while tying the knot. The medallion swung in a perfect circle. Chad followed the path with his eyes.

"What did you ask, man?"

"If the Braves will win the Pennant," Scotty replied, a wry smile on his face. "No, I should not be so flippant. I asked if we were going to find home again." He placed the pendant on the blotter and reached for another. Deftly, he worked the next string.

"It said no." Chad stated.

"No," Scotty smiled at him. "The pendulum has always been contrary with me. The circle is yes."

Chad exhaled loudly, rewarded with a rich laugh from Scotty. They finished in silence. Chad tucked them in his pocket.

***

The rippling voices greeted them in the dining room. Jeff pulled a chair out nodding to Chad. Scotty slipped in between Mac and Colby, patting Colby's hand. Tori carried rolls in a basket followed by Harry porting cheeses and preserved meats.

"Miss Tori. I'll handle the rest." Harry reached for the kitchen door but Tori pulled back an empty chair.

"Now, sugar, you need to join us." She grabbed him by the shoulders and danced him around to face the table. Harry tried to slip away but ran into Jessica.

"Harry, haven't you learned not to argue with a woman?" She kissed him on the nose. "Sit down. I'll get coffee. The cake needs to stay in the kitchen until we're all finished or ..." She looked over her shoulder at Mac, "it will disappear before we're all ready." Mac feigned a look of innocence.

Harry glanced at Sami. She motioned to the chair. He shrugged and sat on the edge.

Chad stared into his soup bowl. The spoon in his hand shook. Murmuring played in the background. *How can they act so relaxed knowing what we're facing tonight?*

Scotty's voice calling his name shook him from his downward spiral. "Chad, will you explain the plan for the amulets?"

Chad flushed, fumbling the medallions from his pocket. "I tried to do everything the Rabbi instructed."

He passed one to Jeff and another to Sami. Jeff fingered the iron disc, rubbing his thumb over the design without looking at it. He handed it to Tori. Sami passed hers immediately to Mac then scrubbed her fingers with a napkin.

"When you get close to Kay or Niki, slip the cords over their heads." Their looks went from doubtful to speculative.

Charlie took the amulet by the cord, avoiding the iron's touch. He dropped it on the table. "What will happen then?" He asked, without taking his eyes from the disc.

"I don't know." Chad hurried on at Charlie's sharp glance. "I would expect the demon or imp won't tolerate its touch, forcing it to flee." Chad slumped in his chair, their scrutiny making him uncomfortable.

"Will they work?" Mac asked.

"Of course, they will." Chad snapped, pulling himself up straight. "I may not know what will happen—smoke … convulsions … or whatever—but I do know I've done a good job. It's the best I can give." He pulled on the red string encircling his wrist, cutting into the flesh. "It's my faith in it." He studied the amulet laying in his palm.

Mac held out the amulet across the table. "I didn't mean any offense. Sorry, man."

Chad accepted the amulet, a wave a reassurance flowing from Mac's touch.

"Gentlemen," Nigel broke in, "we are all tense and I, for one, could use a brandy."

Harry jumped to his feet before Tori could catch his arm. He returned with snifters and the carafe. Nigel let out an ahhh.

Sami touched Chad's arm. "Chad, what will the demon do once it's released?"

Chad paused, studying the way Sami phrased the question. *She doesn't doubt me.*

"Most only tolerate this reality, frantic if they have been held here too long. They'll flee back into the void. Or they will exact a price for their servitude." His voice dropped to a whisper, "Usually a blood price from the summoner. Just don't get in their way."

Silence descended around the dining table. Chad stuffed the amulets into his pocket. *Faith, it's all about faith. Uncle Bernie, help me be strong.*

Charlie rose and piled up additional bowls.

"Well, gentlemen," Sami rose signaling to Colby. "It will take the ladies a bit longer to dress. Looks like you will be left alone with your coffee. Colby, why don't I explain my plan for getting upstairs? Tori, I'm sure you'll approve." She mounted the stairs with Colby and Tori bending their heads to catch her quiet instructions.

Jessica patted Chris on the shoulder, "Let's take Maeve for a quick walk. Then I'll help the ladies dress. Those damn corsets will keep them busy."

Hearing her name carried on the wind, Maeve bounded to the door.

CHAPTER 56

Edward surveyed the guests in the ballroom. *How amusing to see all in such baboon finery.* He caught his wife's evocative scent, his spine stiffening. He searched the crowd.

He studied her in astonishment. Gone was the dowdy brown wren that disgraced his breakfast table. Her alabaster skin and the crescents of her breasts rose above her dress in sharp contrast with the very particular blue highlighting her eyes. Her hair shone, the drop diamond earrings drawing his attention to the hollow behind her ear. He smiled remembering the intense sensitivity at that particular spot. His eyes gleamed, anticipating the first dance with her, imagining his hand on her small waist, her beautiful figure no longer hidden in camouflaging fluff. He stepped toward her, but not quickly enough. Nigel appeared from the crowded and whisked Genevieve into his arms. The orchestra struck up *The Reine Waltz*.

My favorite dance, my wife, and, my painfully annoying brother. Enough. Edward tapped his fist against his leg. *My altar will have two sacrifices tonight. Nigel shall not block me any longer.* He glared at the swirling couples. The tall Texan he met at dinner swept the auburn-haired beauty onto the dance floor. He placed his hand below her shoulder blade positioning his elbow to support her arm along his own. His posture matched the gentlemen on the dance floor, his hand holding hers at her eye level. Edward ground his teeth at the upstart American.

Delighted laughter drew his attention back to Nigel. His anger rose with each glimpse of Genevieve's smiling face.

***

Turning with the music, Jeff frowned at the scowl crossing Lord Ramhill's face, Edward's eyes riveted on Nigel. Jeff spotted Mac standing near the door conversing with the portly gentleman from the dinner at the Stanton-Smythes. He tapped into Mac's thoughts.

"Do you believe dinosaurs still exist?" Conan-Doyle queried.

"There are areas in the world, Africa, Australia, South America, unexplored." Mac responded. "I'd put my money on South America."

"So Gordon said. At night, he heard roars and screams echoing through the valleys, sounds not made by any animal with which he was familiar. And he was a very well-traveled chap."

"I've been to Uruguay where there are valleys and plateaus which are inaccessible" Mac leaned closer, dropping his voice. "Areas protected by native taboo and superstition, tales about lizard-like creatures walking on two legs." Mac felt Jeff's mental nudge. He searched the dancers, locating his friend.

Keep an eye on Nigel. Lord Ramhill isn't happy with his antics.

Will do.

Mac shook hands with Conan-Doyle and moved into the crowd.

"Jeff," Colby spoke softly then more insistently, "Jeff." He looked down at her smile. "Where did you learn to dance?"

"MIT." Her face showed confusion. "I dated a girl whose passion was ballroom dancing. She belonged to a performance group specializing in the waltz, complete with period costume. My only experience, at that point, was the two-step."

She pursed her lips as if in disdain.

"Too plebian?" he asked. Color spread across her cheeks. "You dance beautifully."

"I love to dance." She brightened. "Jon and I've won several competitions at the club. He's a marvelous dancer." Her voice trailed off and she stumbled.

Jeff saved her with a gentle pressure on her back, lifting her arm. He noted the name but kept his eyes over her shoulder, locating each friend, giving her time to catch her breath.

Chad attempted to disengage from a young woman arrayed in pastel rose, the pale dress signaling her availability for matrimony. His face betrayed his discomfort with the feminine hand on his chest. Scotty wove his way through the standing crowd, speaking and nodding but avoiding being detained until he arrived at Chad's side. Chad awkwardly introduced Scotty who stared intently into the young woman's eyes and lifted her hand to his lips. Chad eased away from the pair, snagging white wine from the waiter.

Across the dance floor, Lord Ramhill also lifted a glass from the passing tray and responded to a gentleman guest. He nodded intently during the conversation but his eyes did not leave his wife.

Colby's voice drew Jeff's gaze back. "Being a good dancer is more important than breathing to my mother." She waited for his response but he just nodded. "Lessons were miserable. The sweaty little boys, their sticky hands. I lived with it so my father would dance with me at the country club. Dancing with him is heaven." She looked up at his concerned face. She smiled brightly, "It's a pleasure to dance with a man who can lead. And you do marvelously, Dr. Conray."

The orchestra finished the waltz, the silence filling with light applause. Gentlemen bowed and ladies curtseyed and the dance partners separated.

Edward strode purposefully through the crowd. Nearing Genevieve, he saw the reputed Ramhill cousin bow to her. Before he could speak, Charlie offered his arm and led her to a corner for the next dance, a cotillion. Edward swung on his heel nearly running into Sami. Her amber eyes widened. A thrill ran through him. He captured her hand.

He studied her deep lavender gown. "I wish a dance with you, since your husband has stolen my wife. It is the host's duty." The resemblance to Serena, the high cheek bones and deep-set eyes, the delicate nose and lips intrigued him. He did not believe for a moment she was Gordon's niece. He did not wait for her response. A tremor shook her hand and he tightened his grip.

"Lord Ramhill, my apologies, but I'm not familiar with this dance. Please accept my regret." She tried to pull away from him.

"Then let me obtain wine for you." He pulled her closer. "Did I mention how very much your husband reminds me of my late brother Nigel?" He looked around for a waiter.

Scotty appeared at Sami's shoulder, two glasses in his hands. He offered one to her. "Sami, I've been negligent in Charles' absence."

He kissed her on the temple before turning to acknowledge Edward with a slight bow.

Edward scoffed at the impropriety.

"Lord Ramhill, please accept my compliments on your home. I am Scott McMillan from Inverness."

A polite smile frozen on his face, Edward studied Scotty. "Any relation to Garad MacMillan, the laird?"

"Yes." Scotty deflected the conversation, "I was most impressed by your protégé. Her insight into my particular penchants was startling." He looked around the crowd. "I was hoping to speak with her again. Is she in attendance?"

"No. She is plagued with sick headaches. Those psychically gifted often are. I believe there may be some talented—or at least, well informed— members within your party."

"We each seek spiritual enlightenment in our own way."

"Is that so? And what is your personal interest?"

"Time, sir. Since the publications by H.G. Wells, specifically *The Chronic Argonauts*, I have been fascinated with time and travel. Have you read his works?" Scotty said.

"No, young man, my time is spent in more profitable pursuits than fiction." He shifted his gaze once again to Sami. Scotty placed his arm around her waist and pulled her close.

"Forgive me, your lordship but Mrs. Stanton-Smythe has requested Mrs. Ramhill's presence." He turned Sami away from Edward. Over his shoulder, he continued, "I must complete the errand placed on me by the gentlewoman." Not waiting for a reply, Scotty guided Sami through the crowd to an alcove between the windows.

Finding no one waiting there, Sami looked at Scotty, "Where is she?"

He pointed across the dance floor at the statuesque brunette and her marriageable daughter surrounded by young men. "Over there. We'll work our way through the crowd in a moment but you'll have to come up with something to say to her."

"You mean, she didn't ask for me?"

"No." Feeling Edward's eyes on him, Scotty did not turn around to look back but took Sami's elbow and moved her through the crowd. When he no longer felt the lord's gaze, he slowed their pace.

"Thank you." Sami looked around. "He's quite mad. He called Nigel 'his late brother'." Her eyes clouded. "He's wearing the family ring. It burned when it touched my hand."

He stiffened, wishing to spirit her away.

"Burned with great evil." Her eyes cleared and she scanned the room. "We must stop him, Scotty."

Scotty nodded. A musical flourish rippled through the air and the dancers emptied the dance floor. Charlie and Genevieve intercepted them.

"Saminthea, my dear." Genevieve pressed Sami's hand. "Your charming husband is an excellent dancer. Are you enjoying yourself?"

Sami smiled. "I was on my way to speak with Mrs. Stanton-Smythe."

"Excellent!" She surveyed the gathering. "There she is. Come along." She held Sami's hand in her own.

CHAPTER 57

Chris drove the runabout up the hill, staying just below the ridge. He jumped from the seat and secured the reins to a spindly bush. The old mare nudged his hands.

"Old girl, I'd rather not have ye out here in the dark but I promise a rub down when this storm is over." He scratched the soft tissue around her nostrils. She exhaled hot breath with a sigh, the steam swirling around them.

Jessica swung to the ground, her greatcoat, spreading, settling heavily around her ankles, a dark bird folding her wings. Her jaw worked while she surveyed the roiling clouds on the western horizon. "That storm is carrying lightning. It shouldn't be too hard." Her voice cut like the cold wind. She flipped the horse blanket over the mare, securing the belly strap, and headed for the top of the hill.

Chris buckled the chest strap. He leaned his forehead against her warm side to calm his racing heart. "Be good, old girl. I'll be back to check on ye in a few minutes," he whispered. She nodded, dropping her head against the wind.

Cold mist glazed his face. He stood on the crest searching the brush. A long moment passed with no movement, no sign. He studied the blackness. Lights from the Ramhill estate drew his eye, torches moving around the manor.

"Come on, girl. Be kind to me. Move or something. You're making me nervous." The wind carried his words away into the clouds. He considered returning to the runabout for a lantern, but a warm breeze swirled around him, carrying Jessica's musky perfume. He followed the direction, feeling the wind shift to push at his back. He counted twenty paces across the rough terrain before he saw her pale face. She sat, leaning against a rock outcrop, a heavy blanket across her knees. Without taking her eyes from the clouds, she lifted one edge, a clear invitation.

Chris settled beside her, pulling his hat firmly on his head. Jessica nudged him and he wrapped his arm around her shoulders. He felt her sigh. Sensing her rising tension, he hugged her to him.

"It'll be okay, lass," he whispered into her hair.

"How strange is it that I'm preparing to damage my husband's heritage. I mean, when we get back ..." The unspoken *if* rang in his mind.

"When we get back," she started again, "I will probably find a written account in a diary. Each Lady Ramhill kept one." She rubbed her hands together. "Except me. Not my style." Tucking deeper into the blanket, she looked at him. "Now, my question is, would the tower fall from some other cause if we weren't here. Or are we changing history? If Lord Ramhill is a demonologist, it must influence his son and then his grandson. All the way to my Damian."

Chris tensed at her possessive claim. He tried to suppress the rising desire to kiss her—*not just to comfort*—, he decided honestly. *This would be a lovely evening to watch the oncoming storm.* He felt her hand on his heart, *if only* .... He stopped his thoughts.

"You'll worry yourself daft thinking about this Gordian knot." The lightning play high in the storm clouds. Small ice pellets mixed with the rain stinging his face. He pulled his hat down lower over his eyes. Waiting for Jessica to continue, he lifted the blanket from her shoulders to enfold her hair. She edged closer to him.

"I know. But what if something goes wrong? What if someone is killed—not just one of us—but someone who has influence on the next generation?" She rushed on. "Alternative realities fascinate my brother Lionel. He's always talking about what if." She moved away from him, pulling her hair back from her face. The cold wind poured between them, sending a shiver up Chris's spine.

She faced him. "What if somehow Charlie, for instance, isn't ever born? Sounds like madness because we all know him but if something is changed and he isn't, then how can we be sitting here waiting on this hill?"

"Jess, you are driving me to madness." Chris burst out. "We are here, lass. That means Charlie is fine. He brings us all together. How else could we get here?"

"Okay." She shrugged. "But what if there *are* more subtle changes. What if?" Chris heard Damian's name in her thoughts. "What if Charlie isn't the same man, is somehow affected by this action to be more like his brother. More inclined to follow the family obsession?"

Chris pondered her question and found no words to soothe her.

Jessica shuddered, arching her back and staring intently into the distance. "The storm is weakening, Chris." She unfolded from the blanket. "We can't let it. We have to pull the clouds back together or we won't have enough charge in the atmosphere." She rolled to her feet and shook out her skirt. "What time is it?"

Chris pulled back his cuff, grateful Scotty gave him the watch. "Eleven forty." He rose and stepped to her side, formulating his question. He stuttered, trying to find the way to ask for her guidance, to gain her faith he would follow her lead. He wrapped his arm around her shoulders but she stepped away from him. He tensed for her angry rebuff and jumped violently, his wrist burned on fire.

"Gods, girl, you don't have to hurt me. I'll keep me hands to meself!" Chris burst out.

Jessica looked at him, her eyebrows furrowed in question. The pain intensified. Chris fumbled at the strap. He ripped it off and dropped it to the ground. The dial flared in the darkness.

CHAPTER 58

E dward nodded to Westfield. Placing his hand on Nigel's shoulder, he smiled at Genevieve. "My darling, I wished for a dance with you but we will have a fine closing for this lovely fete with the fireworks. I need to confer with Nigel on that very topic." Edward kissed her on her cheek. "We should inspect the arrangements." Edward steered Nigel through the patio doors and down the steps

Jeff?

Mac's call cut through any romantic thoughts in Jeff's mind.

Lord Ramhill just dragged Nigel from the room.

Mac moved through the crowd using evasive maneuvers from his football days. He opened the garden door and disappeared into the dark.

Jeff drew Colby close. "Our timing just changed. Good luck, babe. I want a spectacular welcome home kiss and I'm not taking no for answer … no matter how well Jon dances."

She pulled back from him but he held her tight.

"Whatever you planned, please proceed." Jeff grinned.

Colby twisted away, swinging her hand flat against his cheek. Everyone near them turned at the resounding smack. Colby stood ramrod straight, glaring at him. "Kiss you? How dare you!" Colby pushed her way through the staring couples. She flounced to Sami, lips trembling.

"The nerve. I'm mortified." Her hysterical voice carried through the crowd. She fanned herself with her handkerchief. Behind the fabric, she whispered. "Watch this." She staggered and sank into Chad's arms.

All eyes on the kerfuffle, Jeff slipped out through the glass doors.

Genevieve touched Chad's arm, distress on her face. "Mr. Alton, would you carry the young lady upstairs so she may compose herself?

There is an open chamber on the right." Her voice indicated her ire at her guest's histrionics. "Charles, you and your wife need to accompany Miss Fairmont to maintain propriety."

She confronted Tori. "Miss Madison, it is best you join them. My staff will notify your coachman you are ready to depart." Her tone carried dismissal. She raised her hand and a maid appeared at her elbow.

"Find Mr. Ramhill's coachman and instruct him to bring the carriage around immediately." The maid preceded the group through the crowd. The orchestra finished the waltz and launched into another reel.

Chad took two steps up the stairs. Colby squirmed in his arms attempting to free her legs. "Now, now" Chad whispered, "you shouldn't recover so soon. We're being watched." Colby relaxed back against his chest.

Charlie and Sami followed to the top. Charlie stopped Sami with a hand on her arm. "Love, I can't come with you. They don't know how to get into the labyrinth. He means to kill Nigel. If I don't go to help them, they may not survive." His hand beat against his leg.

Chad set Colby on her feet. He fumbled in his pocket and tossed Charlie an amulet. "Put this around Uncle Nigel's neck if you have any worries."

Charlie caught the amulet.

"Yep. I'm an overeager cook. I made more than I thought I would need. Good luck, man. Don't worry about me. I'm in good hands here." Chad looked at the women.

"Don't you understand yet Uncle Nigel is the only Ramhill with a sense of humor? Protect my wife or I'll kill you myself." Charlie ran down the stairs.

"Yeah, yeah, Always with the threats. I survived Uncle Nigel's driving. Nothing scares me, now." Chad took the next flight two at a time. "Sami, got the chloroform? I don't want to use it, but ..." Chad's pace quickened with Tori at his elbow. "You guys okay?" he called back.

"Chad, just keep going." Sami removed her shoes. Colby followed suit. They climbed to catch up. The stairs became steeper.

On the third-floor landing, Chad stopped, waiting for them.

"Never ... ever ... will ... I ... wear ... a ... corset ... again." Colby panted. She swiveled her head from right to left. "Two chambers."

Tori pushed open the door on the right. "No one's here." She swept back into the hallway. Chad pushed the second door.

"It's empty, too." Colby said.

Tori rounded on her. "How do you know?"

"I just do. Okay?" Colby shot back.

Sami pushed Chad into the room and beckoned for the other two. She swung the door closed.

She picked up a hair brush from the dressing table. "She was here." Lightning flashed at the window. "We've got to hurry. The storm's almost here."

"But to where?" Chad looked around the room. When his eyes met Colby's, she shrugged.

"Scotty had better be right about this." Tori sank to the floor. She pulled a folded onion skin paper and the crystal pendulum from her evening bag. She unfolded the paper, smoothing it out on the floor. "The tower is here," she pointed to the circle on the drawing, "and the wings go off this way. From Nigel's description, the north wing is a library on the first floor and family chambers on the second. The south wing is kitchen below, dining room, a study on the first floor and guest chambers on the second. I guess the servant's quarters are on third floor. So..." She lifted the pendulum to eye level, staring into the crystal.

She held it over the north wing. It hung motionless for three heartbeats then swung back and forth. Tori pulled it up and away from the drawing. She lowered it over the south wing. The pendulum swung in a circle.

"I'd wager she is not in the guest chambers. That would be an affront to Lady Ramhill. We should try the servant's quarters."

Chad offered Tori his hand. She swept up the paper and accepted his help. "Let's go." They started down the stairs.

"I hope we don't have to go all the way back to the ground floor," Sami said

"I don't think so," Chad scanned the next landing. "I think the tower connects with the wings on the second floor." He beckoned them around a corner into the main hallway. They sprinted down the hallway passing by Ramhill ancestor portraits. Chad reached the end, the walls blank. He turned to look at the women, arriving breathless behind him.

"Where are the stairs, Chad?" Tori demanded, her breath returning first. Chad shrugged, a stricken look on his face.

Colby pressed her hand to the stitch worrying her ribs. "Hidden panel" she gasped.

Chad ran his fingers along the wainscoting and up the paneling on the walls. His heart beat faster, his breath coming in shallow gasps. His vision narrowed. He fingered the talisman in his pocket, murmuring a prayer for guidance. Running his hand over the panel again, he heard a click. The panel swung out revealing the stairs within the wall.

Sami took a deep breath and disappeared up the stairs. Chad followed. Tori shooed Colby into the narrow space then pulled the panel partially closed. She examined the opening, feeling the latch from inside. She closed the panel.

The stairs opened out into a narrow hallway. Doors set into the plain walls lined the hall. A single lamp at each end did little to drive away the darkness. Sami pointed to the third door. "There's light under that door."

The door opened and a slight figure stepped into the hall. Hands on her hips, Anna stared at them.

CHAPTER 59

Scotty's watch flared again. "Something's gone wrong!" Chris cried. "Jess, go on. They're in trouble." He stared at the Ramhill estate desperate to find a clue. The movement around the estate appeared unchanged, the men and dogs patrolling the ground. He concentrated on the gardens near the labyrinth.

"There. Someone's going in." He pointed to the labyrinth. "See the torch. Ye gads, they're going in a straight line. Can't be. It's a maze for gods' sake." Things are moving faster."

He pulled Jessica to the rock outcropping. "Find your spot, girl. I'll back ye up." He grabbed her by the shoulders. "I'll give ye whatever ye need but you're in charge." Chris' fear ran through him, the dark, the storm, the dogs. He grasped the feeling, filling himself with terror, setting off the adrenaline rush for extra power. He pulled her to him, kissing her hard on the lips. "You can give me a good slap when we are back where we belong. Now, do what you do!" He turned her to face the storm.

Jessica planted her feet, lifting her face to the sky, the icy rain coating her eyelashes. The wind whipped with increasing force, pulling at her clothes and leeching away warmth from her body, stealing away the feel of his lips. She raised her arms.

"Come, Jebediah, assist me. Come, Zachariah, heed my call." Her voice rolled, a wordless tune sighing in a new language, gaining speed. The winds increased their keening.

Chris closed his eyes, allowing the tune to wind around him until it rose in his throat. His deeper tones joined hers accelerating the wind's chaotic dance. He squinted against the falling ice crystals, watching the roiling clouds spider-webbed with lightning. Jessica's thoughts flashed through his mind, her litany, winds, windlings, gusts and breezes in a horde. *Mariah, Anoria, Madjica, Zephyr, Coronia.* Exhorting them to attend her.

Lightning flashed from cloud to cloud, bunched in one plane, arcing blue white from the sky. Dark tendrils rose from the tower's base, crashing into the downward bolt, exploding in midair. Blue electric fingers ran up the tower, cascading off the top and swirling in the winds. A second bolt streaked across the sky, the answering updraft from the labyrinth's center. Thunder rolled across the hills.

Jessica staggered, her arms dropping to her side. Chris grabbed her and held her close. He studied her face. His heart hammered at the blue cast to her lips.

"Jess." He coughed, his voice raw in his throat. "Are you done in?" He glanced toward the manor noting the tower still stood, the eldritch fire gone. "Have we done enough?" he said, worry echoing in his tone.

Jessica pulled away, again planting her feet on the icy ground. Raising her arms, she took up the chant. Reaching out, she enfolded Chris in her sphere, feeling him startle when sparks ran up his legs and across his back. His fine hair stood out in all directions, his hat lost. She pulled his energy from him, draining his muscles. She welcomed him into the storm, sending a cold wash through him. The winds ran ghostly hands down his body, his muscles languid under their touch. Cold sweat beaded on his forehead. He felt the lightning bolt before it raced down to meet the rising dark column.

The wind died. *Stillness ...so quiet.* Chris wondered if he could hear at all. *No, I can hear the ice hitting the dried grass. How can I be frozen and broiling at the same time?* He listened, catching a ghostly murmur from Jessica.

She stood, her head down, her long arms hanging loosely at her sides. Her hair rippled as each windling ran through it, caressing her neck and face. She spoke a word to each before it departed. The last ran his long fingers across her cheeks, touching her eyelids and lips. Chris looked away.

"Pray for me. Pray for Damian. Jebediah, pray for us all." She covered her eyes with both hands.

Chris stood silent, his arms and legs aching. He shuffled his feet, willing feeling back into his calves. He took a small step toward her. Hearing the movement, Jessica looked at him.

"Chris, thank you. You're a wonderful friend." Dark circles grew under her eyes.

Chris enveloped her in his embrace. Distant baying raised the hair on his neck. His heart pounded and he held Jessica tighter. Fire flared in his peripheral vision.

"Jess, look!" Flames surrounded the tower. Shouting carried the distance. Several men pushed the pump wagon around the corner. Figures straightened and bowed, pumping frantically. Moments passed. Water sprayed from the hose, directed against the fire but disarrayed by the swirling winds. A cheer died on the grounds men's lips.

Jessica turned in his arms, her back against his chest. He felt her tense.

"No." she said through gritted teeth. "I won't let innocents be hurt."

She whistled loudly, the note starting low and rising beyond his hearing. His ears ached. Grass and scrub flattened, approaching them at great speed. She pulled her arm free from his grasp and pointed toward the manor, uttering sounds in a staccato string. The wind swirled around them, rose into the sky, a dark form coalesced. It dove toward the manor. The waterflow straightened, pouring onto the tower. The men pumped faster. Their cheer reached the Downs. White steam billowed from the tower. Grinding stone signaled its collapsed, dust plumes overwhelming the waterfall.

Jessica fell, deadweight in his arms.

CHAPTER 60

A nna shook her head. "These are the servants' quarters. Guests are not allowed."

"Anna, we're here to help." Sami stepped toward the girl.

"How do you know my name?" Anna eyed her.

"Mr. MacIntyre told us about you." Sami took another step. She held her handbag behind her and shook it toward Chad.

He pulled the bag from her wrist and fumbled it open, his activity in Sami's shadow. He found the small, stoppered bottle.

"Anna, we're looking for Miss Kasavina. Do you know where she is?"

"I've strict instructions, ma'am, so don't go trying to convince me you ladies and this here gentleman have good intentions." Anna's voice shook but she continued blocking the doorway. "Please, ma'am, go back downstairs or I will call for Mr. Westfield." She drew in a breath to shout, but froze, Kay's hand on her shoulder.

"Anna, these are the people I was telling you about. Lord Ramhill sent me to see them yesterday."

Chad dabbed Sami's handkerchief on the top of the bottle. Fumes filled the small space. Kay's nostrils flared. She pushed Anna aside and elbowed Sami against the wall. Kay's pupils narrowed into vertical slits. Captured by their gleam, Chad froze. Her hands reached for his throat, fingers twisted into claws.

Sami grabbed Kay by the arm. Kay shook her off without breaking eye contact with Chad. He backed away, crashing through the door to the room opposite. The bottle slipped from his hand and shattered on the floor. Kay's black aura filled the doorway and blocked the feeble light. Chad stared at her red eyes, fumbling for the amulet. He held it up. Her eyes rolled but she did not stop.

He backed up until he felt the window at his elbow. Lightening flashed, the window rattled. He glanced over his shoulder. Seeing her reflection closer to him, he whipped back around.

"Now, Kay," he said, "I have this lovely necklace for you. I know it's a little crude but it comes with many good wishes."

She drew within reach, her hands grasping for his throat.

"If you will let me put this on." He raised the loop in both hands, weaving away from her. Movement drew his attention.

Anna clung to the door frame barring Tori. Grabbing her shoulders, she tried to push the young maid aside.

"No, ma'am, Lord Ramhill will be fierce angry with me."

"Anna, she's going to hurt him." Colby ducked past Tori then grabbed Anna by the wrist. She twisted Anna's arm tightly behind her and held her motionless.

Lightning illuminated the window. Beyond Kay, Chad saw Tori's eyes grow large, staring at the window behind him. He batted the grasping hands away and glanced back.

The she-raven flung herself against the glass, claws scrabbling at the pane. It tumbled away in the wind, the screeing cry fading. Chad felt Kay's nails dig into his neck. He pulled at her hands. The window exploded, sending glass fragments raining into the room.

The raven landed on his shoulder and sunk its beak into Kay's hand. Tori grabbed her from behind. Kay's eyes flamed. She shook free, undaunted by the raven's attack. Chad hunched his shoulders. With a growl, he rose up between her outstretched arms and looped the amulet over her head.

All motion stopped. The raven launched itself through the jagged glass. It fell away in the swirling winds.

A heavy hand landed on Chad's shoulder, He flinched back.

"Your work is crude but effective, young sir." The gravel voice crawled through Chad's bones. "My thanks to thee for setting me free." Kay threw back her head and keened a high note. Chad buried his head in his arms. Thunder rattled the glass shards in the windows and washed the high notes from the air. Smoke billowed around her, spilling along the low ceiling and pouring out into the night. Her knees crumbled.

Chad folded her over his shoulder. "Looks like it's my night for carrying the ladies."

Sami socked him in the arm. "Hopefully, the chaos downstairs will cover us. Anna, come with us."

Anna looked at the women surrounding her, eyes narrowed. After a moment, she nodded. Colby let go.

A loud explosion rocked the floor. Doors blew open in the narrow hallway. Multiple lightning flashes and fireworks illuminated the sky.

Chad ran for the stairs. "Okay, ladies, they're playing our song." He barreled down the narrow stairs grunting under Kay's dead weight. He staggered, fumbling to open the door into the main hallway. It held fast.

"Damn, damn," he muttered under his breath, jumping when Tori squeezed by him. She fingered the mechanism, pushed the panel open and ran ahead. He ran to the main stairs, praying Colby and Sami were behind him. Thunder rumbled up the stairs. Cracks crawled rapidly across the walls. White plaster dust showered down.

"Come on, ladies, move." Kay stirred. He dropped her feet to the floor maintaining an arm around her waist. She clung to him. He waited for the women. They held their sides and panted in the tight dresses. "C'mon, you're harder to herd than cats. Let's go. Let's go." He hurried them down the stairs into the crowd pouring from the ballroom. Smoke filled the hallway, billowing along the ballroom ceiling.

Genevieve directed the guests to the door. She studied each face. Anna ducked around Sami to reach Lady Ramhill.

"Ma'am, I'm so sorry. I tried to keep them out. The master will be so angry with me!" Tears ran down her face.

Lady Ramhill shoved several capes in Sami's direction before turning to the shivering maid. "Anna, you have done everything you can. Go with Miss Kasavina and stay with her. She will need you to brew the tea I gave you." She leaned close to the young woman. "Do you still have it?"

Anna felt for the packet in the apron pocket and nodded.

"Good girl. Now, on with a cape." She draped it around Anna's shoulders. "Go. You are safe with Mrs. Ramhill." She propelled her along. Shooing the others ahead, she pulled Sami aside. "Your carriage is along the south wall. Harry will find you." She hugged her. "I will see if I can help your Charles and his friends. Be safe, dear one." A deep rumbling grinding, stone against stone, filled the hallway, freezing her reply. The wooden timbers cracked. Dust and smoke billowed from the ballroom doorways.

"Come on!" Colby pulled Sami backwards toward the front steps. Genevieve disappeared into the smoke and dust.

Outside, four men bent and straightened over the pump engine's great seesaw handle. Livery coats festooned the ground around the steps. The flaccid hose swelled larger with each stroke. Water streamed toward the house, showering the running guests.

"This way, Miss Sami." Harry's voice drew Sami's eyes from the roiling smoke. He tucked her under his arm, held his cape over her head and steered her through the carriages and skittish horses. He handed her into the carriage followed by the others. Climbing to the box, Harry shook the reins and guided the horses through the crush.

CHAPTER 61

Charlie's harsh whisper competed with the howling wind. "Jeff. Mac. Let me catch you. Please." He willed his eyes to adjust to the darkness. Lightning on the horizon drew his gaze to the Downs.

Blessings on you, Jess. Chris, keep her safe. He sent his thoughts toward the hills. He ran down the stone stairs and onto the slick winter grass, scanning the lawn. He drew back against the supporting stone wall, eyes wide in the darkness.

Westfield rounded the tower with Niki beside him. Niki's head drooped on his chest, his movements stiff. When he stumbled, Westfield placed an arm around his shoulders, pulling him toward the labyrinth. Westfield paused at the hedge.

Charlie crept closer.

"You're doing as you're compelled." Niki's slurred words carried to Charlie. "In another time, I think we would have been friends."

"Thank you, sir." Westfield said. He stuck his arm into the hedge and a narrow segment swung outward.

"Yew." Niki ran his fingers through the branches. "Ironically appropriate, Westfield. To the Celts, the yew is a symbol of death and rebirth." Niki chuckled. The two figures disappeared into the gap. The panel swung closed.

Charlie froze, sweat running down his neck. *A direct path. The others have gone the long way. They'll be too late.* A loud crackling raised his hackles. Jagged lightning coursed downward into the hedge beyond his vision. Momentarily blinded, he tasted ozone.

Oh god, Jess. Not too close.

He willed himself to move, running to the hedge. Scrabbling through the branches, his fingers searched for a lever or handle. His shoulders dropped, his throat too tight to allow in air. He rubbed his face, straining against the constriction.

"One, two, three, take a right. Find the path's true beginning. Find the way or feel your life force dimming." He ran to the entrance, chanting, his steps in cadence. He plunged into the first corridor and skidded on the icy grass.

* * *

Edward propelled Nigel into the labyrinth's center.

"See here, Edward, you have had your little fun trying to scare me but don't you think you've behaved badly long enough?" Nigel struggled in his brother's grip.

Edward released him. He shrugged his shoulders to settle his coat and eyed Nigel. "I plan to behave badly for quite a long time. You have unrealized talent I will put to better use." He stalked past Nigel toward the altar, pulling the athame from his boot. Nigel stared at him, eyes wide.

The hidden panel swung open. Dressed in a dark robe and carrying the boline, Adrian gave Nigel a disdainful look.

"You see, dear brother, I will have your bones. I will invoke many demons with your talent at my disposal." He paced a circle around the dark stone, running his hands across the scarred alter and examining the ground. His face grew grimmer with each step.

"It will do." Edward grabbed Nigel by the arm.

Lightning blinded the three men, the thunder deafening. The altar stone exploded. Hot, metallic air seared Nigel's lungs. He doubled over and sank to his knees, fighting the urge to inhale. Blinking against the whiteness, he crawled toward the spot he last saw his nephew. His hand found Adrian's face, coming away with blood on his fingers. He felt for the carotid. *His heart still beats.* He settled back on his knees, shaking his head. For a long moment, there was no sound.

Nigel wondered if his hearing were gone until Edward roared. Nigel peered through tearing eyes. Edward stood at the altar staring at the large cracks in the stone.

"Damn you, damn you … whoever you are. My demons will hunt you down! I will have you. Will cut your heart out!" He shook his fist at the roiling clouds, his face florid in the torch light. He hauled Nigel from the ground. "I know somehow you are involved in this travesty." He shifted his grip to Nigel's wrist. Tearing back Nigel's shirt sleeve, he exposed the white forearm.

"Damn lightning weakened the circle." Edward mumbled.

Nigel looked into his brother's crazed eyes. "Edward, what about your son?" He pointed at Adrian's crumpled body. "We should see to him. He is breathing but he may be injured. Come on, old man, think about Adrian." He twisted in his grasp. Edward's grip on his wrist tightened.

"Quit squirming, Nigel! I swear I'll stab you right here!" He stooped to retrieve the boline lost from his son's limp fingers. "What I need is a simple thing." He smiled, madness glinting in his eyes. He slashed Nigel's arm.

Nigel stared at the blood welling up in the long cut and running into his palm. Edward held the hilt against Nigel's wrist. Blood stained the handle and dripped from the blade. He pulled Nigel along to pace the circle, reinforcing it with each drop. Nigel's gaze fixated on the blood pulsing with his quickening heartbeat. He alerted to Edward's voice in mid-sentence.

"… and while I would appreciate some remembrance of you, well, you just don't…."

Nigel's head swam, he stumbled. Edward's iron grip pulled him along.

The hedge panel swung open. Westfield supported Niki through the opening. He stiffened seeing Adrian on his hands and knees, his head down. He dropped his grip on Niki and knelt to wrap his arms around Adrian's shoulders. Adrian's bewildered gaze focused on Westfield and he leaned against the retainer.

"Lord Ramhill, the young sir needs medical attention. Permission to take him to the house." Westfield's voice shook.

"Denied." Edward pushed Nigel toward the hedge wall. Nigel slumped to the ground holding his arm against his chest. Edward grabbed Niki's bound hands dragging him toward the altar. Niki tripped, landing on his knees, his hands an inch from the bloody circle.

"No!" Edward jerked him backwards. He hauled Niki to his feet. "Westfield, carry him."

A spasm of agony rolled across Westfield's face. He released Adrian and stumbled toward his master. He lifted Niki and stepped over the circle. Edward strode to the altar, gesturing impatiently for Adrian.

Westfield laid Niki on the cold stone. He looked down at him. "My Lord, spare this one. There is something special about him."

"Compassion, Westfield? Perhaps my control is slipping. I may have to replace your demon when I am through with this."

Westfield winced.

"Now, go stand at the entrance. I do not wish any more disturbances. See to it!" Edward's voice rose.

Westfield took his place, his eyes downcast.

CHAPTER 62

Step, step, stepping to the right. Use good sense back to the light. The words poured through his memory. "Je—Oomph." Strong arms knocked the breath from him but kept him from falling into the hedge.

"Damn, Charlie, don't you know anything about sneaking up on people?" Mac whispered. "Listen, Uncle Nigel's in real trouble. What's the fastest way through this nightmare?"

Charlie shook off Mac's hands. "I know he's in trouble." He snapped at Mac, his voice husky "And Westfield took Niki in just now."

"How the hell did they get past us?" Mac demanded.

Let him tell the story. Jeff's thoughts bounced in Mac's head.

Mac nodded. Charlie bristled at their unspoken communication. He shook himself to slough off the negative emotion. "They went through the hedge. There are doors. I couldn't find the release to open the panel." He rubbed his hands down his legs, trying to stop the shaking.

"Then it's the long way." Jeff nodded to Charlie.

Heartened by Jeff's confidence, he clapped them both on the shoulders. "Do exactly as I do. You can make fun of me later."

"I'd never belittle rituals." Mac punched Charlie in the arm. "I've been raised better than that. Lead on."

Charlie ran the rhyme through his head once … twice. He counted the openings on the wall. At the third one, he turned left. *It feels right*, he let out a breath. *Right, another right, then a left*. He stopped. He felt Mac and Jeff behind him. He rehearsed the correct phrases.

"Repeat after me," he whispered, and then sang words that made no sense to them. The melody pulled them into the incantation. Their voices blended, intertwined. The last word hung in the air. They stood still, waiting. "Good" Charlie murmured and ran into the darkness.

Voices alerted Jeff they neared the center. He took an extra stride, grabbing Charlie by the shoulder.

"What? Jeff—" Charlie whipped around in surprise. Jeff put his finger to his lips. Edward's baritone voice rang in the air. "He's begun. Hurry."

Jeff melted into the darkness toward the last opening. Mac moved beside Charlie.

"What?" Charlie looked up into Mac's face.

"He's tracking." Mac whispered. "When he comes back, we'll know what we're facing."

Charlie shook his hands, his fingers numb, and worked his jaw relieving his clenched teeth. His thoughts arrowed to Sami. *Please be safe, my dearest heart.*

Jeff reappeared. "Westfield to the right. Lord Ramhill center at the altar, Adrian behind him. Nigel's on the ground to the left. He's bleeding."

"Niki?" Mac demanded.

"He's bound on the altar." Mac tried to push past him.

A black streak ran between Mac's legs and scrabbled to turn the corner.

Hurry, Pyewacket yowled at them, *I smell blood.*

"No more waiting." Mac shouldered by Jeff, throwing him off balance. He rounded the corner. Charlie reached out to steady Jeff but he'd regained his balance and followed Mac faster than Charlie thought possible. Charlie's heart raced.

Mac bowled into the open space. He pivoted to tackle Westfield, bearing him to the ground.

Pyewacket stood on hind legs, clawing frantically at the air above the bloody circle, unable to get through. Niki stirred. He opened his eyes and turned his head to look at him. Pyewacket strained to hear Niki's thoughts. The inscribed circle burst into flame forcing Pyewacket back. He paced, growling. His tail lashed back and forth.

Lord Ramhill continued chanting, his eyes following Jeff. Jeff tested the unseen wall with his hands, the heat reddening his palms.

A banshee cry sounded above the hedges. Black wings sliced through the air, the raven's body barreling down. She threw herself against the ritual wall, lashing out with claws and beak.

Charlie knelt beside Nigel, tearing strips from his shirt to staunch the bleeding. He glanced over his shoulder to see the raven scrabbling in midair. Nigel's voice pulled his gaze back to his uncle.

"They can't get through the circle without you, my boy." Nigel said, winking at Charlie.

Charlie nodded. Rising, he moved to Pyewacket's side. He ran his hand across Pyewacket's back. Pyewacket arched and hissed at him, raking Charlie's hand. Bloody streaks blossomed across the back.

He stared at the blood. "Thank you, Pye," he said. He pulled the boline from his boot and touched the blade to the scratches. The blade remained dark. Charlie frowned. He dove inside seeking the moment when he rebelled against his brother's domination. Cold fire bloomed in his chest. He slashed across his wrist, bathing the blade with blood. The blade glistened but did not respond.

His eyes pulled to Niki, a wry smile on Niki's face.

Charlie returned the smile. Dismissing his anger, he dove into his heart chakra. *Home, I want everyone …* he looked again at Niki. *Everyone, even you and your nasty cat, home.* His unfinished melody played through his mind. He sang the words, his voice cracking but keeping true. The blade flared in the darkness, drops of blood shimmering with light.

Charlie's aura grew, silver-grey wings looming over his head. He sliced downward cutting through the flames, embedding the knife in the burning ground. The flames shot higher, waivered then died.

The hot wave hit Pyewacket, bowling him over.

"Sorry, Pye," Charlie grinned. "No time to warn you."

Pyewacket leapt toward the altar, bounding up on Niki's chest. Sparks flew from his whiskers. Fur standing up in all directions, he clawed Edward's arm.

Lord Ramhill swung the athame in the air, trying to drive off the raven. Her claws raked his face. The knife sliced into her wing. She wheeled away, feathers trailing smoke. Edward scanned the sky. She dove at him. He swung the knife wildly, slicing at her.

She grasped the athame's blade and wrenched it from his grasp. Her blood sprayed across his face, burning his eyes. She beat her wings in the air once, twice, rose disappearing into the storm, the knife in her claws.

Wiping his face, he snatched the boline from Adrian. With a swipe, he knocked Pyewacket off Niki's chest. "You will not escape me." He leaned over Niki, grabbed his bound hands and pulled them above Niki's head. He sliced through Niki's shirt, a red streak blooming across Niki's chest.

Pyewacket bounded back onto altar, leaping to Edward's shoulder, clawing at his head. "Damn you, animal." He grabbed Pyewacket by the scruff and flung him at the hedgerow. Niki struggled to sit up. He pushed Niki back onto the slab. "You have magick in you. It will summon the demon. I will have your blood on my altar." Edward stopped, staring at the blood on the boline. It bubbled, acrid smoke rising into the air.

***

Niki retreated into the darkness within, pulling the small demon to its feet, brushing its scaly skin as if a friend who had fallen into the dust. "You've been a good guest but it's time for you to go." He propelled it into the ether.

The demon shook itself, scales rattling. It met Niki's blue eyes with its own blackness. Niki tensed for a confrontation but the demon bowed to him, twisted in midair and disappeared. Niki opened his eyes. Grey-black smoke boiled from his chest, rising, enveloping Edward. Edward staggered back, falling from the altar step into Jeff's arms.

"Don't touch him!" Niki shouted.

Jeff released his grip, stepping away. Oily smoke poured over the hedge wall, glowing red eyes swirling in the waves. Edward dug at his own neck, pulling against unseen hands.

Jeff leapt onto the altar step, trying to untie the knots binding Niki's wrists. Westfield pushed him aside. Jeff spun, fist pulled back. Mac grabbed his arm.

"Pardon me, sir," Westfield said, the iron amulet around his neck glittered in the torchlight. He pointed to the cords. "A special knot … a family thing … I can undo it more readily." He pulled the strands apart. Niki rubbed his wrists, his hands shaking. Westfield removed his coat and wrapped it around him.

"Charlie," Mac whispered in Jeff's ear, admiration in his voice. "He waded in between us to put that thing around Westfield's neck. Then the man vomited black smoke. Like the exorcist. Hugely gross." Laughter bubbled deep in his throat. Jeff joined in.

Jeff scanned the clearing. Charlie held Nigel on his feet. Adrian backed against the yew hedge, staring at his father struggling with the ink black apparitions, more flowing over the hedge wall. Adrian's eyes shimmered wide. Jeff stepped toward him.

Mac pulled Niki into a tight embrace, his warmth flooding through the coat. Niki's shivering ceased and he closed his eyes. Pyewacket squirmed between the two men. Mac scooped Pyewacket up in one hand, depositing him in Niki's arms.

***

The hidden panel swung open. Genevieve, her hooded cloak pulled close, surveyed the scene. Blood and sulfur burned her nostrils and unsettled her stomach. Through the swirling smoke, she identified Nigel and Charlie. She nodded, relieved her brother-in-law still lived. Westfield wrapped the young mage in his coat, the amulet's shining aura evident to her second sight.

To have such loyal defenders. She observed Mac shepherd Niki from the altar, the black cat nestled in his arms. Her gaze settled on Adrian's ash white face, his stare fixed on his father's convulsing body.

"Quite a mess he has created, isn't it?" A lilting voice spoke at her shoulder. Scotty's arm settled around her waist. She felt his smooth probing, silk running over her thoughts.

She smiled at him.

> *I have heard about the Northern guardians but never had the pleasure."*

He returned her smile, bowing slightly.

"Yes, they have gotten quite out of hand." She tucked her hand around his arm.

Scotty's face sobered. "Beware, my Lady, what he has set loose will not be easy to return to its rightful place. There has been mixing of powerful bloods." He met her brilliant eyes. She nodded, her expression serious.

***

Jeff looked up. Scotty and Lady Ramhill entered the center, the torchlight, flickering in the wind, eerie shadows playing across the hedgerow. He nudged Mac.

> *Always unruffled, that one*, Jeff commented. Mac snorted in response.

Genevieve pulled her skirts back from the smoldering grass. She uttered a staccato phrase. The smoke swirled away.

"Gentlemen." She raised her voice, the soft tones carrying on the wind. "You must hurry along. Rogers has orders to kill any who precede Lord Ramhill from the maze."

Westfield raised an eyebrow.

"I am sorry, Thomas, but Lord Ramhill is not a trusting man. Rogers covets your position. He would not hesitate to improve his standing." She stepped around the circle, her eyes on her husband. He struggled against the void engulfing him.

Harsh baying cut through the air.

Genevieve felt Jeff cast his awareness out to find the enraged animals. She commanded Jeff's attention. "Yes, it is well to be concerned. Now that my husband," her eyes flicked to Edward, "has lost control, the imps are driving the dogs mad. I assume you have plans for such a contingency."

She drew a deep breath, searching for any untainted energy in the clearing. The wind blew warm around her face. She paused, searching for the source. Smiling, she touched Nigel's arm. "Nigel, dear, will you stay or go? You are always welcome here but your wound should be attended to and there is not likely to be a clear mind left amongst the guests."

"Genevieve, your concern is touching. I will go with these gentlemen. I am certain young Charles will see to my welfare." Nigel reached out to pat Charlie's hand. Charlie nodded, slipping his arm around Nigel's shoulders. Nigel's knees buckled nearly pulling Charlie to the ground. Jeff joined him on Nigel's other side.

"Very well, then." She stepped close to Edward. His eyes rolled back. His harsh guttural utterances grated on her ears. She found no words in them.

She motioned to Westfield. "Thomas, you must go with them … with my blessing. You will not be welcome here when his Lordship recovers."

Westfield bowed. "Thank you, my lady. Please follow me, gentlemen." He led them toward the direct path. The baying hastened their steps.

"Genevieve, help me," Edward's garbled words finally made sense to her. "For God's sake, woman, do something."

"Edward, I warned you about this eventuality. It is not as easy to undo as you may think." She looked down at him, staying away from the swirling dark. "You have three demons here. I felt two amulets at work. The third was expelled by your young man. You underestimated him, my dear."

Edward's face reddened. "Genevieve, enough gloating. Help me this instant." The black smoke flooded into his mouth, his eyes bulging at the intrusion. Choking, convulsions racked his body.

"Mother," Adrian's voice echoed loud and demanding, "do something!"

Genevieve turned to her son. "The first thing you will relearn is respect. You will not speak to me in that tone. You will burn everything in his study. These events are not to be spoken of."

Adrian glared at her then melted under her stern gaze. "But you can't let him die." He said, his tone mild. "It is against your beliefs."

Genevieve stared at Edward. Stronger convulsions rippled through his torso. "I will not let him die." Her words rang in the air, one long string wrapping around the shifting essences. One by one, they split apart rising into the air, the winds tearing them away. *I hope there are no more.* Scorching fingertips ran along her throat. She shivered, then shook herself.

"Go find Rogers. Then attend to the study." Adrian hesitated, looking back at his mother, her head held high and the wind whipping her cloak.

"Yes, Mother," he said, obedience the best path … for the moment.

CHAPTER 63

They crossed the first turn in the labyrinth. Westfield held out his hand, stopping the group. He pushed the panel and eased around the edge. Waving them on, they entered the hidden doorway on the far wall.

"This is amazing." Mac mumbled. Niki looked up at him, his long bangs falling away from his eyes. "The direct path." Mac answered the unspoken question. "I couldn't figure out how they could walk directly into the center. This maze doesn't double back on itself like it would have to if there were a straight unbroken corridor. We must have almost run into you. We were that close." Mac shook his head and adjusted his grip around Niki's waist. "You doin' ok?" He frowned at the dark circles under Niki's eyes and his cracked lips.

Niki nodded, "Just need water but I can wait." Pyewacket squirmed in his arms, butting his head against his chest. Niki squeezed him tighter. Mac looked back over his shoulder assuring himself Charlie and Nigel were close behind. The corridor grew darker as Jeff pulled the last panel shut behind them. Scotty moved up beside Nigel, taking his weight from Charlie and holding out a handkerchief.

"Best tie up your arm." He nodded at the blood dripping from Charlie's fingertips.

Charlie stared then chuckled under his breath, drawing a surprised look from Nigel. "Couldn't tell if it was your blood or mine, Uncle." He wound the cloth around his arm, tucking in the edges. "We have to get him to a surgeon, Scotty. He's bleeding heavily." Jeff edged past Charlie and lifted Nigel into his arms. Nigel protested. Jeff tucked him into his shoulder, raising an eyebrow at Charlie, pointedly looking at the bloody cloth.

"I'll keep up. Don't worry."

"I'll walk with you, Charlie." Charlie felt an arm around his shoulders. He shivered releasing himself into Scotty's firm grip. They hurried across the slippery grass. "It's getting colder. We need to get everyone home."

Home, Charlie thought. *Yes, home.* He pictured Sami in her white painter's shirt and black leggings. She stood on the hearth, the light from the Yule log shining off her golden hair. She held out her hand to him, smiling. *Home, yes, I want to go home.*

"We'll be there soon, Charlie," Scotty whispered.

They stopped at the last doorway. Westfield stepped through the narrow opening and disappeared from view. Charlie stared at the flickering figures across the expansive lawn and the fires raging in the ballroom windows. Grounds men and dogs prowled the area. Westfield stepped back into the narrow corridor.

"The men are patrolling the grounds." His voice carried just to their ears. "Some are still loyal to me. They will walk the north side the next few moments. We need to draw the other dogs off." He stepped to Jeff's side. "Mr. Nigel?"

Nigel raised his head from Jeff's shoulder.

"Forgive my presumption." Westfield reached inside Nigel's coat and pulled out a silver flask. Uncorking it, he held it to Nigel's lips. A long draught produced a sigh and Nigel relaxed back against Jeff. Charlie caught the amused glint in Jeff's eyes. Westfield handed the flask to Niki.

Scotty stepped to the front. "The second carriage is behind the stable. There is a narrow lane leading out the back gate near the Downs." He cut off the unspoken question. "Chad found it when he retrieved Pye."

"Looks like there is enough distraction." Mac glanced at the black smoke billowing into the sky. Fireworks exploded at odd intervals.

Westfield pulled aside the panel and led them along the shadows cast by the labyrinth wall. Stopping to scent the air, he motioned for them to proceed across the dark lawn to the manor wall.

Charlie stumbled on the icy grass. Scotty grabbed his arm and supported him in a quick jog, Charlie's feet barely striking the ground.

The group clustered together at the steps. Westfield motioned to the right. He slipped through the shadows staying close to the wall.

Acrid smoke poured from the broken windows. Mac turned his head into his shoulder to breathe.

Sorry, Niki.

He swung Niki and Pyewacket into his arms. He put his head down and drove forward as if linebackers were trying to sack Jeff in the last high school game. Wild baying sounded behind them. Jeff reached out to Westfield, drawing him back. "Take Nigel." He rolled Nigel into Westfield's arms. "Get them to the carriage. I'll distract the dogs."

"Sir, I know their sounds. That is a killing bay. They are hunting blood and will know no master." Westfield implored him.

Jeff, it's too dangerous. They're mad with the demons released."

Get them away, Mac. Jeff disappeared into the smoke and haze.

Mac shrugged. He knew the iron will in Jeff's stance.

Good hunting, Lobo.

Charlie raised his head from his concentration on moving his feet. He looked around. "Where's Jeff?" he shouted.

Scotty pulled him back into motion. "He'll be along."

"No, I don't see him." The smoke swirled around them. The baying drew nearer. Wind cleared the smoke for moment. Charlie strained to make out the large form. "Scotty, is that a wolf?"

"Come on, Charlie. It's a wolf all right. Biggest I have ever seen." He dragged Charlie another step. "We have to get to the carriage."

Charlie nodded, accepting Scotty's support.

***

Pyewacket struggled to escape Niki's grasp.

Nik, he needs me. Pyewacket launched himself off Niki's chest.

"What the hell, Nik?" Mac shouted in his ear.

"Pye wanted to go." Niki shifted his weight. "Mac, I can walk."

Mac held him tighter. "But you can't run." He wove to the right rounding the tower, sidestepping the men manning the hose. He plowed on until he stood at the empty carriage. Looking back, he saw the pack veering off toward the cliffs. His prayer played silently in his mind, unwilling to distract Jeff.

He pulled the door open and deposited Niki on the floor. Niki crab walked back, rising to his knees when Westfield leaned in laying Nigel on the seat then offered an arm to Charlie.

The horses stamped and snorted, eyes wild. Mac vaulted into the seat, grabbing the reins.

Scotty pushed Westfield toward the carriage. "You need to come with us. You are no longer safe here."

"But there are those I care about." Westfield tried to break Scotty's iron grip.

"If you mean Anna, she's in the carriage with the others." The resistance in Westfield's eyes faded. "Nigel needs you." Westfield nodded and mounted the step, pulling the door closed behind him.

Scotty climbed to the forward seat. "Around the garage to the left," he shouted in Mac's ear. The horses reared, foam flicking from their mouths, their eyes white. Sparks blew across the lane. The sky lit up, fireworks filling the sky above the garage.

"Jeff?" Scotty shouted over the noise.

"He'll catch up." Mac urged the horses to a faster pace. He pulled back at the closed gate. Scotty vaulted from the seat and swung the wooden structure open. He scrambled onto the carriage seat, lunging for a hold before Mac shook the reins and the team barreled through the mist.

***

The coach pulled up to the front steps. Lights spilled from the parlor windows. Mac leapt to the ground meeting Westfield swinging out the door. They lifted Nigel and bundled him to the front door. The foxes climbed down from their pedestals to nose Nigel, encouraging the men to hurry.

"It's quite all right, sirs. I am just fine. No need for all this fuss." His words slurred and his eyes rolled.

Charlie levered himself out the door, wincing, the bleeding begun anew. Sami stood in the door, her hair lit from behind by the hallway candles. She met his eye, her face beaming with relief then clouding at the blood staining Nigel's sleeve. Her eyes flicked back running down his frame stopping at the bloody cloth on his arm. He nodded toward Nigel and she hurried them up the stairs.

Sami opened the door to the first chamber. Westfield set Nigel on the bed and peeled off his damp coat.

"I must protest, young madam. I love the attention but this just isn't proper." She unbuttoned his shirt and pulled it swiftly over the wounded arm. Nigel pushed at her hands.

"Nonsense, Uncle Nigel, if I'm sufficient a surgeon for Maeve, I can take care of you, too. I'm not your adoring niece at this moment. I'm a hoary old man with bad eyesight and fetid breath." Sami peered down at him, sticking out her chin and hunching her shoulders.

Westfield laid him back on the bed and lifted his legs. The door opened and Harry's steady footstep approach. "Miss Sami, Sir Nigel will appreciate a little restorative." Harry's voice lilted in his ears.

Not yet, he struggled to say, not a Sir yet, but his eyelids grew too heavy and the words too complicated for his tongue. A gentle hand lifted his head and held a glass to his lips. The scent stung his nostrils and he swallowed.

"No, dear lady," he mumbled groggily, "I do not like pain. Another sip or two would be the best thing for it, now wouldn't it?"

CHAPTER 64

Charlie stumbled up the porch steps. Scotty's firm grasp saved him from falling. He pulled Charlie's coat from his shaking shoulders, accepting the towel Colby offered.

"To the kitchen, Charlie." Colby held his uninjured arm. "We'll see to that wound right away."

"Didn't know you could stand blood." Charlie shuffled, his feet leaden. Scotty wrapped an arm around him.

"You don't know everything about me," Colby said. "Was the only one in my troop to earn the First Aid Badge." She pulled the chair out. Charlie sank onto the seat, his wounded arm on the table.

"Now what do you want to drink? Cognac, bourbon?"

Scotty tore free the last bloody layer. "Scotch," Charlie gasped. Fresh blood welled up. Cold sweat broke out on his forehead.

Colby returned with the water basin and a tumbler. She slid the basin to Scotty and placed the tumbler on the table. Taking Charlie's face in her hands, she looked into his eyes.

"Where's Jeff?" Her voice drew him back to the kitchen and he focused on her.

"I don't know." He felt the cloth wiping across the wound, drawing breath with a hiss. He tried to turn back but she held his face firmly. "I don't know." He shook his head, dropping his eyes from her gaze. He emptied the glass. He shuddered, color flooding his face. "The last I saw was the wolf … a dire wolf." He shook his head. "I am delusional."

Colby looked at Scotty. "He'll be along, Colby. Don't worry." He nodded toward the empty glass. Colby refilled it and slid it into Charlie's hand.

"You don't need stitches and I've cleaned it the best I can." Scotty wrapped Charlie's arm in white gauze, tying it securely.

Charlie nodded.

Scotty pushed aside the basin.

"Where is Kay?" Charlie looked around. "And Chad? Are they all right?" His tone rose in panic.

Colby placed her hands on his shoulders. He felt her energy pouring into him. "Kay is upstairs with Tori and Anna. Chad is outside looking for the raven. He's always disappearing outside. We'd best call him in soon … before he succumbs to hypothermia. Again." She rose. "Harry said to have coffee ready." She raised the pump handle several times until water gurgled from it, filling the pot. She set it on the stove.

Charlie shivered, shoulders drooping with fatigue.

"Come on, Charlie." Scotty lifted Charlie to his feet. "You need to sit by the fire. The others will be along."

"But Jessica and Chris. Where are they?" Charlie struggled to escape Scotty's grasp. *I can't rest. There is no rest until everyone is safe… until everyone is home.*

"They're in the parlor." Colby turned him toward the door.

"The Yule log." Charlie burst out.

"Charlie, it's okay." Colby said. "Chris saw to it right away." She pushed him gently ahead of her.

The foxes set up a keening, sending Scotty to the back door. He surveyed Jeff's torn clothing and the blood down his neck. The foxes rubbed against Jeff's legs then ran back into the gloom.

"I need to change. Glad everyone is elsewhere except you." Jeff studied Scotty's face.

Scotty returned the eye contact. "Did I see what I think I saw? What Charlie saw?"

Before he could answer, Pyewacket shot through the door, climbing his leg and settling on his shoulder.

Scotty laughed. "We'll talk about it another time. Go change before Colby sees you."

***

Standing at the bathroom sink, Jeff wiped his face with the warm water. Closing his eyes, he expanded his awareness throughout the house, noting Charlie on the loveseat, Nigel's gentle snoring, Sami wrapping his wound in clean linen and the soft conversation between Tori and Anna as they helped Kay into a dressing gown. The emotional clouds—concern, anxiety, fear—washed over him, running a shiver down his spine. Lifting his head, he spread out his hands on the sink, his eyes unfocusing. Exhaling, he drew energy up from the earth offering a prayer to each directions and to Foxie … thanks for those safely within the house.

Jeff? Mac's thoughts slid smoothly into his mind. *You okay?*

Jeff sensed the horse's rough coat Mac groomed with the curry comb. The chestnut mare buried her head in the oat bucket. Mac's aura bristled with the fluctuating ley line energy.

Yes. Jeff stretched. *Chad? Jess and Chris?*

Pacing with Maeve at his heels. Home safe, getting dry.

Jeff turned from the sink into Colby's embrace. Wrapping his arms around her, he pulled her to him and rested his cheek against her hair. "Hey, beautiful. You've got quite a right. Remind me to never make you mad for real." He rubbed his cheek.

***

Chad flipped up his collar against the cold wind "Where are you, Raven Soul Keeper?" He called, searching the sky. The stars shone a cold light through the last rolling storm clouds. "Help her find her way," he pleaded with the stars. The wind whipped around him, raising his fears for the frigid night. He paced around the corner.

"I can't just stand around here. I need to go find her." His pace increased. *She needs me.* He raised his hands to the heavens.

The she-raven plummeted and strafed his head, her raucous cry splitting the air. Blood drops spattered his face. The frayed wing beat frantically. She plunged through the conservatory window. He ran to the back. Broken glass winked at him from the roof's edge.

Chad burst into the kitchen, slamming the door against the wall. He careened around the counter. Harry grabbed his arm, spinning him through the hallway door. Coat tails flying, he ran down the steps to the conservatory. His voice echoed in the wooden foyer. "Get Kay to the parlor!"

He stumbled, crashing into the potted plants "Where are you?" he called. "Light. I need more light, please?" He stood still, waiting, confident his plea was heard. The walls glowed a warm amber, spreading light across the ceiling and down through the foliage. His heart pounded in his ears.

A mewling cry pulled at him. Moving aside the giant fronds, he peered into the ferns. He stepped farther in the foliage and extended his hand. She drew back her head, black eyes shining in the shadowed light. Her beak streaked toward his hand, stopping before drawing blood. Chad gritted his teeth and wrapped his hands around her wings. He lifted her, blood dripping from her leg.

He shifted her into his arms, cradling her against his chest. He ran his finger over the silky head. "It's been a long, hard journey." He caressed her with his voice and his aura bent around her. He stepped out of the foliage, his boots crunching on the broken glass. She trilled in protest. Chad held her close, walking to the parlor with slow steady steps, humming.

At the parlor door, Chad nodded his head at the raven nestled in his arms, asking for silence. He eased into the wingback chair.

"Do you think she'd prefer brandy or bourbon? And shall I get her steak tartare?" Chris put a hand on Chad's shoulder.

"Probably, beer and some chili." Chad said. "But for now, some raw meat." He sighed when Jeff entered the parlor carrying a familiar bowl and bandages. Charlie took the bowl and drew the towel from his arm. Jeff raised an eyebrow.

"My turn." He knelt beside Chad. Charlie stretched the leg out from under Chad's arm. The raven's eyes glittered, following his every move. Charlie worked with one wary eye on the beak laid across Chad's arm. She held still. He wrapped gauze around the leg, tearing the end and tying it off.

"There," Charlie rose from the floor. Jeff traded the refilled brandy snifter for the bowl. Charlie clutched the glass and limped to the loveseat, staring once again into the fire.

Chad stroked the raven's head. "Well, at least, I'm warm," he mumbled "and holding a beautiful female." The raven cocked her head, tilting it from side to side following his words. He chuckled, "Maybe not in the form I would choose, but—" Chad's face lit up when Niki appeared in the doorway.

"Niki!" Chad's heart jumped in his chest. He followed Niki's eyes, noting the amused twinkle at the raven gnawing determinedly at Chad's hand.

"Save it, okay?" his voice thick with affection and relief. "You're entitled to dish out all the crap you want after we get Kay settled. My friend here," he looked down at the agitated bird, "wants to be free." Niki and Charlie chuckle in unison at the obvious statement.

***

Niki nodded, acknowledging the price Chad offered in his steadfast care for the raven. Westfield helped him to a seat by the fire. Jeff offered him a snifter. Niki searched their faces. He felt his throat tighten at their smiles, relief reflected in their eyes. *They've all paid a high price for me. And Kay.* Kay entered the room, flanked by Tori and Anna. His eyes filled with tears.

Westfield offered her his hand. She looked up to his face and studied him for a long moment.

"Thank you, Mr. Westfield," she said accepting his hand. He conducted her to the loveseat next to Charlie. Tori stepped to Scotty's side, slipping her hand into his. "Those are the first words she's said since we left the manor." she whispered. He nodded, not taking his eyes from Kay's face.

Jeff and Mac carried in mugs filled with steaming hot chocolate. Westfield took one tray, nodding to Anna to follow suit. The two served the drinks around the room, paused to bow and curtsey in the doorway and disappeared toward the kitchen.

"Harry said we all needed chocolate ... a restorative." Colby stepped to the hearth beside Niki. "Personally, I think a brandy would do better, but who am I to argue with Harry? My mother never won an argument with him, no reason I should even try."

"Oww," Chad exclaimed, the raven once again making her presence known. "Okay, before I bleed to death, can we get on with this?" All eyes on him, he gulped. The crackling fire broke the silence. They waited for Chad to continue.

"Okay, okay, I'm not sure about this. I hope that proximity will be enough but here goes." He stepped over the coffee table and sat on the edge nearest Kay. She stared at him, without a glance at the squirming raven. The pendant's red eye flashed. He reached one hand out to touch it but pulled back sharply.

"We couldn't touch it, either," Tori voice came from behind him. "I asked Kay to take it off but she won't respond to any requests." Chad looked around the room, searching Jeff's face, then Mac's, finally resting on Charlie. He heard a soft groan. Niki rose from the loveseat and edged around to sit at his side.

Niki took Kay's face in his hands and whispered several words to her in a soft tongue Я тебя люблю (*I love you*). Her eyes filled with tears, her gaze remaining vacant. Niki ran his hand down her cheek, trailing his fingers along her neck and finally slipping his hand under the silk cord. He lifted the pendant from her chest, grimacing at the sharp pain. He bumped Chad's hand, his eyes locked on Kay's face. The raven stretched her neck to lay her head in Niki's hand. White light flashed from the raven's chest to surround the pendant. The silk cord disintegrated under Niki's hand and the pendant dropped into Kay's lap. She gasped and closed her eyes, the color draining from her face.

Charlie wrapped his arm around her shoulder, holding her upright on the loveseat. Niki dropped his hand to stroke the raven's head, shaking visible to all. Colby retrieved Niki's mug from the floor and held it to his lips.

Kay straightened, pulling away from Charlie. She struck him across the face with her open palm. Charlie jerked back.

She glared at him. "If you or any one of your godforsaken family touches me or anyone I love ever again, I will track you to hell's deepest trench and kill you with my bare hands."

The room spun in the silence.

Sami's eyes darted from Kay's stiff back to Charlie's reddening cheek. Taking a deep breath, he chuckled low in his chest. He locked eyes with Kay and nodded to her.

"Fair enough. I accept your pronouncement and declare my intention to use all the skill at my disposal to prevent that scenario from occurring." He caught Sami's eye, "I will earn your trust."

Without waiting for reply, he rose, extending his hand to Colby, "and I think, my dear sister-in-law, this calls for champagne. I will pour if you will serve." He pulled her around the loveseat, his arm passing over Kay's head.

The raven squirmed free, launching herself from Chad's numb hands and landing on Charlie's outstretched arm. She sidled up to his shoulder and rubbed her head against his ear.

Jeff's chuckle broke the silence. "Looks like you've made a conquest, Charlie."

Charlie looked back over his shoulder and left the room. The front door opened.

Kay sank to her knees and wrapped her arms around Niki, her shoulders shaking. Sami embraced them both, burying her face in Kay's hair. Slinking along the floor, Pyewacket nosed his way between them, climbing up Niki's leg and squirming into his lap. Kay looked up, her eyes focusing on the others for the first time.

Rising, she embraced Tori, murmuring her thanks then moving on. A moment with each person led her back to Chad, sitting on the coffee table, his lips moving in a silent prayer. She knelt and grasped his hands. His lips formed the words soundlessly. She spoke softly in coordination, her fingers trailing down his arm healing the small wounds from the raven's beak. Finishing in unison, she embraced him.

"Thank you," she whispered. "For your faith and steadfastness. I owe you my soul."

Charlie returned. Colby took the tray and eager hands reached for the bubbling liquid. Charlie took his place on the hearth. Holding his glass up, he said, "My family and friends, it is with heartfelt gratitude to each I offer the blessings this beautiful home holds and wish you a Happy New Year!" They raised their glasses, milling to touch rims with beloved friends.

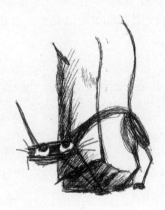

CHAPTER 65

Light filtered through his eyelids. He lost his nighttime vision of Sami's smiling face, brushing her hair from her eyes and dropped her head to nuzzle his neck. Sorting out reality from dream, he reached for her, not finding her there. He stroked the pillow, his fingers searching for warmth. Lilac from her hair rinse tickled his nose. Charlie moaned, torn between the intense desire to recapture his dream and increasing anxiety.

Please, he pleaded, *please let us be home. Let this all have been an incredible nightmare.* The ache in his arm dispelled any hope. *At least, let us be home.*

Barking destroyed the last hope for sleep. Jeff's firm tone commanded Maeve to fetch. Charlie threw back the covers. *Damn, if Maeve is still here, we cannot be home.*

Finding wool pants and starched shirt, he slammed the wardrobe doors. *What more do you want from us?* He pulled at the trousers, the buttons on the stiff shirt befuddled his sleepy fingers.

"Charlie?" Sami held out a steaming mug. He took it in one hand and wrapped his injured arm around her. She brushed his lips with her fingertip, studying his eyes. Rising on tiptoe, she placed her hands around his face and kissed him. He felt his grip on the mug loosen. He pulled away from her, laughing, trying not to spill the tea.

"To what do I owe that lovely greeting?"

She straightened her white lace blouse and tucked it back into the green taffeta skirt. "You looked so worried," she said, "and I love you."

She buttoned his shirt, her fingers brushing his skin. He wished she were going in the opposite direction. "Why are we still here? We've rescued Niki and Kay." A plaintive tone slipped in. "Why aren't we home?"

Sami opened the wardrobe and sorted through the cufflinks. "Perhaps because Uncle Nigel's in the house." She grabbed his cuff pulling it down over the bandage. "He's better this morning ...actually this afternoon." She answered his unspoken question and created another.

"Afternoon?" He looked at her amused face. "What time is it?"

"Two, slugabed." She finished the second cuff and pulled a vest from the hanger. "Everyone else has been up for hours!" She dragged the last word out sufficiently to impress any high school girl.

Charlie stuffed his arms in the blazer she held next.

"Okay, boy-o, you're on your own for socks and shoes. I can't possibly bend over in this corset." Blowing him a kiss, she turned toward the back stairs.

The kitchen scents swirled around her. Harry looked up from the oven, his hands swathed in heavy toweling. He lifted out two steaming brown loaves. At the kitchen table, Anna arranged petit fours on a porcelain plate.

"Harry, smells heavenly." Sami spread butter on the tops.

"Thanks, Miss. You look lovely. Lady Ramhill will be here any moment." The wrinkles around his eyes betrayed his pleasure.

"Thank you both for the lovely treats." Sami ran a finger along the butter cream icing and licked it. Harry smacked her hand when she reached for more. She laughed and danced for the parlor.

Sami surveyed the scene. Nigel sat in the wing chair, his arm resting on the pillow in his lap. Dark circles ringed his eyes, sunken in his pale face but his smile contained the zest she'd come to treasured. Niki sat on a stool at Nigel's feet, their conversation low and animated. She walked up behind Niki and placed her hands on his shoulders. He kissed her hand and continued his conversation with Nigel. She stared down at his fine blond hair.

Amazing the difference a hot bath will make. She remembered his bedraggled appearance the night before. A dark shadow fell across them. Looking up, she found Westfield holding out a snifter to Nigel. The retainer nodded to her, the lonely question forming in her mind.

"Mr. Westfield, I'm glad you've remained with Uncle Nigel. I appreciate everything you've done."

Westfield bowed to her, his eyes lighting. "You are most gracious, Mrs. Ramhill."

Niki chuckled, swiveling off the stool and rising to stand beside Sami. He wrapped his arm around her waist. "Thomas, I'm certain Sami would prefer her first name."

Westfield laughed. "My apologies, sir, but that would be too much for my system to handle. It is bred in my family."

"Dear boy," Nigel drew their attention, "you will think differently after a few months in America."

"America, Uncle Nigel?" Sami raised an eyebrow at him.

"Yes, my sweet girl. I have asked Mr. Westfield and the lovely Anna Simpson to accompany me across the pond. I think some time in the New World will do me good. I may not be welcome back at the ranch." Nigel laughed raucously. "Is that the correct vernacular?"

"Indeed, it is, Uncle Nigel," Jeff joined the conversation. He and Colby entered arm in arm. Maeve dragged along behind them, edging past them to flop on the hearth. She heaved a sigh.

"Jeff demonstrated his best passing style. He threw the stick for Maeve at least fifty times, poor thing." Hearing her name, Maeve's tail beat a slow rhythm on the floor, her eyes rolling in Colby's direction. Colby sat on the loveseat.

"Where's Mac?" Jeff asked.

"Mac and Kay are out walking with Scotty and Tori," Sami explained. "They'll be in soon."

Harry appeared in the doorway, his white apron exchanged for white gloves. He held out a small silver salver. "Lady Ramhill's card, Madam." Sami lifted the linen card from the tray and studied the gold lettering, one edge turned down.

"Please, Harry, invite her in." She followed him to the front hallway.

Jeff raised a questioning eyebrow at Jessica. "Doesn't the turned down corner mean an unexpected visit?"

Jessica nodded.

"But Sami told us at breakfast Lady Ramhill would be here for tea." He glanced at Colby, her cheeks coloring. "Practicing, are we?"

Colby punched him in the leg. He bowed to the two ladies, and settled on the floor next to Maeve. She flopped her head across his lap. Stroking her wiry fur, he closed his eyes.

Anna pushed in the tea cart, arranging it beside the Christmas tree. She unfolded the leaves and spread out the sandwiches and small cakes. Pyewacket stretched up to snag the linen cloth. Niki scooped Pyewacket into his arms and settled back onto the stool beside Nigel's chair. The older man took the last sip.

"What in the world got into Mac?" Kay's soft tones preceded her. Scotty appeared in the doorway, a woman on each arm.

"He said he heard a carriage, Sugar." Tori found a seat by the fire.

Kay bent to brush her lips across Niki's silky hair. A loud voice echoed in the hallway. She shivered, then drew herself sharply to her full height

"Sir, I must insist you put my mother down this instant." Adrian's voice cracked. "Mrs. Ramhill, please, control your guest." Adrian backed into the room.

"Adrian," Genevieve's voice came from the hall. "American exuberance is a condition we should appreciate."

Mac appeared in the doorway, carrying Genevieve in his arms. "Why, ma'am, I'm glad you appreciate the situation. After all, it would not be fitting and proper for your beautiful dress to be dragged through the mud. It snowed last night and the driveway is a frightful mess." Mac looked at the amused faces. "And I didn't have a cloak to emulate Sir Walter so this is the best I can do."

Sami placed a hand on his arm. "I do believe the mud stopped at the steps, Mac. You may set Lady Ramhill down now."

"Sami, that might be the case but I know Anna scrubbed these floors this morning and they might still be slippery. I just couldn't live with myself if any harm came to this beautiful lady."

"Mr. MacIntyre, I appreciate your concern for my person. I do wish you had been a little kinder to my home." She patted him on the cheek. "But, sadly, my son is correct. It is not proper for you to continue to hold me in your arms."

Mac mugged a long face and placed Genevieve in the wingchair beside Nigel's. "There you are, ma'am. Safe and sound."

***

Charlie appeared in the door, working at his tie. He studied the amusement on everyone's face.

"Lady Ramhill." He bent over her hand.

"Charles, thank you for hospitality shown my brother-in-law." She nodded in Nigel's direction without taking her gaze from Charlie's face. "You have brought wonderful friends with you." Releasing Charlie's hand, she turned to Nigel. "I am concerned for your injury."

Nigel raised his arm in its sling, wincing but beaming at her. "Not bad at all, my dear. I have received the best care." Nigel smiled at Sami. "I had hoped she would embroider her lovely face into my arm. Unique scar. It would make quite a conversation piece."

Genevieve motioned to Niki. "Young man, come here." Niki knelt at her feet. "I am relieved to see you looking somewhat refreshed." She ran her hand over his bruised cheek. "I am deeply distressed you were ill-used and wish I could make amends."

"Lady Ramhill, your kindness sustained me." Pyewacket rubbed along his leg and leapt into Genevieve's lap. Niki reached for him but Genevieve stayed his hand.

"And you, little warrior, you scared my kitchen staff. We are lucky Anna was there to provide you a safe exit." She rubbed Pyewacket's ears then massaged along his jaw. Pyewacket stretched his neck, eyes closed in bliss. A deep rumble escaped, his tail twitching in Niki's face. Niki chuckled and batted at it, unable to distract the cat. Genevieve paused and Pyewacket settled into her lap, purring.

Pulling her silk purse from under him, she opened it, holding out a closed fist to Niki. She placed a wooden talisman with a leather cord in his hand. She closed his fingers around the warm wood. Lowering her head, she said, "This is from a friend ... a cantankerous old man, if I do say so. Your tale interested him. He sent a proper Solstice gift. Examine it later." He nodded his compliance placing the object in his coat pocket.

"Lady Ramhill." Genevieve turned to see Jessica, her eyes reflecting her curiosity. Jessica did not flinch. "Was anyone hurt—last night—in the fire or the storm?"

"Genevieve, may I introduce my dear friend, Jessica Hamilton?" Charlie stepped to stand beside Jessica. He put his arm around Jessica's shoulder.

"Lovely, my dear." Genevieve appraised her, watching color blossom in Jessica's cheeks. "I regret I did not meet you at the ball last evening ..." she nodded "but I suspect you were not far away."

Jessica stiffened. Charlie tightened his grip on her shoulder.

Genevieve continued. "One grounds man sustained a broken arm and one maid fainted, bumping her head but they will recover. The house ..." she directed her comment at Mac, "it will be a long road to restoration. The wonderful contraption Nigel insisted we purchase contained the fire." She turned back to Jessica, "The wind seemed to cooperate with my erstwhile firemen, saving the main house."

"And Lord Ramhill?" Charlie blurted out.

"He suffered a stroke. I am assured he will recover but how long it will take is unknown." Genevieve accepted the tea cup. "Thank you, Anna."

Jessica exhaled. She rolled her shoulders. She used the break in the conversation to drop a curtsey and leave the room. Mac half bowed to Genevieve and, pivoting on his heel, strode after her, the cold wind from the opening front door blowing the fire into a roar.

"Lady Ramhill, my apologies for Jessica—" Charlie burst out. Genevieve waved him to silence.

"Not at all, Charles. She needs the open sky. I take from her stride and her outfit, she is a horsewoman. A good choice to bring new vitality to the family." She patted Niki on the arm in dismissal.

Niki rose to stand by Sami. Genevieve observed the greenness in Charlie's eyes before he covered it with a cough.

"Saminthea, please sit with me for a moment." Sami sank onto the stool, holding herself erect. Genevieve searched her face. "Saminthea, you are your mother's beautiful reflection. I see her steel in your eyes." Sami glanced at Charlie. "Yes, my dear, I do not know how you are here as you are but you are Serena's child. Without a doubt."

"What can you tell me?"

"Your mother and I are dear friends." She lowered her eyes to her hands, fingering the same Ramhill wedding ring she had seen on Jessica's hand. "The Ramhill men demonstrate a covetous trait. Particularly when thwarted. I do not have any evidence but I suspect my husband's father had a hand in your mother's disappearance."

"I've all the more reason to search for my family." Sami clutched the locket hanging around her neck. Tears glistened in her eyes. Charlie reached out his arms to her. She looked at him for a long moment then rose and entered his embrace.

"Miss Kasavina, I must speak to you, too." Genevieve commanded their attention.

"Please, Lady Ramhill, call me Kay." She stood in front of Genevieve.

"You are making my task easier. I must apologize for the treatment you received. I would offer to pay any price you feel is appropriate." She paused at her son's startled face, his guilt evident to her.

"Mother, you need not offer such penance." In a long stride, Adrian went to one knee, reaching for Kay's hand.

She stiffened but allowed him to take her cold fingers.

"I offer my profound apologies for the grievous abuse you suffered." He looked down. "I did not wish to see you harmed. It is poor grace to claim it was beyond my control." His lips found her hand. She ran her other hand through his hair, smoothing the small cowlick at the crest. He looked up.

"Adrian, I'm well aware your father forced you. I hold you no ill will." Kay's smoky voice offered forgiveness.

"You are gracious, my lady." He rose and, with a nod from his mother, continued out the front door.

"My son learned a great deal from meeting you all. I see hope in undoing his father's example." Genevieve said. She stood and looked down at Nigel struggling to untangle himself from the lap robe. "No, Nigel, you must rest. I will, however, expect a luncheon before you embark on your adventure." She nodded to each. "Mr. Westfield, will you and Anna please see me to the door?" Genevieve swept from the room leaving behind her lavender scent.

Westfield and Anna attended Lady Ramhill in the front hall. Pulling two envelopes from her silk bag, Genevieve held them out.

"Thomas, you have been steadfast. I am grateful to you. Here, a severance for you both. I am pleased you are going with Nigel. He needs your care." She touched Anna on the arm. "Do not worry about your mother. I will see that she is comfortable. Now, I do expect a missive occasionally to share Nigel's adventures." She pulled the strings tight on her bag.

Westfield opened the front door to the cold afternoon sun. Genevieve beckoned Charlie. In two steps, he stood at her side and she tucked her hand around his arm. "Charles," she said. "I am grateful to have the chance to encourage Adrian to follow a better path." She stopped at the drive. "Do not let the Ramhill darkness overwhelm you. You descend from many good men … and better women." She ran her fingers down his face, cupping his jaw in her hand.

She glanced at Sami standing in the doorway. "Trust your friends for they are strong and bring their gifts to your aid. Especially Nikolai."

A cold wash tightened his throat.

Genevieve turned his chin, bringing his eyes back to her own. "Do not let the dragon destroy your chances. The small owl will not forget the dragon's great heart … and courage on his behalf." Charlie's brow knit but she shook her head. "I have said too much already. It is a puzzle your spirit will have to unlock." Rising on her tiptoes, she kissed him on the forehead and turned in a swirl. Without a backward glance, she accepted her son's hand into the coach.

The hackles on the foxes smoothed back into place.

***

"My dear children," Nigel accepted Niki's arm to rise. "It is time we depart."

"Uncle Nigel, we would not have been successful without you." Sami smiled. "I will miss you."

"And I will miss you all. You have freed me to set about my grand exploration!" He grinned. "Why, after the Americas, we may go on to the Orient and perhaps cross the Himalayas." He turned to Charlie, excitement in his eyes. "We have relatives in India … Uncle Cyrus and Aunt Charlotte and many cousins. The randy old gentleman!" His braying laughter filled the parlor, the fire dancing in time.

"Uncle Nigel," Charlie said, "all I want is to go home, back to electric lights and central heating."

"My dear boy, where is the adventure? The thrill—"

"Mr. Nigel," Westfield stood at his shoulder. "The carriage is here, sir."

Nigel shook hands and received kisses. His eyes filled with tears when Jessica took him in her arms and hugged him tightly.

"I wish we had more time, my dear." He whispered to her. "I know you will weather the storm with grace. You have the will to awaken the goodness in your husband. Don't give up on him." She brushed his lips and stepped away.

Clearing his throat and continuing in a husky voice, "I will not prolong this. It is too hard. God speed to you all." He stepped out the door, caressing the vixen with his good hand. He looked back at Charlie. "But, Charles, do remember to come tell me all about it!"

Charlie stood with Sami on the steps, watching another carriage depart. Notes from the harpsichord—*Invention in F minor* by Johann Sebastian Bach—reached his ears.

Sami turned in his embrace. "I hope we see him again, Charlie. I don't know how or when." She laid her head against his chest.

He held her until the chill seeped through their clothing. Leading her back into the foyer, he closed the oak door against the coming night.

CHAPTER 66

Light filtered through his eyelids. Sorting out reality from dream, he reached for Sami and found her not there. *As usual*. He stroked the pillow. Lilac from her hair rinse tickled his nose. His anxiety rose.

Please, he pleaded, *please, let us be home.*

He pulled himself up from the warm blankets, wincing at the cold floor. The light through the windows announced midmorning and he groaned, wishing to throw himself back into bed.

He pulled open the wardrobe, his eyes tightly closed. Peeking through his shaggy bangs, he found grey flannel pants, a white cotton shirt and a grey fisherman's sweater. He stared, his breath tight in his chest.

"Charlie? You awake?" Sami danced into the room dressed in his white cotton shirt over black leggings and ballet slippers. She held out a steaming mug. He took it in one hand and wrapped his free arm around her. He reveled in her body against him.

She brushed his lips with her finger, studying his eyes. Rising on tiptoe, she placed her hands around his face and kissed him. He felt his grip on the mug loosen.

Oh hell. He let the mug slip, tea splashing across the floor. He wrapped his arms around her, lifting her, spinning her around the room. He sat on the bed and swung her onto the rumpled bedclothes. He rolled on top, bearing his weight on knees and elbows but leaving his hands free to caress her face and hair.

"Charlie, stop," Sami put her arms around his neck pulling close for a long kiss. "Stop," she murmured through their joined lips. A shiver arced through him. He lowered his body onto hers, laying his head on her breast. She stroked his fine hair, running her fingers around his ear and down across his neck.

"Charlie."

"Ssshhh," he countered. "I am listening to the most magnificent beat in the world."

She giggled. "Charlie, we have to go downstairs. The fire around the Yule log is low."

"Yule log?" He pushed himself up and rolled to sit on the edge. Sami curled up behind him, running her hands along his back and shoulders. "But it's after New Year's. Are we going to keep it going until Twelfth Night?" He scrubbed at his face.

Music from an electric guitar rippled across the driveway. His head snapped up and he rose from the bed. "New Year's! We missed the gig. Sami …" he spun on his heel, grabbing the poster for support. "We missed the gig in Baltimore—oh, man." He dove into the wardrobe pulling out clothes then heading for the bath. "Tell them I will be right down, will you, love?" His voice faded under the running water. "I've got to talk to Niki."

Sami leaned against the door frame, watching Charlie lather his face. "Charlie," she called over the running water. "Charlie, it's December twenty-second."

"Can't be, dearest," he mumbled pulling the razor across the skin under his nose. "We rescued Kay and Niki on New Year's Eve and then saw Genevieve on the first."

"Foxie brought us back to December twenty-second," she explained.

"Are you sure?" He lowered the razor and looked at her reflection in the fogging mirror.

"Jess is reading the New York Times and Tori has the Charleston paper. They agree." She stepped from view. "It's time for lunch. Much to Harry's chagrin, Jeff's chili didn't disappear in all our travels."

Charlie stared at the idiotic grin on his face in the mirror. Sobering, he peeled the bandage from his arm. The skin glowed pink and healthy. He made a fist and flexed his wrist. *Surely, she can't be right.* The guitar introduction to "Pretty Woman" sounded faintly in the distance. He shook the lather from the razor and hurried into the shower.

***

Careening down the narrow back stairs, a black streak shot between Charlie's legs knocking him off balance. He threw both hands against the stairway walls.

"Damn it, Pye!" He shouted at the black tail disappearing around the doorframe. Charlie stepped into the kitchen in time to hear a chuckle from Harry. The gentleman stirred a large pot on the gas stove, holding himself carefully away from the steam. The coffee maker gurgled and belched.

"Please, sir," Harry wiped his streaming eyes. "Tell me to throw this hellish concoction away. I will be forever in your debt."

Charlie shook his head. "Jeff's chili is sacred to the band. Along with Jeff and Mac singing 'Ring of Fire.' It's spicier with each batch … a plot to bring us to our knees with the Scoville rating."

Harry's shoulders drooped. "I have tea for you, sir. Lunch …" he looked disdainfully at the pot, "will be in a bit."

Charlie settled at the table. His thoughts flashed to the spilled tea on the bedroom floor. *Maybe you'll help me out, dear Foxie and make that go away.* He shook his head at the insane plea. Spying a newspaper on the seat beside him, he pulled up the Arts section. Opening it, he looked for the date.

Can't be. He felt guilty to doubt Sami.

"But it is, sir." Harry said placing hot biscuits in the warmer. Charlie folded the paper. "We are back on track." Harry held out a plate with two biscuits.

Charlie took the plate, his stomach growling. He tucked into a bite before he felt the rubbing against his calf. A black tail flicked in and out under the table.

"You bugger," Charlie pinched off a piece and dropped it on the floor. "Thank god, you are all right, too. Now astound me some more and actually eat that thing, you inveterate carnivore." A moment later, soft padding accompanied Pyewacket's exit into the hall. Charlie leaned over to retrieve the crumb. He stared at the floor. *It's gone.* He chuckled. The guitar intro to "Stairway to Heaven" filtered through the back door.

"Harry," Charlie grabbed the second biscuit. "Do you know where everyone is?" He rose and set his dishes on the counter. Harry swept them into the soapy water.

"Yes, sir. Madam is in the library with Dr. Kasavina. Master Niki is in the parlor, asleep on the loveseat, I believe. Dr. Conray, Mr. MacIntyre and Mr. Alton are in the studio. Mr. Miles has driven Miss Madison and Lady Ramhill into town for some Christmas shopping. And Mr. Thomas is moping on the porch." Harry ticked off each without taking a breath.

Charlie smiled at the elderly retainer "Why is Mr. Thom ... Chris moping?"

"Maeve, sir. He hasn't seen her this morning. She wasn't in his room when he rose." Harry stacked the clean dishes in the cupboard.

"But she was back then, wasn't she?" He furrowed his brow.

"Sir, it has to do with the love involved." Charlie waited for him to go on but Harry did not look up.

"Harry, Sami showed me the house would provide anything we wanted. Why do you prepare the meal by hand? Why not just ask for it?"

"Well, sir," he said, "why would you ask for something you could provide for yourself? Why play music when you have multiple recordings?" A slight smile crinkled around his eyes.

Charlie nodded, leaving to attend the Yule log. He paused in the doorway not wishing to wake Niki but worrying when he saw the feeble fire. Niki lay on the love seat, his head on one arm and a pillow propping his shoulders. The dark circles against his pale skin attested to the days—the missing days—between.

Charlie tried to grasp this reality, his head spinning. *Get a grip, old man, everything is all right.*

"It's okay, Charlie, come in." Niki spoke, his eyes still closed. "I'm not asleep."

Charlie stepped to the hearth and picked up the brush to remove the ash. He cleared his throat then started working without comment.

"Thank you, Charlie." Niki's voice barely reached his ears.

"What?" Charlie turned to look down at him. "What did you say?"

"I said thank you for helping Kay … and me." Niki opened his eyes.

Charlie stared at him for a long moment then turned away. "Well," he said speaking into the fire, "it's not like we had much choice. I doubt the house would let us come back without you."

Wind swept through the house and the piano strains to "Walking in Memphis" rode on its back. Charlie paused listening until the sound disappeared when the back door closed.

"I'm surprised you aren't out in the studio." Charlie tried to be conversational.

"I don't want to intrude while Chad's learning the set. Besides, I've been listening." Charlie glanced at Niki, once again his eyes closed, his hands folded across his chest.

"Listening? Is this another psychic trick?" The hackles rose on Charlie's neck.

Niki raised a small remote control. Clicking the button, the room echoed with the unusual guitar and piano arrangement Charlie had created. Charlie stared at the crown molding, tracing the sound. Small speakers studded the corners in the octagonal room.

"My Christmas gift to Sami … and you." Niki said. "As the studio neared completion, Sami struggled to go out to see. I figured she might feel left out when you don't rehearse in the parlor anymore. This way, she can hear what's going on." He looked up at Charlie. "There's a set in the kitchen, too. The main unit is in the library but you can control it with this." He held the remote out. "From anywhere on the first floor."

Charlie took the remote and examined the zone buttons and controls. "Niki, thank you," he said "This is very thoughtful." He clicked the system on.

"Damn, but this is good shit!" Chad's voice rang clear followed by Jeff and Mac's laughter. Charlie hastily lowered the volume looking at the parlor door.

"That's the downside. Sami can hear everything that goes on." Niki chuckled.

"Niki, you need to be working with Chad. He'll never catch up in time. We only have days." Charlie felt the anger rising again. He swallowed, struggling to contain it.

"Don't worry, Charlie. I still intimidate him. He has this odd idea about Niki Kaye. How, I don't know."

"What?" Charlie burst out. "After all the pushing he did about the red strings, surviving Uncle Nigel's driving and freeing the raven?"

"Charlie, how people acted then isn't necessarily who people are now. Don't get your hopes up for a permanent change."

Sami's fearful face flitted before his eyes, a pain stabbing his heart.

"There were other influences at work." Niki rose on one elbow to stare at Charlie's flushed face.

Cold emanated from his ice blue eyes, freezing Charlie in place. Charlie's vision narrowed to stare at the blue orbs, grey reptilian eyes reflected in them. He blinked, the image remained. Charlie stepped back, his heel striking the wood piled on the hearth. He grabbed the mantle with his free hand. Fear clutched him, the labyrinth walls rising in his vision. He shook himself, insisting his body live in the present. The conversation from the studio irritated him. He clicked off the sound, holding the remote over the fire.

A shout drew his attention. Wild barking shattered the air. Sami ran past the parlor and flung open the front door. She charged into the cold. Charlie moved to follow her but Niki's voice stopped him.

"It's okay, Charlie, let her go out by herself. It's just Maeve coming home ... to Chris."

"Home? To Chris? But we can't take a dog on the road. He can't possibly think we'd be able—"

"She'll stay here with Sami."

"Sami doesn't want a dog. And Maeve is from then." Charlie stated flatly.

"She's not just a dog, Charlie. She's family." Niki smiled. "Isn't it what you wanted? A companion—a dog by your definition—who will protect her when we're gone?" Niki lay back on the couch and closed his eyes.

Charlie stared at him, envying Niki's relaxed posture. Wild laughter rose in his chest. *This is bloody mad.* He looked back to the hallway.

Maeve bounded into the house. She flew across the threshold, skidding into the newel post, rebounding to leap toward him. Rearing, her paws on his shoulders, her long tongue swiped his face. He grabbed her paws and let go his laughter, her enthusiastic greeting washing away his distress.

Sami swung around the doorframe with one hand. She wrapped her arms around the rough-coated chest and buried her face in Maeve's golden shoulder. When she let go, Charlie lowered Maeve's paws to the ground.

"If you're going to be family, a few manners would be appreciated. Sit." Maeve sat, her long tail beating a tattoo on the floor. "Good girl," Charlie ruffled her ears.

"You see, I told you she's a princess if she's treated well." Chris stepped in the door and pulled it shut. Maeve looked over her shoulder. She turned back to look at Charlie, cocking her head to one side, a quiet whine whistling through the air.

Charlie laughed, "Okay, princess, you may go." Maeve leapt straight into the air, pirouetting for the kitchen. Sami pecked Charlie on the cheek and danced after her.

Charlie swept up the remaining ashes and poked at the log for good measure. He sat on the loveseat, remembering the foxhounds he treasured when he was young. Maeve's presence eased his heart. Swinging his legs up onto the arm, he found a comfortable position and closed his eyes. Only a moment seemed to pass before he heard voices in the hallway.

Grrrooowwlllffff!!! Meerrrrooowwlll. Pyewacket rocketed through the air toward him.

"Oof! Pyewacket! I am not a bloody trampoline? Off me, mate." Charlie sat up, the squirming cat clawing at the air. Polydactyl paws caught in Charlie's fisherman sweater, unwinding a loop or two. Charlie fought the swift swipes.

Sami carried in a small bowl in her hand and a reed basket over her arm.

What is that lovely scent? Pyewacket paused, the yarn forgotten. *"Sardines!"*

A squirm, a lunge and the pulled yarn hung forlornly down Charlie's front.

Pyewacket glanced back at his achievement then skidded to a halt beside Sami. The cat rubbed her legs, running from nose tip to tail's end.

Please, why not set that down? You may continue on your way to whatever task you have. I will guard it with my life. Cats can be trusted with little fishies. Really!

Sami held out the bowl to Niki. Pyewacket leapt, landing on Niki's stomach then sat, eyeing the bowl. Not a whisker moved, his excitement betrayed only by the flicking tail.

Sami raised her eyebrow at her husband's disintegrating sweater. "Charlie, for Pete's sake." She set the basket on the table

Charlie glared at Pyewacket and Niki. Before the words left his mouth, Charlie glanced down at the red string on his wrist. His expression softened. He looked up to see Niki fend off Pyewacket's attempts to snag a sardine from the bowl.

Sami tucked a cloth napkin across his chest carefully avoiding Pyewacket's lightning strikes. She handed him a fork. "Shall I get you some coffee or wine?"

"Thank you, no. Pye and I are happy with the sardines."

Charlie's stomach growled. Sami giggled. "Harry has lunch ready in the dining room. You seem to be having a difficult day coping with your wardrobe. Why don't you change into your red sweater? It's more festive."

Charlie laughed out loud, nodded at Niki and took the front stairs two at a time.

In a moment, he descended the stairs, pulling the new sweater over his head. Voices from the dining room heralded the party to be at full number. His chair stood empty, the chili bowl already in place. He glanced at each friend, engaged in conversation or rapt attention on their plates.

His heart lurched, missing Nigel. He slipped into his chair. Sami grabbed his hand and pulled him close enough to plant a firm kiss on his lips, then push a warm biscuit and honey into his mouth.

"Hmmm." He tucked into the chili, appreciating the burn in his throat. Harry refilled water glasses and offered more biscuits, his expression concerned for the tears rolling down Mac's face.

"Jeff, buddy, I think you got this batch almost right. But I can still feel my nose. When Ma makes it, my nose goes numb."

Scotty choked, his laughter catching him in mid-swallow. Mac clapped him on the back. Scotty scrambled for the water.

"My dear gods," Harry murmured, escaping into the kitchen, his exit prompting more laughter.

Mac looked around the table, *déjà vu* running down his spine. "Where's Niki?" he asked.

"I checked on him before I came in. He and Pye were busy sharing the sardines and crackers." Charlie looked Mac in the eye and smiled. Mac nodded, a smile on his face as well.

Tori stretched. She leaned to look down the table at Charlie. "Kay and I are going to Charleston today. I ..." She glanced at Kay. "We have an open house at the office tomorrow night and I have promised everyone my new partner will be there. But Sami has invited us back for Christmas. Is there anything special we can bring y'all from Charleston?"

Charlie smiled, "We will miss you both." He looked from Kay to Tori. "And I would like some water crackers and kippers. If you can find any—"

Jessica laughed out loud. "Kippers? Charlie, those are awful." Her face reflected her opinion, sending laughter rippling around the table. "Fortunately, I won't be here to watch you eat them. My plane leaves this evening for Chicago and Anita is waiting for me."

"Jess, why don't you come back after New Year's and stay longer?" Charlie pleaded.

"I'd love to but Damian called Anita last night. He's going to join me for the holidays." She looked down at her plate, fidgeting with her napkin. "I'm certain he'll expect I fly back with him after Christmas. We host the New Year's ball, remember?" She pushed back her chair. "It's been wonderful meeting everyone. Perhaps I'll be able to come back in the spring but now I'd better pack. Have a wonderful holidays."

"Jess," Charlie called. "I'll be up in a moment." He looked around the table. "Anyone else leaving today? I hope not."

"I am." Charlie turned to look at Jeff's somber face. The muscles in Charlie's face twitched. Jeff maintained eye contact with him. "Chad went through both sets with us this morning. He's got a good feel for our style. He'll do a great job … after some rehearsal with the whole gang."

"Yeah," Mac growled, "so great we may not need a has-been lead guitarist by mid-January." Tori ducked as Jeff reached over her to punch Mac in the arm.

Chad's head jerked up and he half rose from his seat, "Hey, I don't want to replace you. Not what I want at all." His face paled. He looked from Jeff to Charlie.

"Hey, Chad, it's okay. I was just joking." Mac smiled at him. Not reassured, Chad looked again from Charlie to Jeff.

"If Jeff says you will do a good job, that's good enough for me. After Niki works with you. But you won't be replacing Jeff. He'll be back." Charlie looked at Jeff. He nodded. "And we'll probably need you both by then. There are several pieces I would like to have a bigger sound."

CHAPTER 67

Colby sat mute, the word 'leaving' echoing in her head. She didn't dare lift her eyes from her plate. She twisted her napkin into a knot then lost it under the table. She pushed back her chair and mumbling "excuse me," fled from the dining room. She stopped in the parlor. Her downcast eyes studied the wind rose under her feet.

It's over. You ninny, it never started. He didn't sit by me at lunch. He hasn't spoken to me all morning. What a dope to think there might be anything. She ran her tongue across her lips remembering his kiss in this room. The design swirled around her feet, subtle colors rising in smoky wisps.

She stood in the airport terminal filled with blinding sunlight, heat rippling across the tarmac. Jeff exited the gangway with a long stride, an excited smile on his face. A young, strawberry blonde threw herself at him. He dropped his knapsack, wrapping her in his arms and swinging her around in the air. Her warm laughter filled Colby's ears. Setting her on her feet but not releasing her from his arm, he snagged the knapsack and they sauntered down the concourse, their bodies touching. Colby's breath came in shallow gasps, wavering on her feet.

A hand settled around her shoulder. She pulled away, turning to stare into Niki's face. Her face heating, she shook her head against the tears.

"I'm … I'm just fine. I'm not going to lie down and let that floozy ride roughshod over me. Who does she think she is? By God, I'll show her what spunk is! I've got packing to do. He's not going anywhere without me." She flounced up the first few steps before Charlie caught her.

"Colby, wait. Your mum's on the line." He stretched the cord from the library to its farthest reach, forcing her to descend the steps. She snatched the phone from his hand. "Wants a quick word before they head out to sea."

She retraced the phone line into the library. Niki and Pyewacket followed her. Pyewacket leapt onto the dark walnut desk and sat washing his paws while Niki examined the titles on the books along the wall.

She huffed. "Yes, Mother, I remember the plans for the New Year's … with Jon. There isn't cell reception here, Mother. That's why."

She paused. "Give him Sami's number, for Pete's sake." Niki heard a muffled exclamation from the receiver. "That phrase is not a vulgarity, Mother. Besides, it's not the point, here is it?"

She tightened the muscles around her mouth, choking on unsaid words. "Oh? You spoke to Mrs. McGann? I think she's lovely, too, but nothing's been said and you two mustn't be thinking—"

She listened, tapping her foot.

"He went to the diamond district? Oh …" Colby's voice shook. "Talked to Ira Leibowitz? Ira's very expensive."

Niki pulled a volume from the shelf and buried his nose in it. Colby glared at him.

"Jon's just a resident. I understand about his family's money, but he's firm about his independence." Cold poured down her back. "No, I don't think you should offer to help him. There haven't been words said between us, Mother!"

"No. Now stop that talk right now. You listen to me, Mother! You want another elopement? I don't ever want to hear you compare me to Sami. If you want to be at my wedding, no matter who I marry, you'll never refer to me as your perfect daughter again. I'm ashamed how you treat her, do you hear me? Ashamed." Heat flushed up from her neck to her temples.

"No, this time, you think about how you've behaved! Merry Darn Christmas to you, too! Hope you and Daddy have a fine time!" She slammed the receiver into the cradle.

Colby stood with her head down for several moments, her shoulders rising and falling with ragged breathing. She whirled around coming nose to nose with Niki. Pyewacket shot to the floor between them.

Colby stamped both feet. Pyewacket froze, curling his tail close to his body "Now, you two, listen. Not one word to anyone. No one! No how. Do you understand?" Niki nodded and Pyewacket crouched lower to the floor. She stomped toward the stairs.

Loud ringing filled her ears. She paused, drawing in a deep breath, dreading the next moment. The ringing stopped. She climbed the first step.

Niki held out the receiver, "Colby, there's a gentleman for you."

"For Pete's Sake!" She snatched the phone from his hand, shooing them away. "Hello?" she snapped. Her voice softened. "Jon. Yes. Merry Christmas to you, too." She felt the tears flooding her eyes. "Yes, I know. It's been awhile." She listened, her hand shaking. "New Year's? Yes, I remember." She wiped her eyes, trying to ignore the man and the cat just outside the door.

"No, no, just been out walking in … cold air. Maybe some allergies." His deep blue eyes appeared in her mind. "I'll ask Harry to whomp up some lemon tea. I'll be fine." A tear ran down her face. She rubbed her nose, fighting the sniffle. "What? Whomp? Well, I've been consorting with some very odd people."

She glared at Niki and Pyewacket. "I'm looking forward to seeing you, too." Her shoulders slumped and she sagged against the desk. "What? I'm so sorry. Maybe I'm working on a little cold." She closed her eyes and swallowed. "I promise I'll be more myself by New Year's." She gulped, praying to ring off before she collapsed into sobs. "Yes. Can't wait. Get over that cold soon." She slapped her forehead. "Oh, it's my cold. How silly. Merry Christmas." She gritted her teeth against the chattering. "Yes. Yes. Bye now." She pulled the receiver away from her ear, "What? Oh, love you, too."

Colby hung up the phone. She shambled by Niki, her shoulders stiff. Niki glanced at Pyewacket who raised a paw for a thorough wash.

CHAPTER 68

Mac shoved his hands deep in his pockets. He sighed, biting his tongue to stop once again challenging Jeff's decision. Jeff set his knapsack and satchel in the trunk.

"Can't you stay one more day? Just to celebrate all we've been through?" Mac burst out. "I mean, everyone is okay and we haven't even talked about what happened."

Jeff closed the trunk. The grim line around his eyes and the set to his jaw answered Mac's question.

"Mac, you know what a call from Grey Wolf means." He brushed the dust from his jeans. "I want to stay but ... I have to go."

"Well, aren't you at least going to say goodbye to Sandwich Lady?" Mac regretted his words seeing pain flash across Jeff's face. "Hey, man, you can't just walk away. I know what you're feeling for her."

"Mac, sometimes you need to stay out of my head." Jeff punched him in the arm. "I tried twice but she was on the phone both times. And the last call was from her almost fiancé. Sami suspects a proposal at New Year's. I won't get in the middle. And you know it would never work with my family."

"She's scrappy. I bet she'd hold her own." Mac walked to the driver's door. He fixed Jeff with a sharp gaze. "I don't try to tell you what to do very often, but ..." Mac struggled to finish his sentence. "But you need to go tell her goodbye." Jeff shrugged and opened the passenger door. "No, man, I mean it. You'll wish you had."

Jeff glanced at the house.

"Okay, you're right. I have to say goodbye and ...."

Mac waited.

"Just goodbye. I'll be right back. We don't have much time." He swung onto the porch and bolted through the kitchen door.

Sami looked up from the cookie dough, the gingerbread man cutter in her hand. She smiled at him, flour on her cheek.

"I didn't say goodbye to Colby. Know where she is?" He continued past her to the doorway not waiting for her answer.

"Upstairs. Jeff, be careful—" her words were lost in the stairwell. He took the steps two at a time.

Charlie grimaced and called, "Jeff, I don't think—"

"That's okay, man," Jeff's voice receded up the stairs. "I've thought too much already!"

***

Colby reached the front landing, Jeff seemed to materialize from the opposite direction at the same time. His enthusiasm faded when he saw her tear-stained face.

"What's wrong, babe?" He ran his hands down her arms. Colby jerked away.

"I'm not your babe. That's never been my option, now has it, Dr. Conray?" Colby straightened her sweater.

"I wanted to say goodbye properly." He paused studying the cold glint in her eye. "And tell you, I'd like to see you again."

"Yes. Well, indeed." She flipped her hair and edged past him to her room. "It's been splendid. Next time, I'll give you the sandwiches and take you and your girlfriend up on any dinner invitation extended. I hope you have a lovely reunion. Safe flight and all that. Bye now." She walked into her room. Jeff stepped toward the door. She froze, her back rigid.

"Don't. You know you can't mean it. Go. Please." She closed the bedroom door without looking back.

Jeff stared at the wooden panel. *Girlfriend? What in the hell?* He raised his hand to knock, his motion arrested. He closed his eyes and leaned his forehead against the door, the bobcat's amber eyes staring at him from the dark.

When he reached the kitchen, Sami grabbed him around the waist and hugged him.

"You and Charlie have great holidays." He ran his fingers through her golden hair, lifting a lock to tickle her nose. "You know I love you both." She hugged him again, listening to his rapid heartbeat. "You believe I'll be back, don't you?"

She pushed back from him to see his face. "I know you will. Don't give up on her. She just needs some time to see things clearly."

Jeff hung his head. Sami bit her lip. "You know we're too different. And she's got someone who's serious."

"She and Jon go way back. They've been paired up by our mothers since sixth grade. But I don't think she loves him enough to marry him. I think," she reached up on tiptoe to hold his face in her hands, "she loves you."

"Funny way to show it."

Mac honked the horn.

"Got to go. Merry Christmas." He picked her up in a tight hug and swung her behind him. He nodded to Charlie and ran for the car. Harry stood by the passenger door. The two men shook hands and exchanged a few words before Jeff ducked into the car.

Charlie stepped up behind her and pulled her to him." "Is he okay?"

"I think so. I guess he didn't get the send-off from Colby I hoped for. But she has to work things through in her own way."

"Well, I'm going to have a word with Jess while she packs." He kissed her neck.

The timer on the stove rang and she opened the oven. "Charlie, would you mind checking on Colby before you come back down?"

Metallic fear tinged his tongue. "Of course," he said. *Oh God, maybe she'll be downstairs before Jess and I are done. Please!*

He knocked on the door, pushing it open at her response. She stood by the bed, layering the last sweater in the open suitcase.

"Charlie, just in time. Will you close this for me? Sami insisted I take the sweater I admired. Said it was too big for her." Jessica tucked her white blouse into the corduroy skirt. The quilted vest glittered with gold thread embroidery in an elegant leaf pattern.

"Jess, you look lovely." He snapped the locks and handed her the key. He closed his fingers around hers and pulled her into his arms for a quick hug.

She looked up at him, "Harry said it'll be two hours to the airport. I can't miss this plane. There just aren't any other reservations before Christmas." She smiled, "You see, I did try and change my plans." She picked up her purse.

"Okay, but will you please call? Don't you find it odd Damian would travel during the holidays? Doesn't he have responsibilities to his constituents and the social circle?"

"Of course, he does. I suspect he wants to make certain I … have company on the return trip." She reached for the suitcase but he snatched it up. Without looking at him, she smoothed the counterpane. "Maybe he misses me."

He followed her down the front stairs.

Harry stood at the bottom, Jessica's heavy woolen coat over his arm. Charlie slipped past and out the front door to drop her suitcase in the trunk.

A tight hug for Sami and a quick kiss for Charlie and she was ready to leave. Frantic barking sounded from the stable. Maeve bounded around the corner, barreling toward her, snow flying with each leap. Charlie stepped into Maeve's path but the lithe dog eluded his grasp, spinning him to his knees in the snow. Jessica caught her paws as she leapt at her, Maeve's long tongue reaching for her face.

"Maeve, let the lass be." Chris pulled at Maeve's collar, gasping for air. "Come on, girl, sit."

Maeve backed up and sat, her wagging tail sending snow in Charlie's direction. He scrambled to get up, pulling Sami to the ground when she tried to help him. They ended up wrapped in each other's arms.

"The little lass was afraid she'd not get to say good bye and Merry Christmas so her enthusiasm ran away with her …she …ah…"

"No apologies, Chris, I would have missed saying good bye to her, too." She brushed her lips across his cheek. "Thank you … for everything. I hope you have a Merry Christmas." She looked toward Charlie "I know the concert in Baltimore will be everything you hope." She rubbed Maeve's head then took her seat.

Harry pulled the limousine down the long drive.

"Colby!" Charlie said. Sami looked at him. "You asked me to check in on her. I carried Jessica's bags downstairs." Sami turned for the front door. "No, I'll go." Charlie hugged her and took the front stairs two at a time.

CHAPTER 69

Colby scolded herself, tears leaking from between her pressed eyelids. "Stop! I don't want to redo my makeup. It's your decision to leave, so stop being such a drama queen." Lingerie clutched in one hand, she snatched up her suitcase. The handle slipped from her fingers and the case flew across the room. She stared at her broken fingernail, the ragged edge white against the crème Brule polish. She collapsed on the bed and curled up, clutching the silk panties to her streaming eyes.

Light tapping sounded on the door. Colby sniffed, ignoring the request. Charlie stuck his head around the door. His face displayed concern and great discomfort. "Um, are you all right, then?"

Colby waved, trying to send him away, her breath coming in hiccups. "I just broke a nail. Nothing to worry about." Another deep sob shook her.

Charlie hazarded a step forward. "Are you bleeding? Shall I get you a sticking plaster?" His face brightened. "I know, I'll just run down and fetch Sami."

"No, Charlie, don't! I'm fine." She rose from the bed and shoved the panties into her coat pocket. Retrieving the suitcase, she threw it on the bed. She tossed her shoes willy-nilly. "Just go tell Jess I'll take her to the airport."

Charlie drew breath to protest. "But she is—"

"No, no argument. I have things to do and a …" Her words caught in her throat. "A date for New Year's. Not every lucky girl gets New Year's twice."

"But they—"

She waved her hand at Charlie. "Go, before she leaves with Harry. He doesn't need to make the long round trip."

Charlie nodded backing out, not removing his eyes from her face.

"Here, take my bag with you."

Charlie snatched up the case and bolted for the door.

Good Grief! Nothing like scaring my brother-in-law to death. I should have confronted that villain in England if this is all it takes! Would have undone him right on the spot. Giggles bubbled into laughter refusing to be quelled.

***

Sami pulled the last tray of cookies from the oven just as Charlie hit the bottom step

"Charlie," Sami's voice stopped him in his tracks, "Why do you have Colby's bag?"

"Oh, she's packing." He held up the suitcase. "She said she's leaving. Would take Jess but I could not get a word in to tell her they are already gone. I assume she will want the Mercedes."

"She's what?" She ran up the stairs.

***

Colby looked up, mascara streaks staining her face. Sami stepped in and closed the door. Colby gulped twice but no words came.

"Why are you packing?"

Colby looked at the suitcase, rolling her eyes back to stare at Sami.

Sami took a deep breath. "Charlie's practically whimpering you have him so unnerved." She retrieved a shoe from under the bed. "He isn't usually that easily discommoded." She picked up a blouse from the suitcase, shook it out and reached for a hanger discarded on the bed. The silence stretched on. She turned to Colby, a smile on her face.

Colby stared at Sami's slow, graceful movements maneuvering the hanger into the neck. Feeling Sami's eyes on her, she shook herself free from the fascination and grabbed the blouse. Throwing it back into the suitcase, she snapped, "Sami, stop it! You can't just sweet talk everything back into place." She refused to be placated. "And listen to yourself ..." A puzzled look crossed Sami's face.

Colby charged onward, acid dripping from her words, "Thanks so much for asking me how I'm doing! Oh, I apologize for discommoding your darling husband and I ..." she stood, punctuating each word shoving a shoe into the case, "will—get—out—of—your—way—right—now." Tears rolled down her cheeks. "And not bother him—or you ..." She scrubbed at her eyes with her palm, refusing to look at Sami. "Or anyone else in your newfound family."

Colby sensed Sami's numeric litany, her own heart beating as fast as her sister's counting.

Not my sister. She shoved her hair brush into the overfilled case. Straightening, she found herself face to face with Sami.

Startled she had not taken flight from her tirade, Colby's voice softened, "Oh, Sami, I wish you well, but." Her ire rose again. "I've been watching. You've many chosen ..." she searched for the correct word to carry her hurt, "brothers and sisters. I don't think you need lil ol' me any longer." Unable to turn away from her sister's stare, Colby snorted realizing she'd used Tori's words in her own voice. Her hands shook. She looked at them in disgust.

"Are you quite through?"

Colby's jaw dropped at the steely sarcasm in Sami's voice. Caught off guard, she rose to the challenge. "Why didn't you tell me he had someone in Texas? You could've warned me but, no, you set me up. I believed you c-c-cared about me just a little ... even if we aren't r-re-really sisters."

The color drained from Sami's face.

Colby lost steam. She turned away again, terror at what she was doing chilling her. Life without Sami loomed bleak and lonely, inevitable as the long-legged beauty at Jeff's side.

"Just give me a moment and I'll be gone." She snapped the suitcase closed. She desperately tried to maintain her momentum, fighting regret.

"But, Colby, he never said anything about anyone ...."

"Then he's playing us both." Colby grabbed the case and her purse. She bumped against Sami on her way to the door.

Sami snagged the handle of the purse, spinning Colby around. Wrestling the purse free, she opened the wardrobe door and placed the purse inside. Closing the door, she stood with her back against it.

"You're not going anywhere until New Years. I know you have a date with Jon and I won't let you miss it. But you're my sister and you're a member of this family. And you will stay."

Colby stuck out her lip and pushed Sami away from the wardrobe. "I won't be told what to do." She pulled at the wardrobe door. It refused to open. She beat the wood with her fist. "Foxie, open this door immediately!" She banged her head against the door.

Sami put her hand on Colby's shoulder and turned her around into a tight hug. Colby surrendered to her embrace.

"I don't know what you saw in your visions but I know Jeff. He's an honorable man. There has to be an explanation." Sami released her, handing her a handkerchief.

Colby sniffled, then blew her nose. She drew a shuddering breath. "Did you mean what you said? That I'm still your sister?"

Sami laughed. "Of course, silly. I love you as my sister. I need you as my sister."

Colby hugged her again. "Okay, I'm being hysterical for all the wrong reasons but..." She pursed her lips "I want to know who that floozy is. And you may trust him but I don't. Do you still want me to stay?"

Sami nodded.

"Then ask Foxie to give me back my purse. I need my lipstick."

The wardrobe door swung open.

***

Sami looked around the kitchen for something to occupy her hands. The counter tops, the sink, everything was immaculate. She wondered how things were going in the studio. Fingering the button on the remote control, she heard Scotty's clear voice singing the words to *Right Here Waiting for You.*

I pray they find a way to each other, she thought, recalling the look in Scotty's eyes when Tori and Kay pulled away. *He deserves happiness.* "They all do."

"They all do what?" Colby's voice sounded from the back stairs. Sami remained silent, listening to the group discuss the song. Chad ran through a different lead pattern and Chris played a descant for the last chorus.

Her heart beat in time with Charlie's drumming. She heard paper rustling.

Charlie cleared his throat. "Gentlemen, this needs work … but I want to include it for New Year's. Charlie's voice counted them into the next song. He joined in on the chorus, their voices blending.

Her heart skipped a beat listening to the words.

> When I feel this exultation
> Instead of dire lamentations
> This sense of warmth and healing
> That brings me straight to you
> I'm lifted up straight to you

The music unwrapped the longing and the love. The flute floated above the melody. Closing her eyes, she envisioned Charlie's head bobbing, playing the drums, sweat on his face, his eyes partly closed.

Scooping up the remote from the counter top, she flourished it in the air. The music died. She handed a platter of cookies to Colby and picked up the coffee pot. "Come on. I want to hear it in person." The back door swung open. "Thank you, Foxie."

Chill wind pulled at her hem. She studied the distance from the porch to the open stable door yawning in the greying afternoon. Her heart raced in her chest too fast to count.

Snowflakes tickled her face. A black shape separated from the swirl, dove toward her, landing in the driveway. The raven cocked her head, her dark eye fixing Sami in place. Ruffling her feathers, she marched toward the stable door. She looked back, whistling and crooning. The shadow inside the door shifted and Maeve's nose appeared from the gloom. She barked, prancing by the door.

Sami walked through the snow to the stable door.

Pyewacket nudged Colby's calf. He leapt from the porch, prancing, tail high. He looked back, waiting for Colby to join him.

Be sure and visit our website for more adventures of Pyewacket and the gang:
www.FoxhavenChronicles.com

Carolyn Houghton

I admit it. I am a spiritual child of Walter Mitty, James Thurber's character who lived his real life in stories he made up while coping with his every day, humdrum life.

I loved to pretend. I still do. Writing about time travel, being a musician, a goofy (but brilliant) member of the English elite, is a wonderful way to spend my time. I hope you'll also find a fine escape as well in the *Foxhaven Chronicles* and, soon to come, *Waterton* series.

When I'm not wandering around in alternate universes, I'm the proud mother of Celia Ann. She looks at the world in quite unusual ways. My children's book, *Celia and The Land of Discouraging Words* is the result of an evening's conversation. The town I lived in for many years provided love and support when one of my family members was seriously hurt. *I love Summer the Best* is my love letter to the town that was more than willing to help.

Music provides the heartbeat in my life. You'll find lyrics in the back of the books that reflect Charlie's love for Sami, and Mac's worries about zombies. You just never know who will have a story to tell in lyrics.

My writing partner has helped me to grow in many ways. It's so wonderful to think about the following questions: What am I seeing, tasting, smelling, touching and hearing. She reminds me that the world doesn't always center around dialogue. I'm grateful to have her constancy and brilliance in my life.

The Carrolton Writer's Guild has provided wonderful support for my story telling and poetry. I urge you to find a group that will help you to refine your stories.

Contact her at Carolyn.Houghton.Writer@gmail.com or visit on Facebook at Carolyn Houghton, Writer.

Elyse Wheeler, Ph D

 Elyse Wheeler spent many summers hidden away in the small library in northern Illinois trying to figure out who she wanted to be. Following in the path of the scientists/physicians in her family, she completed a PhD in Human Physiology and Biophysics and training in medical technology. She led laboratory services in two major medical centers. Along the way, she published several scientific articles and wrote three book chapters. To finish out her career in science, she designed and implemented two programs (BS and MS) in clinical laboratory sciences and retired from education after 15 years' service.

Raising her son and introducing him to Dungeons and Dragons at an early age has kept her fantasy worlds rich and robust. She is now free to pursue writing the stories she always wanted to read (and let's be honest, live.) With her co-author, she is currently writing the second volume in *Foxhaven Chronicles* and editing the companion series *Waterton Zoo*. She is also writing a YA fantasy novel about a young troll girl and a Pegasus colt.

She celebrates the collaboration with her life-long friend and writing partner, Carolyn Houghton with whom the first three novels have taken form.

She lives in Georgia close to her son, Colin, his wife, Dante and two grand-dogs, Sumner and Ashby. The household includes CH, Tikva the yellow lab, and two rescue cats, Axel and Karmel. She enjoys the company and encouragement of the members of the Carrollton Writers Guild. Other hobbies include gardening with the West Georgia Chapter of the Georgia Native Plant Society.

Contact her at Elyse.Wheeler.Author@gmail.com or visit on Facebook at Elyse Wheeler Author.

Mac's Halloween Song

Broken backs and screaming cats
Un life gets in the way
I'm not having so much fun
with zombies climbing from the bay

If we get a good run going
as we leave the cemetery
Well, then I'll stop and ask you why
My life goes on this way.
I meant no disrespect when I said to you in passing
Zombies minds are just decayed.
All zombies could be beaten.
We could out run them
before we got gnawed on."
What in the world do you think got them so mad?
There's talk of a filet of me on
Zombie Food Tonight?

Oh! Broken backs and screaming cats
Un life gets in the way
I'm not having so much fun
with zombies walking toward me and talking etouffee

Well, we've left the graveyard far behind us
But I hear them mumbling now
"I'll take the tall one's shank
 and you can have his upper brow"
I'm not looking to be a zombie po'boy
And I know you don't wanna be a manwich
We need to find a way to find the queen who will
Do what she do to voo doo
Us out of this very bad how do you do.

Broken backs and screaming cats
Un life gets in the way
I'm not having so much fun
with zombies walking toward us their lips dropping on the way.

10/19/2019
Carolyn Houghton

Coming in 2020

Foxhaven Chronicles
Volume Two

Wolf's Fang

EXCERPT FROM WOLF'S FANG

Oooff. "Pyewacket. Get off of my chest. You weigh a ton. Leave me alone. Go away, I said." Colby jerked the blanket over her head, the bottom hem slipping up to her waist. She sat up looking for the cat that couldn't possibly be there. *I'm home ... not at Sami's.*

Nikki said you're petulant, but I disagreed. I know you better than that. And I do not weigh a ton. I'm the perfect weight. You need to help or Jeff will die throughout the ages.

"Pye, what are you talking about?"

He's out there ... has been a long time. I can't reach him alone.

Pyewacket's thought waves sent vibrant dreamscapes of the worst nightmare quality to Colby in her hypnogogic state.

"Pye, slow down". Colby roused and leaned over the edge of the bed, looking under the dust ruffle. "Where are you?"

In your head.

"You mean you aren't really here."

How could I be? You're miles and miles away.

"Okay, so how are you doing this?"

Close your eyes.

Colby stopped herself from saying that wasn't an answer to her question. She closed her eyes. Pye's luminescent green eyes stared at her. She started, pulling the blanket back over her head.

"Pye, how?"

Jeff taught me. I don't know where to find him.

"What makes you think I know where he is? All I know is he's off with his girlfriend." She felt her lip curl as she said the last word.

What's wrong with me? I haven't said it like that since middle school. Her eyes flew open and she was alone again. She closed her eyes.

> *Not this world ... the other one. We must hurry, Colby Bobcat Seer.*

"How do I know where to go? I remember him going up through the clouds."

> *You can see! If you'd only look.*

Colby smacked her forehead. She rolled over and snatched open the nightstand drawer, the force pulling it free. The contents scattered across the floor. The crystal ball rolled away. She dove for it, tumbling and landing on the floor. She pulled the covers off the bed and over her head.

Cupping the ball, she stared, her eyes stinging. The ball remained blank. "Pye, it isn't working." She bit her lip. "It never works when I want it to."

> *Come out with me.*

She started to say she didn't know how, but it sounded too whiny even to her ear. She took a deep breath reaching for the feeling of the bobcat. Her fingers curled in anticipation. Her own musk from the sheets hit her nose and she sneezed. She reached for Mick's handkerchief, huge paws scrambling through the sheets.

> *I did it! Pye, I did it.*

> *Hurry.*

She stared at the crystal expecting to see the bright meadow or the cave where Jeff found Pyewacket.

> *It's dark and cold. I see a wolf ... a really big wolf. He's fighting something holding him ... snapping at it but it keeps wrapping him back up. A big spider web ... sticky and black. Pye, he isn't up there. It's down there.*

> *Find a hole in the ground—any hole—and come on.*

The oak tree in the garden flashed through her mind, the hole at the base between the roots where she had played with her toy animals.

She bounded from the bed and ran down the stairs, paws flying. She passed Mick in the kitchen. She shut her eyes and barreled through the closed backdoor believing she could.

She slammed into the tree trunk, willing herself smaller as she slid into the hole. Wet earth met her paws, roots dangling from the ceiling. She ran, head down, passing through rocks in her path. She felt someone beside her. Pye ran at her shoulder, his feet slipping on the muddy path. She imagined the path dry—better for traction. The two of them flew down into the earth.

***

Don't miss the companion series, **Waterton Zoo**. Charlie's sister, Sherry, travels to the Colonies to direct a zoo in a small river town in upstate New York. She trained in the care of exotic animals and alternate species. Can she save the zoo from ruthless treasure hunters? She'll have help from the midnight shift, including the trolls, the gargoyles and the dwarves, not to mention a wily wolverine and a not-so-persnickety python.

CPSIA information can be obtained
at www.ICGtesting.com
Printed in the USA
FFHW021623231019
55716962-61576FF